Praise for *Blood of the Wicked*

"Entirely absorbing." —*The New York Times Book Review*

"Both a powerful political thriller and gripping crime fiction.... Gage proves himself a true storyteller." —*Florida Sun-Sentinel*

"[A] brutal tale of murder and vengeance.... Gage's inspector is a fascinating character, a man who once dispensed his own brand of Brazilian justice now charged with upholding the law of the land. Highly recommended."
—*Library Journal*, Starred Review

"The book is a murder mystery, but it's also a contemporary tapestry of modern-day Brazil. It doesn't just entertain, it informs. The issues treated within its pages include liberation theology, the excesses of the military dictatorship, the prostitution of children and the current conflict between the landless and the great landowners. It's a book that should have been written by a Brazilian—but wasn't.... *Blood of the Wicked* is certain to put Brazil on the map for many American and European readers." —*Brazzil Magazine*

"Leighton Gage has written a powerful debut mystery. He brings Brazil to life, with the complex politics, and ugliness of the poverty, and, at times, the life."
—Lesa Holstine, *Glendale Daily Planet* and *Blog Critics Magazine*

"In *Blood of the Wicked*, the first in a planned series, author translates easily to authority. Gage's insider view of the landscape, politics, and people of his adopted country are both tender and terrible.... This is a top-notch police procedural as well as an intriguing window into a vast country mostly unknown."
—*ForeWord Magazine*

"Emotionally charged debut.... Gage, a part-time resident of Brazil, vividly evokes a country of political corruption, startling economic disparity, and relentless crime, both random and premeditated." —*Booklist*

"Gage creates a contemporary tapestry of Brazil.... [His] debut builds a compelling foundation for future Silva cases." —*Kirkus Reviews*

"Leighton Gage's debut novel, *Blood of the Wicked*, is a compelling mystery set in modern Brazil amid the conflict between the few large land owners and the many landless in the country.... There are many reasons to recommend *Blood of the Wicked*. The principal characters, Mario Silva and Hector Costa, are fully developed with conflicted backgrounds that serve them well in their current positions as federal officials. The writing is first-rate, descriptive and atmospheric. The primary plot is multi-dimensional, complex and intricate, yet surprisingly easy to follow, no small accomplishment for a book with a strong and varied cast of secondary characters, each participating in intersecting subplots.... *Blood of the Wicked* is a terrific mystery, a strongly written and powerful novel that will be remembered long after the final pages are read."

—*Mysterious Reviews*

"If you are a fan of chilling murder mysteries and have an interest in Brazil, then this is the book for you. Highly recommended."   —Gringoes.com

"Gage neatly combines a hard-hitting police investigation with the issues of land distribution that are at the heart of Brazilian politics. A fascinating tour with enigmatic Silva the perfect guide."   —Mystery *Lovers Bookshop News*

"A more-than-first-rate police procedural in which Silva must contend with corruption, deceit, and violence. The novel also becomes a post-modern morality play in which someone with a wickedly bloody strategy seeks and obtains divine justice in a perversely corrupt world.... If you enjoy chilling, complex, and intelligent thrillers, you really should treat yourself to reading Leighton Gage's novels. You will not be disappointed."   —*Bookloons*

"Once again the New York City-based Soho Press has delivered a winner. A welcome addition to the world of contemporary crime fiction, *Blood of the Wicked* is a finely crafted work that shows none of the usual shortcomings of a first novel.... Blurring the distinction between literary fiction and crime fiction, this is a book that will inform readers, and needs to be read. Gage has done himself proud."   —*Sherbrooke Record*

BLOOD of the

WICKED

BLOOD of the
WICKED

Leighton Gage

Published by
Soho Press, Inc.
853 Broadway
New York, NY 10003

Library of Congress Cataloging-in-Publication Data
Gage, Leighton D.
Blood of the wicked / Leighton D. Gage.
p. cm.
ISBN 978-1-61695-180-1
eISBN 978-1-56947-676-5
1. Catholic Church—Bishops—Crimes against—Fiction.
2. Brazil—Fiction. I. Title.
PS3607.A3575B56 2007
813'.6—dc22
2007007307

Printed in the United States of America

10 9 8 7 6 5 4 3 2 1

This book is dedicated to
Maria Helena Dumont Adams
in thankful recognition of many kindnesses.

The righteous shall rejoice when he seeth the vengeance: He shall wash his feet in the blood of the wicked.

PSALMS 58:10

Chapter One

SOMETHING TOOK THE HELICOPTER and shook it like a jackal worrying a carcass. The bishop gripped the aluminum supports on either side of his seat and hung on for dear life.

"Clear air turbulence," the pilot observed laconically, and resumed chewing his gum.

"*Merda!*" the bishop muttered. He regretted the vulgarity as soon as he'd said it.

"What's that, Your Excellency?"

The bishop's eyes darted to his right. In his fear and discomfort, he'd forgotten the microphones, forgotten the headphones, forgotten that the man could hear every word he said.

And what if he had? Was it not true? Was the helicopter not a merda, a great stinking, steaming merda? And who was the pilot, anyway? What had he ever done in his blessed life other than to learn how to fly the merda? How dare he criticize a man who might, God willing, be a future prince of the Church?

The pilot, whose name was Julio, and who wasn't criticizing anyone, had been distracted by a flock of vultures wheeling in graceful curves over the approaching river. He honestly hadn't heard what the bishop had said. He opened his mouth to repeat the question, then shut it again when he saw the cleric's mouth set into a thin line.

Julio had a paunch, sweat stains under the arms of his khaki shirt, and a habit of chewing gum with his mouth open, all of which Dom Felipe Antunes, the Bishop of Presidente Vargas, found distasteful. But it was nothing in comparison to Dom Felipe's distaste for the helicopter.

The bishop glanced at his watch, wiped his sweaty palms on his silk cassock, and resumed a death grip on the aluminum supports.

Forty-seven blessed minutes in the air. Forty-seven minutes.

"It won't be long now, Your Excellency."

Was that amusement in the man's voice? Was he enjoying himself? Did he think fear was funny?

On the floor beneath Dom Felipe's feet there was a thin (he was sure it was thin) window of Plexiglas. He tried to avoid looking down, but some perverse instinct kept drawing his eyes back to that dreadful hole in the floor. They were over the river now, sand bars protruding through chocolate-colored foam. The sand looked as hard as the rock-strewn banks.

Do helicopters float?

A rowboat drifted in mid-river, two fishermen aboard, a huge net piled high between them. They looked up at him, shielding their eyes against the morning sun. One waved.

Reflexively, Dom Felipe waved back. Then a flash, like the strobe on a camera, caused him to snap his head upward and seek the source of the light.

Far ahead of him, beyond the bug-flecked windshield, the flash came again. He squinted and . . . yes, there it was. Sunlight of an almost blinding intensity reflected off an expanse of glass. It couldn't be anything other than the Great Window. And that meant that the brand-new church of Nossa Senhora dos Milagres was in sight.

The window was almost five meters in diameter and had come all the way from the Venetian island of Murano at a cost of almost 200,000 reais, not including the shipping, which, together with the insurance, had amounted to R$30,000 more. When the sun hit it just right—as it was doing now—the window would cast rays of glorious blue light all along the nave of the new church.

Dom Felipe made a conscious effort to hold that image,

focusing on the blue light, as if it were a meditation. But then the pitch of the engine changed, dragging him back into his dreadful reality.

The Lord is my shepherd. . . .

A landing spot had been marked out: a Christian cross in stones the size of golf balls, and just as white. A rectangle of sere grass surrounded it, hemmed by dusty palm trees. Yellow plastic tape ran from tree to tree, holding back the crowd. Men in the gray uniforms of the State Police were stationed at intervals along the length of the tape, their backs to the cross, keeping the landing area clear.

The crowd started moving like a living thing. Signs of welcome were raised. Others, already aloft, were turned to face the approaching helicopter. White and brown faces looked upward. And there were banners, too.

Dom Felipe bit his lip in vexation. The banners were red, blood red, the unmistakable standards of the Landless Workers' League. The league seldom missed an opportunity—no matter how inappropriate—to turn a gathering into a political event. The bishop knew that. Still, he'd been hopeful that, in this case, the consecration of the new church . . .

There was the slightest of jolts as the helicopter's skids met the grass.

It's over! Hail Mary, full of grace. . . . Never again.

Julio pulled a lever and threw a switch. The engine died.

Above the swish of air from the still-spinning rotor blades Dom Felipe could hear, for the first time, the cheers of the crowd. He took off his headset, handed it to the pilot, and raised his right hand in benediction.

Insolently, the red banners waved back at him.

Dom Felipe suppressed an uncharitable thought and bent over to retrieve his miter, untangling the lappets before placing it on his head. Then he composed his features into a beatific smile and waited for the pilot to open his door.

Julio, unaccustomed to ferrying bishops, finally seemed to realize what was expected of him. He removed his headset, skirted the nose of the aircraft, and reached Dom Felipe's side just as the bishop opened the door himself.

Dom Felipe waved off the pilot's offered hand, put his feet on solid ground, and started searching the crowd for the face of his secretary, Father Francisco, the man who'd hatched the helicopter plot.

If Francisco thinks I'm going back to Presidente Vargas the same way he got me here, he's got another think coming. I'll return by car, he'll have to find one, and it had better be one with air-conditioning.

Francisco was nowhere in sight, but Gaspar Farias was. Dom Felipe could clearly see his corpulent body, wrapped in a black cassock, standing in the shadow of the vestibule. Involuntarily, the bishop scowled.

A choir of adolescents dressed in identical cotton robes was standing against the tape, a rectangle of blue in the multicolored collage that made up the crowd. The children were close enough to read the bishop's scowl and seemed to be puzzled by it.

With the skill born of practice, Dom Felipe forced a smile onto his lips. The youngsters' puzzlement vanished, replaced by beams of welcome. A woman in an identical robe, her back to the bishop, her face toward her charges, started to wave her arms and the children broke into song, their young voices murdering the English words, "Why do the nations . . ."

Handel? A Protestant? Who in the world chose that?

Dom Felipe raised his hand in another benediction and silently mouthed words of thanks, conserving his voice for the sermon and for the all-important interviews that were sure to follow.

It was the dry season and, to make it worse, a great deal of construction was going on. From the air, the city of Cascatas do Pontal had seemed to be covered by a dome of red dust. He could feel some of that dust right now, abrading his neck where it met his collar, coating his lips, working its way into his throat. He'd need a carafe of water on the pulpit. Francisco could take care of that. Not Gaspar. Dom Felipe didn't want anything from Gaspar, didn't even want to talk to him.

The bishop shifted his body to face another sector of the crowd and raised his arm. His silk sleeve slid downward, just enough to expose his watch. A practiced flick of his eyes confirmed that he wasn't early. He was a stylish seven minutes late.

So where is the blessed reception committee?

He didn't want to stand there looking like a fool, so he folded his hands under his chin, bowed his head, and offered a prayer.

In recognizance of the solemn moment, the singing faded, and then stopped. The cheering abated. Dom Felipe kept his head down, and his eyes closed, until he heard the rustle of people working their way through the crowd. Then he lifted his head and unclasped his hands. Immediately the cheers erupted anew, and the singing started all over again, right from the beginning of the piece.

One of the policemen grasped a segment of the yellow crowd tape and held it shoulder high. One by one, the members of the reception party slipped under it, seven men in all, and started crossing the empty space toward him.

Cascatas do Pontal was an agricultural town, an informal place. The jackets and ties the men were wearing all looked new. Despite the welcoming smiles they'd plastered on their faces, the local dignitaries looked uncomfortable. All seven of them were red-faced and sweating in the heat.

The bishop took an impulsive step toward them, and then stopped.

They'll think it more dignified if I let them come to me.
It was the last decision of Dom Felipe's life.

WALTER ABENDTHALER snapped off another shot with
the Pentax, advanced the film and reached for the motor-
driven Nikon. Some of his contemporaries liked the digital
gear, and all of the kids used it, but not Walter. Walter pre-
ferred film. He was an old-fashioned kind of guy.

Maybe *too* old-fashioned; at least that's what the agency
art directors were telling him these days. A few lines on your
face, a little gray in your hair, and they all thought you were
over the hill.

Scheisse! Why didn't they concentrate on his portfolio
instead? His pictures clearly demonstrated that he had a better eye for angles than most of the young punks now getting
into the business. *But did they appreciate that? No, they didn't.*
Instead of focusing on his pictures, art directors had a ten-
dency to focus on his gray hair.

Walter would have been willing to bet good money—
something he happened to be short of at the moment, or he
wouldn't have been in Cascatas at all—that not one of
those overestimated punk kids, not even that *Scheisskerl*
Chico Ramos, would have had the foresight to do what he'd
done.

He was on the church steps, almost in the vestibule, just
below Gaspar Farias, the crow that ran the parish. (The
black soutanes priests wore always reminded Walter of crows
so that's what he called them.) That put Walter seventy-five
meters from the helicopter, maybe even a little more, but
that was the beauty of it, the action of a man who knew his
business. The punk kids always tried to get in close, instead
of letting the lens do it for them. And now, while they were
all down there in the crush elbowing each other out of the
way, Walter had a spot all to himself, high above the heads

of the crowd. There was nothing, nothing at all, between him and the Chief Crow. He had an unimpeded view.

Exactly as he'd foreseen, Walter's medium-length telephoto, the 300mm, was the perfect lens for the job. His frame ran from slightly below the knees to the tip of the bishop's miter.

Walter hit and released the shutter button. The Nikon clicked and whirred.

Ha! Gotcha sneaking a peek at your watch.

He'd save that one, maybe blow it up and put it in his portfolio. They'd never print it. Then it got boring: His Crowness bowed his head, concealing his face under his funny hat, and stood there for a long time doing absolutely nothing.

Walter didn't bother to waste any film.

At last the head came up and the kids started singing again, their high voices carrying well over the murmur of the crowd.

Walter knew the music, a passage from the *Messiah*, and he hummed along, pleased with himself.

The bishop took a few steps forward and stopped.

Just to the cleric's left, Walter had the logotype, the whole logotype, solidly in the shot. The telephoto altered the perspective, brought the background closer, made the logo look even bigger than it was. The client would love it.

Love it, because Walter's assignment wasn't to register the arrival of the bishop. It was to register the *link* between the Church and Fertilbras, Brazil's largest manufacturer of fertilizer.

Providing this day's transportation was a public-relations ploy for the company. Running the chopper cost them 1,800 reais an hour, and they intended to get their money's worth by making sure that Walter's photos, the ultimate selection of which would be made by Fertilbras's chairman himself, appeared in every newspaper in the state of São Paulo. Or at least in those newspapers where Fertilbras's advertising budget gave them leverage with the editorial staff.

In one of his sarcastic moments, of which there were many, Walter, no Catholic, had commented to his wife, Magda, that there was a similarity between what the Catholic Church and his client offered to the public. Magda hadn't laughed, so he'd had to explain: "The Church peddles bullshit, another form of fertilizer. Get it?" She still hadn't laughed. Magda was from Zurich and had the same sense of humor as her parents: none at all.

The Chief Crow had turned out to be as handsome in the flesh as he was in the photos Walter had seen. Dom Felipe was still young, well under sixty, but his abundant, carefully coifed hair was already a snowy white.

Colored, for sure. His eyebrows are still dark.

Unfortunately, the 300mm didn't bring Dom Felipe close enough to display the blue eyes that women were prone to gush about. Walter hoped for better luck when the bishop got his act together and moved toward him.

The guy's got charisma, I'll give him that. Looks like he has a poker up his ass. Stands more like a soldier than a priest.

Walter momentarily took the viewfinder away from his eye and glanced at the film counter.

Six. Thirty shots left on the roll.

He switched off the automatic focus and made a minor adjustment.

Uh-oh.

A cloud slipped between Walter's subjects and the sun. He had to open up. One, no, two stops. *Two whole stops! Scheisse!* It was playing hell with his depth of field. If the bishop moved any further away from the background, Walter was going to have to choose between staying sharp on either the man or the logotype. And that was, as the English put it, Hobson's choice: no goddamned choice at all. Unless the sun came back from behind that fucking cloud, the link he was supposed to capture would be gone, and he'd have one unhappy client.

Walter saw blurry movement on the bottom left of his frame. He lowered the camera to check it out, and then clapped the viewfinder back to his eye.

The reception committee.

He left the focus where it was. The group was getting sharper and sharper as it approached the bishop. Then one of them stepped right between Walter and the logotype.

In a spasm of anger, Walter pressed the shutter.

A fraction of a second later, a hole appeared in the front of Dom Felipe's cassock.

The shutter stayed open long enough to register both the entry wound and the red mist that spurted into the air behind the bishop's back.

A less-experienced man, one of those young punks, might have started looking around to see where the shot had come from. But not Walter Abendthaler.

Walter, old pro that he was, kept his finger on the shutter button. The motor drive kept advancing. The shutter opened and closed, opened and closed, capturing shot after shot.

In successive frames, the bishop took a step backward, looked down at his chest, sunk to his knees, and pitched forward onto the ground. And then, in the very last exposure before the film ran out, the top of his head seemed to explode.

The crowd was horrified.

Walter Abendthaler was ecstatic. He was damned near positive he'd captured the very moment of the bullet's impact.

Chapter Two

"UGLY," SAID MARIO SILVA, Chief Inspector for Criminal Matters.

"Ugly is right," Nelson Sampaio, Silva's boss and the Director of the Brazilian Federal Police, agreed.

He pushed another photo across the burnished mahogany of his desktop and tapped it with his forefinger.

"Here. Look at this one."

The photo, like all of the others in the stack, was in color. The bishop was staring down at the red hole in his chest. His miter had tumbled from his head and the camera, clearly working at a high shutter speed, had caught it frozen in the air. Silva couldn't see the prelate's eyes, but he could imagine the look of mingled shock and horror that must have been written there. When the death was quick, as it was in this case, such looks often remained on the face of the corpse.

"We're on the spot," the director said, dealing out another photograph as if he was manipulating a deck of oversized playing cards. The photo would have slid off of his desk and onto his thick green rug if Silva hadn't caught it with his fingertips.

This time the bishop was already prone, and the top of his head was partially obscured by the bloody red mist that ensues when a high-velocity bullet penetrates a human body. Silva had seen the same effect before but never in a photograph.

"That's the last one in the sequence," the director said. "Did I mention that the Pope called the president?"

Twice, Silva thought. "Really?" he said.

At that moment, Ana Tavares, the director's gray-haired secretary, came in without knocking. Silva had known her for fourteen years, thirteen longer than the director had. She put some papers into one of the elegant hardwood trays situated to her boss's left.

"Good morning, Director," she said.

"You can't just murder a bishop," Sampaio went on, ignoring her. "This is Brazil, for Christ's sake. Brazil, not some little Central American pesthole."

Ana raised her eyes to heaven and walked out, gently closing the door behind her.

Central American pesthole? Then Silva remembered: A bishop, murdered while he was celebrating a mass. Salvador? Nicaragua? One of those places. They'd made a movie about it.

"And this guy wasn't just *any* bishop, either. This guy was on a fast track for promotion to cardinal."

"How do you know that?"

"Because the president told the minister of justice and the minister told me. And for all I know, the Pope told the president. Now look, Mario, I don't care what else you're doing—"

The director broke off abruptly, his attention caught by a hangnail on the forefinger he was pointing at Silva. He opened his top drawer, rooted around until he'd found a nail clipper, and applied himself to the offending digit. Silva crossed his arms and waited. About ten seconds later the director tossed the instrument back into the drawer and took up exactly where he'd left off.

"—but whatever it is, drop it. From now on, and until you catch the *filho da puta* who did it, this is your first priority."

Sampaio sounded as if Dom Felipe's murder had been an offense to him, personally.

Silva knew that was unlikely.

The director, an appointee without a single qualification in law enforcement, had the politician's gift of being able to hide his true emotions behind a fog of words. In this instance, the fog probably concealed an underlying nervousness. And with good reason: If the murder of the bishop went unsolved, Sampaio's enemies would smell blood. They'd be all over him like piranhas on a wounded tapir and they'd pressure him to kiss his political ambitions goodbye.

Not, Silva thought, *that there was any chance whatsoever of the director doing that.*

Anyone who really knew Nelson Sampaio also knew that the director reserved his kisses for his mistresses, photo opportunities with babies, and even occasionally his wife. His ambitions were another matter. As far as Sampaio was concerned, being Director of the Federal Police was just another step on his Long March to the Presidency and woe betide anyone who got in the way, including his top cop.

Silva reflected upon that and winced.

"Why are you doing that?" the director said.

"What?"

"That thing with your face. What do they call it? Wincing?"

"It was that last photo," Silva said, glancing out the window at the façade of the Ministry of Culture, "All the blood and brain matter. It got to me."

The director narrowed his eyes and said nothing. He wasn't buying it.

"So who took the photos?" Silva asked, in an attempt to get the conversation back on track.

"Some goddamned Swiss photographer," Sampaio said, after a pause just long enough to let Silva know that he wasn't fooling anyone. "He sold the lot. They'll be in tomorrow's papers."

"And how did they wind up with you?"

Sampaio's lips took on the aspect of someone who'd just been sucking on a lemon.

"Romeu Pluma dropped them off. Personally."

Romeu Pluma was the Minister of Justice's press secretary. He'd been a journalist and when the minister's term was done he might well go back to being a journalist. But one thing was for certain: He sure as hell wasn't going to serve in any ministry headed by Nelson Sampaio. Sampaio hated his guts.

"So the minister—"

"Knew all about it before I did. That's right. And is that supposed to happen? Is the Minister of Justice supposed to know about crimes before the Director of the Federal Police does?"

"No, Director, he's not."

"Damned right, he's not. You should have seen the look on Pluma's face. It was . . ."

Sampaio sought for the right word.

"Condescending?" Silva offered.

"Supercilious. It was downright supercilious."

Silva imagined the scene and decided he rather liked Romeu Pluma. He tried not to let it show.

"He got all of these little snapshots," the director continued, "from one of his newspaper-editor buddies. And then he went right in and showed them to the minister. And what do you suppose happened next?"

"The minister called you?"

"Wrong. What he called was a press conference."

"Oh," Silva said. *Merda*, he thought. His concern showed on his face.

"You're not pleased?" Sampaio asked, picking up on it immediately. "Well, I wasn't either. I don't suppose I have to tell you what he said?"

"Let me guess."

Silva had been in Brasilia for a long time. He probably could have written the speech himself. "Promised that the whole business was going to get his personal attention?" he hazarded.

"Right. Go on."

"Said something about applying the 'considerable resources' of the federal government?"

"Right again. What else?"

Silva sighed. He could feel a headache coming on. "Something about assuring the public that the perpetrators would be swiftly brought to justice?"

"Actually," the director said, "the word he chose was 'quickly,' not 'swiftly,' 'quickly brought to justice.' And here's something you're really going to like: The 'considerable resources' part includes you. He mentioned you by name."

Silva's headache took a turn for the worse.

The director lowered his eyes to the desktop and stared at the last of the photos, the one that showed the destruction of Dom Felipe's cranium. It seemed to hold a morbid fascination for him. He put a hand to the side of his head.

"Is it always like that?" he asked.

"What?"

"If someone's shot in the head, does it always do that much damage?"

"Not always. Depends on the weapon. A .22, even at close range, usually makes a hole no bigger than the diameter of a pencil. And the bullet stays inside the skull."

The director shuddered and focused on another aspect of the photo.

"Dom Felipe had just climbed out of a helicopter. He was going to consecrate a new church. Look, you can see it in the background."

Silva leaned over and scrutinized the shot. "The church?"

"The helicopter. It was owned by that fertilizer company, Fertilbras. They must have loaned it to him."

"Umm," Silva said, nodding. He turned the photo over. There was nothing on the back.

"Where did it happen?" he asked.

"Some little hick town called . . ." The director consulted a paper on his desk, "Cascatas do Pontal, wherever the hell that is."

"State of São Paulo, far western part. Not so hick. Population must be almost a quarter of a million by now."

"For me, that's still hick," the director said.

He proudly hailed from São Paulo, the capital of the state of the same name. It was a city boasting a population ten times larger than that of Brasilia and at least sixty times larger than Cascatas do Pontal.

"How the hell do you know about Cascatas do Wherever?"

"Pontal."

"Right. Pontal. I never even heard of it," the director said.

"There were some killings. A month ago, maybe a little more."

"Killings? What killings?" the director asked and leaned back, awaiting an explanation. It was Mario Silva's business to know about such things.

"An agricultural worker, his wife, and their two kids. A nasty business."

"Was it in the newspapers?"

"A couple of paragraphs, no more."

"A couple of paragraphs, eh?" The director leaned forward. "It doesn't matter how little there was. If it was in print at all, that bastard Pluma will know about it and you can bet your ass he'll mention it to the minister. Fill me in."

"I don't think it could possibly have anything to do with what happened to the bish—"

"Fill me in, I said."

"As you wish. Ever hear of Luiz Pillar?"

"Who in this town hasn't? What's Pillar got to do with it?"

Luiz Pillar, the spokesman for the Landless Workers' League, was a notorious gadfly, a major critic of the government's policy of land reform and a thorn in the side of Brazil's big landowners. He was not one of the director's favorite people.

"Seventy-five years ago—"

Silva got that far before the director cut him off.

"I don't care about history. I asked you what Pillar had to do with it."

"Bear with me. I'm getting there." Silva waited for a nod of assent before he picked up the thread.

"Seventy-five years ago," he repeated, "ninety-five percent of the land around Cascatas was owned by the government. These days, less than two percent of it is. The rest is in private hands, all concentrated into big estates."

"So?"

"So, Pillar claims that it was all done with fraudulent documents. He wants the landowners to give it back, and he wants the government to redistribute it to the poor."

"Give it back?" Sampaio said. "Ha. Fat chance."

Big landowners were also big contributors to election campaigns. Their political clout far outweighed that of the poor and landless.

"A lot of that land isn't cultivated," Silva observed.

That brought the director up short.

The Brazilian government had a constitutional obligation to appropriate untilled land and distribute it to the landless. In practice, however, local politicians and a corrupt judiciary were almost always successful at blocking any attempt to break up the great estates. Populist presidents, ministers— and politically ambitious directors of the federal police— didn't like to be reminded of that fact.

"So this agricultural worker, he was some kind of an

activist?" Sampaio asked, picking up a pen and tapping it impatiently on his desk.

"As I understand it, yes."

"Worked with Pillar."

"Probably. Most of them do."

"And some landowner had him killed?"

"Maybe a single landowner, more likely a group of landowners. That would be my guess."

The director dropped his pen and raised his hands in the air. "So why don't you do something about it?"

Silva held his ground. "With respect, Director, I think you know the answer to that."

The answer was that the federal police, except in rare and very specific cases, had no mandate to investigate murders unless they occurred on federal property. The director knew that as well as Silva did.

"You're my man for criminal matters, and this is clearly a criminal matter. Put a stop to it," the director said, just as if Silva could, and should. "I have no sympathy for Pillar and his crowd, but we can't just stand idly by while people go around killing people. Where the hell do those landowners think they are, Dodd's City?"

Silva thought Sampaio probably meant Dodge City, but maybe not. Maybe there actually *was* a place called Dodd's City.

"The minister's going to call the Governor of São Paulo," the director went on, "and he'll talk him into requesting our help in the investigation of the bishop's murder. And while you're there, you'd better sniff around and see what you can learn about who killed that activist. It might help to keep Pillar off our backs."

While you're there? Silva didn't like the sound of that. "Can I keep those?" he said, reaching for the photographs and rising to his feet.

"Not so fast," the director said.

Silva withdrew his hand.

"Sit down."

Silva sank back into his seat, knowing what was coming, knowing he wouldn't like it.

"The first man you should talk to when you get there," Sampaio continued, "is a colonel in the State Police" —he consulted the same paper he'd looked at before—"called Ferraz. He's the man in charge."

"Are you suggesting I go personally?" Silva said it innocently, as if he hadn't seen it coming all along.

The director's eyes rounded. He leaned back in his chair, his face transformed into a perfect expression of surprise. He would have made a first-class thespian.

"Are we on the same page here?" Sampaio spoke as if he was addressing someone who wasn't fluent in the language. "I *told* you. We—are—on—the—spot. This is top priority. It has to be perceived that we regard it as such. I'm not suggesting anything. I'm telling you. You can use that hotshot nephew of yours, what's his name?"

"Costa. Hector Costa."

"Yeah, him, and anybody else you think you might need, but you're going too, Mario. I'm supposed to call the minister at noon, and I'm going to tell him that."

He glanced at his watch.

Silva caught the signal for dismissal. Once again he rose to his feet but the director held up a hand.

"I want a report twice daily, at noon and at six, and I want to be able to get through to you anytime. Take a new cell phone, don't use it for outgoing calls, keep the number confidential, and tell Ana what it is."

"Understood," Silva said, trying not to let his irritation show. *And, if I feel like it, I may even pick it up when you call,* he thought.

Cell phones in Brazil were notoriously unreliable. The director might suspect that a lack of response was intentional, but he could never really be sure.

"And make sure you answer when I call," the director said, fixing his subordinate with a steely gaze. "By the way, did I tell you that the Pope called the president?"

Chapter Three

IN THE LARGEST CITY south of the equator, springtime is generally too warm for comfort and the spring of 1978 was no exception. In those days, automobile emission standards had yet to be established. To make it worse, a thermal inversion persisted over the city for twenty-nine of October's thirty-one days. The resulting smog reduced visibility to less than 500 meters. Eyes stung. People buried their noses in handkerchiefs and addressed each other with gravelly voices emerging out of irritated throats. In Liberdade, the Japanese neighborhood, residents took to wearing surgical masks. The black waters of the Tietê, the river that flowed in a sluggish crescent around the city's western boundaries, generated vapors strong enough to bring nausea to queasy stomachs. Socks, clean and white in the morning, were peeled off at night, begrimed with black soot so fine that it penetrated shoe leather. The smell of rotting garbage hung in the air. It was a typical springtime in São Paulo.

Back in those days, long years before the bishop's murder, Mario Silva was at peace with the world. His legal training was behind him. So, too, was the exam that admitted him to the OAB, the Brazilian Bar Association.

In the week before his world fell apart, he'd spent his days setting up a law practice. Nights were reserved for courting Irene Camargo, a petite brunette he'd met in law school.

The twelfth of October, Irene's twenty-second birthday, was an event her parents had insisted she celebrate at home. The young couple reserved the night of the thirteenth for themselves. Friday the thirteenth. Silva didn't give the portentousness of that a second thought until much later.

The evening began well. They dined at the Ca d'Oro, one of São Paulo's finest restaurants, and one that Mario Silva avoided forever after. Next, they drove out onto the Rapouso Tavares, a highway lined with high-rotation motels. Silva and Irene had to wait in a long line before they could pass through one of the dimly lit kiosks. They put the car into the enclosed garage, ordered a bottle of champagne, and frolicked in the whirlpool bath while the tiny sauna came up to temperature. Afterward, they lingered in bed to talk.

It was almost 4:00 by the time Silva dropped her off, approaching 4:20, when he arrived at the house he shared with his parents. In the driveway, where his father's big Ford Galaxy should have been, was a black and white sedan. Leaning against it, puffing on cigarettes, were two men in uniform. They squinted in the glare from Silva's headlamps and then stood upright. In the seconds before he cut the lights, Silva noticed the seal of the city of São Paulo and the words POLICIA MUNICIPAL painted on the car. The lamp over his front door was dim, but it cast enough light to read their expressions. Those expressions were grim.

"You Mario Silva?" the older cop asked, not unkindly. He had a protuberant blue vein on his forehead, just below the hairline.

"Yes."

"You got a sister named Carla?"

"What is it? What happened to her?"

The cop pursed his lips. "Nothing," he said. "Nothing's happened to her. Not as far as I know. Do you know where she is?"

"Probably at home, asleep."

"She doesn't live here?"

"No. She's married. She lives with her husband. What's this all about?"

The cop threw his cigarette to the macadam and ground

out the glowing butt with his heel. "Sergeant Mancuso," he said, extending a hand, "São Paulo PD." His palm was moist. "This is Officer Branco," he continued. The younger cop nodded, but didn't offer to shake hands.

"Is it about my parents?"

Mancuso gave a little nod.

"Your mother's in the hospital," he said, then added quickly, "She's fine. She's going to be okay, but your father. . . ."

He made a little grunting noise in his throat.

"What? What about my father?"

Mancuso reached out his hand, gripped Silva's upper arm and gave him a squeeze of sympathy. The younger cop, fat and with a baby face that made him look like a cherub, answered Silva's question.

"They shot him."

"*Shot* him? Is he—"

"Dead," the cherub said, bluntly.

Mancuso, the older cop, bit his lower lip. Even in the pale light, Silva could see the lip turning white.

"Dead?" Silva blinked, trying to get his head around the idea. After a moment, he said, "Who did it?"

Mancuso gave his arm a final squeeze and let go. "How about we go inside?"

In a daze, Silva unlocked the front door and led the way into the living room. Without being invited, the cherub sat down on the couch. Mancuso remained standing. Silva walked over to the piano, picked up the wedding picture of his parents and stared at it. "How did it happen?" he asked, trying to get his head around what they were telling him.

"Your dad screwed up, Senhor Silva," the cherub said. "He stopped for a red light."

Silva felt a sudden flash of anger. He looked up. "I'm sorry, Officer. What was your name again?"

"Branco."

"My father *always* stopped for red lights, Officer Branco."

"Yeah? Tell me something, Senhor Silva. How long did he live in this town?"

"All his life. He was born here."

"A native-born Paulista, huh? Then he should have known better. You can't stop for a red light. Not after midnight. The best thing is to slow down and keep rolling. That's what most people do."

"I know what most people do, Officer, but my father isn't . . ." Silva swallowed " . . . wasn't like that. As far as I know, he never broke a law in his life, never even got a speeding ticket."

"Too bad everybody's not like him," Mancuso said.

Silva searched the older cop's face for a sign of irony. There wasn't one. He put the photo back on the piano. "Where's my mother?"

"At the Hospital das Clinicas. They got her under sedation," the cherub said, "so it's not going to make any difference to her whether you get there in twenty minutes or two hours. Why don't you sit down a little? I'll tell you the rest."

"I'll stand."

"Suit yourself, but when I finish you're going to wish you were sitting."

Mancuso narrowed his eyes at his partner. "That's enough, Paulo," he said. "Let me tell it."

"Well, *excuse* me," the cherub said petulantly, and crossed his arms in front of his chest.

Mancuso turned his back on him and addressed Silva. "Your mother was pretty hysterical before they put her under," he said, "so we still don't have all the details. Basically, the story is this: Your parents were coming home from some kind of a party—"

"A charity affair," Silva said. "A dinner to raise funds for a new wing at Nossa Senhora de Misericordia. My father is . . . *was* a doctor there."

"Right. So they were coming home, and your old man stopped for a red light, and two elements came up on your mother's side, tapped on the window and pointed a hand-gun at her head. Your father did the right thing. He did-n't resist. I mean, it's only money, right? No matter how much they take, it isn't worth losing your life for. We always tell people—"

"Please finish the story, Sergeant."

"Okay. So your father unlocked the door. The two perps hopped into the back seat. Your mom said the guy holding the gun put the muzzle up against your father's neck, like this."

Mancuso walked around behind his partner and demon-strated, putting the tip of his extended index finger up to the back of the cherub's neck. The cherub didn't move, kept his cold eyes fixed on Silva.

Silva shook his head in disbelief. "And shot him? Shot him just like that? With no warning? For no reason? For nothing?"

"No," the cherub said, apparently finding it impossible to keep his mouth shut. "Not then. The punk told him to drive up to the Serra de Cantareira."

The Serra, a mountain range that looked down on the city from the north, was a place of unpaved roads, few houses, and thick vegetation. There were monkeys up there and brightly colored tropical birds.

"Why? Why the Serra de Cantareira?"

"Yeah, well, I was getting to that," Mancuso resumed. He looked pained. "It's isolated. There wouldn't be anybody around at that time of night. They weren't likely to get interrupted."

"What do you mean 'interrupted'?"

"They . . . well; first they took everything of any value,

money, watches, jewelry. Then they told both of your folks to get out of the car."

The cop paused to light a cigarette. He didn't bother to ask Silva if he minded. It was the 1970s. Nobody asked back then. He took a deep drag, expelled the smoke and looked around for an ashtray. There was one on the coffee table. He leaned over and dropped the extinguished match into it.

Silva was about to snap at him to finish the goddamned story when he realized that the cop was stalling for time, trying to find a gentle, less painful way to say what he had to say.

Mancuso couldn't find one. In the end, he just blurted it out, "They raped her."

"They *what*?"

"Raped her."

"Sergeant Mancuso, my mother is fifty-three years old. She's overweight, she's diabetic—"

"They wanted your father to stand there and watch it," Mancuso said, talking faster now, eager to get it over with. "He wouldn't have it. He went after the guy who was holding her down. The other guy shot him twice in the head. It was quick. He didn't suffer, didn't live long enough to see what they did to her."

Silva put his hands over his eyes and started to cry.

Mancuso stood and put a hand on his shoulder. "But your mother's okay. You hear me? She's okay. They took the car. We're looking for it. It's one of those big Ford Galaxies, right?"

Silva nodded.

"There aren't too many of them," Mancuso said, "so they're easy to spot. If they hold on to it for any time at all, we're going to nail them."

At that moment, Silva couldn't have cared less about the two punks. "And . . . my mother. What happened then?"

"When they were . . . done, she managed to get herself back to the main road."

"She walked?"

"Crawled is more like it," the cherub said.

"Shut up, Paulo," Mancuso said. "There's not much traffic up there after nine or ten at night and she was . . . well, she was bleeding, so she just didn't have it in her to go any further. She propped herself up under a streetlight and started waving at the cars that went by. After a while, somebody had the guts to stop."

"Who?"

"We don't know. He called it in from a phone booth, left her by the side of the road, told us where to find her, said he didn't want to get involved. It happens. At least he stopped for a look. Not everybody would have."

Dr. Silva's Galaxy was found later that morning abandoned on a suburban back street. The killers had removed the tires. They'd also taken the radio. If there were any latent fingerprints, the cops didn't find them. The truth of the matter was they hardly tried.

Silva's parents weren't particularly prominent people. The incident drew no bold headlines. São Paulo was one of the major murder capitals of the world, and the municipal police had other priorities.

Silva was told that such things are solved within the first 48 hours or not at all. It was something he refused to accept. If the cops wouldn't do anything about it, Silva was bound and determined that *he* would. He questioned his mother again and again. There were some things she couldn't bring herself to talk about, others that her son couldn't bring himself to ask, but a few salient facts emerged: both men were mulattos, in their twenties, clean-shaven, curly haired. Both had distinctive accents. They were from the northeast,

Bahia perhaps, or one of the neighboring states. One of them had a tattoo, a snake that started on his chest, wrapped once around his neck, and ended in a protruding tongue that pointed at the lobe of his left ear. The other one, a man missing a couple of his front teeth, had done the shooting.

The cops' initial questioning hadn't brought out the details about the snake or the teeth. Silva thought they were important clues. The investigators didn't.

"It'd be different if we had something to cross-reference," a detective named Valdez told him, "like a list of all the punks with tattoos, or all the punks with dental problems. But we don't. And we sure as hell don't have the manpower to put people on the street trying to find somebody who knows somebody with a tattoo like that. Best thing for your mother to do is to put it all behind her, put the whole thing out of her mind. Jesus Christ! It's been three weeks already, and that's much too long. Let me level with you, Senhor Silva, we haven't got one chance in a million of catching these guys, and it's not going to do her any good to keep dwelling on what happened to her."

Detective Valdez was right. It didn't do Carla Silva any good at all, but she was unable to dwell upon anything else.

For three months, she cried day and night. Then she ingested twenty of the sleeping pills she'd been hoarding. Silva laid her to rest in the family crypt, turned his back on a legal career, and joined the Federal Police.

Chapter Four

MARIO SILVA'S TRAINING AT the Federal Police Academy took seven months. He graduated first in his class and was assigned to the field office in Rio de Janeiro, working drug control.

That kept him busy for five days out of every week. The other two he spent in São Paulo, a 45-minute flight away. Partly, it was to pursue his courtship of Irene, but mostly it was to follow up on what he then considered to be his best lead. His mother's wristwatch had vanished along with the rest of her jewelry. It was a Patek Phillippe in yellow gold, unusual anywhere, unique because of the inscription on the back of the case:

> *To Carla,*
> *Who enriches my autumn*
> *As she enriched my springtime.*
> > *Mario*

Mario had also been his father's name.

Canvassing all of the jewelry stores in São Paulo was a big job. There were thousands of them and some, no doubt, specialized in stolen goods. He thought it best to represent himself as a potential buyer, not a cop. After months of disappointment, Silva no longer felt a surge of adrenaline when he saw a watch that resembled his mother's until the day he turned one over and found his father's words staring up at him.

It was the end of November, 1979. His mother had been dead for ten months.

"If she's Clara, and you're Mario, this is definitely the watch for you," the man behind the counter said, pushing the sale, trying to make a joke of the inscription.

He had buck teeth and was young, too young to own the place. He wore an expensive black suit and a silk tie covered with little butterflies. Silva, who'd pegged him as the business's heir apparent, didn't reply, didn't even smile. He just kept staring at the watch, running his thumb over the words on the back of the case.

The clerk continued his pitch. "I've got to be honest with you. We considered polishing it off, but the engraving is too deep. That's why it's such a good deal. Do you have any idea what one of these things costs when it's new?"

He was distinctly displeased when Silva produced his warrant card and demanded to know how the watch had wound up in the shop.

THE YOUNG man's father, as Silva had suspected, owned the place. He wasn't particularly surprised to be told that the watch was stolen, and his previous experience with such things had taught him to keep meticulous records of his sources.

The trail led to a pawnshop near the center of town. It was a place with a frontage no more than four meters wide, but it was at least twenty deep, and stuffed with everything from musical instruments to household appliances.

"Sure, I remember it," the pawnbroker told Silva. He was a little man with a bald pate, a shock of surrounding white hair, wearing wire-rimmed glasses and a denim vest. "One of the best deals I ever made. The guy had no idea what it was worth. I didn't figure he was coming back, and he didn't, but I kept it for the full ninety days anyway."

"Why did you think he wasn't going to come back?"

The owner hesitated. "I just didn't," he said, avoiding Silva's eyes.

The man in the vest knew more than he was telling.

"You got a name? An address?"

"Sure. It's the law, right?"

According to the man's records, the watch had come into his possession five days after the murder. Still, Silva didn't get his hopes up. The address was probably false.

First, he thought, he'd go check it out. Then he'd come back and squeeze the pawnbroker for whatever else he knew.

An outdated map of the city, and two stops to ask for directions, brought Silva to a little street in the working-class suburb of São Caetano.

The house was identical to the buildings on either side, hastily constructed out of white stucco, showing fissures in the mortar. In contrast to the green and flowery gardens of the neighbors, the short path leading to the front door was hemmed by dusty red earth. The door was blue, but its paint was peeling, showing the cheap pine beneath. The tiles on the front steps were cracked, and one was missing altogether, the impression of its ribbed underside still visible in the gray cement.

Silva tried the doorbell.

It didn't work.

He knocked.

There was no answer, but he could hear a baby squalling from somewhere inside.

He knocked again, louder.

The woman who finally opened the door had prematurely graying hair and a crying, red-faced baby in her arms.

"*Boa tarde*, senhora," he greeted her. "Does José de Alencar live here?"

To his surprise, she nodded. An appetizing smell of garlic sautéing in olive oil was coming from the kitchen. It reminded Silva that he hadn't had lunch.

"Is he home?"

"Who wants to know?" she said, suspiciously.

Silva flashed his warrant card.

"Federal Police. I want to talk to him about a case."

"Let me have a closer look at that," she said.

He reopened his wallet. She scrutinized his credentials.

"Yeah, okay," she said. "He's here. Come in."

As he stepped through the front door, she put the baby over her shoulder and started patting it on the back, but the squalling continued.

"You're lucky," she said. "He just switched over to the eight PM to four AM shift. If you'd come last week, you wouldn't have caught him." She'd raised her voice to make herself understood over the baby's crying. Now, she raised it still further. "José, you got company."

She showed a distinct lack of concern about an unexpected visit from the police. The reason became clear when her husband walked in, buttoning his shirt. There were stripes on the sleeve and insignia on the lapels.

José de Alencar was a sergeant in the São Paulo Police Department.

That explained the reticence of the pawnshop owner. Nobody wanted any trouble with the SPPD.

"I've got lunch on the stove," the woman said.

"You want me to take him?" the sergeant asked, pointing at his son.

De Alencar was in his mid-thirties, pale skinned, with a cruel mouth and gray eyes that turned soft when he looked at his offspring. He had a thin but well-tended mustache on his upper lip.

The woman smiled at him. "No," she said, "He's okay. Just a little bit of colic, I think. Come soon. I don't want you bolting down your lunch." A moment later, she and the squalling baby were gone, leaving the two cops alone.

Silva glanced around the room. An expensive stereo

system, a brand-new television set, a leather sofa and two leather armchairs, a table that looked to be made out of jacaranda wood. None of it fit. Not with the house's external appearance, and certainly not with a guy who was supposedly surviving on the salary of a municipal cop.

"So you're José de Alencar?"

The sergeant picked up on Silva's tone of voice. His gray eyes went from soft to hard, seemed almost to change their color, becoming a shade darker. "Yeah. Who are you?"

Silva's credentials were still in his hand. He held them out.

De Alencar took a step closer and read them. "A federal, huh?" he said curiosity turning to hostility. "What do you want?"

Silva's mother had described her assailants as in their early twenties and mulattos. This guy was in his thirties and white. His teeth were good. He had no tattoo. There was no way he could be one of them.

"It's about a watch you pawned," Silva said. "A gold one with an inscription on the back."

"When was this?"

"October of last year. You left it with Gilson Alveres, who owns a pawnshop on Rua Rio Branco. Your signature's on the ticket."

"So what?"

"I want to know where you got it."

"What's it to you?"

"It belonged to my mother. Someone stole it."

The sergeant's face reddened, but whether in embarrassment or irritation, Silva couldn't tell.

"Well, I sure as hell didn't," he said. "I found it,"

"Found it? Where?"

"On the street."

"Where on the street?"

"I don't remember?"

"Try."

"I told you, I don't remember."

"And you expect me to believe that?"

"I don't give a shit what you believe. Fuck you."

Silva saw red. He reached out his left hand and grabbed the sergeant by the front of his shirt. "Where did you really get that watch?"

The sergeant was at least twenty kilograms lighter than Silva, and maybe ten centimeters shorter, but he didn't back down.

"You got any idea who you're dealing with? You take me on and you're going to have the whole damned force on your back. Let go of my shirt."

The sergeant was right. The municipal cops stuck together. It was the only way for them to keep on doing what they did.

Silva released the sergeant, took a deep breath and a step backward. "The way I figure it is you lifted my mother's watch off of some lowlife punk. And you know what? I really don't care. All I care about is his name and where to find him."

"Who the hell do you think you are, coming in here and making accusations like that? Get the fuck out of my house."

"I need to know, Sergeant. Those filhos da puta killed my father and raped my mother."

The sergeant's red face turned even redder. "Tough. My heart bleeds. But I had nothing to do with it. Now, get out of here before I call some friends."

AT 4:30 the following morning, Sergeant de Alencar, sleepy from a long night at work, was walking along the deserted street, and less than five meters from his house, when he felt cold steel on the back of his neck.

"It's a revolver, and it's cocked," a voice said. "Keep your hand away from your holster. Pass your front door and keep walking."

"I don't know who you are, senhor, but you're making a big mistake."

"Shut up. Now, cross the street, stop next to the green car, and put your hands on the roof."

The sergeant did as he was told. The man behind him relieved him of his revolver, patted him down, and pocketed a small Beretta 7.65 semi-automatic that de Alencar was carrying in an ankle holster. Then he used the cop's own cuffs to shackle his hands behind his back and opened the rear door of the car.

"Get in."

"What is this?"

"Just do it."

The sergeant felt the revolver again, pressing into the back of his neck. He did as he was told. When the man slipped in beside him, de Alencar glanced at his face.

"You!" he said.

"Me. Tell me about the punk you got the watch from."

"There wasn't any punk. I already told you—"

Silva cut him short by smashing him in the face with the butt of his .38 Taurus. The sergeant began to bleed profusely from his nose and lip. Silva reached behind him and threw him a towel. He'd come prepared.

"I know what you told me. Now listen to me very carefully. If you tell me what I want to know, and then keep your mouth shut about it, it stops here. If you don't, I'm going to kill you, and then I'm going to go into your house and kill your wife, that baby of yours, and anybody else who's in there. Your choice."

It was a bluff. He would never have done it, but the sergeant looked into Silva's eyes, black as death, and believed him.

THEY WERE just a couple of punks, the sergeant said, just like the hundreds of others he'd shaken down in his lifetime.

He'd been on patrol with two rookies, teaching them the ropes, teaching them how to get along on the *salário de merda* that was supposed to keep a roof over their heads and food in their bellies and didn't.

It had been broad daylight, maybe 2:00 or 3:00 in the afternoon. They were cruising along Avenida Faria Lima, not far from that big shopping center, Iguatemi, when Flores, one of the rookies, spotted a Rolex. Everybody, even a green kid like Flores, knew what a Rolex was, right?

Silva nodded. There were gangs in São Paulo that specialized in lifting that one brand alone and sending the watches off to Paraguay for resale. But he wasn't there to talk about Rolexes.

"Get on with it," he snapped.

"I *am* getting on with it. See, the thing about this particular Rolex was that the guy who was wearing it was a lowlife punk with dirty sneakers and a fucking Palmeiras shirt."

He remembered the shirt, the sergeant told Silva, because, just the previous night, Palmeiras had stolen a game from Corinthians, four goals to three, because of a blind referee who, in de Alencar's opinion, had no place on a soccer pitch and should never have been given a whistle.

Silva told him to shut up about soccer teams and finish the story.

De Alencar swallowed, and continued. "The punk with the shirt . . . no, that was wrong, it wasn't a shirt. It was more like a jersey—"

Silva waved the pistol.

"—well, he wasn't alone. There were two of them. And both of them were punks. The other guy was dressed in one of those fucking, stupid-"

Silva narrowed his eyes and took in an audible breath.

De Alencar cut short his sartorial criticism and hastened to tell how he and the two rookies had taken both punks into a convenient alley for a quick search. The watch was a Rolex all right, stainless steel with a black face. They'd gotten six hundred cruzeiros for that one. The other watch, the one Silva was talking about, was in the pocket of the other punk. Because it was gold, it brought three times that. They'd split the money, half going to him, half going to the two rookies. He was a sergeant, after all, and that's the way it worked. The senior guy always got half the take.

All the while they were being shaken down, the punks didn't say a word. What could they say? That the watches were family heirlooms? Yeah, right! So they just emptied their pockets and asked de Alencar and the two rookies to leave them enough change for the bus. No hard feelings on either side. That was just the way it worked.

Names? No. It had been over a year ago. How could Silva expect him to remember names? He hadn't seen them before, he hadn't seen them since, and after all this time, he sure as hell wouldn't recognize them from a mug shot.

They were *Bahianos,* he remembered that much. Well, maybe not from Bahia, maybe from Pernambuco, or Alagoas. It could be anywhere up that way, because all of those fucking northeastern accents sounded the same to him, and in the sergeant's opinion, all of those lazy bastards should be crammed into a fleet of buses and shipped right back to where they belonged because, more than anybody else, it was them that were fucking up the city.

"And that's it? That's all you can remember?" Silva said, cutting the social commentary short.

"Yeah. That's it."

Before he'd smashed de Alencar in the face, Silva had lowered the hammer of his Taurus. Now, he cocked it again.

"What are you doing?" the sergeant said, nervously. "Watch out for that thing."

"Think hard. Give me something else."

The sergeant swallowed, crimped his eyes shut, opened them again. "There was one more thing," he said.

"What?"

"One of them had this tattoo. It was a snake that started under that fucking jersey, maybe down on his chest. Then it curved all the way around his neck and the head and tongue were just under his ear."

The tattoo clinched it for Silva.

The man in front of him had been face-to-face with the men who'd killed his father and raped his mother. De Alencar had been close enough to smell them, close enough to reach out and touch them. But now they'd vanished again, and Silva's lead had run out, all because of the venality of three municipal cops.

Only the thought of the woman and baby sleeping across the street caused him to stay his hand. The sergeant never realized how close his wife had been to becoming a widow.

Chapter Five

EMERSON FERRAZ, THE COLONEL in charge of Cascatas do Pontal's State Police Battalion, had clumps of hair protruding from his nostrils, pockmarked skin, a forehead about two fingers high and a personality as ugly as the rest of him.

When Hector Costa, after a thirty-minute wait, was admitted to his presence, Ferraz didn't even look up. For a good minute-and-a-half Hector stood in front of the colonel's desk like a schoolboy called up for disciplinary action. All the while, Ferraz scratched away on a yellow legal pad with a Mont Blanc fountain pen. The pen, dwarfed by his pudgy fingers, looked out of place in the hands of a man earning the salary of a cop.

The office stank of sweat and cigar smoke, both of them stale. Topping the clutter on Ferraz's desk was the business card Hector had handed to the uniformed policewoman—no beauty herself—who functioned as Ferraz's secretary.

Tiring of being ignored, Hector sank, uninvited, into one of the two chairs in front of the colonel's desk.

"Sure. That's right. Just make yourself comfortable," the colonel said, putting down his pen and raising his head. He stared at Hector out of a pair of porcine brown eyes and then screwed up his face as if his visitor had just passed gas. "I've heard about you," he said. Ferraz emphasized his words by jabbing at Hector's card with a pudgy forefinger.

Hector groaned inwardly. He knew what was coming.

"Your boss is Mario Silva, who just happens to be your uncle, am I right?"

Hector hated it when people brought that up.

"Yeah, I thought so." Ferraz said, responding to Hector's nod, as if he'd just wrung a confession from some criminal he particularly disliked. "Well, let me tell you something. I don't need your help." He picked up Hector's card, ripped it in half, and dropped the pieces into a wastebasket. "And I don't need your *uncle*, either." He made the word "uncle" sound as if it was some kind of epithet.

Hector was tempted to tell him that neither he, nor his uncle, needed, or wanted, Ferraz or his damned case either, but the colonel wasn't finished.

"Something else. I don't talk to messenger boys. If that uncle of yours wants anything from me, tell him to come himself."

Ferraz picked up his pen and went back to doing whatever he'd been doing when Hector arrived. For some time the only sound in the office was the constant whir and clank of heavy construction machinery drifting in through the closed windows and the scratching of the colonel's pen on paper. Hector waited him out, saying nothing.

After a while, Ferraz looked up and blinked theatrically. "Still here?" he said.

"He *is* coming himself," Hector said, picking up where Ferraz had left off, "but he had to clear his schedule. He'll be here tomorrow morning."

"Here?"

"Here. In Cascatas."

"The almighty inspector-general himself?"

"His title, Colonel, is Chief Inspector for Criminal Matters."

"No shit? Chief Inspector, eh? Well, don't expect me to be waiting at the airport with a brass band. And tell him that if he wants to come here"—Ferraz stabbed the desktop with the same forefinger he'd used to jab the card—"he'd better call for an appointment."

As if emphasizing what the colonel said, someone on the floor above flushed a toilet.

Hector crossed his arms and leaned back in his chair."Do both of us a favor, Colonel," he said, choosing his words carefully, but letting his irritation show. "Answer my questions. It'll save you time in the long run."

Ferraz didn't appear to be ruffled by the absence of cordiality. In fact, he seemed to welcome it. "Okay," he said. "How about I give you five minutes of my time. Starting . . ." he glanced at his watch " . . . now."

He took a box of thin cigars from the drawer of his desk, chose one, and replaced the box without offering it to Hector.

Hector had already noticed that Ferraz had a slight wheeze when he talked. *Probably*, he thought, *because he inhales the damned things*. He wasn't looking forward to the colonel lighting up that cheroot.

The colonel seemed to sense it. He licked the cigar to moisten it and rolled it back and forth between his palms, staring at Hector all the while.

Hector had made inquiries about Colonel Emerson Ferraz before leaving São Paulo: *Politically connected and close to retirement*, a friend at the State Police had told him. *Wasn't born rich, didn't marry into money, but drives some kind of fancy imported car, owns a really big fazenda, and takes vacations in Miami*.

What Hector's friend *hadn't* told him was that Colonel Ferraz, in addition to almost certainly being a crook, was also a nasty son of a bitch.

Ferraz bit a piece from the end of his cigar and spit it across his desk, narrowly missing the chair to Hector's right.

"What do you want to know?" he asked.

"Do you have any leads?"

"Not a one," the colonel said contentedly. He removed a

box of long wooden matches from his breast pocket, lit up, and blew some smoke in Hector's direction. The cigar was Bahian and the smell was everything Hector had feared it would be. He started breathing through his mouth, a trick he'd taught himself after being exposed to too many rotting corpses.

"Speed it up," the colonel said. "You've got four minutes and forty seconds."

"Where did the shots come from?" Hector asked.

"The north tower of the new church."

"How can you be sure?"

"We found the murder weapon."

Ferraz opened the drawer of his desk.

Hector sniffed. A telltale smell filled his nostrils. *A photo. Recently processed.* Hector was blessed, sometimes cursed, with an extraordinary sense of smell, a sense so acute that he could have made a living as a perfumer or a wine taster. He'd already found the stale sweat and the cheap cigar smoke hard to bear. Now, despite the trick of breathing through his mouth, there was the dominant top note of a photographic print hardly dry.

Ferraz handed it over. The paper was still damp.

The image was of a firearm, a rifle with a telescopic sight and a leather sling. It had been photographed against a white background, perhaps a Formica table.

"Looks like a Sako Classic with a Leupold scope," Hector said.

Ferraz tipped some ash into an ashtray. "It is," he said, a reluctant note of admiration creeping into his voice.

"What was he firing?"

"Nosler ballistic tips," the colonel said, and then, glancing at his watch, "three minutes and twenty seconds."

Hector kept staring at the photograph. In Brazil, the rifle and ammunition were unusual—sniper stuff—but these days, you could buy just about any firearm you wanted in the *favelas* of São Paulo and Rio de Janeiro. The drug gangs smuggled them in from Paraguay or bought them from corrupt quartermasters in Brazil's armed services. The crooks were as well armed as the police and often better.

"Latent prints?"

The colonel put the cigar back into his mouth, held it firmly between his teeth, and tipped it up at a jaunty angle. "Not one. Wiped clean," he said through clenched teeth.

"My people are going to want to inspect the rifle."

"Be my guest. It's in the evidence locker downstairs."

"And no one saw anyone going in or out of the tower?"

"Nope."

Ferraz took the cigar out of his mouth and bared his teeth, more of a grimace than a smile. The teeth were tobacco-stained and as crooked as the tombstones in an old cemetery.

"Have you sealed off the tower?"

"Of course I have. What do you take me for?"

An ugly, unpleasant son of a bitch. But Hector didn't say it. He took a shallow breath and let it out slowly. "Any theories about the motive?"

"Seven, to be exact."

"*Seven?*"

"Seven. The reception committee. They're all landowners and each and every one of them thinks the bullets were meant for *him*."

"They think the bishop was shot by mistake?"

"What did I just say?"

"Why?"

"Ever hear of the Landless Workers' League?"

"Sure."

"How about Aurelio Azevedo?"

Hector shook his head. "Aurelio who?"

"Azevedo. He was their leader around these parts, a real

pain-in-the-ass. About a month ago, somebody killed him. His buddies figure it must have been a landowner and they're out for blood."

"What do *you* think?"

The colonel took another deep drag on his cigar. "They're wrong. The bishop was the target." He expelled the smoke and coughed. He brought up some phlegm and leaned over to spit it into the wastebasket next to his chair.

Someday, Hector thought, *those cigars are going to kill him. But not soon enough to suit me*. "What makes you so sure?" he said.

"When the first shot was fired the whole reception committee, all seven of them, stopped dead in their tracks. The closest one, the mayor, was still four meters away, maybe even a little more. The second shot hit the bishop just above the line between his eyes, took off the back of his head. That sound to you like the shooter didn't know what he was doing? No way. He was aiming at Dom Felipe, all right. No doubt about it."

Ferraz pulled up his cuff and ostentatiously displayed his watch. It was a gold Rolex. "You've got two minutes left."

"Tell me more about this guy Azevedo."

Ferraz took another puff. The smoke was beginning to sting Hector's eyes.

"Azevedo was a field hand out on the Fazenda da Boa Vista," he said. "No criminal record. Never made any trouble until those League people got to him. Then he started going to meetings and rallies and the next thing you know he's running around in a red shirt, waving one of those banners and organizing a group to occupy Muniz's land."

"Muniz? Orlando Muniz? The industrialist?"

"And banker, and God knows what else. He's richer than God. He owns the Boa Vista, and his son, Junior, runs it."

"Tell me more about what happened to Azevedo."

Ferraz studied the ash on his cigar, twirled it, tapped it gently on the edge of a large brass ashtray, and took another puff. "Not much more to tell. He turned up one morning nailed to a tree in front of his shack. They'd cut off his cock and stuffed it in his mouth. His wife and kids were inside the house. All of them shot through the back of the head."

"No suspects?"

Ferraz shrugged. "The League people got it into their heads that it was Junior, accused him of bringing in hired guns from Paraguay to do the job, but they could never prove it. You got one minute left."

"All right. Let's get back to the bishop. Despite what the mayor and those other six guys on the reception committee think, you're convinced that the bishop was the target and that the Landless Workers' League had nothing to do with it. Is that right?"

"Did I say that?" Ferraz took another puff, but offered nothing more.

"Explain," Hector said, shortly.

"Dom Felipe was new in the job. The old bishop died about six months ago, and not a minute too soon, if you ask me. Mellor was his name. Dom Augusto Mellor. He was a piece of work, the old bastard, a big supporter of the League. He had his priests out recruiting new members, showing up at their rallies, helping them to plan occupations of fazendas, all that kind of shit. He was no better than a fucking communist. Now, Dom Felipe, he was different."

A small piece of ash fell off of Ferraz's cigar and onto his gray shirt. He brushed it off with a practiced gesture.

"Different? How?"

Ferraz glanced at his watch and grinned.

"Time's up," he said.

Chapter Six

By three o'clock in the afternoon the sky over Cascatas do Pontal had turned a pinkish white.

"Dust," the desk clerk at the Hotel Excelsior told Hector, "kicked up by all the construction. It's a good thing. It means the town is growing."

The clerk sounded as if someone had told him to say that to visitors, as if he didn't quite believe it himself. He was a young fellow, probably not more than twenty-one or twenty-two, with the flat nose, jet-black hair, and coppery skin that betokened Indian blood. He and Hector were the only two people in the lobby.

Hector leaned one elbow on the counter. "Where's the church?"

"Which one?" the Indio said with a touch of pride. "We have lots of churches, senhor. There's Santa Mari—"

He had his fingers out in front of him, his thumb extended upward, ready to count the rest of them off, but Hector cut him short. "The one the bishop was coming to consecrate."

"Ah," he said, his hands falling to his sides. "That would be the new one, Nossa Senhora dos Milagres."

"Who's the priest?"

The clerk looked blank. "Senhor?"

"The priest at Nossa Senhora dos Milagres. What's his name?"

"That would be Father Gaspar."

"New in town, is he?"

"Oh, no, senhor. He used to be at Santa Cecilia's on the Rua Governador Quercia, but it's closed now. They're going to tear it down and put up a school."

"Where do I find this Father Gaspar?"

The clerk reached to one side and pulled a street map of downtown Cascatas from a nearby stack.

"We're here," he said, circling an intersection with a red ballpoint pen. "And the church is . . . here." He made a cross. "Father Gaspar lives next door. You can't miss it."

THE CLERK was right. You couldn't miss it. The priest's house was three stories tall and had an enclosed garage. It was built of the same red brick as the church, an obvious annex to the much larger building.

The young man who answered the doorbell had tawny skin and reddish-brown hair that hung low over his forehead. He had a single earring, a nose that showed signs of having been broken more than once, and mismatched lips. The upper one was thin and the lower one fleshy. He was wearing white duck pants, an open-necked white shirt, and a white jacket. His black shoes were highly polished. His manners weren't.

"Got an appointment?" he said, before Hector had a chance to utter a word.

"I'm here to see Father Gaspar."

The young man raised his eyes and sighed. "I didn't think it was to see me, so I ask you again. Have you got an appointment?"

"No, but—"

"Then call and make one."

He started to swing the door shut, but not quickly enough.

"Hey," he said, "get your foot out of the—"

Hector didn't wait for him to finish. "Tell Father Gaspar that it's police business."

The door swung open again, relieving the pressure on Hector's foot.

"You're a cop?"

Hector nodded. "I'm a cop. Federal Police."

"Prove it."

"Jesus Christ," Hector said, but he reached for his wallet.

"We don't take the name of the Lord in vain around here," the young man said, reprovingly. He studied Hector's ID. "You got a business card in there?"

Hector fished one out and handed it over.

"Okay, wait here. And take your foot out of the door."

Hector did, and the surly servant slammed it shut.

A few minutes later the servant was back. This time he swung the door wide, led Hector toward the back of the house, and ushered him into a room where a fat man in a black cassock was waiting for him. Limpid brown eyes stared at Hector from beneath bushy eyebrows.

Hector took the hand he was offered. The priest exerted only the slightest pressure before he let go.

"Father Gaspar Farias," he said.

"Pleased to meet you, Father. Hector Costa, Federal Police."

Completely bald, Father Gaspar had slightly protuberant eyes, a wide mouth, virtually no neck and a double chin. His head seemed to be out of proportion to the rest of his body. He reminded Hector of a huge frog.

The priest's study was a high-ceilinged room lined with bookshelves. A rustic dining table had been pressed into service as a writing desk. Two cane chairs were situated in front of it, and a more comfortable one, in black leather, was behind.

A strong floral perfume hung in the air. Hector sniffed. *Lilacs?* The priest was using a scent more suited to a woman than to a man, and to an older woman to boot.

"Have a seat," Father Gaspar said, indicating one of the cane chairs and sinking down in the other.

When Hector sat he felt a cold blast of air-conditioning on the back of his neck. He glanced upward and discovered that his chair had been placed directly under the vent. He shifted his seat and tried leaning forward slightly, but it didn't seem to help. The priest showed no sign of noticing his discomfort.

"Am I the first to welcome you to Cascatas, Delegado?"

Father Gaspar was using Hector's title, the one on his business card, a clear improvement on the treatment he'd received from Ferraz.

"Yes, Father, you are. Not the first person I've spoken to, mind you, but certainly the first person to welcome me."

A look of consternation came over the priest's face. "I'm sorry. Euclides can be a bit abrasive at times."

"Euclides?"

"The young man who answered the door, my self-appointed watchdog. Sometimes a bit too zealous, but—" The priest broke off when the door swung open.

Euclides came in carrying a tray with coffee, already poured. He put a cup and saucer in front of each man.

Hector picked up his cup and took a sip. The coffee was nauseatingly pre-sweetened, and cold. He glanced over at the priest and saw a thin wisp of steam arising from the other cup. Determined not to give Euclides any degree of satisfaction, Hector drained the remainder of his coffee, and smacked his lips, as if he'd actually enjoyed it.

The servant's thin smile faded. He leaned his back against the wall, settling in.

"Thank you, Euclides," Father Gaspar said pointedly. Then, when his servant still didn't seem to get it, he added, "That will be all."

Euclides narrowed his eyes and left without a word. Hector had no doubt he'd be listening on the other side of the door.

"What can I do for you, Delegado?"

"I'd like to talk to you about Dom Felipe."

Father Gaspar furrowed his brow. "A terrible thing, that. A terrible thing."

"You knew him well?"

There were four picture frames on Father Gaspar's desk, all with their backs toward them. The priest leaned forward, picked up the largest one and handed it to his visitor.

"That's him, there, on the right."

In the photo, Dom Felipe's hair hadn't yet turned white. There were three men in the shot. The man standing on the left was a younger, and much thinner, Father Gaspar. The third man was the Pope.

"Taken . . . let me see . . . seventeen years ago this April in the garden of the Vatican. Autumn here, but it was springtime in Europe. Winter had been mild that year. You can see that the flowers were already in bloom." He took the photograph back from Hector and stared at it.

"The bishop and I were great friends," he said. "Longtime friends. I shall miss him. The church will miss him." He seemed to make a conscious effort to shake off his melancholy. His voice took on a more businesslike tone when he said, "Have you made any progress in discovering who did it?"

"Not yet, Father. Were you there when it happened?"

"Yes, I was. I was standing in the vestibule of the church. I saw it all. The first shot hit him in the chest. The second . . . ."

His words tapered off. He shook his head, rubbed some dust off of the top of the frame, and returned the photo to its original position.

"Sorry, Father. I'm sure this must be painful for you, but—"

"No, Delegado. Don't apologize. I want to be of any help that I possibly can. Please, ask away."

"Thank you, Father. I'll try to be brief. Can you think of any reason why someone would want to kill him?"

Father Gaspar hesitated. Hector noticed, and gave him a gentle push. "Did he have any enemies?"

"Everyone has enemies, Delegado. Even priests."

Hector sat back in his chair and crossed his legs. His instincts told him Father Gaspar was holding something back. "Could his death have had something to do with ah . . . an intimate relationship?"

Father Gaspar looked confused.

Hector was forced to explain.

"Women, perhaps? Or boys?"

"Certainly not," Gaspar said, reddening.

"Money, then? Was he particularly fond of money?"

The priest shook his head. "To him, money was only an instrument, an instrument he employed to help the less fortunate. And to celebrate the glory of God."

"You're not giving me much to work with, Father. In my world, unless they're insane—and, believe me, I'm not ruling out that possibility—people kill each other for revenge, jealousy, money, and very little else."

"And do you think, Delegado, that *your* world is so very different from his or, for that matter, from mine?"

"Frankly, I hope it is. Mine can get pretty ugly at times. But, if he wasn't killed for revenge, or for jealousy or for money. . . ."

Hector let the unasked question hang in the air.

Father Gaspar folded his hands over his ample stomach, and blinked. It made him look all the more like a frog. Then he nodded, as if he'd made a decision.

"Are you familiar with liberation theology, Delegado?"

"Familiar with it? No. I've heard the term, that's all."

"The expression *liberation theology* comes from the title of a book, a book written more than forty years ago by a Peruvian priest named Gustavo Gutierrez. He entitled it *The Theology of Liberation*."

"I don't see—"

"Bear with me, Delegado. I don't know any other way to

explain this, and I think it's something you should be made aware of."

Hector inclined his head.

The priest continued. "Liberation theologians believe the church should be involved in what they call 'the struggle for economic and political justice.'"

"Struggle?"

"That's the word they use. Struggle." Father Gaspar lifted a forefinger like a teacher anxious to make a point. "They maintain that there are two kinds of Christianity: their kind, liberation theology, which proposes radical change, and another kind, one that favors the status quo."

"And by the 'status quo,' they mean?"

"The current distribution of wealth, more specifically of land."

"What's land got to do with theology?"

"For them? Everything! They maintain that rural people who don't own at least a small piece of land are doomed to live as an underclass. On the other hand, they say that the ownership of vast tracts of land defines membership in a group that exploits and oppresses the poor."

"And you, Father? Do you subscribe to that?"

The priest looked shocked, as if Hector had just accused him of something morally repugnant. "Of course not! But all liberation theologians do. They also believe that priests who defend the status quo, priests like Dom Felipe and myself, are lackeys to the rich. They say we're brainwashing the poor."

"Brainwashing?"

"Brainwashing. Their phrase, not mine. They accuse us of convincing the landless that they should be patient here on earth because that's what God wants. Then, when they die, they'll get their reward in heaven."

"Land in heaven?"

Hector smiled, but the priest didn't.

"Unfortunately, some of the simpler people interpret it exactly that way. It's a lie! We don't teach them that. We teach that paradise awaits for all good men, both rich and poor. Liberation theologians, on the other hand, postulate that everyone has a God-given right to a certain degree of wealth *in this life*. They want to force radical change. They propose redistribution of wealth, redistribution of land, here and now."

"Sounds like Marxism."

"Similar, but different. The concept of sin is alien to Marxism, but not to liberation theologians. To them, *not* overthrowing the ruling class, *not* fighting to redistribute wealth, is a sin, a sin of the gravest nature, perhaps the gravest one of all."

"So they basically advocate some kind of a holy war, a crusade, a Christian jihad?"

"Exactly. And they embrace anything it takes to achieve their ends."

"Even violence?"

"Even violence. There was a classmate of Gutierrez, a priest by the name of Camilo Torres. He was killed fighting with the guerillas in Colombia. When they found his body he had a weapon in his hands."

Hector shook his head. "How can the church tolerate something like that?"

"The church doesn't. Not anymore. Liberation theology has been condemned."

"Condemned?"

"By the Sacred Congregation for the Propagation of the Faith, the body that rules on such things.

"And Dom Felipe . . ."

"Devoutly carried out the dictates of his superiors."

"Which brought him in direct conflict with the liberation theologians?"

"Exactly. But he welcomed the conflict. Dom Felipe saw it as his duty to bring them to heel. He made it clear that priests who were liberation theologians had to renounce the doctrine or leave the Church."

"Which wouldn't have made him popular with the people from the Landless Workers' League."

"Just so. Simple people—and most landless farmers *are* simple people—interpreted his action as a rejection, by the Church, of everything that the league stood for. The good Catholics among them became concerned that they might be doing something wrong, even impious. They quit the league in droves."

"Which gave the league a good reason to dislike Dom Felipe."

"Exactly."

"Enough to kill him, do you think?"

"Perhaps, but that's not my point."

"What *is* your point, Father?"

"There are still priests out there who ignored Dom Felipe's clear instructions. They're recruiting for the league, battling the landowners, planning the occupation of fazen-das, doing all the things that Dom Felipe expressly told them to stop doing."

"And what, Father, does all of this have to do with the murder of Bishop Antunes?"

Father Gaspar looked surprised.

"Isn't it obvious? I'm trying to tell you, Delegado, that the man who killed Dom Felipe could have been a priest."

Chapter Seven

THE DOOR TO ORLANDO Muniz Junior's bedroom, a door he kept locked and bolted, shattered. Most of it crashed to the floor. What was left flew back on its hinges. Orlando rolled onto his left side and reached for the revolver he kept in the drawer below the lamp, but before he could close his hand around the grip a heavy body fell on top of him.

"Somebody get the lights," a voice said.

Somebody did, and they dazzled him. He opened his mouth to call for Anselmo, and shut it again when he felt cold metal against his forehead. The muzzle of his own revolver. He heard the weapon being cocked and stopped struggling. They stripped off the sheets that covered him and dragged him out of bed.

Orlando was tall with blond hair and blue eyes and had once been handsome. Once. These days, he had a thick waist, a veined cherry of a nose, coarse skin, and permanently bloodshot eyes.

Some said his early good looks had been passed down from his paternal grandmother, a German immigrant to Rio Grande do Sul, Brazil's southernmost state. Others, less charitable, ascribed Orlando's Teutonic genes to a schoolteacher named Ernst Koppel, who'd been beaten to death under mysterious circumstances some six months before Orlando was born. Those same people offered, as support for their argument, the comportment of Orlando's mother, Solange, who'd been seen to shed more tears at Koppel's funeral than anyone else including Koppel's wife of almost a decade. Solange's husband, Orlando Muniz Senior, didn't attend the funeral. While it was taking place he was seen in the bar just across the square from the church. He'd seemed to be having a very good time.

Whatever the truth of his origins, one thing about Orlando Muniz Junior was certain: He was a drunk. Not just an ordinary drunk, but a world-class drunk. He started the day with a tumbler full of cane spirit and an ice-cold beer. He had more beer and more cachaça for lunch, often to the exclusion of anything else. And he consumed at least two bottles of wine at dinner, usually following them with multiple doses of Macieira, a Portuguese brandy to which he was partial, a case of which never lasted him more than a month.

Orlando seldom went to bed before 2:00 in the morning, and often found himself awake at 4:00 or 5:00 AM, his body craving more alcohol. Recently, to assure a good night's sleep, he'd taken to consuming a healthy dose of a sleeping potion that his doctor had refused to prescribe, but that one of the local pharmacists was all-too-willing to provide. So it might have been the alcohol, and it might have been the drug, but one or the other had dulled his wits and slowed him down just enough to prevent him from getting his hand around the grip of that revolver. And either one or both also caused him to stare stupidly around him, shaking his head to clear it, blinking his eyes in confusion and trying to absorb what was happening to him.

The room was filled with men, all of them wearing hoods, a few of them holding guns and most of them clutching makeshift weapons: mattocks, pickaxes and machetes. The man who had Orlando's Taurus .38 pointed it in the air and slowly released the hammer, demonstrating that he knew how to use a revolver.

There was a commotion at the door. Anselmo, his face bloody, his holster empty, was hustled into the room. The man behind him, hooded like all the others, was wearing a red T-shirt bearing the logotype of the Landless Workers' League. While Orlando watched, the man threw a loop of white cord over Anselmo's head. There was a wooden toggle at either end.

They wouldn't dare, Orlando thought.

But they did.

The man gripping the toggles changed hands and started pulling outward, tightening the garrote around Anselmo's neck.

Anselmo's tanned brown face began to flush, only slightly at first, and then becoming redder and redder, as if he was lifting a heavy weight. The capanga's mouth opened and his tongue popped out, but no sound escaped his lips. He needed air in order to cry out and he wasn't getting any. His legs scrabbled, as if he was running in place. Suddenly, the room filled with the smell of excrement, and a spreading stain appeared on the front of Anselmo's faded jeans. His eyes rolled upward and his legs collapsed.

The man in the red T-shirt kept up the pressure until he was quite sure the capanga was dead. Then he motioned to a short man with a prominent Adam's apple just visible under the fall of his hood. Together they dragged Anselmo's lifeless body out of the room.

Orlando was waking up fast. His throat was so dry he had to swallow, twice, before he could utter a word. The word he chose to utter was "please." That was about all he could manage, but it seemed to help. He could hear them relaxing, shuffling their feet, some of the tension going out of them.

"Please? Did you say *please?*" the spokesman said.

"Yes. I said please. Please, don't hurt me." The words were coming easier now.

"Did Aurelio Azevedo ask you not to hurt him when you nailed him to a tree? Did he ask you not to geld him like one of your cattle? Did his wife and children beg you to spare their lives?"

Orlando started shaking his head, stopped when he felt the shooting pain behind his eyes. The brandy always gave him a headache when he didn't have time to sleep it off. "I had nothing to do with any of that," he said.

The spokesman put his hooded face only a few centimeters from Orlando's own, so close that Orlando could smell the tobacco on his breath.

"No?"

He searched Orlando's eyes.

"No," Orlando said. But he looked away.

"You're lying," the spokesman said, and then, raising his voice only slightly, "Carlos."

The man with the red T-shirt, the man he'd called Carlos, came back into the room, his garrote doubled back into a loop and dangling from his right hand.

"Kill him."

The executioner stepped forward and slipped the white cord around Orlando's neck.

"No. For the love of God—"

"Answer me, then. What did Aurelio do when he knew you were going to nail him to that tree?"

Orlando shook his head. He lifted one hand and got two fingers between his throat and the cord. The man with the garrote gave a little pull on the toggles, enough to let his victim sense that mere fingers weren't going to be enough to save him.

"We know you did it. So tell us the truth," the spokesman said, "or die now."

"It wasn't me. I swear. It was Anselmo. Anselmo did it."

Some of the men in hoods looked at each other, but the spokesman didn't take his eyes off Orlando.

"And cutting him? Whose idea was that?"

"Anselmo. It was Anselmo's idea. He said it would frighten the others, said that real men are more afraid of losing their cocks than losing their lives."

"Did Aurelio beg you not to kill him?"

"No. No, he didn't. He spit in Anselmo's face."

"And then?"

"And then Anselmo . . . well, he got angry . . . and he did what he did."

"And you made Aurelio's wife watch you murder him?"

"Not me. Anselmo."

"What happened next?"

"She started to cry. Asked Anselmo not to kill the kids."

"But you did anyway, didn't you?"

"We had to. Can't you see? They weren't babies anymore. They saw our faces."

Orlando swallowed.

The spokesman inclined his head, giving a sign. Orlando wet himself in fear, certain that the garrote was going to tighten, but he was wrong. To his immense relief, he felt it being slipped from his neck.

They dragged him down the long hallway, through the living room where embers were still glowing in the fireplace and the smell of brandy still hung heavy in the air and out onto his front porch. One of his trucks was standing at the foot of the steps, the engine already running.

The early morning air and the adrenaline that was pumping through his veins helped to clear Orlando's head. He still had a headache, but now he was able to think. *How did they get into the house? Where the hell are the rest of my bodyguards? Where are they taking me? How am I going to explain this to the old man?*

The old man was his father, Orlando Senior, who had never thought much of his son's abilities even at the best of times and the best of times were several years in the past. These days, fed up with Orlando's drinking and mismanagement, he'd gotten to the point of threatening to cut Orlando off without a cent.

Money! That's it! This is all about money. About ransom. Suppose they ask for too much? What if the old man says no? What then? And how much is too much, anyway? A million? Would he pay a million?

They hustled him down to the truck, pausing at the tailgate. The spokesman went up front and climbed into the cab. They bound Orlando's hands behind his back with a piece of wire and tossed him into the bed like a sack of garbage. He landed hard on one shoulder, his head bouncing against the metal floor.

For a moment, he thought he was going to pass out, but he didn't. When the dancing black spots faded, he found he was looking at the answer to one of his questions. The other capangas were with him in the truck, and like their boss, Anselmo, they were dead. All six corpses were crammed, one on top of the other, into an area between the side of the truck and an oblong object covered by a piece of tarpaulin.

His abductors found places on the floor, on the oblong object, and even on the bodies of the dead. The last man to climb aboard was the man in the red T-shirt, his garrote now dangling from his belt like a watch chain, the toggles stuffed into a pocket of his jeans. He signaled to the driver by pounding on the roof of the cab with his fist. The truck set off with a jerk.

Orlando twisted his body and craned his neck to look back at the house. His front door had been smashed. Splinters of blue wood were lying on the porch. The shutters, blue like the door, were still closed and locked.

Why didn't Anselmo stop them? He must have been drunk. All of them must have been drunk. Stupid bastards! The old man, damn him, had been right again: If you're only willing to pay peanuts, what you're going to get is monkeys. He'd hired Anselmo for peanuts. And Anselmo had hired the others for peanuts. And now the old man was going to tell him that it would never have happened if he'd been smart enough to hire good people.

Dust welled up behind the truck, blocking the view of his home. Tears began to run from Orlando's eyes. *It's the dust. Just the dust.* But he knew it wasn't. And it wasn't fear, either. It was rage, rage and frustration. Every damn time his father came to the fazenda, it was nothing but criticism, criticism, criticism. And now this. The old tyrant was richer than Croesus, but he parted with every centavo like it was the last one he had in the world. No matter what the amount of the ransom was, he'd bitch about it forever.

They passed the tobacco sheds, where the leaves were cured, and the old deposito, where they kept the coffee. The driver didn't hesitate when he came to the fork. He seemed to know exactly where he was going, but it still surprised Orlando when they suddenly screeched to a stop. Surprised him, because the driver had stopped in the middle of nowhere. There were no nearby buildings, no other vehicles. There was nothing but a steep hillside on the right and level cane fields sweeping off to the left. The cane had been harvested less than a week before, and except for some stubble, the land was bare. Orlando could see all the way to the trees hemming the river, almost a kilometer away.

Two of his abductors grabbed his arms and bundled him, none too gently, out of the truck. The spokesman and the driver climbed out of the front seat. Four of the men removed the tarpaulin from the oblong object and lowered it to the ground. It turned out to be a wooden box about two meters long. The other two dimensions were about a quarter of that, no more than fifty or sixty centimeters wide and high.

"What have you got in there?" Orlando asked.

"Start climbing," the spokesman said.

"This hill?"

"You see anything else to climb? Get moving."

Orlando was overweight. The only thing he ever exercised was his drinking arm. Before he was even halfway up the slope his heart was pounding, and he was struggling to breathe. He tried to slow his pace, but when he did the strangler kicked him in the buttocks to speed him up. By the time they reached the top Orlando was sweating like one of his horses after a sharp gallop in midsummer.

The sun's disk was just peeking over the horizon. The golden light cast long shadows from two shovels standing upright in a pile of earth. The shadows fell over a trench, freshly dug at the very summit of the hill.

The four men who'd been carrying the box set it down. Then the whole gang gathered around the hole and took off their hoods.

Orlando gaped at the face of the spokesman.

"You!" he said.

"Yes, you swine, *me*. Surprised?"

Remembering Azevedo's gesture, Orlando tried to spit. But he couldn't. His throat was too dry. He tried to tell himself it was the wine, knew it wasn't. He studied every face and recognized three more: Flavio, who'd worked for him for years and was still working for him, damn him; Lucas, who he'd fired last August—no, September—for impertinence; and, finally, the killer in the red T-shirt. Carlos Something. He couldn't remember the rest of the name, but he did remember that the association had circulated a photo of him, a photo meant to ensure that he never got a job on any ranch owned by a member.

Orlando let his eyes sweep around the group, scanning the other faces, trying to commit each and every one of them to memory.

The entire circle was looking back at him with contempt and with no pity at all. In an attempt to avoid their eyes he looked down at the hole and had a sudden and very ugly thought. *No. They wouldn't do that. It wouldn't make any sense. They're just trying to frighten me.*

He strove for reassurance. "How much is it?" he said, nervously.

The spokesman gave him a quizzical look. Orlando felt a shiver of fear go down his back, but he tried again. "The ransom. How much is it?"

The spokesman's brow wrinkled. "Is that what you think this is all about? Money?"

Orlando swallowed.

The man in the red shirt grinned, but no one else did.

"We're not interested in your money," the spokesman said.

Up to that very moment Orlando had always thought that *everyone* was interested in money. It was very late in his life for him to discover that some people weren't. He struggled with the thought.

Far away, in the trees by the river, a parrot shrieked. The sun was warm on his cheek. A gentle breeze ruffled his hair. He could smell the freshly turned earth. Despite his persistent hangover, Orlando felt very much alive and he wanted to stay that way. There was a space between the spokesman and the man in the red T-shirt. Orlando tensed his tired muscles, prepared to run.

Something struck him on the back of his head. There was no pain, just a flash of light, and then blackness.

But it wasn't the end.

He awoke lying on his back. Thin slivers of light shone through planks that were only centimeters from his face. He tried to lift his hands, but they were still bound behind him, the wire cutting into his wrists. He tried to raise a knee. It wouldn't move. His feet were wired together at the ankles.

He called out for help, and as if his call had been something they'd been waiting for, he felt them lifting him up and then lowering him down. When the movement stopped, he found himself resting at a slight angle, his feet somewhat higher than his head.

Then began a series of thuds. He didn't recognize them for what they were until something fell onto one of the small cracks above his face, and some of it trickled through and landed on his lips. He opened his mouth to taste it. Dirt!

And then he knew: Those thuds were the thin red earth of his fazenda falling on his coffin. The bastards were burying him alive.

He cried out for them to stop, drummed against the top of the box with his knees, beat against it with his head.

The shoveling continued at the same rhythmic pace. He screamed, screamed as loud as he could, and while he was still screaming they began to sing.

It was that song of theirs, the one he hated, the one they always accompanied by waving their left fists in the air, the one about brotherhood and justice and all that other crap.

It was the anthem of the league.

Chapter Eight

THE FBI NATIONAL ACADEMY is located on the grounds of the United States Marine Corps Base at Quantico in Virginia. It shares the same campus with the FBI Academy, and bears a similar name, leading some people confuse one with the other. They are, in fact, separate institutions.

The FBI Academy exists to train special agents for the bureau. The FBI National Academy is an advanced course of study for experienced law enforcement officials. Among them, there is always a handful of senior officers from countries outside of the United States. The benefit to those countries is that their most talented cops have an opportunity to share ideas, techniques, and experience with their American counterparts. The benefit for the United States is that lifelong relationships are established, relationships that transcend national boundaries.

In June of 1983, four and a half years after his father's murder, Mario Silva received an invitation to go to Quantico. He was the first Brazilian to be so honored. His law degree, fluent English, and the spectacular results he'd achieved in Brazil's combat against the drug trade had all contributed to his receiving the coveted opportunity. There could have been no clearer indication that his superiors destined him for greater things. For ten classroom weeks, in the company of 250 other police officers, he took courses in behavioral science, leadership development, communication, health/fitness, law, and forensics. Forensics interested him most of all.

Upon his return, he was transferred to Brasilia, the federal capital. The expectation of his superiors was that he'd be able to put some of the things he'd learned into practice. Those were the days when experienced law enforcement officers, not political appointees, ran the Federal Police. The man who held the job, Helio Fagundes, was a consummate professional who recognized talent when he saw it. And he saw it in Mario Silva.

"How BIG is this thing?" Fagundes asked. They were in his office. Silva had been back from the United States for about a week.

"About like that," Silva said, as if demonstrating the size of a fish he'd caught, "and like that, and that," tracing the other dimensions in the air.

"That small? Jesus!" Fagundes leaned forward, leafed through the proposal on his desk, and looked at the bottom line. "Cheap, too," he said, "Compared to those monsters we've got downstairs. Okay, you've got a green light. I'll send you the paperwork. Go buy the thing."

The "thing" was an IBM Personal Computer. The device, less than two years on the market, was just beginning to come into use in law enforcement agencies in the United States. Silva had seen his first one when he was in Quantico.

The computer was duly installed in a small room down the hall from Silva's new office. Silva started learning how to use it, and with the blessing of the director, he hired a young man to help him. The young man was Cicero Morales. Cicero had a sparse goatee, a developing potbelly, thick horned-rim glasses, an acne problem and unkempt hair. Years later, and thirty kilograms fatter, he would become the head of the Federal Police's forensic laboratory. Even then, at twenty-three, Cicero was an unusually perceptive man.

"This whole project of ours," he said to Silva one night when they were working late, "it's not just for the greater glory and efficiency of the Federal Police, is it?"

"What do you mean?"

Silva stared at Cicero out of hooded, black eyes. "Oh, come on, Mario, this is me you're talking to," Cicero said, ripping open a bag of potato chips. "There's something personal about this business. Why don't you just admit it?"

"What makes you think it's personal?"

Before he replied, Cicero stuffed a handful of the chips into his mouth, chewed, and swallowed. "Are you telling me it's not?"

"That's what I'm telling you."

"Chips?" Cicero offered the bag.

Mario shook his head. Cicero took out another chip, nibbled it up in two bites. "Why did you choose São Paulo for the pilot project?"

"Why not? I wanted to give this thing an acid test."

"I'm not buying it, Mario. Brasilia would have been much better, and you know it."

"I don't know any such thing."

Cicero took in an exasperated breath and let it out in a snort. Some fragments of potato chip came with it. He grabbed one of the napkins he kept next to his workstation and wiped his mouth.

"You want me to spell it out for you? Okay, I will."

Cicero crumpled the empty bag and tossed it. Then he gripped his right thumb with the other hand and started to count off his reasons. "First, because São Paulo is just too damned big. It doesn't make the job *twice* as hard, it makes the job *twenty times* as hard. Second reason: We're here, so instead of being able to put on pressure locally, we have to do it by telephone and letter. Third reason: We—and by that I mean the federal police—are a force in this town. Here in Brasilia it's relatively easy to get the data we need to input. It's much harder in São Paulo. We're not much of a player in that shithole. Oops! You're from there, aren't you? Sorry about that."

"No, Cicero. You're not sorry, and you know damned well I think it's a shithole too."

"Maybe I do, but getting back to the subject: Being from there doesn't have anything to do with choosing São Paulo for our pilot project, right?"

"No. Not a damn thing. And will you please back off?"

"Temper, temper, Mario. No need to get huffy about it. No need to deal in falsehoods, either. Your secret is safe with me."

"Secret? What secret?"

"That you're more concerned about tattoos and a lack of front teeth than you are about scars, or moles, or birthmarks. Have I got that right?"

"No, you don't."

"Well, I hope not, because what we're supposed to be doing is to set up a database that'll make it possible to zoom in on a felon based on *any* identifying characteristic. That's the brief, isn't it? Collect *any and all* identifying characteristics and get them into the computer so they can be sorted and cross-referenced? *Any and all*, not just tattoos? Not just teeth?"

"Right."

"And there's nothing personal about anything we're doing?"

"How many times do I have to tell you, Cicero. There's nothing personal about this. Not a damned thing."

SILVA KNEW, all too well, that he was working against the clock. The director hadn't specifically said it, but unless his new system for identifying repeat offenders proved its worth within the first six months, it was likely to be written off as a failure.

Department heads were constantly filing into the Director's office with their hands out. The budget of the Federal Police was never sufficient to do everything that everyone wanted to do, and the fact that Silva had gotten any financing at all was proof positive that Fagundes considered him to be on a fast track.

Every day Silva prayed for results. Four months into the experiment, and long before their database was anywhere near complete, his prayers were answered.

Estrella Alba was a white woman in her mid-thirties with a red birthmark, about the size of a strawberry, on her left cheek. Her previous arrests, two for shoplifting, one for assault, and one for prostitution, coupled with her prominent facial feature, had brought her into Silva's database.

Digital photography was still some years in the future. All of the references were verbal. In Estrella Alba's case, the keywords were, in order of importance, BIRTHMARK, CHEEK, LEFT, and RED.

At ten o'clock one morning, and only a few days after Cicero had made the entry, an inquiry came in: A woman with a red birthmark on her left cheek was being sought for the holdup of a bank on São Paulo's Avenida Paulista. Could they help with an identification? By noon, Estrella's name had been telexed to the inquiring officers in São Paulo. They located her a little before 3:00 in the afternoon. And, by 6:00, after a little coercion, she confessed.

The news spread quickly throughout the law enforcement community. From that time on, Cicero and Silva no longer had to beg people to make the necessary contributions to their database. Other successes followed, first only a few, then many more as the database grew. They bought another computer, then another.

Silva got a promotion. He was no longer entrusted with the day-to-day operation of the database, but he still made it a part of his daily ritual to check the computer for the references he'd been seeking all along: TATTOO, NECK, SNAKE, all of them together in one file. In October of 1985, almost seven years to the day after his father's murder, he found them.

Chapter Nine

His name was João Miranda.

Most people called him by his nickname: Cobra.

The word, in Portuguese, means snake, any snake, not just those of the mantled variety. As it happened, however, the snake depicted in Cobra's tattoo was one of those. It started on his chest, went up to encircle his neck and ended just below his ear. That's where the mouth was, and the mouth was red, and open, and had a little pink tongue flicking out as if it was trying to touch his earlobe.

Cobra loved that tattoo. It had been with him since he was sixteen years old. He'd chosen it out of a book in a one-man tattoo parlor wedged between a bar and a cheap hotel in Pelourinho. That had been back in Bahia, long before he ever thought of coming south to São Paulo.

The original design was smaller, and the snake was coiled up. Making it bigger and having it twist around his neck was Cobra's idea. The guy with the needle was so pleased with his work that he'd asked Cobra to let him take a picture. He wanted to put it into his book and offer the same tattoo to other people. He thought Cobra would be pleased.

Cobra wasn't. That tattoo was his, his and nobody else's. The very next night, just as the artist was closing up shop, Cobra had gone back and slit the man's throat.

People in São Paulo, if they thought about it at all, figured that Cobra's nickname came from the tattoo. It wasn't true. The kids in the favela where he grew up were already calling him that before he was thirteen. The name fit, because little João Miranda, just like a snake, was quick to

anger, quick to strike, and had eyes that showed no com-
passion at all.

By the time he was eighteen, he was already well
known—too well known for his liking—to the cops in his
native city of Salvador. Back in those days, he was just an
ignorant kid, still learning how to steal and kill and get away
with it. They'd busted him more times than he had years,
even managed to keep him behind bars for a while, until his
brothers raised enough money to buy him out. By that time,
he'd learned that only chumps served out their sentences.
And that was only if they were sentenced in the first place,
which they generally weren't, because the cops and the
judges were just as crooked as the prison guards.

The situation, he soon discovered, was no different in São
Paulo. With one exception: the Municipal Police. They
were real bastards, as bad as anybody working the street.
They'd shake you down just because they didn't like the
color of your skin, or the clothes you were wearing, or for no
reason at all. But, he didn't let it bother him. He'd steal from
others, and they'd steal from him. It was just a cost of doing
business, right? One thing they hardly ever did was to put
him away. It just didn't happen if you weren't stupid. This
time, he'd been stupid.

He'd just smoked his last rock, and he was uptight about
where he was going to get another one. Without the crack
in his system, or if he hadn't been in such a hurry, he
would have pegged the two guys sitting at the bar as the
off-duty cops they were. Hell, one of them was even wearing the trousers that went with his uniform. There were
red stripes on the outside seams, and they ran all the way
up his legs. Who else wore that kind of pants? Answer:
nobody. Just cops.

They had their pistols out less than a second after he'd pointed his own at the guy behind the cash register. He was lucky

that the cachaça the cops had been drinking had made them mellow. Lucky, too, that he'd had the presence of mind, high on crack or not, to drop the gun the instant they told him to.

So here he sat, stuffed into an overcrowded cell packed with drunks, transvestites, and juveniles. It just took one kick to somebody's balls to communicate to his cellmates just where he stood in the pecking order. And when he went a little further, and smashed the guy in the face with his steel-tipped workman's shoes, they even cleared a corner for him.

He'd hit the bar in the early hours of a Monday morning. Another mistake. There was bound to be a big backlog of cases from the weekend. It could be two days, maybe even three, before he'd be called up for arraignment. Three days in the stench and the shit. He didn't even want to think about it. God help him if he fell asleep.

Before they'd brought him to the cell, one of the cops showed an interest in his tattoo. Cobra didn't find it unusual. A lot of people were interested in that tattoo. After all, it was the only one like it in the whole world, at least as far as he knew. But what Cobra *did* find unusual was that the cop pulled out a measuring tape, measured the snake from head to tail, and wrote the measurements down in a little book.

"What the fuck are you doing that for?" he'd asked.

"Watch your mouth when you talk to me, you fucking punk," the cop said, and walked off.

Then, at around three o'clock on Tuesday morning, almost twenty-four hours after they'd locked him up, something else happened.

He wasn't asleep, not even dozing. He'd propped himself up with his back against the wall, and was keeping a wary eye on his cellmates, when he heard the jangling of keys in the corridor. He lifted his head and watched a guard insert one of those keys into the lock on the door of his cell. The guard was a young guy, somebody Cobra hadn't seen before, and he wasn't alone. The guy next to him was wearing a gray suit and had cold, black eyes and a thick mustache on his upper lip. Cobra pegged him for a detective.

"Where's João Miranda?" the cop called out.

It was a common name. Two men stood up. Cobra wasn't one of them.

The cop shook his head. "The Miranda with the tattoo," he said, impatiently. "The one with the snake."

Heads turned toward Cobra's corner.

"You," the cop said. "Get on your feet and get over here."

Cobra took his time about it. He figured to be back in the cell before long, and his cellmates would be all over him if he let a couple of cops intimidate him.

"Hurry up, you punk," the guard said.

When he reached the door, the man in the gray suit pulled out a pair of handcuffs and spoke for the first time. "Turn around. Put your hands behind you," he said, in an emotionless voice.

"For Christ's sake," Cobra said, "It's the middle of the night. Can't a guy get some sleep?"

"Shut up and turn around." This time the man let a bit of irritation show.

Cobra figured he'd done enough. He'd made a show for his cellmates, but he didn't want to wind up getting the shit kicked out of him. He turned and allowed the cop to shackle him, staring down the other men in the cell while it was happening. Most of them avoided his eyes, proof that he'd played it right. To solidify the impression of a tough guy, he didn't speak again until they'd gone through the steel door and into the corridor outside.

"Where you taking me?"

"Brasilia," the guard said.

"Brasilia? Why Brasilia?"

"You'll find out soon enough."

* * *

SILVA WAS surprised when he saw the little man in the cell. For almost seven years he'd been imagining someone who was tall and strong. The punk who offered his wrists to be cuffed didn't even reach his chin, and Mario Silva wasn't a particularly tall man.

But the tattoo was there, and it was just as his mother had described it. There couldn't possibly be another one like it. Or could there? Doubt plagued him. He'd have to get the punk to open up. He'd have to be sure.

Getting João Miranda out of the *delegacia* was no problem. The military dictatorship had ended in January, but it had persisted for twenty years and old habits die hard. Silva was a federal cop. He'd come all the way from Brasilia. He had clout.

The SPPD was all too happy to deliver their charge, and even happier when Silva told them they could dispense with the paperwork. Someday, some bureaucrat might discover forms that showed they'd once had a punk by the name of João Miranda in one of their holding cells. Someday, someone might even remember that a federal cop had come in, given them some story about Miranda being a material witness in a drug case, and taken him away.

But, even so, nobody would give a damn, and in the unlikely event that they did, Silva had a story all worked out. There would be an escape report filed away in a place that no one would look for it unless he told them it was there.

Ostensibly, he'd been bringing Miranda over to the federal building for questioning in a drug case he was working on. They'd stopped at a light. He'd seen a couple of punks trying to assault an old couple. He'd hopped out of the car to help. When he got back the felon was gone. End of story.

Silva shackled the punk's thin ankles together with a second pair of handcuffs, tossed him into the back of his rental car, and started driving through the early morning streets.

There was little traffic. The punk gave him the silent treatment for a while and then started to talk. By the time he did,
they were already outside of town and climbing into the
Serra de Cantareira.

"What kind of a cop are you, anyway?"

"Federal," Silva answered shortly.

"Your *colega* said you were taking me to Brasilia? Why
Brasilia? I didn't do anything in Brasilia."

"Meaning that you only did stuff in other places?"

"Meaning nothing. What's this all about?"

"It's about a rape and a murder."

"I don't know nothing about no rape and no murder."

"It was a long time ago. Seven years."

"Seven years! Shit, I can't remember back seven months.
Except I never raped nobody. Never had to pay for it neither.
I got women lining up to fuck me, I do."

Silva drove on in silence, giving no sign that he'd heard
what Miranda had said. The car began to jolt when he hit the
unpaved road. A light rain had been coming down when they
left the *delegacia*, but had tapered off before they entered the
forest. The air was heavy and tinged with the smell of rotting
vegetation. When Silva braked to a stop, it was gray dawn over
the road, still dark under the shade of the trees. The place had-
n't changed since his last visit. The little depression in the
ground, the surrounding vegetation, the large rock with the flat
face, all were just as he remembered them. Silva had been back
to this place many times over the course of the last seven years,
at first to walk the ground and investigate, later to meditate
about what he might do here, and to pray for his father's soul.

He opened the back door, pulled João Miranda out by his
heels, and started dragging him across the ground.

"Hey," the thug said when his head hit a rock. "Hey, no
need to get rough. Let me up. Let me walk."

Silva didn't respond. He kept dragging Miranda until they

reached the place his mother had pointed out to him, the place where his father had been shot.

"You know where you are?" he asked. "You know why you're here?"

The punk shook his head. Silva gave him a kick in the ribs. "Answer me," he said.

"I don't know what you're talking about."

"I'm talking about you and a friend of yours. I'm talking about a man you shot to death, here on this spot."

"I didn't shoot nobody."

Silva kicked him again. The punk assumed the fetal position, protecting his soft parts, his genitals and his abdomen.

"Talk, you filho da puta."

"I told you, I didn't shoot nobody."

"The next kick is going to be in the balls."

That was the only threat Silva had to make. Despite his façade, the punk was a coward at heart. "It wasn't me," Miranda said. "It was Escorpião. Escorpião did it."

The name meant *scorpion*.

"Who?"

"Dante Correia. Escorpião. It was an old guy, right? We were gonna do his wife and he came on strong, and he took a swing at Escorpião and Escorpião shot him in the head."

"How many times?"

"Twice. He shot him twice."

"Where's this Escorpião now?"

"Dead."

Silva kicked him again. "Don't lie to me."

"No. I swear. You know the Commando Vermelho?"

The Commando Vermelho was a drug gang, one of the largest. They were in constant warfare for control of the trade. The battles were fought out in the favelas, the shantytowns.

"Yeah, I know the Commando Vermelho," Silva said. "What about it?"

"He was one of their soldiers. Got himself shot dead, maybe five years ago. I swear. You're a cop. You can look it up. Dante Correia. Escorpião. It was in all the papers."

"And he pulled the trigger on the old man who was shot here? Is that what you're telling me?"

"That's what I'm telling you. Why are you making such a big thing out of this? It was years ago, for Christ's sake. What's it to you?"

"The man was my father. The woman you raped was my mother."

João Miranda's eyes got so big that Silva could see white encircling both pupils.

"Jesus," he said.

"Yeah," Silva said, and pulled out his revolver.

HE HAD a shovel in the trunk of his rental car, a new one he'd bought just for the purpose. He dug a hole, stripped the handcuffs from Miranda's wrists and ankles, and buried him just below the place where his father had died.

He'd been looking forward to doing that for seven years, but in the end, it didn't bring him the satisfaction he thought it would.

When he'd been at Quantico, he'd heard a lecture from some psychiatrist. The man talked about "closure." Closure, like you could just walk away and close a door behind you and that would be it. Could it be that there really were people who could do that?

The next day, he looked up the records on Dante Correira, the man Miranda had called Escorpião. Miranda had been telling the truth. Correia had been dead for almost five years.

Silva felt a little surge of relief. He'd never before killed a man in cold blood. He didn't want to do it ever again.

But two years later, he did.

Chapter Ten

CARLA, MARIO SILVA'S ONLY sibling, shared her mother's name and her father's features. She had the same jet-black hair, the same black eyes, and the same determined set to her jaw.

In character, she resembled her brother. Once she'd made up her mind that something, or someone, was worth pursuing, she did it with singleminded determination.

In September of 1974, she made up her mind about a fledgling electrical engineer named Claudio Costa. In August of 1975, they were married.

At first, her parents greeted the news of her engagement with protest. Not that they didn't like Claudio. They just thought the match was premature. The young people had, after all, known each other for such a short time. Then there was the matter of Carla completing her education at the University of São Paulo.

Carla admitted, and promptly brushed aside, the matter of the relationship's short duration. As to the degree, she said, one thing didn't preclude the other. She'd keep on studying.

Dr. Silva and his wife had to admit that they'd never known Carla to promise anything she couldn't deliver. Backed into a corner, they reluctantly gave their consent. A very pregnant Carla Costa was awarded her diploma in June of 1976. Her son, Hector, was born a week later. He was two years old on the night his grandfather died, eleven when he witnessed the murder of his father.

* * *

IT WAS a Saturday, a week before Christmas. The Costas lived in Granja Viana in those days, a residential suburb about twenty kilometers from the city center. On the morning of the murder they were stuck in a traffic jam, mostly composed of people who, like themselves, were on their way into town to do some shopping.

Claudio was behind the wheel. Carla was seated next to him, her attention absorbed by a notepad into which she was jotting names and gift ideas. Hector was in the back seat, manipulating a little plastic puzzle.

They heard the man before they saw him.

"Your watch," he said. "Hand it over."

Carla looked up to see a man with a day's growth of beard pointing a revolver at her husband's head. The man was standing just outside the car, on the driver's side. The muzzle of the gun protruded through the open window.

Carla looked around for help. People in the neighboring cars were staring straight ahead or in other directions. They'd seen the gun. Nobody wanted to get involved. Carla looked back at the gunman. The muzzle of the revolver was trembling, the man's brown eyes glazed and distant.

Drugs, she thought.

"Do it," the man said to Claudio. "Do it, now. Take off the goddamned watch." As if to emphasize what he said, he cocked the revolver.

Carla watched the cylinder spin, heard the click, saw Claudio's Adam's apple bob as he swallowed. Both of her husband's hands were frozen on the wheel. She knew the watch had been his father's, knew he didn't want to give it up.

"Claudio," she said, calmly. "Please. Take off the watch and give it to him."

But Claudio didn't. Instead, he made a sudden lunge for the revolver, trying to grab the barrel.

The man with the beard took a quick step backward, extended his arm, and pulled the trigger.

The bullet caught Claudio in the chest. Carla screamed. Little Hector started to bawl. The man opened the flap of a leather haversack, put the revolver inside, and walked away. No one tried to stop him.

The police did what they usually did in such cases: They wrote up a report and took no further action.

The day after the funeral, her brother, Mario, came for her. "Would you recognize him?" he asked.

She nodded. Recognize him? She'd never be able to forget him.

"Come with me," he said, reaching out and taking her hand.

They spent the next few days searching the neighborhood, the same streets, over and over again, centered on the place where it had happened. She drove. He sat on the front seat beside her.

Mario had been a cop for almost nine years by then. She knew almost nothing of his professional life, but she knew her brother. He would be good at anything he turned his hand to.

Once, years earlier, he'd talked to her about vengeance for their parents. She'd told him she didn't want to hear anything about it, that it wouldn't change anything. He'd never brought the subject up again. Now, with Claudio, she felt differently. By the third day she was beginning to wish that Mario wasn't a cop, that he wouldn't be forced to act like a cop was supposed to act, that they could just deal with the assassin themselves rather than deliver him to judgment by the court.

On the afternoon of the fourth day she saw the killer hurrying down the street. He'd shaved, but he had the same leather haversack dangling from his shoulder.

"There," she said.

"You're sure?"

"I'm sure. It's him."

"Go home. I'll call you later."

"What are you going to . . ."

She let her voice trail off. Her brother had already slammed the door and was following the man with the haversack.

The driver in the car behind her leaned on his horn.

She did what Mario had told her to. She went home.

As promised, he called her. It was just after midnight, more than five hours after he'd left her car.

"You were right," he said. "It was him."

"He confessed?"

"He confessed. It's late, Clara. Go to sleep."

"Tell me about him, Mario."

"No."

"No? Mario, he—"

But her brother had hung up.

The next day, and the following day, she scanned the paper looking for news of the arrest.

There wasn't any.

They never discussed the subject again.

SOME FAMILIES seem to be cursed with tragedy. Mario Silva's was one of those, and his suffering wasn't over.

In the years that followed the death of his parents, the lights of his life had been his sister, her family, his wife, and his son. The next light that died wasn't snuffed out with the suddenness of a gunshot. It faded slowly.

IRENE AND he had married in the summer of 1980. Their son was born in 1981. It was a difficult birth, rife with medical complications. When it was over the doctors told him their baby was destined to be an only child.

They named him Mario, after his father and grandfather before him. He was a baby who hardly ever cried, an infant who always smiled, a toddler who old ladies passing on the street wanted to pick up and hug. In late 1988, he contracted leukemia. It took him five months to die. His parents dealt with it in entirely different ways. Mario threw himself into his work. Irene started to drink.

First, it was just a little, to help her, as she said, "to get through the night." First, it was sweet concoctions, *caipirinhas*, with the rinds and juice of limes, or *batidas* made with mango juice, or coconut milk. Then, gradually, she'd eased off on the fruit juice and the sugar, claiming they were making her fat. Within a year it had become straight cachaça, pure cane spirit, with no sugar and no juice at all.

The stuff was killing her as surely as the leukemia had killed their son. Perhaps Irene knew it, but she wasn't willing to admit it. She insisted that she was still a "social drinker" even though almost all of her imbibing took place at home and when she was alone. She only drank at night, but it was *every* night, and her nights started at five o'clock in the afternoon. She was generally sleeping it off when Mario left for work, drunk by the time he returned home.

In the beginning, he tried drinking along with her, trying to be companionable, seeking common ground through a haze of alcohol. But the solace he found was only temporary, and the hangovers weren't worth it. In the end, he communicated with her by trying to call her several times a day, trying to catch her when she was still sober. He never contemplated divorce, nor did he sleep with other women but what remained between them was only the ghost of what their relationship had once been.

As for Hector Costa, having his father shot to death in front of him turned him into an old little boy. For almost a year he lost the gift of laughter.

Carla thought it best to get him out of São Paulo, away from the memories. They moved to Campos de Jordão, a little town in the mountains, north of the road linking São Paulo with Rio de Janeiro.

It was a place where people went in the wintertime to sit in front of fireplaces, bundle up in woolen sweaters, and drink hot chocolate; where the summers were times of empty hotels and unending boredom, and where people who shot people tended to know their victims.

Mario had always doted on Hector, but after the death of his son, and the boy's father, the two of them reached out for each other. The little boy came to idolize his uncle. By the time he was fifteen, he'd already decided he wanted to follow in Mario's footsteps and become a cop.

At first, Carla treated it the same way she'd treated his previous aspirations: to be a teacher, a fireman, a soldier. But time passed, and he mentioned no other vocation. She was momentarily relieved when Hector started law school. You had to be a lawyer to achieve officer rank in the Brazilian Federal Police, but she remained hopeful he'd become enchanted by some other aspect of the law and find something else to do with his life.

But he didn't. Even before he'd received his law degree, he submitted his application to join Silva's organization.

She hoped he'd be rejected.

He wasn't.

Six months later, he was posted to São Paulo. As far as Carla was concerned, that was just about the worst thing that could have happened. There was no more dangerous place for a cop to work.

Chapter Eleven

THE CASCATAS AIRPORT WASN'T in Cascatas at all. It was just outside the city limits, in the neighboring municipality of Miracema.

The airport consisted of a single unpaved strip of red earth and a white stucco building with blue trim reminiscent of a farmworker's cottage. There were no hangars, and there was no control tower.

The twenty-odd aircraft sprinkled here and there on the dusty grass were all high-wing monoplanes except for a vintage Cessna 310B and an old biplane that looked like something out of a World War I movie.

The airplane Hector was waiting for started out as a speck in a cloudless sky, a sky free of dust and therefore much bluer than the one back in Cascatas. As it got closer, he could see that it was an Embraer Bandeirante, a twin-engined job that dwarfed anything else parked on the field. The markings of the Brazilian Air Force were prominent on the tips of the wings and above the cabin windows.

Hector waited until the pilot had cut both of the engines and some of the dust had settled. Then he drove his rental car right onto the strip.

The man who opened the door to the cabin wore an open-necked blue shirt with chevrons on his sleeves. Once he'd lowered the steps he snapped a salute and made way for the familiar figure of Mario Silva.

Hector's uncle was in his working uniform, a gray suit. All of Silva's suits were immaculately cut and all of them were exactly the same color. It was one less decision he had to make when he got up in the morning. His mustache, a bushy island of vanity between his nose and upper lip, didn't quite match the color of the suit but only because a few isolated strands of black hair gave a salt and pepper effect to the gray.

Waving off the sergeant's attempt to help him, he carried his own bag down the steps, tossed it into the back seat of the car, and climbed into the front.

They embraced.

"Thank God for air-conditioning," Silva said, when the mutual back patting was done. He reached for his seatbelt, fastened it with a click, and pulled out a handkerchief to mop his brow.

"You think the heat is bad? Wait until you get a lungful of the dust."

"Dust?"

"Dust. The whole town is one big construction site. You want to stop by the hotel and freshen up?"

"No. Let's get right into it. Did you see that colonel? Ferraz?"

"I saw him," Hector said. He let out the emergency brake and slipped into first gear. "He doesn't want any help from us."

"Well, we've run into that before, haven't we?"

"Yeah, but most people feign politeness. Ferraz doesn't. He gave me five minutes of his time and then he threw me out."

The air conditioning was coming up to speed. Silva mopped the remaining perspiration from his forehead and started folding his handkerchief. Hector turned onto the road that would take them back into town.

"You learn anything in your five minutes?" Silva asked.

"A bit."

Hector briefed him on the weapon, the location the sniper had chosen from which to make the shot, the lack of leads, and the little that Ferraz had told him about the political situation. Then he recounted the details of his other interview.

"A priest, eh?" his uncle said when he heard Gaspar's theory.

His voice expressed neither shock nor surprise. There was very little that shocked or surprised Mario Silva.

"That's what he said. Are you familiar with this liberation theology stuff?"

"Oh yes. There was a time when it was considered subversive activity. A lot of those priests were tortured. Others disappeared."

Hector nodded and turned off the main road onto a street lined with warehouses. He didn't ask where the priests had "disappeared" to. The military regime had ended twenty years before, but the clandestine graves of dissidents were still being discovered.

He pulled out a newspaper that he'd stuffed between the two front seats. "The local rag," he said, handing it to his uncle. "The editor is a woman by the name of Diana Poli."

"So?"

"So that's our first stop. They say she knows everything and everybody. I made an appointment."

DIANA POLI turned out to be a short, heavyset woman in her mid-thirties with a Marlene Dietrich voice and John Lennon spectacles.

Her only jewelry was a Russian wedding ring—red, yellow and white gold in three interlocking bands—which she wore on the third finger of her right hand. Her hair was prematurely shot with gray, and except for lipstick of an indifferent red, she wasn't using any cosmetics. Her outfit, black jeans and a man's dress shirt, completed a distinctly masculine impression.

The *Cidade de Cascatas*, her newspaper, occupied a

rectangular metal building with galvanized external walls, a tile roof, and a pervading smell of printer's ink.

Diana met them at the reception desk, studied the business cards they gave her, and led them past a rumbling press into a glass-walled office at the back of the building. When she shut the door the noise dropped off by a considerable number of decibels. It wasn't what you'd call quiet, but it was possible to hold a conversation without shouting.

"Double glazing," she said when Hector looked surprised. "Call me Diana. Everyone does. Nice of you to stop by. Saves me the trouble of looking you up. How's the investigation going? Any leads?"

Hector speared her with his black eyes. He didn't actually say, *I'm the cop, I'll ask the questions,* but he might as well have.

It didn't work. She wasn't in the least intimidated. She leaned across her desk, putting her face closer to his.

"Look, Senhor—"

"Delegado."

"Okay, Delegado . . . what was your name again?"

"Costa."

"Costa. I'm not just the editor around here. I'm the principal journalist, and I own the newspaper. And before you ask how that came to be, it's because my daddy's rich, I love journalism, and he dotes on his only daughter."

"Senhora Poli—"

"I told you, it's Diana, and it's not senhora, it's *senhorita*. Let's get a couple of things straight. I'm a serious reporter, not a fucking gossip columnist. If you want anything out of me, you've got to make it a two way street."

"Meaning?"

"Meaning that if you expect any answers to your questions, you'd better have some to mine."

"Look . . . Diana, we've just started this investigation. I can't—"

She held up a hand.

"Hear me out. The bishop's murder is the biggest story ever to hit this town. There are reporters flocking in from all over."

"Yes, we know," Silva said unhappily.

"And I'm the soul of discretion. Ask anybody. If you tell me it's not for publication, not yet anyway, I won't publish it. I just want an inside track."

"How about this," Hector said, "how about we talk about your story after you answer our questions?"

"How about we don't."

"Then how about we charge you with impeding an investigation?"

"Don't you threaten me, Delegado. That won't stick and you know it."

Hector flushed. Silva put his hand on his nephew's arm.

"Let's start all over again," he said. "Hector has been in Cascatas since yesterday. He's a bit upset with the level of cooperation we've been getting."

"So?"

"So he's a little grumpy."

"A little?"

"Don't take it personally."

Diana sat back in her chair and smiled. "Okay," she said. "I won't. Lack of cooperation, huh?"

Silva nodded.

"Ferraz?"

He nodded again. "But that's not for publication," he said.

"What else do you know that isn't for publication?"

"Ferraz has what he claims to be the murder weapon. It's what you might call a sniper rifle, a Sako Classic with a Leupold telescopic sight, if that means anything to you."

Diana picked up a pencil and made a note. "It doesn't, but it will. I'll look it up. What else?"

"The weapon and the cartridge casings are apparently free of fingerprints. The shots seemed to have been fired from the north tower of the new church. That's where the rifle was found."

She made another note. "Have you been able to trace it? The gun, I mean."

"Not yet. We're working on it."

"The killer didn't file off the serial number or anything like that?"

"No. But that probably only means he knows the weapon won't be traceable."

She tapped the paper she'd been writing on. "Why don't you want me to publish this?"

"The ballistics tests haven't been completed. We're not absolutely sure that the rifle is the murder weapon."

She leaned forward. "When will you know for sure?"

"Maybe tonight, maybe tomorrow morning."

"And you'll tell me when you do?"

"I will if you help us."

She leaned back. "Okay, we have a deal. Do you think the murderer was somebody from around here?"

"I'd be guessing."

"Guess."

"Probably. According to the bishop's secretary, the decision to arrive by helicopter was made the day before the murder. There wouldn't have been much time for an outsider to plan the shot, and he probably wouldn't have known how to get access to the tower."

"Okay," she said. "What else can you tell me?"

She held her pencil poised.

"At the moment, nothing else. Your turn."

"What do you want to know?"

Hector, calmer now, picked up the questioning.

"Why did you smile when you mentioned Ferraz? What do you know that we don't?"

She dropped the pencil into a coffee mug she'd pressed into service as a penholder. SÃO PAULO. 450TH ANNIVERSARY, it said. Red letters on white porcelain with a black outline of the city's most prominent buildings.

"Because I think—as a matter of fact I *know*—that Ferraz doesn't want the Federal Police snooping around Cascatas."

"And how do you know that?"

"Because I'm doing a little investigation of my own. Not about the bishop's murder. Something else."

"What?"

Diana hesitated, and then shook her head. "It has nothing to do with your case."

"Why don't you let us be the judge of that?"

"Because I've been working on the story for weeks, and I don't want to tip my hand. You can read it when I publish it."

"And when will that be?"

She picked up a cardboard desk calendar and consulted it. "The fourteenth. That's a week from this Friday."

Hector let his displeasure show.

Silva didn't.

"What can you tell us about the Landless Workers' League?" he asked. "Not the movement. I know about that. I'm talking about the local picture. Who runs the league here in Cascatas? What have they been up to recently? Who opposes it?"

Diana pulled another pencil out of the mug. "Why do you want to know?"

Hector and Silva exchanged glances.

"There's been a suggestion made—" Hector said.

"By whom?"

"I can't tell you that, but there's been a suggestion made

that Dom Felipe was acting against the best interests of the league. They might have wanted him out of the way, might have killed him."

She dropped the pencil on her desk and made a dismissive gesture. "I don't believe it. Not for a minute. Okay, Dom Felipe came down on liberation theology, and that hurt the league, but that's no reason for them to kill him. As far as the higher-ups in the church are concerned, liberation theology is a dead issue. People like Dom Felipe don't make the rules. The Vatican does, and they're sure to appoint somebody with the same views."

"So liberation theology is dead?"

"I didn't say that. I said it's a dead issue *in Rome*. Here, on the local level, it's different. There are still a few priests who are—how shall I put this?—sympathetic to the doctrine."

"And who might they be?"

She narrowed her eyes. "Why do you want to know?"

"Another suggestion was that a priest, one of those liberation theologians, might have committed the murder."

She looked at him as if he'd given her a personal affront. "That's insane. Who put an idea like that into your head. Gaspar?"

"I'm not at liberty to say. Why do you think it might have been Father Gaspar?"

"Ah, so it *was* him. Why do I think so? Because he's like *that*"—she crossed her index and middle fingers—"with the landowners. One of his favorite themes for a sermon is the inviolability of property. The people from the Association love him."

"The association?"

"Landowners' Association, set up to oppose the league."

Silva nodded knowingly.

"Oppose? How?" Hector said.

"Don't you read anything other than the sports pages?"

Hector reddened and opened his mouth to reply. His uncle stepped on his foot.

"Ever since the government in Brasilia shifted to the left," Diana continued, "the big landowners have been feeling like orphans. The bureaucrats have been grabbing their uncultivated property and giving it away."

"So what?" Hector said. "It's legal, isn't it? And it's not like they don't get paid for it."

"Legal, yes. And, yeah, they get paid for it—eventually— but most of them don't want the money. They don't need it. They want to keep the land. And there's something else, too."

"What's that?"

The definition of 'uncultivated.'"

"Seems pretty clear to me."

"As it does to the people from the league. For them, anything that isn't actually planted with food crops is 'uncultivated.' The landowners don't see it that way. Some of them run cattle, some plant trees for the paper industry, some of them have land they're allowing to lie fallow for crop rotation. The league goes in anyway. Next thing you know they're setting up tents, occupying farm buildings, planting their own crops, and petitioning the government. It drives the landowners crazy. That's why they set up the association."

"To lobby the government?"

"That too. But also to force the eviction of league members who occupy their fazendas."

"Force how?"

Diana shrugged. "By any legal means possible. But, for some of them, by using capangas, hired gunmen. They contract them in Paraguay and up north in places like Piauí. And sometimes they hire the local cops."

"Like Ferraz?"

"You said it. I didn't. The landowners call the league

people communists and anarchists. The league calls the landowners despots and terrorists. The truth of the matter is probably somewhere in the middle. Who wrote that line 'in a true tragedy both sides are right'?"

"I don't remember," Silva said, "but from what you're saying, it sounds appropriate."

"It does, doesn't it?" she said, picking up her pencil and making a note to herself before continuing. "There've been excesses on both sides, but most people are only capable of seeing one side of the question. Even the priests."

"Okay, let's get back to them. Where do I find liberation theologians?"

Diana's smile was back. "You don't find them. They no longer exist. Not officially, anyway. They wouldn't be permitted to stay in the church if they did. But if you want to know something about how they *used* to think and what they *used* to do, go talk to Brouwer."

"Brouwer?"

"Don't give me that innocent look, Delegado. I wasn't born yesterday. If Gaspar talked to you about liberation theology, he must have talked to you about Anton Brouwer."

"I don't recall telling you that Father Gaspar talked to me at all."

She sighed. "Okay, have it your way. *Father* Anton Brouwer. He's a Belgian from some little town in Flanders near Antwerp. He's been living here for years, helping the Indians, the orphans, AIDS victims, the street kids, you name it."

"Is he involved with the league?"

She hesitated. "He was once," she said, cautiously. "But since the bishop started cracking down. . . . Well, I can't say."

"Can't or won't?"

"He's a good guy, Brouwer is. He does what he thinks is right."

"You're not answering my question."

"No, I'm not. And I don't intend to. But I'll say this: Brouwer is a priest, not a landless worker. That means he wouldn't qualify for membership, much less leadership, in the league."

"Who runs it?"

"Luiz Pillar."

"Not him," Silva said. "He's in Brasilia. I'm talking about here, locally."

"Most people don't know," she said.

"But you do?"

She thought about the question for a moment and decided to answer. "I do, but I don't print it."

"Why?"

She sighed. "Because when certain landowners manage to identify league leaders, those leaders have a way of turning up dead."

"Like that guy they nailed to a tree?"

"You heard about that, did you? His name was Aurelio Azevedo. Ferraz was in charge of the investigation. He never arrested anyone. Why am I not surprised?"

"You think Ferraz is in bed with the landowners?"

"I think he's a whore who gets into bed with anyone who pays him, and the association pays him. Don't quote me. I can't prove it."

"Who runs the association?"

"The Munizes, father and son. Orlando Senior is the national president. Junior runs the local chapter. He also runs a big ranch—and I mean a *really* big ranch—that his father owns about fifteen kilometers east of here, the Fazenda de Boa Vista."

"And his opposite number? The guy who runs the league locally?"

"Roberto Pereira. Don't spread it around, okay? I don't want his murder on my conscience. By the way, did you know that Pillar is in town?"

"Luiz Pillar? Here?"

Silva was surprised. Pillar spent most of his time lobbying politicians in Brasilia. He'd been particularly successful with the President of the Republic, a man who'd been a labor leader long before he had political ambitions.

"Yeah. Here," Diana said, "and staying at the Hotel Excelsior."

"We're at the Excelsior as well," Hector said, giving his uncle a sideways glance.

"Of course you are," Diana said. "It's the only game in town except for the Hotel Grande, which is anything but grand, except, maybe, for the size of the cockroaches."

"What brings Pillar to Cascatas? Any idea?"

"No, but whenever he shows up things have a way of happening."

"They do indeed. This guy Pereira, you know where to find him?"

"No."

Hector lifted an eyebrow.

"No," she repeated. "I really don't, but if there's a demonstration or if they occupy somebody's property—and with Pillar here it's got to be one or the other—you're going to find him right up front."

"Capable of violence?"

"Roberto?" She thought about it for a moment. "I'm not sure," she said, massaging the lobe of one ear between a thumb and a forefinger. "If you'd asked me a year ago, I would have said 'definitely not.' But he and his wife were great friends of the Azevedos. Their kids used to play together. After the murders he—"

She was interrupted by a knock. The roar of the press

increased in intensity as a young woman stuck her head through the open door. She was in her early twenties, had short blonde hair and multiple studs on her ears.

"Can it wait?" Diana had to shout to make herself heard. "I'm almost done."

The blonde shook her head. "You'd better come out here," she shouted back.

Diana went out, closing the door behind her.

"Bitch," Hector said, as soon as she was gone.

"I rather like her," his uncle said. "Refreshingly candid." And then, to soothe his nephew's ruffled feathers: "Good idea. Coming here, I mean. At least you and the lady seem to agree about one thing."

"Yeah. Ferraz."

Before he could say anything more the roar of the press was back. Diana bustled in, holding what appeared to be a box full of paper. She kicked the door closed with her left foot and put the object on the desk. The word IN was written with blue marker on a piece of masking tape stuck to one end.

"I didn't touch it," she said, breathlessly, "but my secretary did. You'll probably need her fingerprints for comparison. Read it."

She pointed. Silva stood up, took out his reading glasses, and leaned over the paper that topped the pile. The note wasn't anything fancy. It had been block-printed with a ball-point pen:

ORLANDO MUNIZ, THE MURDERER OF
AURELIO AZEVEDO, NOW HAS ALL OF THE
LAND HE'LL EVER NEED: IT'S TWO METERS
LONG AND FIFTY CENTIMETERS WIDE.

There was no signature.

"Delivered by a street kid," Diana said, "in a plain white

envelope with nothing but my name on the front. The envelope is outside in the wastebasket. The kid's already gone."

"Orlando Muniz. Would that be Junior?" Hector asked.

"No doubt," she said. "The old man lives in Rio de Janeiro most of the time. If it had been him, you would have felt the ground shake. They say he's got half of the politicians in Brasilia in his pocket, but that's probably an exaggeration. Personally, I don't believe that it's more than a third of them."

When Diana said the word "politicians," Hector glanced at his uncle.

"Merda," Silva said.

Chapter Twelve

"WHAT?"

"Is that a comment on what I just said, or do we have problems with the telephone line?" the director asked testily. He hated to repeat himself.

"The line," Silva lied.

It was two minutes past 6:00, and true to his promise, the director was calling for an update.

"I said Orlando Muniz is on his way to Cascatas," he repeated, switching into his *I'm-speaking-to-someone-who-doesn't-know-the-language* mode. "He'll be there tomorrow afternoon. Be nice to him. He was a major contributor to the president's campaign."

"Muniz contributed to the president's campaign."

Silva started the sentence as a question, but managed to kill the rising inflection and turn it into a statement. "Why would he do that?"

"Why not?" the director said.

"Because the president leans to the left and Muniz's politics are said to be somewhere to the right of Attila the Hun's."

"Yeah, but he's not stupid. Every poll predicted that the president was going to win, remember? Anyway, that's no concern of yours. Just make sure you don't piss Muniz off."

"Don't worry. I couldn't if I wanted to."

"What's that supposed to mean?"

"Just what I said. I won't even *be* here when he arrives."

"Why the hell not?"

"I'm going to Presidente Vargas."

"What for? What's in Presidente Vargas?"

"The seat of the diocese. The bishop's secretary. We have an appointment."

"Cancel it. Send somebody else."

"Didn't you tell me my top priority was to—"

"Yeah, well now you have *two* top priorities: The murders of the bishop *and* Muniz Junior. I don't want to see you back here until you've solved both."

"With all due respect, Director, we're not even sure the Muniz kid is dead."

"Kid? The man's thirty-seven, or he *was* thirty-seven. Whichever. And if he isn't dead, so much the better, but I want you to stay there until you get to the bottom of it. Oh, I almost forgot. I have something for you. Information about the rifle, the one Ferraz's men found in the tower. The bullets that killed the bishop were definitely shot from it. They traced the serial number."

"And?"

"And a Belgian arms dealer by the name of . . ." Silva heard the director rustling through some papers, "Hugo van Aalst bought it directly from the manufacturer."

"A Belgian? Did you say a Belgian?"

The director took in an exasperated breath and grunted. "Yeah. So what?"

"Nothing. Go on."

After a pause, the director did. "That's Aalst with two 'a's.' *He* sold it to the Paraguayan army, and he has an end user certificate to prove it. The Paraguayans say they can't find it. Sound familiar?"

"Too familiar."

Not a few Paraguayans made a very lucrative living by supplying contraband to their neighbor to the north. Most of it came across the so-called "Friendship Bridge" near Iguaçu Falls. Scotch whiskey, cigarettes, and weapons were all popular items.

The registration of the weapon was a dead end. They'd never be able to trace it to the killer, but Silva didn't think it would be a good idea to stress that fact at the moment.

"Hang on," the director said.

He left the line without waiting for a response, but he was back less than five seconds later: "Minister on the other line. Keep me posted." He hung up without saying goodbye.

Silva looked at his watch. It was already too late to call Irene. With a shake of his head he got up, crossed the living room of their suite, and knocked on Hector's door. His nephew, wearing a bathrobe, his hair still wet from the shower, opened it immediately.

"You don't look happy," Hector said.

"I'm not," Silva said, but he didn't elaborate. "That Poli woman said that Pillar is staying here, right?"

"Right."

"Get some clothes on and see if you can find him. Try to keep it friendly. Invite him for a drink."

"In the bar?"

"No. Here. In twenty minutes."

THE YOUNG man behind the reception desk confirmed that Pillar was, indeed, registered in the hotel.

"Room four-oh-seven," he said to Hector, "in the back of the building. Certainly not one of our best, but he asked for the cheapest—"

"Where's the house phone?"

"Over there, senhor."

Hector had already turned his back when the clerk added, "But if you're going to call Senhor Pillar, I'm afraid you're not going to find him."

Hector turned back to the clerk. "No?"

"No, senhor. There are quite a few messages for him, some of them urgent, so I tried to call him when I came on duty."

"When was that?"

"At five. When he didn't pick up, I asked the chamber-maid to check the room. His bed hasn't been slept in."

"How about his room key?"

"He left it with me at about this same time last night. I don't think he's been back since."

Hector was breathing hard when he got back to the suite. Too impatient to wait for the elevator, he'd run up four flights of stairs.

His uncle's aplomb immediately deflated him.

"So you don't think he was kidnapped?"

Silva shook his head. "By the landowners? Unlikely." He set aside the thick folder he'd been leafing through and picked up the scotch and water he'd prepared for himself. "Muniz is their local leader, and he's gone missing."

"Well, then, maybe somebody else organized it."

"Maybe. But I doubt it. You leave a message?"

Hector nodded. "And a tip to the desk clerk to make sure it stayed on the top of the pile. Some pile, by the way. He has more people trying to get in touch with him than you do. What's that?" He pointed to the folder Silva had been perusing.

"Pillar's dossier. I brought it from Brasilia. Pour yourself a drink and have a look."

Hector did just that.

The dossier had been opened back in the days of the military dictatorship, before Pillar had been forced to flee to asylum in Uruguay. Kept current to the present day, it chronicled, in great detail, the life of one of Brazil's premier activists.

Hector didn't see eye-to-eye with Pillar's politics, but as he skimmed the pages, he started building up a grudging respect for the man. Pillar was a firebrand, but he certainly wasn't a megalomaniac. When he spoke, and there were summaries of many of his speeches, he always stressed that he wasn't the President of the Landless Workers' League. The organization had, he insisted, no chief executive, no board of directors, no hierarchy. They were all comrades, all equals in the struggle for land reform.

And Pillar certainly wasn't in it for the money. He lived simply, drove a sixteen-year-old Fiat and resided alone in a studio apartment in one of the less-fashionable neighborhoods of Brasilia. An exhaustive examination of his financial dealings seemed to indicate that he was scrupulous in accounting for the contributions made to his organization and that he regularly paid his taxes.

In dictatorships, people like Pillar are imprisoned and tortured, often killed. In the great democracies they sometimes become candidates for president or prime minister. But they seldom win.

More than 1,500 of Pillar's colleagues had been murdered in the land wars of the last decade. He was more visible than any of them, but the threat to his life didn't seem to make him afraid, only angry. If Pereira, the local man, was anything like him. . . .

The telephone rang. Hector started to close the dossier, but his uncle stood. "Keep reading. I'll get it."

Silva identified himself, said "yes" twice, gave his room number, and replaced the receiver. "Better conceal that dossier after all," he said. "That was Pillar. He's on his way up."

LUIZ PILLAR was older, and thinner, than he looked in his photographs. His brown eyes were sunk deeply into their sockets. His cheekbones showed sharply under his brown skin. He was certainly a man under pressure. Perhaps he was ill. He reminded Hector of a painting by Edvard Munch, the one called *The Scream*. He was dressed in faded jeans and a red T-shirt emblazoned with the logotype of the league, a crossed hoe and pitchfork on a circular white field.

Silva offered him a hand and after a moment of hesitation Pillar took it.

Hector offered him a drink and Pillar refused.

"Are you here to arrest me?" he asked.

"Why would you think that?" Silva said.

Pillar shrugged and smiled. The smile was surprisingly gentle. "Because policemen, when I meet them, almost always do. Arrest me, I mean."

Pillar wasn't exaggerating. He'd been arrested tens of times. He'd been convicted, too, but that didn't necessarily mean anything. Policemen and judges often worked hand-in-hand with vengeful landowners. Juries often *were* vengeful landowners.

"You have nothing to fear from us, Senhor Pillar. We work for the federal government," Silva said.

"I know who you are, Chief Inspector. Your reputation precedes you."

"Yours, too. Now, will you sit down?"

Pillar sank into the offered chair.

"What brings you to Cascatas?" Silva asked.

"League business. You?"

"Murder. Initially, the murder of Dom Felipe Antunes, the Bishop of Presidente Vargas, and of your colleague, Aurelio Azevedo. More recently, the probable murder of a landowner by the name of Orlando Muniz."

Pillar's eyebrows shot up in surprise.

"Senior?"

"Junior."

"Too bad."

"You mean too bad it wasn't his old man?"

"Isn't murder a local matter?" Pillar asked, as if he hadn't heard Silva's question.

"Normally, yes. But the minister asked us to help the local police with their inquiries."

Pillar smiled again. "Assisting Colonel Emerson Ferraz with his inquiries? And is the colonel grateful?"

"Not particularly."

"No. I wouldn't think so. Still, your presence means that he's probably working harder to find the murderer of the bishop."

"But not to find the murderer of your colleague?"

The smile vanished. "No," Pillar said. "The colonel doesn't give a damn about what happened to Aurelio. What do you want from me, Chief Inspector?"

"There's been a suggestion that members of the league might have been involved in the murder of the bishop."

"Ridiculous."

"How about in the murder of Orlando Muniz Junior?"

"Now, that one I could understand. But I deny it, of course."

"Of course. You knew him?"

"Not personally, no, but I knew the bishop. He was misguided, but he was a well-meaning man, true to his convictions. I can't say I liked him, but I certainly didn't hate him, and neither did anyone else in my organization. That's not the case with Muniz. We all hate his guts. He's an exploiter of the worst kind."

"You just told me you didn't know him."

"*Personally*, I said. I'm basing my opinion on things I've heard."

"Heard from whom?"

"People who worked for him. Other people who knew him."

"You think he's dead?"

Pillar shrugged. "Dead or alive, I had nothing to do with it. His father won't believe that, of course. The old bastard will probably come after me next."

Silva took in a breath and let it out slowly. Before he uttered his next words, he already knew they'd be wasted but he said them anyway. "There's no end to this. Whenever you kill one of them, they're going to come right back and kill one of you. You know that, don't you?"

"I know more than that, Chief Inspector. I know that when one of them is murdered they go out and kill fifty or even a hundred of us. They've killed more than fifteen hundred of us in the last ten years."

"Yes, I know."

"But we're still going to win."

"What makes you so sure?"

"Because we have the numbers on our side. There are less than fifty thousand of them. There are almost five million of us out there." He pointed at the window as if all of them were just outside the hotel. "Five million landless workers. We've got them outnumbered by a margin of more than one hundred to one. We can't lose."

"There are laws in this country, Pillar—"

"Laws?" Pillar snorted. "We occupy unused farmland to force the government to do their duty and expropriate it. Is that a crime?"

"In fact, it is. It's called trespassing."

"Trespassing. And that *serious* offense, that *major* crime, merits the attention of the Federal Police?"

"Spare me your sarcasm. How long have you been in Cascatas?"

"What you're really asking is: Was I here before the disappearance of young Muniz?"

"Yes."

"When did he disappear?"

"Sometime during the night before last."

"Then the answer to your question is yes. Yes, I was here in Cascatas."

"Sleeping here at the hotel?"

"Yes."

"And last night? Did you sleep here last night?" Silva asked, already knowing the answer.

Pillar didn't hesitate. "No," he said.

"Then where *did* you sleep?"

"I didn't sleep at all. I've been up all night."

"Doing what?"

"Helping my brothers from the league to cut through Muniz's fence and occupy a part of his fazenda."

"A part of his—"

"Less than ten percent of his holding. Land he's never used, but the greedy bastard doesn't want to part with any of it. We're going to stay where we are until our demands are negotiated."

"That's senseless. "

"You're referring to the new law, I presume, the one that blocks appropriation in the case of occupation?"

"I am."

"The government hasn't been enforcing that one. Not since the new president was elected. He can't come right out and say it, but he's on our side."

"In his heart he may support you, but in practice, he won't. He has to enforce the law. You're pushing him too far."

"I don't think so. I think time will prove me right."

"My God, Pillar, do you have any idea who you're dealing with? Old man Muniz is one of the most powerful men in this country. You think he's going to think it's a coincidence that his son disappears one day and that you occupy his fazenda the next?"

"I don't give a damn what he thinks. He can't prove a thing."

"Proof? You think he needs proof?"

"That's the law."

"He's the kind that picks and chooses his laws, just like you do. You mentioned Ferraz—"

"The best cop money can buy. If he was an elevator operator, you'd have to bribe him to let you off on the right floor."

"Very funny. But this isn't a joke. The two of them, old man Muniz *and* Ferraz, are going to come after your people, and I won't be able to do a thing about it."

"Maybe that wouldn't be such a bad thing."

"Are you crazy?"

"No, Chief Inspector, I'm not crazy at all. Think about it. Right now, this town is full of reporters. They didn't come for us, they came for the bishop, but I intend to use them. What the league needs, more than anything else, is publicity for our cause. If Muniz and Ferraz crack a few heads—"

"They'll do more than crack a few heads. They'll kill people. Back off, Pillar. This whole thing isn't worth spilling blood for."

"No? Then why did *they*? You mentioned Aurelio Azevedo. He was my friend, Chief Inspector. They nailed him to a tree. They shot his wife, Teresa. They even killed Paulo and Marcela, their two kids. Paulo was fourteen. Marcela was only nine."

"A tragedy, I admit that, but—"

"Not only a tragedy. A travesty. A travesty of justice. You think we don't know who did it? You think we don't . . . ah, why am I wasting my breath. What's the use of talking to you? You can't help."

Luiz Pillar lifted his wrist and glanced at his watch. The face of it was scratched, and it had a cheap plastic band. "Look, I'm busy. If you want to continue this conversation you'll find me at our encampment, out on the Fazenda Boa Vista."

He left without offering either one of them a hand.

Chapter Thirteen

DIANA'S HEART GAVE A leap when she heard the sound of a key in the lock. A moment later someone forced the front door against the chain.

"Diana? Are you there?"

Lori's voice. Diana breathed a sigh of relief.

"What's going on?"

Lori had her mouth against the narrow opening between the door and the jamb. There was an edge to her voice.

"Coming," Diana said, making an effort to keep her own voice cheerful and nonchalant. Hurriedly, she closed the file she'd been working on, exited the word-processing program, and switched the computer off.

"Diana?"

Lori kicked the door. Hard.

Diana slipped off the chain and tried to relieve her partner of one of the brown paper bags, but Lori brushed by her, hurried into the kitchen, and set both of them on the counter. She kept her back turned to Diana.

"Are you alone in here?" she said.

"Of course I'm alone."

Lori spun around and eyed Diana suspiciously. "Then why the chain?"

"You're jealous?" Diana said.

"Have I reason to be?"

"No, Lori, you don't. The door was on the chain because I . . . I didn't want anyone to walk in on me while I was working."

It was the truth, but even to her it sounded like a feeble excuse.

"Including me?" Lori said. When Diana didn't reply to that, she continued, "Because I thought no one else except you and I have keys to this apartment." Lori turned her back again and started taking groceries from the bags, setting them on the counter with just a bit more force than was necessary. "So what are you hiding?" she said.

"I'm not hiding anything," Diana said. "I'm just being careful. Here, let me help you."

Diana picked up a six-pack of yogurt and put it into the fridge. Lori opened the door to one of the cabinets and stood poised with a can of chickpeas in her hand. She was a short woman and had raised herself on the tips of her toes. Now, without putting the can away, she sank back onto her heels.

"Why careful?" she said.

"I can't tell you."

"You-can't-tell-me?" Lori doled out the words one by one.

"Not because I don't want to," Diana said, hastily. "It's because I promised someone I'd—"

"Hold it right there! You promised someone you were going to keep secrets from *me?*"

"It's for your own good, darling. Be a sweetheart and hand me that package of butter."

Lori handed her partner the butter and leaned her derriere against the sink. She crossed her arms and watched Diana put the package into the compartment at the top of the refrigerator door.

Diana glanced at her. "What?" she said.

"You don't trust me." It was an accusation, not a question.

Diana closed the door to the fridge and breathed out in exasperation. "Of course I trust you."

"Then tell me."

"No."

"Why not?"

"Because . . . because it's dangerous. If a certain party gets wind of it before it's published, God knows what he'll do."

"Who is he?"

Diana shook her head.

"Have it your own way," Lori said.

She turned her back, went into their bedroom and slammed the door. Diana heard the key turn in the lock. She sighed to herself, returned to her office and rebooted her computer. Lori would come around. Eventually. But until Diana had her work in print she wasn't going to get a good night's sleep, and not just because she'd be spending all of those nights on the couch.

Her biggest threat came from the kids themselves. Those kids were used to selling their bodies, which aside from being humiliating, was often more painful than selling information. If it occurred to one of them that Ferraz would pay him for what he knew, the kid would betray her in an instant. And whatever most of those kids were, they weren't stupid. At least one of them was bound to figure it out before long. That's why she and Anton had agreed that it was safest not to tell Lori anything. If Ferraz came for her, the less Lori knew, the better.

Up until that moment, the moment she resumed her seat, Diana had taken only minimal precautions. She hadn't typed up the interview transcripts at the office. She hadn't left any record of what she was working on in the computer there. She'd been careful on the telephone. She'd even made sure Lori hadn't caught her working at home. Until now.

The risk hung over her head, and it was a deadly risk, but it was worth it. This was going to be *the* series of her journalistic life. She didn't want to rush it into print. She wanted more color, more human interest, more juicy details. That's what sold newspapers. That's what won prizes for journalism. That's what could catapult her into the big time.

And once Lori read her work, then she'd understand, and all would be forgiven. Lori could be temperamental at times, but Diana had grown confident about the depth of their love. It was a far cry from their first few months together, when Diana was always asking herself how a blonde goddess with fashion sense could be interested in a square-shouldered woman with no waist.

She glanced at her watch. The bank was open late. She could just make it.

She transferred everything she was working on, transcripts and all, onto a CD, put the CD into a large envelope, added the memory sticks from the camera and the copies of the audiotapes. Then she typed out a short note, put it into a smaller envelope, and added stamps.

She went to the door of their bedroom and tapped lightly. "Lori?"

No response.

"Lori, I'm going out. Just for a little while. I'll be back for dinner."

Still no response.

Diana gave it up, picked up her knapsack, and left the apartment, locking the door behind her. Down in the garage she fired up the Honda Valkyrie, her favorite bike. Her business at the bank took no more than ten minutes. She mailed the letter to Anton Brouwer on her way home.

Chapter Fourteen

SILVA AND HECTOR DEDICATED the day following their conversation with Luiz Pillar to the procedural ritual. They visited the murder site, spoke with the medical examiner, and interviewed the members of the bishop's reception committee. Nothing brought them closer to a solution.

They were back at the hotel, and Silva was nursing a cold beer, when his cell phone, the one for which only the director had the number, started to ring. He fished it out of his breast pocket.

"Good evening, Director."

"Silva?"

It wasn't the director.

"Who is this?"

"Orlando Muniz. One of your superiors should have talked to you about me. Did he?"

"Yes. How did you get this number, Senhor Muniz?"

"Never mind that. I've arrived. I'm in suite nine hundred at the Excelsior. Where are you?"

"In my room. The same hotel."

"Good. Come up."

"Right now?"

"Something wrong with your ears?"

"I assumed you'd be staying at your son's place."

"It's not his place. It's *my* place, and it has two broken doors. I'll move out there when they're fixed. Suite nine hundred. Make it quick. I'm waiting." Muniz hung up.

"And good afternoon to you, too, Senhor Muniz," Silva said. Then, to Hector, "How about another beer?"

* * *

THIRTY MINUTES later, a flinty-eyed man wearing an empty shoulder holster answered the door of Suite 900. A pistol, a Glock .40 just like the one Silva was wearing under his jacket, was in his right hand, pointing at the floor.

"Senhor Muniz?" Silva said.

"Who wants him?" the bodyguard said.

"Costa and Silva, Federal Police."

"Took your own sweet time getting here," a voice grumbled from inside the suite, and then, giving an order, "Let 'em in, Jair."

Jair stepped aside. After they walked past him he stuck his head into the corridor, looked left and right, and then locked the door behind them.

Muniz's suite was a good deal larger than Silva's, but it was on the top floor of the hotel, just under the roof, so the air-conditioning wasn't equal to the task of cooling the place. It was uncomfortably hot. If Muniz had shown him a bit more courtesy, Silva might have told him that the hotel had other, cooler, alternatives.

But Muniz hadn't and Silva didn't.

Muniz had another visitor and, by the look of things, he'd already been in the suite for some time. Both men were stripped down to their shirtsleeves, had opened their collars, and had circles of sweat under their arms. There was a full ashtray on the coffee table. The same table held a number of empty glasses, an ice bucket, and a bottle of Logan's Twelve Year Old. The bucket was transparent. It only had a few slivers of ice in the bottom and about a centimeter of water. A strong smell of tobacco was in the air and enough haze to make Silva's eyes burn.

Muniz stood. He was a short, swarthy man, with a wart to the left of his nose. Earlier in the day, Silva had received photos of his son. There was no physical resemblance.

The other man also stood. Muniz introduced him. "Judge Wilson Cunha."

The judge offered his hand, first to Silva and then to Hector. He was short and his erect posture and protruding chest reminded Silva of a pigeon. His hair, moist from perspiration and immaculately coifed, was somewhat long for a man of his age and station. It hung slightly over his ears.

The other two men in the room, the fellow who'd opened the door, and another who could have been his younger brother, apparently didn't rate introductions.

Muniz wiped his forehead on his sleeve, snapped his fingers, and pointed to the chairs surrounding a dining table. "Put two of those"—he pointed to a spot on the opposite side of the coffee table—"right there."

The men with the flinty eyes did what he'd told them to do and then retreated to opposite corners of the room.

"Sit down," Muniz said, making it sound more like a command than a courtesy. He sank back into his seat on the couch.

Cunha adjusted his armchair to form a united front. He was obviously going to be on Muniz's side, whatever it was.

Silva expected to be offered a drink. It didn't happen.

"You find my boy?" Muniz began without preamble. In Brazil, where manners dictate that virtually every conversation open with some kind of chitchat, it was a clear discourtesy.

"Not yet, senhor," Hector said.

"I was talking to your boss, not you," Muniz said, sharply. "What about the note?"

"No prints," Silva said. "Written with a ballpoint pen in block letters."

"Get it. I want to see it."

Silva shook his head. "I sent it to Brasilia for analysis.

Maybe there are fingerprints. We may learn something of interest from the ink or the paper, but I doubt it. We may be able to confirm the identity of the writer if we catch him, but then again—"

"Maybe, maybe, maybe. That's all you've got? What's the matter with you people? How many of those agitators have you questioned?"

"League members, you mean?"

"Who else would I mean? Do you know what happened last night?"

"The occupation of your son's, sorry, *your* fazenda?"

"So you're not completely uninformed? Good for you. You think that threat was bullshit, or is my boy really dead?"

"They made no demands. I'd expect the worst."

Judge Cunha nodded sagely, as if he'd already made the same point. Then he reached over, used his fingers to extract some of the remaining ice from the bucket, put it into his mouth, and cracked it with his teeth.

"Why haven't you arrested some of the bastards?" Muniz went on.

"As Judge Cunha here will undoubtedly be able to tell you, there's the issue of proof—"

"Proof?" Muniz exploded. "Those maggots are crawling all over my fazenda. Do you think it's a coincidence? Haul the bastards in on a trespassing charge. I'll be happy to question them myself."

Silva's jaw tightened, but he kept a close rein on his temper. "It's possible we may be dealing with two unrelated issues," he said.

"It's possible that the blessed Virgin Mary had two balls and a cock," Muniz said, "but I doubt it."

The judge looked shocked. But then he reached out, tentatively touched Silva just above his kneecap and cleared his throat. "You have to understand, Chief Inspector, that my friend Senhor Muniz is justifiably upset. He's worried about his son, as any father would be, and he's outraged that those . . . people had the effrontery to invade his property."

He paused, and appeared to be waiting for Silva to respond. When Silva didn't, the judge continued. "Before you arrived, we were discussing Senhor Muniz's legal recourses with respect to the occupation. The situation seems very clear to me."

"Does it? I'm told that Senhor Muniz's son wasn't using that land."

"What the hell has that got to do with it?" Muniz snapped.

"The law states," Silva said, "that the government can appropriate uncultivated land by paying a fair price for it. The law further states that the government can grant land thus appropriated to landless farmers. If you, Judge, would entertain an act of appropriation, I'm sure the league people could be convinced to leave the property until the case is settled."

It was Muniz's turn to look shocked. "Are you insane? Whose side are you on, anyway?"

Before Silva could answer Judge Cunha intervened. "Do you own any land, Chief Inspector? I'm not talking about a piece of property with a house on it, or a little *chacara*. I'm talking about *real* land, a fazenda."

"No."

"No. I didn't think so." The judge looked at Muniz and gave a faint nod, as if he'd just scored a point. "Then we could hardly expect you to understand, could we?" he said to Silva.

Muniz stood. The interview was over. "We'll solve it our own way," he said. "The way we always have. We don't need your help anymore. Go home."

116 *Leighton Gage*

"I'm afraid I can't do that," Silva said. "I wasn't sent here because of your son, and I have my orders."

"We'll see about your orders. Get out."

"MERDA," THE director said twenty minutes later, and he said it loud enough to cause Silva to move the cell phone away from his ear. "I told you to treat him with kid gloves. What am I going to tell the minister? Get on a plane and get out of there. Muniz won't stay for more than a day or two. You can go back just as soon as he's gone."

"You're the boss, but . . ."

"But what?"

"It's pretty obvious what Muniz is up to. He's got a local judge in his pocket, and I have no doubt he's got more than the two capangas I saw in his suite. He'll have brought them in from one of his other fazendas, or from Paraguay. This town is already packed with people from the national press. If Muniz gets his way there's going to be a slaughter, and when there is, the journalists are going to spread it all over the media."

The director reflected for a moment, considering the consequences.

"I'll have the minister talk to him," he finally said.

"As you wish. But if you do, and if Muniz ignores him and goes ahead with his plans, the minister won't have any deniability. He might not thank you for that."

There was a long silence on the other end of the telephone. Finally, the director said, "Well, then, get that State Police Colonel Whatshisname to stop it."

"With respect, Director, Colonel Ferraz will do what Judge Cunha tells him to do, and the judge will do what Muniz tells *him* to do. Ferraz, by the way, has a large landholding of his own."

"A cop with a fazenda?"

"Yes, Director, a cop with a fazenda, and that should give all of us an idea about what kind of a cop he is, don't you think? Anyway, he's got no sympathy for the league. If they need his protection, the odds are that he'll be somewhere else. He might even be the person they'll be needing protection from."

"Can't you get that judge to do something?"

"No. But I'm sure Muniz can. I'm also sure that, if he does, we're not going to like it."

"So what do we do?"

"I'll try to defuse the situation. Meanwhile, I'll keep trying to find out what happened to the bishop and to Muniz's son. It's possible the two events are connected."

"Connected? How?"

"I'm not sure, and I could be wrong. I just have a hunch."

"What's your next step?"

"I still want to go to Presidente Vargas and talk to the bishop's secretary."

"That again? We've been through that already. You want to leave Cascatas? At a time like this? Not on your life."

The director seemed unaware that he'd just undergone a complete reversal of position.

"Just for the day," Silva said. "I—"

"Out of the question," the director said. "Not on your life. You stay right where you are. Send that nephew of yours."

Chapter Fifteen

Father Francisco Caporetto was in his mid-thirties and darkly handsome. When he met Hector in the reception area, he was wearing a tailored black suit that fit him like a glove. They shook hands, and he led his guest down a long corridor toward the back of the building.

"This is—was—Dom Felipe's room," he said, opening a door. "Shall we sit over there?" He pointed at two chairs nestled into the alcove of a bay window.

The late bishop's office was a spacious chamber with white-painted walls, modern furniture, and an oil painting which Hector thought might be a Pignatari above the fireplace.

The two men sat, and the bishop's erstwhile secretary rang for coffee.

The novice who brought it, a girl of seventeen or eighteen, couldn't seem to take her eyes off Father Francisco. She used no makeup, was radiantly beautiful, and smelled of toilet soap. Hector suppressed a libidinous thought and waited until she left before he got down to business.

"Have you been with Dom Felipe a long time?"

"Since before he took up his most recent appointment. It would have been three years, this June," Francisco said, without betraying whether he thought three years was a long time.

"You were his friend?"

"I was his secretary, Delegado. I don't believe the bishop had any friends."

"*De mortuis nil nisi bonum,* eh?"

Father Francisco smiled, but not, Hector thought, because he found it funny, only to show that he understood the Latin. The priest settled back in his chair and crossed his ankles.

"Did you like him?" Hector persisted.

"It wasn't my place to like or dislike him."

"That's not what I asked."

Francisco looked through the bay window. Hector followed his gaze. Two boys were kneeling on the street, playing with a wooden top. Hector hadn't seen a wooden top for at least twenty years.

"Hardly any television here," Francisco said, as if he could read the thought. "No antennas. No cable. Some of the wealthier people have satellite dishes, of course, but most of the children are still being raised without it. They play the same games their parents and grandparents used to play."

"Nice."

"A little dull, actually. But to get back to your question: No, to be frank, I didn't really like him. He was severe with himself and severe with others. Mind you, I'm not saying he was unjust, just severe."

"Father Gaspar called him a friend."

"Did he?"

Father Francisco lifted an eyebrow. Hector waited for him to say more. When he didn't, Hector went off on a new tack. "How about enemies?"

"No one who hated him enough to kill him."

"Pardon me for asking this, Padre, but I have to: A relationship?"

The urbane priest seemed to take the question in stride. "A relationship of a sexual nature you mean?"

"Yes."

"No. I think not. He never struck me as a man who had to struggle to maintain his vow of chastity. He really wasn't interested in women. And he often expressed a distinct dislike of homosexuals and homosexuality. He found it an aberration."

"Money, then. Was he particularly fond of money?"

"Some people might say so. He was always trying to raise money to build a new church, or a new school. He was good at it, too; some of the donors wouldn't have been anywhere near as generous if Dom Felipe hadn't been so persistent."

"What did he think of liberation theology?"

The sudden change of theme caused Francisco's forehead to crease in puzzlement. "I thought you were exploring motives."

"I am. Please answer my question."

"Liberation theology? What did the bishop think of it?"

Hector nodded.

"He opposed it. He had to. It's been condemned by Rome."

"So it's likely his successor will condemn it as well."

"It's not 'likely,' Delegado, it's certain. Dom Felipe's successor will certainly condemn it."

"What would you say to a suggestion that another priest, a liberation theologian, might have killed the bishop?"

Francisco shook his head. "That's absurd."

"Is it? Why?"

"First of all, because there are no longer any priests who are liberation theologians. All of them either renounced the doctrine or left the Church. Second, because any priest, no matter how radical, would know that killing the bishop wouldn't change anything. Liberation theology is a discredited doctrine, and the death of a hundred bishops won't alter that."

"I see."

Francisco leaned forward. The gold frame of his eyeglasses reflected a pinpoint of light from the window. "But there's one possibility you might not have considered. Have you heard of a man called Aurelio Azevedo?"

"The activist? The man they nailed to a tree?"

"Yes, the man they nailed to a tree. Did you know that they killed his wife and his two children as well?"

"Yes."

The priest paused for a moment, as if he expected Hector to comment on the barbarity of it all. When Hector didn't, he went on. "All of us were outraged, the bishop in particular. Several weeks before he died he went to Cascatas and preached a sermon in the old church. He drew his inspiration from Psalm Fifty-eight, verse ten: The passage reads 'The righteous shall rejoice when he seeth the vengeance: He shall wash his feet in the blood of the wicked.' His thesis, in a nutshell, was that whoever spills innocent blood is evil and deserving of having their own blood spilled."

"I gather he didn't believe in turning the other cheek?"

"No, Delegado, he most certainly did not. The bishop leaned toward Old Testament solutions, an eye for an eye. He enjoined anyone with information about the death of Azevedo to come forward, told them their souls would be in peril if they didn't."

"Did he specifically accuse any individual or any group?"

"No. He stopped short of that, but people got the message."

"And those people included the big landowners, I suppose."

"Most certainly. Several of them stood up and walked out while he was still speaking. I was there. I saw it."

"Did it work? Did anyone come forward?"

"Possibly."

"Possibly?"

Francisco looked out the window, gathering his thoughts. Hector followed his gaze. The children who'd been playing with the top were gone.

"About a week after the sermon," the priest resumed, "Dom Felipe received a letter, postmarked Cascatas, and signed by someone named Edson Souza."

Hector made a note of the name. "Go on," he said.

"Souza claimed to have knowledge of a crime and wanted to speak to the bishop personally. He gave a date and a time when he was going to call."

"May I see the letter?"

"It's gone. Missing. After the bishop's death I searched for it, but I haven't been able to find it. I don't think anyone took it, though. Perhaps the bishop discarded it."

"And did this Souza actually call?"

"He did, but the bishop was unable to speak to him. At the date and time specified he had a longstanding engagement elsewhere. He instructed me to give Souza an alternate date and time to call him back."

"Which you did?"

"Which I did."

"What did Souza sound like? Can you describe his voice?"

"Young. Poorly educated. Local accent. I'm afraid I can't be more specific than that."

"What do you mean by a local accent?"

"He's from around here somewhere. São Paulo State for sure."

"Any speech defects? A lisp, perhaps?"

"No, nothing like that."

"When did this conversation take place?"

The priest stood up, walked to the glass-topped desk and consulted a calendar. "The . . . eighth of last month."

"At what time?"

"Eleven o'clock in the morning."

"What number did he call?"

"Number?"

"The telephone number that Souza used to contact you."

The priest rattled off some numbers, and Hector made a note of them. "Then what happened?"

"Souza agreed to call back."

"And did he?"

"He did. He called the next day at the same time. The bishop spoke to him. I was curious, so I went into his office just after he'd hung up. Dom Felipe was staring down at the surface of his desk. When he heard me come in, he looked up. He was as angry as I've ever seen him. At first, I thought it was because of my interruption. But no. He told me to place a call to Father Gaspar Farias in Cascatas."

"And did you?"

"I did."

"What did they discuss?"

"I have no idea. He offered me no information about either call. Not the one from Souza, not the one to Father Gaspar. Not then. Not later."

"And you never asked him?"

The priest shook his head and smiled, as if the question struck him as naïve. "Oh, my goodness, no. I'd never take that kind of liberty with the bishop."

"Do you think the two calls were related?"

Father Francisco toyed with his empty cup and thought about the question. Then he pushed cup and saucer aside and leaned back in his chair. "They might well have been."

"Might they both have had something to do with Azevedo's murder?"

"I'd be speculating, but . . . yes, I think so."

"Why would he talk to Gaspar about it and not to you?"

"I'm here. Father Gaspar is in Cascatas. The bishop preached his sermon in Gaspar's old church, and he was going to Cascatas to consecrate the new one. Perhaps he wanted some information about a parishioner, or wanted Gaspar to take some kind of action prior to his arrival. That's my best guess, but I really don't know."

"Did you speak to Dom Felipe on the morning of his death?"

"No. As you now know, having made it yourself, it's a long drive to Cascatas. I wanted to be there when he arrived. I left very early in the morning, long before he came down to breakfast."

"Why didn't you accompany him in the helicopter?"

Father Francisco shook his head. "He wouldn't have welcomed it."

"Why not?"

"Well . . ." For the first time during the interview Father Francisco seemed to be at a loss for words. " . . . the bishop was—how shall I put this?—publicity conscious." He seemed pleased with his phrasing and repeated it. "Yes, publicity conscious. He was making a grand entrance into Cascatas. My presence on the helicopter would have been . . . a distraction."

"A prima donna was he? A publicity hound?"

"I didn't say that, Delegado."

"No, Padre, of course you didn't. Let me ask you this: Did his arrival achieve the intended effect?"

"Oh my, yes. It was a great success. He must have been very pleased."

"His idea? The helicopter?"

"Mine. More coffee?"

Hector accepted the coffee. His interview with Father Francisco went on for almost another hour, but nothing of any further significance came to light.

SILVA WAS in a taxi when his nephew's call came through.

"Where are you?" Hector asked.

"On my way to see Anton Brouwer, that priest Diana Poli mentioned. You?"

"Just leaving Presidente Vargas."

Hector gave his uncle a quick summary of his conversation with the bishop's secretary. Toward the end of his account, the signal started breaking up. " . . . bring . . . São . . . leg . . ."

"What?"

"I said . . . bring Arnaldo . . . São Paulo . . . legwork."

"You want to bring Arnaldo from São Paulo to do some legwork?"

"Yes. I . . . you fine."

"Well, I can't hear you. Okay, call Arnaldo. Tell him to drive. We could use another car."

Silva could see the cabdriver's face in the rearview mirror. The man's mouth tightened when he heard the part about another car. More cars meant fewer customers for taxis.

"Did you start a trace on the bishop's incoming calls?" Silva said.

" . . . already underway. If . . . home phone, we'll get him."

"Don't count on it. Anything else?"

But Hector was gone.

The cabdriver pulled onto the unpaved shoulder of the road, put one arm over the back of the seat, and pointed with the other.

"Father Brouwer's place is over there. You go down that alley between the banana trees," he said. "You want me to wait?"

Chapter Sixteen

A FRIENDLY MONGREL WITH a gray muzzle came padding up to Silva as he started down the path. He paused to scratch the dog behind the ear. When he resumed walking the animal, panting in the heat, fell into step behind him. The path ended at a little house with a tile roof and stucco walls badly in need of paint. Wooden steps led up to a small porch. The dog brushed by, sought a place in the shade, and lay down with its head between its paws.

As Silva mounted the last step the front door opened and a priest in a black cassock appeared. He smiled at his visitor and then bent his head to light the unlit cigarette dangling from his lips.

The priest was frail and very old. Silva had expected a younger man. "Father Brouwer?"

"Oh, my goodness, no. You flatter me. I have thirty-seven years on Anton," he said. "I'm Father Angelo." The priest stuck out a hand. There were amber tobacco stains on his index and middle fingers.

Silva shook hands and introduced himself. If the priest was impressed to be speaking to a chief inspector of the Federal Police, he didn't show it.

"What can I do for you, my son?" Father Angelo was a small man. The top of his head didn't quite reach Silva's chin, and he had a sparse rim of hair that encircled it like a white laurel wreath.

"Actually, Father, I'm here to talk to Father Brouwer."

"Nothing I can help you with? You sure?"

"I wanted to talk to him about liberation theology."

"You've come to the right place. Have a seat."

He pointed to one of four chairs that surrounded a wicker table. Silva sank into it, and Father Angelo sat down in another. "He doesn't like me to smoke inside the house," he said.

"He?"

The priest ground out his cigarette in the ashtray, fished a half-empty pack of unfiltered Caballeros from somewhere within his cassock, and immediately lit another one. "Anton. Father Brouwer."

The old man coughed, took out a handkerchief, put it over his mouth, and coughed again. Before he put it away he studied the surface of the cloth and nodded to himself, as if pleased. "I'd offer you coffee," he said, his voice like a rasp on hardwood, "but he doesn't like me mucking about in his kitchen."

"I'm fine, Father. Thanks."

"Smoke?"

Silva shook his head. "I gave it up."

"Very wise of you. Sorry about the ashtray. Anton doesn't smoke either. This is his week to do the household chores, but he refuses to clean it. And if I leave my cigarettes lying around, they have a mysterious way of disappearing. It's a little game we play. Now, tell me, what sparks your interest in liberation theology?"

"I'm investigating two crimes: the shooting of Bishop Antunes and the abduction, perhaps murder, of a landowner by the name of Orlando Muniz Junior."

"Ah, yes. Muniz."

"You know him?"

The priest took his time in answering, first studying the ash on his cigarette, then tapping some of it off into an over-flowing ashtray. Most of the ash fell onto the surface of the table. He didn't attempt to clean it up.

"Oh, yes," he said at last. "Everyone around here is familiar with young Muniz. Slavery was abolished in this country in 1889, but that fact seems lost on people like him."

Silva said nothing, suspecting that Father Angelo would have more to say, which he soon did.

"Muniz is a bloodsucker, a modern day slaveholder. You must know how it works."

"Why don't you tell me?"

"It's the old story: His agents recruit people, promising to pay them a fair wage. When they arrive they find they're in debt for the cost of their transport and the food they ate along the way. Then he forces them to buy everything they need from his own store."

"So they never get out of debt?"

"Never."

Silva was all-too-familiar with the practice. The Brazilian government had been trying to stamp it out for more than a century, but it persisted.

"And if they run," the priest went on, "Muniz's capangas go after them, beat them into submission, and bring them back. In your work you must have met others like him."

"Never in the state of São Paulo. The practice is more prevalent up north, in places like Acre."

"It happens here, too. And it's not just Muniz."

"We can stop him, you know. All we need are—"

"Witnesses brave enough to come forward?"

"Yes."

The priest shook his head sadly. He lit another cigarette with the glowing butt of the one he'd been smoking and then stubbed out the butt, causing more detritus from the ashtray to fall onto the table.

"You won't find them. Not after what happened to a man named Aurelio Azevedo."

Silva nodded. "I've heard about him."

"God forgive me. I try to love my fellow man, but I can't help myself from despising some of them. Cascatas is going to be a better place without Orlando Muniz Junior." The priest seemed to realize what he'd just said and added hastily, "If he's really dead, that is."

They stared at each other for a moment. Then Silva said, "It's been suggested to me that he might have been kidnapped and murdered by people from the league."

A wary expression came into Father Angelo's eyes, but the only thing he said was, "Really? The league, eh?"

After a moment of silence, Silva went on, "I'm told that your colleague, Father Brouwer, actively supports the league."

"Told by whom?"

"Sorry. That's confidential."

"Hmm. Well, as to the league, it's probably best if you put that question to Anton himself, but if you think he might have had anything to do with Muniz's death you'd be wrong. He didn't."

"You think so?"

"I don't think. I *know*. We go back a long way, Father Brouwer and I."

Father Angelo settled back in his chair, rested his elbows on the arms and took another puff.

"Where were you on the thirteenth of May, 1976?" he asked.

It seemed like an abrupt departure from the subject, but Silva played along. "I have no idea. Should I have reason to remember?"

"Probably not. But I do. I can remember *exactly* where I was on the thirteenth of May, 1976. I was with Anton Brouwer. He would have been . . ."—he took another puff and made the calculation in his head—"twenty-four at the time. The two of us were suspended by our wrists, facing each other, in the cellar of the State Police headquarters in

Cascatas. They hung us up on the evening of the twelfth. They took us down on the morning of the fourteenth. They had us hanging there for thirty-four hours."

"Why?"

The priest went on as if he hadn't heard the question. "I've always kept a diary. My memoirs. I hope to have them published someday. But I never wrote about that. The whole period of our most recent military dictatorship isn't covered in any degree of detail anywhere in my writings. It was too dangerous to write about then, and I can't bring myself to write about it now. But I talk about it, every now and then. I talk about it to someone like you, someone I don't know too well, or to someone I think should hear the story, and remember. Am I boring you?"

"Not at all."

Father Angelo lit another cigarette from the glowing stub of his last and extinguished the stub in the overflowing ashtray. He dangled the cigarette in his mouth while he rubbed the ash off his fingers. Then he took another puff and went on.

"When the military took power in 1964, they told us they were doing it to reestablish law and order. We soon discovered that law was for the few and order only an excuse for oppression. In reality fear, not law, was the source of their power. Torture was one of their instruments for instilling that fear."

"Why did they pick on you and Father Brouwer?"

"We'd set up a producer's and consumer's cooperative for the small farmers. They said it smacked of communism."

"And they tortured you just for that?"

"Oh, no. In those days, even people who practiced mild socialism got in trouble with the government, but we did much more. We organized adult literacy groups. That interfered with their concept of education. They didn't want the underprivileged to be educated. Education could have led to resistance. That's what they said, anyway. We also established a small newspaper and made the mistake of calling it *The Liberator*. All the major newspapers were censored then. The smaller ones . . . well . . . they just raided the offices, beat the people, and destroyed the facilities. Three days after they'd done that to *The Liberator* they came for us."

He took another puff. There was no breeze. The cloud of smoke hung about him, dispersing slowly in the air. The old dog lying near his feet whined in its sleep. He glanced at the animal, smiled, and continued.

"There was a police captain named Soares. I haven't seen him since the fourteenth of May, 1976, but when I close my eyes I can see his face as clearly as I can see yours now. At about nine-thirty on the evening of the twelfth they brought us into a room in the cellar of the police station. There were no windows. The walls were painted green. There was a drain in the floor, and there were hooks hanging from the ceiling. Captain Soares had several assistants in the room and while they hung us up from the hooks, he told us that there'd been assaults throughout the state. Money had been stolen from banks and some weapons had been stolen from one of the military installations. He said he was sure we could provide information about the people involved. When we told him we knew nothing, he ordered his assistants to strip us. One of those assistants, the only one I ever saw thereafter, is now a colonel in the State Police."

"Ferraz?"

"Ferraz. You know him?"

"Not personally. Not yet," Silva said and then, before the priest could break the thread of his story, "What happened next?"

Father Angelo stubbed out another cigarette and took the pack from his cassock. This time he didn't light another one right away. He held the orange-colored pack in his hands, turning it around from one side to the other, looking at it as if he'd never seen it before. His eyes were far away.

"I told you, didn't I, that they hung us facing each other? They worked on us, one at a time. It was ingenious in its perverted, disgusting way. I could see everything that was happening to Anton, and he could see everything that was happening to me. That made it worse: You not only saw a close friend being injured and broken, you could also anticipate that they'd soon be back to you, doing the same thing."

The priest dug a disposable plastic lighter out of his cassock. It was pink. The color didn't suit him at all. Silva wondered if a woman had given it to him.

Somewhere in the near distance there was the sound of children's voices: "Give it to me," one of them said. "Get your own," another one said. Then there was a slap and a squeal. Father Angelo didn't react to any of it. He went on with his story.

"Captain Soares told Anton to open his mouth to receive the Eucharist. When he did, the Captain put an electric wire into it. A spark lit up the inside of Anton's mouth. I could smell his burned flesh. When he fainted, they threw buckets of cold water on him and turned to me. They only worked on us for about fifteen minutes at a time. Then they'd go away and leave us hanging. Sometimes they'd be back within minutes, sometimes it took several hours. They beat us with little boards, kicked us in the stomach and genitals, put out their cigarettes on our bodies. I still have the scars."

He took a cigarette out of the pack, looked at the end of it, and rotated it between his fingers, remembering. "The more we denied complicity in the robberies, the more they were convinced we had something to hide and the more determined they became to force us to divulge it. Up to a point, of course. After thirty hours or so they began to think differently. They gave us no food. They did give us water—

through a hose—sometimes not enough, other times, far too much. And yet we fared better than the others."

"There were others?"

Father Angelo lit the cigarette with the little pink lighter and took a puff. Then he waved a hand back and forth in front of his face, dispersing the smoke, dispersing the memories.

"Oh, yes. Yes, there were others. Four other priests. Tito de Alencar, they released, but he hanged himself soon thereafter. He wasn't sure he was strong enough to resist if they arrested him again. He . . . knew things, you see."

"What sort of things?"

"It's not important now. It wasn't even that important then, except—"

"Except, if he'd spoken, other people would have been hurt?"

"Yes. I can see you understand. Let it go at that."

"And the other three?"

"Burnier, a Frenchmen, and two Belgians: Lukembein and Pierobom. These days, most priests are Brazilian-born, like me. It was different then."

He drew again on his cigarette.

"What happened to them?"

"Murdered. All three. No one was ever officially charged, much less tried. Ever since then I've had more fear of the police than of being assaulted by a criminal."

Silva shifted uncomfortably in his chair. "Was Ferraz ever prosecuted?"

"No. He really didn't do anything, did he? He just stripped off our clothing and stood there, watching."

Father Angelo paused. Silva had heard other stories, read many reports. The priest's tale was, for him, a variation on a theme already old but no less horrible because of that. They sat there for a while, in silence.

When Father Angelo spoke again his voice continued to rasp, but his tone was lighter as if he'd shaken off a burden by talking about it. "In the end, this country went through twenty years of dictatorship. Twenty years. And there were many like them, like Soares, like Ferraz. You can't prosecute the whole country."

"No," Silva said.

"I've told you all of this to make a point. Bear with me a little longer. I'm almost done."

Silva inclined his head.

"Through most of the long hours that Anton was suspended in front of me he was in pain, excruciating pain, as I was. His body reminded me then, and when I look back on it, it reminds me now, of a painting depicting St. Sebastian. You must have seen such images? The saint perforated by Roman arrows? His body streaming blood from a multiplicity of wounds?"

"Yes, I've seen them."

"Anton cried out in agony, he begged them to stop, but never—not once—did he curse the men who were torturing him. And at no time—no time—did he make a false confession. He had only to give them some names, and they would have stopped, but he refused to do so. *That* is the kind of a man Anton Brouwer is. He's incapable of spilling innocent blood, no matter what the provocation."

There was something in what Father Angelo had just said that triggered a reaction in Silva. A thought, like the flash of a distant lighthouse on a dark night, coursed through his brain and was as suddenly gone. As he attempted to call it back, a battered old truck loaded with farm produce pulled into the alley of banana trees and screeched to a stop. A man got out and waved to the driver. The driver waved back, reversed his vehicle, and drove back the way he came. His passenger turned and started to walk toward the house.

Father Brouwer had come home.

Chapter Seventeen

DIANA OPENED THE DOOR to her apartment and frowned. She took a step inside. There was tobacco smoke in the air, something strong, like—she sniffed again—yes, like a cheap cigar.

Lori didn't smoke. Neither did Diana, and they invited few people who did. They didn't even own an ashtray. The occasional visiting smoker was handed a water glass to use as a substitute and asked to go outside, onto the terrace, before lighting up.

Diana started to back out of the door, but someone gave her a push between the shoulder blades and sent her sprawling. She struck her head against the edge of the coffee table on the way down. Behind her she heard the sound of the door hitting the jamb like a trap slamming shut. She saw a tiny drop of blood fall onto the white carpet. She lifted her hand and touched her forehead. Wet.

A man with a scar on his left cheekbone, wearing the uniform of a major in the State Police, pulled her to her feet and hustled her into her home office. There was something strange about his grip. She glanced at the hand he'd wrapped around her arm. Gloves. The man was wearing latex gloves.

Colonel Emerson Ferraz, also wearing latex gloves, was tapping at the keyboard of her computer. He was wearing something else, too: a white apron, disposable and plastic, like the ones Diana had seen on medical examiners.

Lori was there, tied to a chair, gagged with what looked like a fragment of her own pantyhose. She'd been crying, and her mascara had run, staining her cheeks. Her legs were spread, and her skirt was bundled up around her waist, exposing strands of pubic hair.

"Oh, no," Diana said.

"Oh, yes," Ferraz said. His cigar was resting on a dinner plate. He picked it up and put it into his mouth. The tip glowed.

Diana was frightened, but she was also angry. "You didn't have to do that," she said, pointing at Lori. "I'm the one you came for."

"You've got to be joking," he said, expelling a cloud of smoke. "I wouldn't fuck you with my worst enemy's dick. Besides, Blondie here was just to pass the time until you got home. And she wasn't bad, for a dyke."

"You're an animal. Disgusting. A pig."

Her words seemed to make no impression on him at all. When he spoke again his voice was exactly the same as before: calm, detached, and very cold. "Did you really think you were going to get away with it, really think no one was going to tip me off?"

"Who was it?"

"You think I keep track of their names? I didn't even bother to negotiate. I gave the little bastard what he asked for: five hundred reais. He's a crackhead. I'll get it all back within a week. Okay, enough small talk. I haven't got all day."

He pointed at the computer. "Where are the backups?"

"Backups?"

"Copies, printouts, any duplication of this material in any form."

"There aren't any."

"Really?"

He put his cigar back onto the dinner plate. Next to the makeshift ashtray there were two other items he'd taken from their kitchen: a wooden cutting board and a small meat cleaver. Lori used the cleaver to make Chinese food. She kept it as sharp as a razor. Ferraz picked up the cleaver with one hand and gripped the board in the other. Then he got up from his chair, balanced the cutting board across Lori's thighs and splayed out the fingers of her right hand on the marbled surface. Lori's eyes rounded and seemed to enlarge. She looked at her hand, then at Diana, making a silent appeal.

Ferraz raised the cleaver and held it poised in the air. "No, don't—"

Diana stopped short as Ferraz slammed the cleaver into the board, severing Lori's index finger. Blood gushed from the open wound and would have spattered his clothing if he hadn't been wearing the apron. Lori gurgled through the gag and then, mercifully, she fainted.

Ferraz looked down and frowned when he didn't see the finger. Not relinquishing his hold on the cleaver, he dropped to his hands and knees and finally found what he was looking for behind one of the legs of the desk. He picked it up and held the bloody end in front of Diana's nose.

Diana felt a wave of nausea. The other cop was still holding her right arm. She lifted her left hand and covered her mouth.

"You vomit on me," Ferraz said, "and I'll beat the shit out of you."

She turned her head and let it go. Ferraz took a quick step backward to protect his shoes. When Diana's spasms had passed he said, "Every time I don't get an answer, I'm going to cut off another finger. If I run out of fingers, I'll move to her toes. If I think you're lying, I'll take off a hand. If I still think you're lying, I'll take off another hand. Do we understand each other?"

He threw Lori's finger aside as if he was tossing away the stub of his cigar.

Diana nodded. Her nostrils were filled with the sour smell of her own vomit and the steely odor of Lori's blood.

"Now, who else has seen, or heard, that interview?" He pointed to the screen of the computer.

"Which? Which interview?"

"The one with Pipoca."

"No one."

He looked upward and sighed, as if asking for the blessing of patience. Then he turned around and stretched out Lori's middle finger.

"Stop."

But he didn't. This time, he held on to the newly severed finger and dangled it in front of her nose.

"No one," Diana said desperately. "No one else. Honest to God, no one but me. I didn't even tell Lori."

Ferraz adjusted the cutting board and reached for Lori's ring finger. Lori was wearing her Russian wedding ring, the companion piece to Diana's own. He slipped it off, examined it, and put it into his pocket. Lori didn't react. She was still unconscious.

"Where is the little bastard?"

Diana shook her head. She would have told him if she knew. He raised the cleaver.

She stared, transfixed, willing him to keep the cleaver where it was. Tears rolled down her cheeks. She struggled to speak.

The cleaver smacked into the board.

Diana gave a little squeak. Lori's blood was flowing freely from all of her stumps, dripping off the board, pooling on the parquet floor of the office.

"What's this kid Pipoca's real name?"

"Let me stop the bleeding."

"You want to help her? Talk fast. What's the kid's real name?"

"I don't know. Everybody just calls him Pipoca. Everybody."

Pipoca was a nickname, a street name. It meant popcorn. She'd thought it was funny when she heard it for the first time.

"Where does he live?"

"He wouldn't tell me."

"Who else knows?"

"Anton Brouwer. He's a priest who—"

"I know Brouwer. Who else?"

"No one."

"Why Brouwer?"

"He works with street kids. Tries to get them off drugs, find places to live, get jobs. Pipoca talked to him first. Brouwer convinced him to talk to me."

"Those federal cops, how much do they know?"

"Nothing. I didn't tell them anything."

Ferraz gestured with the cleaver. "I swear," she said in a strangled voice. "I swear to God."

"What else do I need to know?"

"I took photos."

"You did what?"

It was his first sign of anger. She shrank away from him, spoke quickly.

"I used a digital camera so I didn't have to process the film. I worked without a flash. No one noticed me doing it, and no one's seen any of it. No one, except me."

"What's in the photos?"

"You. Your men. Distributing drugs. Taking money."

"Where's the material?"

"Here in the computer."

"Where else?"

"There's . . . there's a memory stick. It's in my safe-deposit box at the Itaú bank, the one on Avenida Neves."

"And the interviews? The original tapes?"

"Same place. And a CD, too, with copies of all the transcriptions."

"So you lied. I should make this a whole hand."

He lifted the cleaver and brought it down again. The severed finger remained on the board. He used the blade of the cleaver to brush it aside, and it fell with a *plop* into the spreading pool of blood.

Diana felt a rush of gratitude. Yes, he was right. He'd told her the rules. He could have made it a hand. *What's he done to me? He cut off all those fingers and I'm feeling grateful. Oh, God.*

"Where's the key?"

"What key?"

"The one to the safe-deposit box, you fucking dyke. Where is it?"

"In my pocket."

"Which?"

"Hip. Left side."

Ferraz put down the cleaver, groped in her pocket, and came up with the key. Then he reached for his cigar, only to discover that it had gone out. He tossed it back onto the dinner plate.

"Anything else I should know about? Anything at all?"

"No. Nothing. I've told you everything."

His eyes searched hers, looking for any sign of duplicity. "You know," he said at last, "I really think you have."

He wiped the bloody fingers of his gloves on Diana's T-shirt, treating it like a dirty rag, kneading her breasts while he was at it.

Then he took out another cigar and nodded, casually, to the cop who was holding her by the arm.

Chapter Eighteen

FATHER ANTON BROUWER WAS a tall man, so tall that he'd developed a slight stoop from leaning over when he spoke to people. He had a nose like the beak of a parrot and a receding hairline of straw-colored blond hair. Like straw, too, it lay every which way on the top of his head. From what Silva had already learned, he was well into his fifties, but unlike Father Angelo he wore his years lightly.

No cassock for him. His blue denim pants hung low on bony hips. Above them, and tucked in at the belt, he was wearing one of those red T-shirts bearing the logotype of the league.

He was smiling when he mounted the veranda, still smiling when the old dog got laboriously to its feet, and he leaned over to stroke it. The smile vanished when he found out who his visitor was. Brouwer rose to his full height. The dog continued to stand there, looking up at him with adoring eyes.

"Chief Inspector Silva and I have been having a pleasant chat," Father Angelo told him. "He's here to talk to you about the league."

"For the league," Father Brouwer said, sinking into a chair, "I have all afternoon. As for you, Angelo, you'd better empty that ashtray and clean the table. That's no way to receive a guest, now is it?"

Brouwer's Portuguese was excellent, but there was the trace of an accent there. Silva had never heard anything quite like it. He assumed it was Flemish.

Father Angelo contemplated the overflowing ashtray. "In

time, my boy. I'll clean it in time. At the moment I'm rather enjoying myself."

"Before we touch on the subject of the league," Silva said, "I have a few other questions."

"About?" Brouwer said. The dog came up to him and stuck its muzzle in his lap. Absently, he scratched it behind one of its floppy ears.

"About Bishop Antunes and about Orlando Muniz Junior. He seems to have disappeared."

Silva was watching Brouwer closely to see how he took the news. Brouwer's expression didn't change. He didn't even nod.

"Let's start with Muniz," Silva said. "Do you have any idea what might have happened to him?"

"Read First Kings Twenty-one," Brouwer said.

Angelo chuckled.

Silva looked from one to the other.

"How about sharing the joke?"

"First Kings Twenty-one," Angelo said, "a passage from the Old Testament. There was a chap by the name of Naboth and he had this vineyard. Stop me if you know the story."

Silva shook his head. The old man went on.

"Ahab, he was the King of Samaria, wanted that vineyard so bad he could practically taste the grapes, but Naboth was like me. The old fellow liked his wine. He made that wine from those grapes, and he told the king to buzz off. Now, Ahab was married to a very unpleasant lady by the name of Jezebel. They decided to . . . what's the phrase you use? Bump Naboth off?"

Silva nodded.

"You also say 'waste them,' don't you? I think I like that even better. So Ahab and Jezebel decided to waste Naboth and lay their hands on the property. They did it, but it was a big mistake. In those days, God used to take a more active role in people's affairs and he was on Naboth's side. The Lord avenged Naboth's death in a most exemplary way: Dogs wound up licking the blood he spilled from Ahab, but Jezebel fared even worse. The dogs ate her. They must have been a good deal fiercer than old Methuselah here."

At the sound of his name, the old dog turned his head and looked at Father Angelo. Father Brouwer picked up where his friend had left off.

"The moral of the story is that if you get greedy for land, you'd better watch out. Muniz should have spent more of his time reading the Bible and less of it exploiting the people who worked for him."

Silva looked from one to the other. "Thank you, gentlemen, for the scripture lesson. What else can you tell me about Orlando Muniz Junior?"

"He was responsible for the murder of an innocent man by the name of Aurelio Azevedo," Brouwer said. "And not only Azevedo himself, but also his entire family, a wife and two children."

"Can you prove that?"

"No. But I'm sure he was. Whatever death Muniz died, he deserved it."

Silva pounced. "What makes you so sure he's dead?"

"Why . . . you said so, didn't you?"

"No, Father, I didn't."

After a moment of silence, Father Angelo spoke. "Chief Inspector Silva is quite right, Anton. He didn't say it. Perhaps someone at the encampment mentioned it to you, someone who was jumping to conclusions."

He turned to Silva. "The night before last the league—"

"—invaded Muniz's fazenda. Yes, I know."

Father Brower shook his head. "Don't call it an invasion. It wasn't. What the league did was to *occupy* uncultivated land within a fence put up by Orlando Muniz Junior. When the government—"

Father Angelo put his hand on Father Brouwer's knee. "I think that Inspector Silva's concerns lie elsewhere, Anton. He's only interested in things that are germane to the cases he's investigating." He turned to Silva. "Muniz's foreman was heard to say that his employer had disappeared and that people were searching for him. Perhaps the rumor about him being dead is simply wishful thinking."

"That must be it," Brouwer said. "A rumor."

There was a moment of silence.

Then Silva said, "All right, let's put Muniz on the back burner for a moment. What can you tell me about the bishop?"

Father Brouwer leaned back in his chair. "I can't help you very much," Brouwer said. "I didn't know him well."

"Did you like him?"

"As I've just said, I hardly knew him."

"Why would anyone want to kill him?"

"You heard about his sermon? Asking people to come forward if they knew anything about the murder of the Azevedo family?"

"I heard about it, yes."

"Well, then, there you have it. My guess would be that he was killed by the same murdering parasites who killed Azevedo: Muniz, or one of his cronies."

"Landowners?"

"Landowners. From all accounts, the bishop wasn't a particularly likeable man, but I can't think of anyone else who would have had a reason to kill him."

"Father Gaspar thinks otherwise. He thinks someone from the league might have done it."

"From the *league*?"

Father Brouwer was genuinely surprised.

So was Father Angelo. "What possible motive could anyone from the league have?" the old priest asked.

"Perhaps because the bishop withdrew church support?"

"Nonsense," Father Brouwer said. "Everyone knew that was bound to happen when the old bishop died. Now, *that* man, the old bishop, he was a saint. He cared more about the poor than he did about the opinions of a few learned—and some believe misguided—old men in Rome. We won't see his like again in our lifetimes. These days, Rome would never appoint a man like him. They'll only appoint someone else who follows the party line. Dom Felipe did. That's one of the reasons he got the job."

"Tell me about the league."

"What do you want to know?"

"Help me to understand them. What kind of people are they?"

Father Brouwer scratched his chin, and then said, "They're the stubborn ones."

"Stubborn?"

"Stubborn. The ones who haven't given up, the ones who've rejected migration to the big cities, the ones who've elected to stay and fight."

"That's well and good, Father, but they shouldn't be doing it by occupying land to which they have no right—"

"No right? No *right*?" Father Brouwer scowled. He took a deep breath then let it out, slowly, through his nose. "Tell me this, Chief Inspector: Who has a greater right to the land, someone who's born on it, sweated on it, drawn his subsistence from it, or some capitalist who paid for it with money, or stole it by forging false documents?"

"Capitalist?" Silva said, raising his eyebrows.

Father Brouwer leaned forward and put his elbows on his knees. "I know what you're thinking. You're thinking Marxist, you're thinking communist. But you're wrong. I'm neither. I believe in God."

"How about liberation theology? Do you believe in that?"

Brouwer exchanged a glance with Angelo. "How could I?" Brouwer said. "After all, my superiors in Rome have condemned it."

"It's forbidden," Angelo said. "I'm surprised you didn't know that."

"Condemned?" Silva said. "Forbidden? So no priest could ever publicly commit to it, right?"

"Right. Not publicly," Brouwer said.

It didn't escape Silva that neither one of the priests had actually denied being a liberation theologian. He looked from one to the other. The conversation was going nowhere. He rose to his feet. "I think I've taken up enough of your time. I'm at the Excelsior. You *will* call me, won't you, if anything else occurs to you?"

"Of course," Father Angelo said.

Father Brouwer didn't say anything at all. He didn't even nod.

WHEN SILVA got back to the hotel he was surprised to find a note from Arnaldo:

If you're reading this, I'm in the coffee shop.

It would have been impossible for Arnaldo to arrive in the few short hours since he'd authorized Hector to summon him. His nephew had clearly jumped the gun. Silva made a mental note to take him to task about it.

Arnaldo was where he'd promised to be. It was still lunchtime, and the restaurant was crammed with people dressed in the fashion of the countryside. At that time of the year, with temperatures peaking around 40 degrees Celsius— 104 degrees Fahrenheit—the men were clothed almost exclusively in thin cotton shirts open at the neck. Arnaldo, in a beige suit, starched white shirt, and blue necktie, stuck out like a penguin in a chicken coop.

He was frowning at a menu when Silva slipped into a seat in front of him.

"A cheeseburger, medium," Arnaldo said to the hovering waiter.

"And to drink, senhor?"

"Guaraná."

"What a surprise," Silva said.

In coffee shops, Agente Arnaldo Nunes always perused the menu from appetizers to desserts, and almost always ordered a cheeseburger and a guaraná.

Arnaldo was an experienced man, considerably older than Hector, almost as old as Silva himself. He was a good cop, but his lack of formal education had blocked his advancement. The law required federal delegados to have a law degree from an accredited university and Arnaldo, having married young, could never find either the money or the time to get one. He was condemned to working out his time as a lowly agente. Silva had known him for over twenty years. They were comfortable with each other, despite the difference in rank.

The waiter offered Silva a menu. Silva shook his head.

"One cheeseburger, medium, and one guaraná. That's it?" the waiter said, looking at each of them in turn.

"That's it," Arnaldo said.

"You got it."

The waiter turned on his heel, managed to look right past an aged couple trying to get his attention, and strolled off toward the kitchen.

"The guy's a real pro," Arnaldo said, in mock admiration. "Those geezers coulda shot off rockets, and he wouldn't have raised an eyebrow."

He scanned the tables around them, leaned forward, and lowered his voice. "We got a trace on the incoming phone call, the one from Edson Souza to the bishop. Turns out it originated right here in Cascatas, from the post office."

"Post office?"

"It's one of those places where you fill in a form and make a deposit. Then the operator sends you to a booth and places the call. After you finish, you go back and get your change."

"And nobody remembered the caller, I suppose?"

"Nobody remembered. But I got these."

Arnaldo took a transparent envelope from his breast pocket.

Silva examined the objects inside: Forms the post office used for requesting telephone calls.

"Why didn't you send them off to have them dusted for prints?"

"I thought maybe you wanted to use that local guy. . . ."

"Ferraz?"

"Yeah, Ferraz."

"No. We'll do it ourselves. Send them to São Paulo. It'll be quicker than going through Brasilia."

"Okay. I took the prints of the clerk for comparison. Same guy was on duty both times."

Silva held the bag closer to his nose and studied one of the forms. The name of the caller and number he'd called were filled in with a blue pen. The amount of the deposit, the cost of the call, and the amount of the balance were written in another hand, in black ink.

"Souza is lefthanded," Silva said.

"How can you tell?"

"The heel of his hand brushed over the wet ink while he was writing. Look here. See?"

Arnaldo took the envelope. He was still studying it when his guaraná arrived. He put the envelope back in his pocket, took a sip, and said, "What's next?"

"Ferraz's men know the town," Silva said. "We don't. As

much as I hate it, I'm going to ask him to help." He glanced at his watch. "He's probably back from lunch by now. I'll go over and have a talk with him."

"Want me to do it?"

"No. He gave Hector the brush-off. He'd do the same to you. Hector says he's a son of a bitch." He briefly summed up what his nephew had learned about Ferraz and added what Father Angelo had told him.

"Sounds like a real sweetheart," Arnaldo said. He would have embellished his remark, but the waiter arrived with his cheeseburger. Arnaldo moved his drink aside and sat back in his chair while he was served. When the waiter had gone he opened the bun and made a face.

"Medium, my ass," he said, and probed the overcooked meat with his fork. "You want company? With Ferraz, I mean."

Silva shook his head. "You start checking available sources to see if we can't get some information on this Souza. Credit cards, bank statements, utility bills, all the stuff that's easier for us to get than it is for Ferraz."

"You think somebody who uses a post office telephone has a credit card?"

"No, but maybe we'll get lucky. Maybe he didn't *have* to use it. Maybe he *decided* to use it. Anyway, we have to go through the motions. Check the phone book."

"I already did. It's thinner than the director's dick and there's no Edson Souza."

"Do you talk about me like that? And how do you know about the director's dick, anyway?"

"Only behind your back, and because the director has been fucking me ever since he got his appointment."

Arnaldo was referring to the current freeze on salary increases. Silva definitely didn't want to get him started on that subject.

"Hector's on his way back from Presidente Vargas," he said. "After I see Ferraz, I'm going to make some telephone calls and turn in early. Let's all meet for breakfast. Here, at nine. I'll leave him a note."

"Okay. Sure you don't want to check out the nightlife?"

Silva shook his head. When the opportunity arose, Arnaldo always asked the same question and he always got the same answer. But asking was part of their ritual.

Arnaldo took a cautious bite of his cheeseburger and grimaced in disappointment. "You really want to have breakfast here? I'll bet the cook in this place can't even boil a fucking egg."

Chapter Nineteen

FERRAZ'S SECRETARY WAS A uniformed policewoman in her mid-forties with a no-nonsense hairdo and an abrasive manner.

"I already told you on the telephone, Chief Inspector. He's in a very important meeting. He doesn't want to be disturbed."

"Just tell him I'm here," Silva said.

She gave him a scornful look, picked up her telephone, and stabbed a button set into the base.

"Chief Inspector Silva is here," she said and then, after a moment, "Yes, here. He asked me to tell you."

She hung up. "You can wait," she said.

A table against the wall bore a pile of magazines—a half dozen dog-eared and outdated copies of *Veja*, three of *Agricultor Moderno*, and two of *Gente*—as well as a tattered copy of Diana Poli's newspaper, *Cidade de Cascatas*.

The headline on the front page caught his eye: ANOTHER HAM: THE FIFTH.

Silva checked the date: Two days before the bishop had been shot. He picked it up and took a chair.

The photo spread across the bottom half of the page made it clear that the headline didn't refer to smoked pork. In Brazil the word ham, *presunto*, has a secondary and more sinister meaning. It's *giria*—slang—for a murder victim who has been bound in a special way, ankles tied to wrists, so that the body takes on a form roughly resembling a ham, and then shot, execution style, with a single bullet to the back of the head.

Making presuntos is a signature of a death squad, rogue policemen who take it upon themselves to thin out the ranks of the criminal population. It was an aberration in law enforcement, and as such, should have been immediately reported to the Federal Police. But no one had. Diana's article was news to Silva.

All five of the victims had been street kids, and all five had been murdered in exactly the same way, at a frequency of about one a month for the last four months.

Silva muttered an obscenity and reread the story from beginning to end, absorbing the salient details. He had plenty of time to do it.

Ferraz kept him waiting for a total of sixty-three minutes. No federal employee could have gotten away with it, but Ferraz reported to the State Secretary for Security, and Silva's department had no power over him. In the interim the colonel received three other visitors.

Two of them were together, a married couple in their sixties who arrived shortly after Silva did. The woman was carrying a toy dachshund with a collar that matched the necklace she was wearing. The gems on both the necklace and the collar *could* have been green tourmalines, but the man was using a gold Rolex watch, which led Silva to believe that he was looking at a dog that was draped with emeralds. Both the man and the woman were wearing jeans, designer jeans but still jeans, wealthy landowners by the look of them. Ferraz received them after a short wait.

They stayed about twenty minutes and came out with smiles on their faces. Their host didn't accompany them to the door.

Another ten minutes went by and another visitor arrived. His uniform and badges of rank identified him as a major in the State Police. There was a thin scar high on his left cheekbone. A scabbard in black leather that matched his holster hung from the opposite side of his gunbelt. The bone handle of a knife protruded from the scabbard. He ignored Silva, nodded at the secretary, and went into Ferraz's office without knocking. Ten minutes later, on his way out, he gave Silva the look that policemen generally reserve for felons, not colleagues.

More time went by. Finally, the secretary's telephone buzzed. "He'll see you now," she said, replacing the receiver. "Go on in." She made no effort to open the door for him as she'd done for the couple.

Silva stepped into a haze of cigar smoke and would have left the door ajar, but she came out from behind her desk and slammed it shut.

The colonel didn't waste any time on pleasantries. He didn't offer Silva a hand. He didn't even offer him a seat. Silva took one anyway.

"Okay, Mario, now that you've made yourself at home, what can I do for you?"

Ferraz said it with an insolent smile. The use of Silva's first name without having such usage offered to him was a breach of etiquette bordering on insult.

"Thanks, Colonel, for coming right to the point. I'm sure you're a busy man and wouldn't appreciate me wasting your time any more than I appreciate you wasting mine."

The smile faded. "Crap. If I'd shown up to see you without an appointment, wouldn't you have kept me waiting?"

"Not if I could help it. And I would have taken your call. You know what brings me here. I can hardly imagine you have anything more important on your agenda."

"What the fuck do you know about my agenda?"

Silva ignored the question. "How come you haven't informed us about those street kids?"

"What?"

Ferraz seemed genuinely surprised.

"The serial murders, Colonel. My business, as much as yours."

"Oh. That."

Ferraz made a dismissive gesture. "Paperwork," he said. "I didn't get around to it."

"The first one was four months ago, Colonel. Four months."

"I thought you were here because of the bishop."

"I am, or rather I was. Now there appear to be other matters that require my attention, notably serial murders, and the disappearance of the fazendeiro, Orlando Muniz."

"Junior," Ferraz corrected him. "Orlando Muniz Junior. How did you find out about the death squad?"

"From the newspaper in your waiting room. So you confirm it's a death squad?"

"Pretty damned obvious, isn't it? But they're only killing street kids, so who cares? It's not like they're knocking off honest citizens."

"It's still serial murder."

"Look, if you want to waste your time, I'll send you the paperwork, okay? I'll try to have it waiting for you when you get back to Brasilia, which I hope is going to be real soon. What else do you want? I'm a busy man."

"Have your men made any progress in investigating what happened to the bishop?"

Ferraz took another pull on his cigar and launched a jet of smoke toward the ceiling. "Nope," he said. "But we don't have to worry, because now we've got the Federal Police in town and if they can't catch the bad guy, who can?"

"You asked me what I wanted. I'm going to tell you. I want you to help me locate someone called Edson Souza."

The colonel blinked, obviously mystified. "Who?"

"Edson Souza."

"Why?"

"I think he might have information about the bishop's murder."

"You got a description? A profession? Age?"

Silva shook his head. "Only a name."

Ferraz puffed on his cigar. "So what makes you think—"

"We talked to the bishop's secretary. This Souza called Dom Felipe a few days before he was shot. They spoke about something so confidential that even the secretary doesn't know what it was. Maybe it's related."

"Okay," the colonel said. He picked up a pen and made a note. "Souza, Edson. I'll get back to you. Don't let the door hit you in the ass on the way out."

Chapter Twenty

THE FOLLOWING MORNING, ARNALDO got to the breakfast table first. He was already poking at a cheese omelet when Silva arrived.

"Look at this thing," he said. "I told you they couldn't even boil an egg."

"That's not boiled."

"The hell it's not. It's boiled in warm oil."

Hector joined them five minutes later, his eyes still puffy from sleep. His uncle made a show of looking at his watch.

"Yeah, sorry," Hector said, and then to the waiter: "Coffee, black. I'll have the breakfast buffet."

"Good choice," Arnaldo said, and put down his fork.

"So, how did it go with Brouwer?" Hector asked. "What did you think of him?"

As if on cue, the buzz of conversation in the restaurant came to a sudden stop. Heads turned toward the door.

A tall man in blue jeans and a Landless Workers' League T-shirt was standing there, scanning the room.

"Speak of the devil—" Silva said.

"That's him?"

"That's him."

The conversation around them resumed, but something about it had changed. There was tension in the air. Eyes followed Brouwer as he walked toward them and stopped at their table.

"May I?"

"Sure. Have a seat," Silva said, indicating the empty chair.

"Padre Anton Brouwer, meet Delegado Hector Costa and Agente Arnaldo Nunes. Coffee?"

"Please."

Hector raised a hand to summon the waiter, who seemed to be the only person in the room who wasn't looking their way.

"I'll go get him," Arnaldo said, and stood. As he lifted his bulk out of the chair, he did a visual sweep of the room. People started taking a sudden interest in their food.

Silva raised his eyebrows. "We seem to be attracting quite a bit of attention. Is it you, Father, or the T-shirt?" He pointed to the league logotype emblazoned on the priest's chest.

"Both," Brouwer said. "This isn't a place for the have-nots. I don't belong here."

Arnaldo came back and caught the priest's last words. "The waiter thinks so, too," he said. "Says the other customers aren't going to like it if you get served. I had to flash a badge at him."

"I don't want to be here any more than they *want* me to be here," he said. "But I had to come. Because of this." He pulled a piece of paper from one of his pockets.

"What's that?" Silva said.

"A letter from Diana Poli to me. Read it."

Silva did.

Anton,
You were right. It's one hell of a story, but now that I know what he's capable of I'm scared to death.

If anything happens to me, tell the Federal Police to look in my safe-deposit box. It's at the Itaú Bank, the one on Avenida Neves. And if you call, for God's sake don't mention this note. He may have tapped my phone.

Love,
D.

Silva handed the note to Hector. Hector read it and passed it to Arnaldo.

"Who's 'he'?" Silva asked.

"I'm not sure she'd want me to tell you that."

Silva let that one go for the moment. He took the note back from Arnaldo and rustled it. "When did you get this?"

The waiter arrived with a pot of fresh coffee, put a cup in front of the priest and went away without looking at any of them.

"It came in this morning's mail," Brouwer said. "I called her right away. She didn't answer the phone at her apartment, so I tried her at the office. She had a meeting set for eight o'clock, but she never arrived."

Hector wrapped his napkin around the metal handle of the pot and filled Brouwer's cup. The priest nodded his thanks and reached for the sugar.

"She's punctual? Reliable?" Silva asked.

"Very. And she has a pager and a cell phone. She's not responding to either."

"You know where she lives?"

"Yes."

Silva pursed his lips. He was getting a bad feeling about this.

"Finish your coffee, Father. I want you to take us there."

THEY TRIED buzzing Diana from the lobby. There was no answer.

"There's probably a *zelador*," Arnaldo said—a live-in janitor, responsible for keeping the public areas of apartment buildings clean and neat.

"Go see," Silva said.

Arnaldo took the stairs that led down to the garage. A few minutes later they heard two pairs of footsteps coming back up.

The zelador was a little brown man with a singsong

Bahian accent. No, he hadn't seen Senhorita Diana, not last night, not this morning. No, he didn't have a key to her apartment, but Cecilia did.

"Cecilia?"

"*Sim,* senhor. Cecilia. Senhorita Diana's *faxineira.* She comes to clean. She'll be here tomorrow morning."

"We can't wait. Come with us. We're going up."

Upstairs, they pounded on the door of the apartment.

There was no answer.

Silva put his ear to the door. He heard a faint buzzing, constantly changing in pitch, and recognized it immediately for what it was.

"Ah, Jesus," he said to no one in particular. And then, to Arnaldo, "Open it."

Arnaldo stepped up to the door and examined it.

"Steel, in a steel frame," he said, "it's gonna be a bitch to break. You want me to call a locksmith?"

"Wait," Hector said. First he looked under the welcome mat. Nothing. Then he ran his hand over the top of the doorjamb. A key came tumbling down, tinkled once against the door and wound up on the corridor's rug.

"Voila," he said, and picked it up.

The steel door had done a good job of isolating the hallway from what was happening inside. The minute Hector cracked it open all of them could smell the stench.

Arnaldo and Hector exchanged a knowing look. Father Brouwer put his hand to his mouth. Silva turned to the zelador.

"There's a dead body in there," he said.

"Stinks, doesn't it?" the zelador asked. He was enjoying it.

"I want you to go downstairs and call the State Police. Wait for them out in front and bring them here when they arrive. Understand?"

"Sure. But—"

"But nothing. Get moving."

The zelador looked at the door to Diana's apartment, back at Hector, back at the door again, and shrugged. Then he turned and walked reluctantly to the elevator, taking his time about it.

Silva walked inside, followed by Hector.

"Let's go, Padre," Arnaldo said. "Follow me, hold your nose, and watch where you step."

They found the bodies in the office. Someone had switched off the air-conditioning and left the door to the terrace ajar. Diana's apartment wasn't just hot, it was stifling. The smell was bad, but the flies were worse. They were everywhere: in the air, on the furniture, the curtains, the walls, the ceilings, the pools of blood on the floor, but mostly on the corpses of the two women.

Diana was lying on her back with her throat cut. Nearby, a woman with blonde hair was bound upright in a chair. She was naked from the waist down. Her head was tilted forward, and they couldn't see her wound, but judging by the blood that covered her blouse it was likely she'd been dispatched in the same way.

"You know her?" Silva asked Brouwer, pointing at the blonde.

He nodded. "Diana's friend, Dolores. Diana called her Lori. They lived together."

"Look at her hand," Arnaldo said.

The other three did.

Brouwer was the first to speak.

"There was something they wanted to know," he said. "They chopped Lori's fingers off, one by one, until Diana told them. Then they killed them both."

Silva remembered the priest's experience of torture.

Arnaldo looked at him with admiration. "You could've been a cop," he said.

"Let's get out of here," Silva said.

"You don't want to wait for the locals?" Hector asked.

His uncle shook his head. "I want to see what's in that safe-deposit box," he said.

Chapter Twenty-one

THE BANK MANAGER MUST have been one of the few people in town who wore a suit to work. He was friendly and helpful, but also a fusspot, determined to go through all the formalities.

"Pardon me for asking, but may I see the warrant?" he said.

"We don't have one." Silva was doing the talking for the four of them.

"An authorization signed by Senhorita Poli would do just as well," the manager insisted.

"We haven't got that either. This is a special case, Senhor . . ."

"Junqueira."

"Senhor Junqueira. Look, Senhor Junqueira, I'm sorry to have to tell you this, but Senhorita Poli won't be signing any authorizations for anyone. Senhorita Poli is dead. Murdered."

The manager opened his mouth, reminding Silva of a fish with eyeglasses.

"Murdered?"

"All I'm asking you to do is to let us have a look in that box. We'll do it in your presence. We won't take anything out or put anything in. You can watch us while we do it."

"Murdered. My God. Well, in that case . . ."

THE WOMAN in charge of the safe-deposit boxes was introduced as Carmen. She had a picture frame on her desk with photos of two little girls who weren't quite as plump as their mother but who were well on their way.

She smiled, offered a hand to each of them—Silva, Hector, Arnaldo, and Brouwer—and started gathering chairs from neighboring desks to seat them all.

"That won't be necessary, Carmen," Junqueira said. "The gentlemen are in a hurry. I'll sign the book,"

"Sim, senhor," she said. "And the key?"

"Ah, yes, the key. I'd forgotten about the key."

"What key?" Silva said.

"There are two keys," Carmen explained. "We keep one, and the client keeps the other. You need both keys to open a box. We have ours. You need Diana's."

Carmen seemed to be on first-name terms with Diana Poli.

"And without that key?" Silva asked.

"We have to drill out the lock. It happens occasionally, people losing their keys."

"Drill out the lock?"

"Yes," she said brightly. "There's a locksmith we always use. But I'm sure it won't be necessary in this case."

"Why not?"

"Well, you're policemen, aren't you?"

"We are."

"Then why don't you just ask Colonel Ferraz for his?"

FERRAZ HAD left an authorization, ostensibly signed by Diana and dated a week earlier. Carmen showed it to Silva. It was short and to the point:

Please allow Colonel Emerson Ferraz, RG 186364682, to access my safe-deposit box, number 3601

                                                    Diana Poli

RG was the prefix to numbers in a national identity card.

"When was he here?" Silva asked.

"Yesterday afternoon," Carmen said, "about an hour after

we closed our doors to the public. He just caught me. I'd finished my paperwork, had my purse in my hand, and was on my way out the door."

SILVA, HECTOR, and Father Brouwer left Arnaldo to wait for the locksmith and adjourned to a *padaria* on the other side of the street. They sat on the terrace where the smell of freshly baked bread battled exhaust fumes from the passing traffic.

Silva and Hector ordered coffee. The priest asked for a mineral water. "I don't expect there'll be anything left in that box," he said.

"No. I don't expect there will be," Silva said. "Now, let me hazard a guess. The man she was referring to in the note was Ferraz, right?"

The priest looked around before he inclined his head. "That bastard," he said, softly. It sounded strong, coming from a priest.

"I think we agree with you there, Father," Hector said. "What's going on? And what's your involvement in all of this?"

A young girl, probably no more than thirteen, came up from behind Father Brouwer and touched him on the arm. He turned in his chair and studied her pinched face, thin arms, and short, dirty hair. She was wearing a tattered smock, once white, and carrying a baby. Father Brouwer looked from one child to the other, sighed, and reached into the pocket of his jeans. "Buy some milk," he said.

The girl nodded, closed her hand around the coin he gave her, and moved off without a word.

"Dear God," the priest said, "let that be her little sister and not her daughter."

Hector gave him a curious look. "How did you know—"

"That the baby was a girl?"

Hector nodded.

"Her ears were pierced," Brouwer said. "You asked me what's going on? Where do I start?"

"Start with yourself," Silva said. "How did you get involved in what Diana was doing?"

"I work with the poor. Not just the league, but anyone who's poor, anyone who needs help: widows, orphans, the disabled, the indigent, street kids. One of the street kids came to me with a story."

"About?"

"The murders."

"The death squad?"

"It isn't a death squad."

"No? Then why do they make hams out of their victims?"

"To make people think it is."

"Why?"

"This is a law-and-order town, Chief Inspector, run by rich people and crooked politicians who want clean streets. No matter what they say in public, privately they tend to agree that those kids are a plague that has to be rooted out. Except that rooting them out by giving them homes, work, and food is too much trouble and too expensive. They'd rather see some of them killed and hope the others will take fright and move away."

"So there's a tacit approval of the murder of those children, is that what you're telling me?"

"Yes."

Father Brouwer picked up his glass and drained it. His hands were trembling slightly, and the glass made a little clinking sound when he put it back on the metal table.

"So why *are* they being killed?"

"Pipoca said—"

"Pipoca?"

"The boy who came to talk to me. All of the children have

street names. That's his. Pipoca. He told me the children were murdered because they didn't pay their debts, not because there was a movement underway to clean up the streets."

"Debts?"

"Drug debts. He said that all of them had to work hard to support their habits and when someone defaulted . . . an example was made."

"So instead of cleaning up the town, it's the other way around. The people doing the killing are forcing the kids to work harder?"

"Yes."

"And that work is prostitution, petty theft, burglaries, assaults. . . ."

"Yes. All of that."

Silva glanced at Hector before he asked the next question. "This Pipoca, does he know who's behind it? The drugs? The killings?"

"Emerson Ferraz."

"Why didn't you come to us?"

"You weren't here. I didn't know whom to trust. I have issues with policemen, as you may know. And it isn't just the policemen in this town who are corrupt. It's the politicians as well. And that judge, Wilson Cunha. He may not be involved in Ferraz's business, but he's certainly in the pocket of the movers and the shakers."

"So you discussed it with Diana?"

"Yes. She's from a wealthy family, people who own a great deal of land, but she's always been sympathetic to the needs of the poor. And not just Diana, but her mother and father too. They've been regular contributors to our work."

Silva's voice took on a harder tone. "And instead of advising you to come to us, as she should have done, she asked you to keep quiet about it so she could write a goddamned newspaper story?"

"You have to understand," the priest said, defensively, "that up to then it was all hearsay. The person doing the talking was a street kid. The man he was accusing was a colonel in the State Police. We needed more proof. Diana set out to get it. She interviewed other street kids. She took photographs."

"Interviews? Photographs? My God, Padre, street kids will sell their own mothers for a vial of crack. Didn't it ever occur to you that it was all going to get right back to him?"

"Of course it did," the priest said, bristling. "No one knows those poor children better than I do. They've been taught to value money above all else, above ethics, morals, friendship, even God. I *knew* it would get back to Ferraz eventually, but I never thought it would be so soon. I thought we'd have more time and I also thought . . ."

"Thought what?"

The priest rested an elbow on the table and covered his eyes with his hand. "Thought . . . no, *hoped*, they'd recognize what would happen to anyone they informed on, and think twice before doing it."

"Then you're naïve, Father. Naïve. Ferraz is a bastard. You said it, and I believe it, but to them he's their source of the magic stuff that helps them to forget their misery. You say you know those kids better than anyone? Well, if you do, you've been a damned fool."

"Keep your voice down, Chief Inspector, and please stop abusing me. I already feel bad enough. I feel responsible for Diana's death."

Silva took a deep breath, then went on in a milder tone. "No, Padre. You're not. Ferraz is. And I will virtually guarantee you that he's not finished. If he found out about the safe-deposit box, he found out about you as well. Take my advice and disappear for a while. Get out of town until we get all of this cleared up. He'll be coming for you next."

"I can't do that. I'm helping the league with the operation they have underway."

"Stay away from them. It would be just the excuse that Ferraz needs to shoot you."

"I'll consider your advice."

"Which is another way of saying you won't take it?"

The priest had been looking down at his empty glass. Now he looked up and met Silva's eyes. "Probably not," he said. "You mentioned Diana's safe-deposit box. How can he justify breaking into it?"

"He's not a fool, Father. He'll justify it, believe me. What else have you got on him?"

The priest shook his head. "Nothing. But we know he killed Diana and Lori. It had to be him."

"We might *know* it, but we can't prove it. He's a cop. You think he's going to leave any evidence behind? Forget it. I can already tell you that Diana's apartment will be as clean as a whistle. He won't have left a shred of trace evidence."

"Oh, dear God. There must be something you can do."

"There are several things I can do, but I'd prefer that you don't hang around while I'm doing them. What's the real name of that kid, Pipoca? Do you know?"

Father Brouwer closed his eyes and put his fingers to his lips, thinking about it.

"He told me, but I . . . no, wait . . . it's . . . Edson. That's it: Edson. Edson Souza."

Chapter Twenty-two

"EDSON SOUZA. I'LL BE damned!" Hector exclaimed after the priest had gone.

"And I asked Ferraz to help us find him," Silva said. "Damn it!"

"You didn't tell Ferraz anything he wouldn't have learned by questioning Diana."

Silva thought about it.

"True," he said.

"Maybe Souza didn't call the bishop about Azevedo's murder. Maybe he called about Ferraz."

"I don't think—" Silva's cell phone rang. He pulled it out of his pocket. "Silva."

"I just heard about the Poli girl," the director began without preamble. "Have you any idea whose daughter she was?"

He didn't wait for an answer.

"Dionisio Poli, that's who. In addition to about half the land in the State of Parana, he also owns Editora Julho."

Editora Julho was the largest magazine publishing combine in the country.

"Merda!" Silva said.

"I couldn't have put it better myself. Don't they murder *un*knowns in Cascatas?"

"I'm sorry to say they do. They kill street kids."

But the director wasn't listening. He was talking. "Jesus Christ. A bishop, then Muniz's son, and now Poli's daughter. The obituaries in that town are beginning to read like a social column. And now the papers here in Brasilia are beginning to pick up on it. The headlines are bad enough, Mario, but the editorials are going to be even worse. You've got to do something. The minister's watching. He's watching both of us. We need results and we need them fast."

"Yes, Director, I'm aware of that. I'm doing my best."

"Any progress?"

"Not yet."

"Jesus Christ," the director said again, this time with an inflection of disgust. "Call me again at six, as usual." He hung up without saying goodbye.

"Him again?" Hector asked.

Silva nodded glumly.

They sat in silence for a while. A chocolate-skinned woman in a red dress went by, swinging her hips. Hector's eyes were still fixed on her retreating derriére when he said, "The minute this Pipoca hears about Diana Poli he's going to panic and try to disappear down some sewer hole."

Hector was decidedly not fond of street kids. Less than a month earlier his former girlfriend, Angela Pires, had been brutally slashed by a thirteen-year-old who was trying to steal her wristwatch. The kid had done the job with a piece of window glass. It had taken five stitches to close the wound on her arm, and she'd bear the scar for the rest of her life.

"With the exception of the sewer-hole part," Silva said, "I agree with you. Look, there's Arnaldo."

Arnaldo scurried across the street, narrowly avoiding being hit by an oncoming truck loaded with rattling, silver-painted gas canisters. He started talking even before he took the seat Brouwer had vacated.

"Empty as my bank account," he said. "Not a damn thing there. Carmen says we owe the bank a hundred-and-fifty reais for a new box. I paid the locksmith. He charged twenty-five reais. I hate to see little guys getting stiffed."

"I gather your generosity doesn't extend to the bank?" Hector said.

"What generosity? I got a receipt. I'm gonna declare it."

"And I'm going to approve it," Silva said. "Now go back across the street and settle with the bank. We need some friends in this town."

Arnaldo shrugged and got up.

Silva and Hector ordered more coffee.

"So what's next?" Hector asked.

"You and I will look into the league. We'll go out to that encampment of theirs, the one they set up on Muniz's fazenda, and ask a few questions."

"You really think they're going to tell us anything?"

"Probably not, but we've got to start somewhere. The league is as good a place as any."

"We were interrupted when the director called. Let's get back to that. What if Souza went to the bishop about Ferraz, and Ferraz killed the bishop to keep him quiet?"

"Unlikely. Souza was already talking to Brouwer and Diana Poli. What did he need the bishop for?"

Hector scratched his head. "Yeah, you're right. So I guess our first hypothesis is the most likely one. Souza must know who killed Azevedo."

"Or thinks he does."

"Or thinks he does. Either way, we've got to find him before Ferraz does. We'll leave it to Arnaldo. He excels at that kind of street stuff."

The waiter arrived with two cups of espresso. Hector added some sugar from the dispenser and picked up one of the tiny spoons.

"What do you make of Brouwer?"

"I'm not sure. Remember Father Angelo?"

"The old guy you told me about? The one who lives with Brouwer?"

"Him." Silva took a sip of his coffee. "He said Brouwer was incapable of spilling innocent blood. That's the way he put it, "spilling innocent blood.""

"There's just one problem with that."

"What?"

Hector drained his cup.

"Suppose Brouwer doesn't think the blood he's spilling is innocent?"

Chapter Twenty-three

THE TASK SILVA GAVE him presented Arnaldo with a dilemma: The only people who could help him find a street kid were other street kids. But trying to start a casual conversation with a street kid wouldn't work. The kid would either clam up or run. And he couldn't just go out and arrest one. Without some kind of a charge that would stick, even a federal cop couldn't get away with that. And, besides, where could he take him? Bringing him to Ferraz's jail would be useless. The kid would be so terrified that he'd never open up. Taking him to the hotel would attract too much attention, and might have fatal consequences if the colonel found out about it.

Arnaldo considered going to a seedy part of town and flaunting his wristwatch and wallet. But, no, that wouldn't work either. He was a big guy, so they'd have to set on him in a group or leave him alone. If they left him alone, he'd be wasting his time. If they set on him in a group, he'd have to pull a gun, but then somebody was liable to get hurt.

Finally, and somewhat reluctantly, he came up with a way to go about it.

The desk clerk at the Hotel Excelsior, the one who looked like an Indian, frowned when Arnaldo asked him the question. "A boy?" he said. "You want a boy who—"

Arnaldo didn't let him finish. "You heard me. And wipe that look off your face. I'm after information, not sex."

"Information, huh?" The clerk smirked.

"Answer the question. Where do they hang out?"

"I wouldn't have any idea." The clerk's smirk was carrying over into his voice.

"No?"

"No. Now, if it was a girl you wanted—"

"I told you what I wanted, and I just told you why. And don't tell me you don't know, because this is a small town and everybody knows things like that. Don't make me lose my temper. You won't like it."

The clerk absorbed Arnaldo's change in attitude, and crumbled.

"The rumor is that they hang around Republic Square," he said, lowering his voice even though they were alone in the lobby. "But they're like tapirs. You don't see them much in the daytime."

Arnaldo thought about it. His first reaction was to go to his room, have a nap, and hit the street after sunset. But, if he did that, Ferraz might find Pipoca first and it would be goodbye Pipoca.

"Where is this Republic Square?"

The clerk gave him directions, adding that it was "in the old part of town."

Until he got there, Arnaldo figured that "old" was a misnomer. Cascatas wasn't really old as towns go, but this part of it sure as hell *looked* old. The square was as dirty and rundown as anyplace you could find in São Paulo, which was almost four hundred years older.

The clerk at the hotel hadn't bothered to mention that there was an open-air market in the square every Tuesday and Friday. That was annoying for Arnaldo, but was a good thing for the businesses that surrounded the square. Because if the market vendors hadn't hosed down the place, as they were doing when he arrived, it might never have been cleaned at all. Unfortunately, the storm drains were mostly blocked with garbage, which meant that the hosing simply served to concentrate the detritus on top of the grates. The air was heavy with the smell of rotted fruit and spoiled fish. The elaborate cast-iron lampposts, once the pride of a new city, were rusting, and in two cases broken off just above the ground. Arnaldo noticed that there was something else about the lampposts: Every single globe was broken. He suspected it had been done on purpose to assure that the square would remain a dark place after sundown.

The buildings surrounding the square were all of a pattern and all four stories tall. Some of the windows on the upper floors bore signs: a homeopathic doctor, a tarot card reader, and several businesses identified only by their names. At ground level, offices were interspersed with a few shops: One sold herbs, small statues and other artifacts for use in the spiritualist rituals of *Candomblé* and *Macumba*, Brazil's equivalent of voodoo. Another was occupied by an ironmonger. The proprietor had stacked wooden boxes containing horseshoes, and funnels of all sizes, beside his door. The ironmonger was flanked, on one side, by a place heaped with secondhand furniture and, on the other, by a bar.

The bar had only a handful of clients, all wearing the aprons that identified them as vendors from the market. They were seated around a rusting collapsible table and drinking straight cachaça. An old man with a day's growth of beard was hovering nearby, making a halfhearted attempt to sell lottery tickets and trying to cadge a drink. One of the men at the table stood up, offered his almost-empty glass to the ticket seller, and strolled off in the direction of his stall. The old man lifted the mouthful of cachaça to his lips and drained it in one gulp.

The housewives had already bought their fruits, vegetables, meat, and fish and had departed. With the exception of the drinkers, the vendors were packing up. Arnaldo decided to wait it out.

It didn't take long.

Half an hour after he arrived, all vestiges of the market were gone, the bar had closed, and the square was virtually empty. It was almost two o'clock by then and getting into the hottest part of the day. Arnaldo went back to where he'd parked his car, stripped off his tie and threw it on the front seat. He left his jacket on to cover his holster. Then he went back and started trolling, walking around and around the square in a clockwise direction.

He was beginning to think he was wasting his time when he heard a voice: "Looking for company, senhor?" The voice wasn't brazen. It was soft, young, almost embarrassed. He looked around for the source and spotted a kid looking at him from the alleyway between two of the crumbling red-brick buildings. The boy might have been a teenager, but Arnaldo doubted it. He looked to be eleven, twelve at the most, and had eyes grown large with hunger. The eyes reminded Arnaldo of a character in one of those Japanese cartoons that his son, Julio, liked to watch on television. A dirty sweatshirt from the PUC hung low over the kid's faded jeans. The PUC—The Pontifícia Universidade Católica— was one of São Paulo's institutions of higher learning. The shirt was as close to it as the kid was ever going to get.

Arnaldo had been offered the bait. Now he snapped at the hook.

"Sure," he said. "How much?"

"Fifty reais," the kid said.

"Twenty."

You never agreed to give a whore, any kind of a whore, the first price they asked for. They'd think you were crazy, or stupid, or maybe they'd think you were a cop.

"Forty," the kid said.

"Thirty," Arnaldo said. "And a tip if I like your work."

"Where?" the kid said.

It was broad daylight, so it wasn't going to happen in the alley. Arnaldo assumed that the kid had a deal with some high-rotation establishment.

"You got a place?" he asked.

The kid nodded. "There's one around the corner. It's twenty for half an hour."

"Good enough."

"Follow me," the kid said. "Not too close."

He sashayed out of the alleyway, wriggling his butt in a travesty of someone of the opposite sex and twice his age. Sewn to one of his hip pockets was a crude red heart, cut out of some feltlike material.

Arnaldo let the kid get about twenty paces ahead and followed. The hotel was a five-minute walk, the building a four-story walkup that looked like it had been constructed to cater to traveling salesmen and had gone downhill from there. The exterior was painted a sickly green.

The guy behind the counter was young and fat, reading a computer magazine. His light blue shirt had sweat stains from the armpits all the way down to the roll of lard above his belt. He leered at Arnaldo and asked for forty reais.

"I thought you said twenty," Arnaldo said to the kid.

It was the fat guy behind the counter who answered: "Twenty for a half-hour, twenty for the deposit. You clear out of there by two-fifty-five"—he'd already shaved a couple of minutes off the time—"you get twenty back. You're not gone by three-twenty-five, I come in and pull the kid off your dick."

"You take credit cards?"

"You out of your fucking mind?"

Arnaldo handed over the forty reais, knowing it would be useless to ask for a receipt, thinking about how he was going to get Silva to reimburse him.

The guy didn't even pretend to put the bills into a cash drawer. He just stuck the money in his pocket. Then he reached behind him, took a key from a row of hooks on the wall, and handed it to the kid.

"Enjoy it," he said to Arnaldo. "They tell me the kid has

a mouth like a vacuum cleaner. Personally, I wouldn't know. Me, I like girls."

"Come on," the kid said. "It's this way."

He led Arnaldo up a flight of stairs. They walked along a dim hallway lit by a few unfrosted bulbs and came to a door. The kid checked the number on the key against the number of the room, nodded, and turned the knob. The door wasn't locked. Once they were inside, he stuck the key in the lock and turned it.

The room's only furniture was a double bed with thin sheets, gray from many washings. Through an open door, Arnaldo could see the interior of a closet where a few metal hangers hung suspended from a crossbar. There was a rusty sink, but no bathroom. An aluminum ashtray was perched precariously on the windowsill. The place stank of leaky plumbing, mold and old cigarette smoke. There was no air-conditioning.

"Thirty reais," the kid said, sticking out his hand.

Arnaldo reached for his wallet and paid him. The kid put the money in his pocket and started to undress.

Arnaldo scanned the room. No mirror, so no two-way glass. Some holes in the wall, but the superficial ones showed plaster, and the deeper ones showed brick. A shade on the window, but it was pulled down. They weren't being watched.

The kid was down to his shorts now, and he was staring at Arnaldo.

"You can hang your stuff in the closet," he said.

"No."

"Suit yourself, then. Throw it on the floor for all I care. Or just drop your pants and I'll do you standing up."

"I'm not here for sex. I'm here for information."

The kid took an involuntary step backward. "What kind of information?" he asked suspiciously.

"I want to know about a kid who calls himself Pipoca. His real name is Souza."

The kid started scrambling for his clothes. "I don't know any Pipoca."

"No?"

"No. And no Edson Souza, neither."

The kid grabbed his sneakers and made a move for the door. Arnaldo got there first and pulled the key from the lock.

"Who said his name was Edson?" he said, softly.

"*Caralho*," the kid said, realizing his mistake. "Leave me alone. They know me here. All I got to do is scream."

"Go ahead," Arnaldo said.

"What?"

"Go ahead and scream. Let's see what happens."

The kid's eyes darted toward the window.

"Long way down," Arnaldo said, but he glanced that way anyway.

Which must have been what the kid wanted because suddenly there was a switchblade in his hand. Where he got it from was a mystery. The kid wasn't wearing anything but a pair of jockey shorts.

"Drop it," Arnaldo said.

But the kid didn't. Instead, he stretched out his arm and leaped forward, aiming the point at Arnaldo's gut.

He'd picked the wrong guy. Arnaldo was skilled in *capoeira*, the Brazilian martial art. In capoeira, blows are delivered by the feet and they're stronger than any punch. The agente tried to be as gentle as he could, but the art hadn't been developed to be gentle; it had been developed to maim and kill. The kid went flying head over heels and wound up in a heap in the corner. On the way, the knife flew out of his hand. Arnaldo retrieved it, snapped it closed and put it in his pocket.

"I'm a cop," he said.

The kid scrambled to his feet and backed up against the wall, as if Arnaldo had said, "I'm a murderer." He held his hands up in front of him, the palms toward Arnaldo, as if he was fending him off. He looked terrified.

"Look, kid . . . What's your name?"

The kid swallowed, twice, before he got it out: "Rambo."

Arnaldo wanted to smile, but didn't. "Okay, Rambo, listen up. I'm not from here. I'm not one of Ferraz's men. I'm a federal cop, and I come from São Paulo. Look."

He reached into his coat, saw the kid flinch when he caught sight of the shoulder holster, then relax when he pulled out his wallet, not his gun. He showed the kid his badge and warrant card. It didn't help. Rambo remained as skittish as a colt. Arnaldo could only think of one reason for him to be acting like that.

"You've been warned about us, right?"

The kid licked his lips.

"Told that anybody who talks to us is going to get hurt?"

The kid blinked.

"Killed?"

The kid looked at the door.

"Okay. Here's the way it's going to be. You're going to tell me what you know about Edson Souza—"

"No. I don't know anything."

"Shut up and listen. You're going to tell me what you know about Edson Souza, or I'm going downstairs and tell that asshole at the reception desk that you did."

"What?"

"I'm going to tell him I'm a cop, show him my badge and tell him you spilled your guts all over this room, tell him you told me everything I wanted to know. Then I'm going to question him, and when he refuses to talk, as he will, I'm going to beat the shit out of him."

"You can't. You can't tell him I told you anything. That would be a lie—"

"No shit? Now if, on the other hand, you tell me what I want to know I'm going to give you two hundred reais, and I'm going to walk out of here with a smile on my face just like somebody who got his dick satisfactorily sucked. I'm not going to like that, first, because I'm going to have to advance you the two hundred from my own pocket and, second—"

"They'll kill me."

"—and, second, because I really would like to beat the crap out of that tub of lard downstairs. Kill you? They'll kill you if they think you talked. Since when would they kill you for giving somebody a blowjob? Isn't that how you pay for the stuff they sell you? How old are you?"

"Sixteen."

"One more lie, just one more, and I'm on my way downstairs. Then, after I finish with that *filho da puta*, I'm going to find some other kid who'll tell me whatever I want to know. I won't bother to come back looking for you because within a day or two you're going to be dead. With two hundred reais, on the other hand, you could easily afford a bus ticket out of town. It's your choice."

He didn't expect the kid to tell him cops weren't supposed to do what he was doing, and the kid didn't. This kid had seen cops do much worse.

Rambo ran his hand through his hair, muttered something under his breath and finally met Arnaldo's eyes. "Give me the two hundred," he said.

Arnaldo handed it over. He was getting low on cash. He'd have to stop by an ATM.

"They're looking for him, too," the kid said, taking the money. He counted it, folded it and stuffed it into the pocket of his jeans. Then he started putting them on.

"Who?"

"The cops. The State Police. Anybody who finds out where Pipoca is gets five hundred reais. Anybody who tells you guys anything gets a bullet in the back of the head."

"What do they want him for?"

"He owes them money. For dope."

"You know that for a fact?"

"No. But that's what it usually is. You stop buying, they beat you up; you don't pay them what you owe, they make a ham out of you."

"Where is he?"

"I don't know."

Arnaldo shook his head and stuck out his hand. "Give me the two hundred back," he said.

"Wait. Will you fucking wait for a second? Listen to me. Honest to God, I don't know. If I did, I would already have told them. Shit, man, they would have given me five hundred reais. You only gave me two hundred."

The kid had a point. Arnaldo dropped his hand. "Where's he from, this Pipoca?"

"Around here."

"What do you mean by 'around here'?"

"Around here. Cascatas."

"Look, Rambo"—Arnaldo tried to keep the sarcasm out of voice when he used the kid's street name—"if I don't find Pipoca before your friends do, they're going to kill him."

"They're not my friends."

"And they're not mine, either. Give me some help here."

The kid thought about it. After a while, he said, "I heard him say he has a mother."

"Everybody's got a mother."

"A mother he visits. A mother he talks to. Somebody who cares about him."

The kid made it sound as if having someone who cared about you was a marvel, like it was the rarest thing in the world.

"Now we're getting somewhere. You got a name?"

Rambo didn't. And he didn't have anything else that would have helped, other than a vague memory that Pipoca seemed to be pretty familiar with a favela by the name of Consolação.

Favelas are shantytowns. There are no numbers on the shacks; there are no names given to the streets; they aren't to be found on municipal maps; there's no mail delivery. If Souza's mother lived in a favela, it might not be easy to find her. Arnaldo recognized that he was going to need help, local help. Not the kid. He'd scamper off at the first opportunity.

"Take my advice," he said. "Use the money to get out of town."

The kid swallowed. "And you won't tell? You won't tell anyone what I told you?"

"No. Put your clothes on and get the hell out of here."

He let Rambo leave first. After a minute or so, he followed him downstairs and walked up to the desk.

"You owe me twenty reais."

Fat Boy lowered the magazine and looked at his watch. "You figure?" he said, insolently.

"Yeah, I figure."

Fat Boy looked Arnaldo up and down. Arnaldo was a head taller and at least twenty kilos heavier. None of it was fat.

Fat Boy reached into his pocket.

Their parting was about as cordial as could be expected. Fat Boy didn't thank Arnaldo for his business, and Arnaldo didn't give in to the temptation to beat the crap out of Fat Boy.

Arnaldo walked around until he found an ATM that would accept his bankcard. The limit was R$500, so he withdrew that. And then he went looking for a taxi.

Chapter Twenty-four

"ROADBLOCK," HECTOR SAID, TAKING his foot off the accelerator pedal.

He put the gearshift in neutral, lightly tapped the brake, and glided to a stop behind a blue truck piled high with bunches of green bananas. On the tailgate, the truck's owner had made his contribution to popular literature:

KIDS ARE LIKE FARTS. MOST PEOPLE CAN ONLY TOLERATE THEIR OWN.

The majority of Brazil's owner-operated commercial vehicles display something similar, pithy expressions of folk wisdom dreamed up by the drivers themselves. This one was surrounded by little painted roses, white and pink.

Silva got out and assessed the extent of the traffic jam. The space between their car and the roadblock, a distance about the length of a soccer pitch, was packed with all kinds of vehicles, mostly trucks.

He got back in. "Plenty of room on the right shoulder," he said.

Hector put the car in gear, spun the wheel, and drove the hundred meters or so to the roadblock.

A man with a paunch, and a gap where his two front teeth should have been, wearing a State Police uniform with sergeant's stripes, saw them coming. He walked toward them with a scowl on his face, flapping his hands at the wrist as if they were wet and he was trying to shake the water off.

"What the hell do you think you're doing?" he said as soon as he was close enough not to have to exert himself by raising his voice. He lisped. It would have been difficult not to with those missing teeth, but it was still funny, coming from such a big man.

Silva suppressed a smile and reached for his badge. "Federal Police."

"You Silva?" the cop said, not in the least impressed. It came out "Thilva."

Silva nodded.

"We weren't expecting you so soon. The colonel said to bring you up when you got here."

"What are you talking about?"

The sergeant scratched the bulge of flab that hung over his belt.

"You're here to see the body, right?"

"What body?"

"Muniz. They found him."

THE ENTRANCE to the Fazenda Boa Vista was a stone's throw from where the cops had set up the roadblock. The sergeant got into their car and went with them to show the way.

"You go left at the fork," he said as they drove through the front gate.

A right turn at the same fork would have brought them to their original destination, a cluster of pavilions surrounding a red banner on a long pole. There must have been at least fifty of the structures, fluttering roofs of black plastic. Around and among them were gathered people of both sexes and all ages. There was a smell of cooking fires, and the distant sound of a baby's crying.

"League encampment," the sergeant said. "Smells real bad if you get too close. Stop over there next to the ambulance. We gotta climb the fucking hill."

The hillside was steep and strewn with gray rocks, some of

them as big as a baby's head. The sergeant picked his way carefully over the ground, going slow and huffing like a steam engine. At the pace he set, Silva and Hector didn't even work up a sweat.

About halfway up, Silva's cell phone rang.

"Director?" he said.

"That Mario Silva?"

"It's Silva. Who's this?"

"Corporal Borges from the State Police. I've got a message for you from Colonel Ferraz."

"How did you get this number?"

"The colonel gave it to me."

Silva sighed. "What's the message?"

"Orlando Muniz Junior is dead. We found the body. The colonel said to meet him at the Muniz fazenda, the Boa Vista. You know where that is?"

"Yes."

"He says somebody will be waiting for you at the gate."

Silva thanked him and hung up without bothering to explain that he was already there.

The flat area on the crown of the hill had once been cleared, probably for grazing, but that must have been quite some time ago. A few stunted trees and some clumps of brush were sprinkled here and there. Silva stood still for a moment and let his eyes sweep around the horizon. Down below there were endless fields, most planted with sugarcane, some lying fallow. At the margin of one vast, empty area he could see the plastic shelters and flapping banner of the Landless Workers' League.

Close at hand, red earth was piled next to a rectangular hole cut into dried grass. Half a dozen cops in uniform, and some who weren't, were hanging around the site. Most were looking at the contents of an oblong wooden box about the size of a coffin.

The spectators didn't include Ferraz, who was standing to

one side, engaged in conversation with the same officer Silva
had seen entering and leaving his office, the one with the
scar and the knife hanging from a scabbard on his belt. The
colonel was dressed in a red polo shirt, jodhpurs, and boots,
as if he'd been out riding when he got the news.

A man wearing latex gloves squatted over the box. There
was a black medical bag standing open-mouthed on the
ground near the man's right foot.

"Colonel."

Ferraz turned at the sound of Silva's voice. "How the fuck
did you get here so fast?"

Silva ignored the question. "Why don't you introduce
me?" he said, nodding at the officer.

Reflexively, the officer nodded back. Ferraz looked from
one to the other and finally said, "Osmani Palmas, Mario
Silva." He didn't elaborate, and he didn't include Hector in
the introduction.

"How did you find him?" Silva asked, pointing at the
makeshift coffin.

"His old man hired a helicopter, had it fly back and forth
over the property. The pilot spotted what looked like a
grave. Turned out, it was."

"Does Muniz know his son's dead?"

"He sure as hell does, and he's on his way. Those league
guys screwed up big this time. He's going to fuck them up
good." Ferraz seemed pleased, almost gleeful.

"There's no proof they did it."

"No proof?" Ferraz laughed out loud. A couple of the other
cops turned toward him. "No proof?" he repeated. "What do
you think *that* is?" He pointed toward the corpse. "How
much more proof you think the old man needs?"

Silva brushed past the colonel and went to talk to the
man wearing the latex gloves, a Nisei with rimless glasses
and a purple birthmark on his forehead.

"Ishikawa," the man said, rising to his feet. "Medical examiner. You?"

"Costa," Silva pointed at Hector, "and Silva," he stuck a thumb into his own chest. "Federal Police. Any conclusions?"

"He was alive when they buried him," the doctor said. He stuck the thermometer he was holding into a breast pocket, pulled out a pencil, and made a note. "He tried to free his ankles and wrists. Cut himself up pretty badly. The marks on his forehead came from battering his head repeatedly against the lid. Maybe he was trying to knock himself out."

Silva looked down at the body. The younger Muniz's pants were pulled down over his thighs. The thermometer the medical examiner had been using was obviously rectal.

"Cause of death?"

"Asphyxiation," Ishikawa said, "unless something else turns up in the autopsy."

The doctor was friendly and more forthcoming than Silva would have expected. Silva was used to dealing with the big-city medical examiners, men and women who were unwilling to hazard a guess about a cause of death, much less commit themselves, until they'd completed an autopsy.

Ferraz came up to stand at Silva's shoulder. "His eyes were open when we dug him up," he said. "The doc here closed them for him. He musta been shit scared."

Doctor Ishikawa winced at Ferraz's tone and lowered his eyes so he wouldn't have to look at him.

"You want to take him now?" he said.

"Hell, no," Ferraz said. "His old man's on the way. He'll want to have a look."

He glanced at the road leading toward the main gate of the fazenda and squinted. Silva followed his gaze. There were three vehicles down there, coming fast, trailing red dust.

"That's probably him now."

Silva took Hector by the arm. "Let's go," he said.

"You mean you're not going to stick around for the old man?" Ferraz asked, incredulously.

"We're going down to see what the league people have to say."

Silva turned to go and then, remembering, he turned back to face Ferraz.

"I've been asked to look into the murder of Senhorita Poli as well."

"So?"

"So I'd like to know why she gave you an authorization to go through her safe-deposit box and what you were looking for."

"Confidential matter between her and me."

"Confidential?"

"Confidential. And she must have made some kind of a mistake, because it was empty."

Silva stared at him. Ferraz wasn't intimidated. As if to prove it he said, "By the way, my boys have been all over the crime scene. The guy who cut their throats was left-handed, just like Major Palmas here. And the blonde was raped, but there was no DNA, nothing under their finger-nails, no strange pubic hairs, no semen. No prints, either. Too bad, huh?"

Silva didn't trust himself to speak. He turned on his heel and started back to where they'd left their car. Behind him, Ferraz and Palmas shared a laugh.

Hector followed his uncle down the slope. A moment later they passed the dead man's father, hurrying upward. The two bodyguards from the hotel were hot on Muniz's heels.

One of the bodyguards stopped to talk, but the other two men brushed by without a word. The old man's anxious eyes were fixed on the crown of the hill.

"Is it him?" the bodyguard asked Silva.

"Yeah. It's him."

"Then God help them."

"Help who?" Silva said, but the man was already scrambling to catch up to his boss.

"Let's get down to the encampment," he said, "before they do."

Another two minutes brought them onto the flat. All three of Muniz's vehicles were pulled up next to Hector's rental car. A driver sat behind the wheel of a black Mercedes. The others were vans and they were packed with armed men.

Chapter Twenty-five

ONE THING SILVA COULD have anticipated, but hadn't, was the presence of the press in the league's encampment.

A pod of them surrounded Luiz Pillar. All were men, except for one very attractive brunette.

"That's all we need," Silva said when he spotted her.

"Wow," Hector said, "That's—"

"Yeah. Vicenza Pelosi." Vicenza was an ex-model turned investigative journalist. If the stories about her were true, she'd gotten her break into journalism by having an affair with the president of the network, but that was ancient history. These days, it was said, she tended to avoid entanglements with men, and had a low opinion of most of them. Her father had been a shop steward in the metalworker's union, mysteriously shot down one night by a person, or persons, never identified. She'd been twelve years old when they'd buried him. By the time she was fourteen, she'd blossomed into a black-haired, olive-skinned beauty with pouting bee-stung lips, an hourglass figure, and intriguing green eyes. She entered a modeling contest and won it. The prize was a contract, and within six months she'd appeared on the cover of half a dozen magazines. The camera loved her, and in another sense, so did the photographers and art directors upon whom her work depended. By eighteen, she'd bedded dozens and her photos had appeared in publications all over the world.

But Vicenza was much more than a pretty face. Early on, she'd realized that the career of a model, no matter how successful, was short. She started bringing books to her photo shoots, reading them while they were setting up the lights or when the other models were being made up. They were the kind of books most photographers and art directors had never read, much less any of the other girls. Marx, Spengler, Engels, Sartre, Camus—she read them all, and kept going back to the bookshops to buy more. While the other girls' closets were stuffed with shoes and dresses, Vicenza's were stacked with paperbacks. While the other girls spent their evenings in nightclubs and trendy restaurants, Vicenza took to staying at home, reading, and going to bed alone, by preference.

She couldn't discuss her books with any of the people she worked with, so she started studying at night. By the time she was twenty-three she'd earned a degree in social sciences from the University of Rio de Janeiro. At twenty-six, she was doing local coverage for the Rede Mundo affiliate in São Paulo. At twenty-eight she went national. And now, at thirty-three, she had her own show, could choose what she wanted to report on, and was a major force in shaping Brazilian public opinion. Everybody in government, from the President of the Republic on down, was leery of getting on her bad side.

"I think she spotted me," Silva said.

"I think she did too. You ever meet her? In person, I mean."

Silva nodded. "In another age, she would have been locked up for being a communist. She and Pillar must see eye to eye. He probably invited her."

"She's beautiful."

"She is that. She's also abrasive as hell."

"Introduce me."

Silva nodded. "Okay," he said, "but don't say I didn't warn you."

Vicenza came walking toward them, trailing a cameraman and a guy with a microphone boom.

"Ah, Chief Inspector Silva. I heard you were in Cascatas."

"Is the camera running, Vicenza?"

She answered him with a smile and another question.

"Are you here to help with the breakup of this encampment?"

Silva just stood and smiled. She repeated the question with exactly the same result. Their activity attracted the attention of other journalists. Some of them started walking toward them like cautious wolves inspecting new prey. Silva didn't recognize any of them but there was a good chance that some of them would recognize him. He turned his back.

"Okay," Vicenza said, walking around Silva so that she could face him. "Take a break, guys." The cameraman took the camera from his shoulder and slipped on a lens cap. The soundman lowered his microphone boom. Then the two of them wandered off in the direction of a blue truck with the Rede Mundo logotype.

The other journalists watched them for a moment, then gravitated back to Pillar.

Vicenza fished a cigarette out of her shoulder bag and lit it. She didn't seem miffed by Silva's unwillingness to play.

"Shall we try again?" she said. "Off the record?"

Hector cleared his throat.

"Who's this?" She flashed her long eyelashes.

"Hector Costa, a delegado from the São Paulo office."

Hector smiled and took a step forward.

"Ah. And your nephew, if I'm not mistaken."

Hector winced.

"Well informed," Silva said, "as usual."

Vicenza redirected her attention to Silva.

"What brought you to Cascatas in the first place, Chief Inspector? Dom Felipe? The Poli woman? Young Muniz's kidnapping?"

"All of the above. What can you tell me about Muniz?"

"Who's the reporter here?" She had a slightly crooked incisor. The small defect served to enhance her smile.

"Help us out, Vicenza. I'll reciprocate."

She cocked her head and thought about it. "Okay. Who do you want to know about? The father or the son?"

"The son."

"Nasty bastard, just as mean and greedy as his father. Thought the league was out to get him, and with good reason. They say he murdered a man by the name of Aurelio—"

"I know about that."

"So he was paranoid. Always locked himself in at night and had a half a dozen capangas guarding the house. He's got a manager who lives here on the property, name of Santos. They were supposed to meet for a late breakfast."

"Where?"

"At the *casa grande*, Muniz's house. Santos showed up on time, but Muniz wasn't there. Neither were any of his bodyguards. The cook and the maid were, but they don't sleep in the house. They've got their own little cottage just on the other side of that hill. They arrived to find the front door and the door to his bedroom smashed and no sign of their boss."

"What time was that?"

"A little after eight."

"Aside from the broken doors, and the fact that Muniz missed his appointment, was there anything else that induced them to suspect foul play?"

Vicenza smiled. "Foul play? *Foul play?* Do cops really talk like that?"

"I'm a cop and that's the way I talk. Answer my question."

Vicenza's smile vanished.

"Please."

The smile came back.

"That's better, Chief Inspector. Be nice. Muniz's car and van were still in the garage. Both are *blindados*, teflon in the doors, windows two centimeters thick and bulletproof. He never traveled in anything else."

"Was he married?"

She immediately caught the past tense. "Why do you say 'was'?"

"I'll tell you in a moment. Was he married?"

She nodded. "And he's got two kids. They spend most of their time in Rio. The wife is a socialite. A spoiled bitch, addicted to dinner parties laced with caviar, champagne, and *foie gras*. If she spends more than a week living on the fazenda she gets claustrophobic."

"Claustrophobic? How big is this place?"

"About half the size of Denmark."

"No kidding?"

"No kidding."

"Jesus. How about their kids?"

"She keeps them with her. Says they can't get a decent education in Cascatas. She's got them in the American School in Rio."

"Muniz's paranoia—the fact that he surrounded himself with hired guns—was that because he feared reprisal for Azevedo?"

"Not only that. He had another reason."

"Which was?"

"This isn't the first time the league has made a grab for some of his property. They tried it about fourteen months ago. Muniz got the State Police to help him evict them. A couple of people were killed, including a seven-year-old girl. The league blames him for that, too."

"I remember reading about the girl. She caught a stray bullet."

"That's what Colonel Ferraz says. The league people tell a

different story. They claim Muniz shot her on purpose, just to make a point."

"Why didn't the league people bring charges?"

"They tried, but the local judge is a friend of the Munizes,' some crook by the name of Wilson Cunha. He threw them out of court."

"The Azevedo thing, was that before or after?"

"Before *and* after. Azevedo was the guy who led the invasion of the property, and he was the guy who tried to press charges for the murder of the little girl. Junior started getting threats. That's when he started locking his doors and, some say, laying plans to make an example of Azevedo."

"What's your best guess about who's responsible for Junior's disappearance?"

"For heaven's sake, Chief Inspector. He disappears one night, and they invade his fazenda the next. What do you need? A road map? It had to be the league. Who else? Your turn now, and I hope it's good."

"Oh, it is, Vicenza, it is."

Silva looked around and leaned closer. Her perfume had a faint lemony scent. "It's not a kidnapping anymore. Muniz is dead. They found his body, on a hill, about two kilometers down that road. His old man just arrived and he's already up there."

She threw her cigarette to the ground and crushed it under one of her black pumps. She'd only taken one puff on it, the one to get it lit.

"A pleasure doing business with you, Chief Inspector. We'll catch up later." Then, with a sideways glance at the competition, she started strolling toward the blue truck as if she was disengaging herself from a fruitless conversation.

Chapter Twenty-six

ARNALDO DIDN'T THINK it would be a good idea to take a rental car into a favela, so he took it back to the hotel and left it in the garage under the building. Then he found a place under the shadow of a jacaranda tree and looked up and down the dusty, deserted street. There was no sign of a taxi. He was thinking about going back inside and asking them to call one when a white-haired lady, trailing a poodle of the same color, came out of a neighboring apartment building. While the dog sniffed at Arnaldo's crotch, and they both tried to ignore it, the lady directed him to the nearest taxi stand.

It turned out to be a three-minute walk away, on a parallel street called the Rua Tiradentes, and consisted of a telephone box bolted to a lamppost. A yellow Volkswagen Beetle with both doors open was parked along the curb. The passenger's seat, the one next to the driver, had been removed to facilitate access.

"We're going to a favela called Consolação," Arnaldo said, folding his considerable bulk into the back and slamming the door on the passenger's side.

The driver, who'd been fanning himself with a magazine while leafing through another, turned around and stared at him. He was a black man with a day's growth of white beard and a bald head. "No, we're not," he said. "Not me. Those people will slit your throat for a few reais."

Arnaldo took out his badge and flashed it. "Consolação," he said, "or the nearest police station."

"Merda," the driver said, but he slammed his door, started the engine, and pushed down the flag.

"Isn't this thing air conditioned?" Arnaldo asked.

"No," the driver said. "Why don't I bring you over to the cab stand near the bus station? You can get an *especial* with air conditioning and the whole bit. You'll be a lot more comfortable."

"Forget it. Get moving."

"No charge. I'll take you for free."

"Get moving, I said. Now, listen up. When we get there you're going to help me find a woman—"

"Look, senhor, if all you want is a whore I can—"

"Shut up and drive. I was talking."

WHAT PASSED for the favela's main street was an unpaved alleyway lined with shacks built of scrap lumber. Every now and then a narrower alleyway branched off to the left or to the right. There was no room for the driver to maneuver, no way for him to avoid the water-filled potholes, any one of which might have been deep enough to engulf one of his wheels. He bounced ahead slowly, cursing under his breath.

"Stop next to that woman," Arnaldo said. "We'll try her first."

The woman in question was carrying a blue plastic washtub on her head and picking her way through the garbage that lined the street. The windows in the back of the cab didn't open, so Arnaldo had to lean over the driver's left shoulder to talk to her.

"Senhora?"

She stopped and gave him a wide, curious smile.

"I'm looking for a woman who has a son named Edson Souza."

"Sorry," she said, "I don't know her." And then, almost as an afterthought, "Senhor?"

Arnaldo leaned forward hopefully.

"If I were you, I wouldn't go driving around this neighborhood."

"You see?" the taxi driver said as they pulled away. "Now you heard it from somebody else, and she lives here, for Christ's sake. Let's get out of here."

"Keep going."

They came next to a group of five youths standing in a circle.

"Stop here."

"Senhor, for the love of—"

"Stop, I said."

The driver stopped and looked down, writing something on a clipboard, avoiding the five pairs of eyes.

The youngest kid was about thirteen, the oldest maybe seventeen. They were all dressed in clothes that looked several sizes too big for them, and they all had shaved heads. Arnaldo was reminded of the school of barracudas he'd once seen while scuba diving. He'd been about thirty meters down, on the wreck of the old *Principe de Asturias*, just off the north coast of Ilha Bela. The damned fish had looked at him then just like the kids were looking at him now, as if they were deciding whether it would be safe to flash in and take a bite.

"What?" the oldest kid said.

No greeting, no smile, just the single word. Arnaldo asked the same question he'd asked of the woman with the washtub.

"What's it worth to you?" the kid asked.

"Five reais."

"Go fuck yourself."

"Ten."

"Let's see the ten."

Arnaldo fished out his wallet. Probably a mistake, he thought. The wallet was fat with the money he'd taken from the ATM. He held it low, so that the kids couldn't see into it, and took out a ten-real note.

The kid stuck out his hand.

"First the information," Arnaldo said.

The kid snarled, then pointed up the street. "You see the house with the blue plywood?"

Arnaldo squinted through the windshield. "Yeah."

"That's it. Give me the ten."

Arnaldo did, and the kid turned his back on him. It was a sign for the rest of the school. They all turned their backs on him, too.

Without being told, the driver crept forward again, glancing nervously in the rearview mirror.

"*Meninos da rua,*" he said. Street kids. He sounded frightened.

He stopped at a shack that had a piece of blue plywood patching a hole to the right of the entrance. Entrance, not door. A piece of rotting canvas hung down to close the opening.

"Keys," Arnaldo said.

"What?"

"Shut off the engine and give me your keys."

"That's not necessary, senhor. I'll be right here, waiting for you when you come out."

"Sure you will. And the Tooth Fairy exists. Keys."

The driver sighed, turned off the engine, and handed them over.

A little too easily, Arnaldo thought. "You have a set of spares?"

"No, senhor, no spares."

"Okay, get out."

"Why, senhor?"

"Don't argue, just do it."

When he did, Arnaldo told him to go around to the back of the car, remove the distributor cap and take out the rotor.

The driver's eyes rounded in fear. He ran a hand over his bald pate.

So he did have another set of keys. "I won't be long," Arnaldo said, pocketing the rotor. "Anybody gives you any trouble, just yell."

"There are five of them, senhor. *Five.*"

"And I'm carrying a pistol with ten rounds in the magazine. *Ten.* If they come over here, tell them I'm a cop. It will save me the trouble, and I can start shooting right away."

"Please, senhor, I don't want any trouble. I have a wife. Three children. You don't know those kids, they—"

"I know kids like them. And, yeah, I know that at least a couple of them are carrying."

"Carrying, senhor?"

"Certainly knives. Maybe a gun or two."

"Senhor, for the love of God—"

"Okay, okay, come with me. Stand in the doorway and keep an eye on your car. If they touch it, tell me."

With a furtive glance at the kids, the driver nodded, and followed.

Arnaldo didn't know what the protocol was when it came to canvas curtains instead of doors. He tried clapping his hands.

It worked. A moment later, the canvas was swept aside, and he was looking into the mistrusting eyes of an old mulatto woman. She had what might have been a piece of firewood in one hand. Or it might have been a club. She stared at him without speaking.

"I'm looking for the mother of Edson Souza."

"Not here."

When she opened her mouth he could see she was toothless.

"Souza's mother doesn't live here?"

"Not here," the woman repeated, smacking her gums. And then added, grudgingly, "She's working."

He'd come to the right place. "Who are you?" he asked.

"Who are you?" the woman said.

He showed her his warrant card. She squinted at it.

"Can you read?"

"No," she said.

He showed her his badge. "Federal Police."

She drew back slightly and took in a breath. "Didn't do anything," she said.

He was beginning to think she wasn't quite right in the head. "I didn't say you did. Can I come in?"

She stepped out of the opening, pulling the canvas aside as she did so.

Inside, the shack smelled of lamp oil, sweat, and human excrement. Arnaldo remembered that places like these didn't have toilets. They dug holes in a corner and used that, covering the holes with boards, sometimes sprinkling lime if they could afford it. They'd fetch their water from a communal spigot. Electricity, if any, would come from an illegal tap.

There were no windows. In the dim light, he could make out that the interior was nothing more than one small room. Three children, the oldest about six or seven, and the youngest no more than two, lay entangled on the bed like a litter of cats. The bed was made of jute coffee bags, sewn together and stuffed with something. There was a single three-legged stool, and there were three wooden crates, but no other furniture. One of the crates supported a small black-and-white television set with a rabbit-ear antenna.

The television was tuned to a channel that was showing an old *Tom and Jerry* cartoon. The oldest kid, a girl, took her thumb out of her mouth and glanced at Arnaldo when he came through the door. The other two didn't take their eyes off the screen.

The stool and the two remaining crates looked incapable of bearing his weight. If Arnaldo wanted to sit, it would have to be on the bed next to the kids. He decided he'd remain standing.

"Yours?" he said to the old woman, inclining his head in the direction of the listless children.

"Marly Souza's," she said. "I take care of them when she's at work."

"Siblings of Edson?"

"What?"

"Brothers or sisters of Edson?"

"Two sisters, one brother. Different fathers."

"You a relation?"

"What?"

"Are you their aunt or their grandmother?"

The woman shook her head.

"She pays me."

"What's your name?"

"Lia."

"Okay, Lia. You know Edson?"

She nodded.

"Where is he?"

"Gone away."

"Where?"

"Don't know."

"When did he go?"

"Don't know."

"Where's his mother?"

"Working."

"Yes, you told me. Where?"

She put a veined hand to her cheek and closed her eyes, thinking. Then she opened them again and went over to one of the wooden crates. She came back with a wrapper from a bar of toilet soap. LUX. THE SOAP OF THE STARS, the label read. There was a photo on the front: one of the actresses from last year's eight o'clock *novela* on Rede Mundo.

Arnaldo turned the wrapper over. On the white paper someone had laboriously block-printed something in pencil.

He took it closer to the light from the doorway and put it near his nose so he could read it. The paper still smelled faintly of the bar of soap it had once enveloped, an artificial smell, only vaguely reminiscent of flowers.

"We going now?" the cab driver asked hopefully. He'd been standing in the doorway, holding the canvas aside and occasionally craning his neck to keep an eye on the teenagers.

Arnaldo showed him the writing on the wrapper:

Dona Marcia
Rua das Bromelias, 142
Jardim Jericoara

"Can you find this place?"

The taxi driver squinted at the paper, moving his lips silently as he spelled out the words. "Sim, senhor. It's not far. Maybe ten kilometers."

"Let's go then."

The driver let the canvas fall and was gone.

The only light in the shack was now coming from the television. In its glow, Arnaldo could dimly see the faces of the occupants. While he'd been talking to the driver, the old woman had taken a seat on the bed. She was holding her elbows in her hands and staring at the screen.

"Thanks," he said, but the woman didn't even look up.

Outside, the driver had the hood open. He stuck out his hand. Arnaldo put the rotor into it and stood there, waiting, while he installed it. Then he handed him the keys.

To get out of the favela they had to make a U-turn and pass the predatory kids. No one made a move, but Arnaldo saw the driver swallow when they got close and continue to shoot nervous glances at his rearview mirror once they'd gone by. When Arnaldo turned in his seat, and looked out of the rear window, five pairs of eyes were fixed on the retreating cab.

Chapter Twenty-seven

THE LEAGUE ENCAMPMENT BEGAN at a rise bordering the road, swept on through a depression in the ground, and petered out at the edge of an empty field. It consisted of tents fashioned from black plastic sheeting supported by limbs freshly cut from the neighboring trees. In deference to the heat of the day, most of the walls had been rolled upward and tied to the crossbeams, affording protection from the sun and allowing a view over the entire campsite. There were at least two hundred people settled there. All but about fifty were children. The smell was a mixture of unwashed bodies, wood smoke, garlic, and onions. At the center of it all, on a flagpole that had recently been the trunk of a scrawny tree, the blood red standard of the Landless Workers' League waved in a listless breeze.

It was there, at the base of the pole, that Pillar had been talking to the reporters. Now he'd drawn aside and was involved in an animated conversation with a heavyset individual wearing a league T-shirt. When he saw Silva and Hector approaching him, he broke off and turned to face them.

"So you decided to grace us with your presence," he said. He laid a hand on the shoulder of the man next to him. "Chief Inspector Silva, Delegado Costa, let me introduce Roberto Pereira. I'm here at his invitation."

Pereira offered the cops a hand, but not a smile. His rimless spectacles were as thick as bottle glass. They magnified eyes that were brown, hard, and wary.

"You must have known Aurelio Azevedo," Silva said.

"He was like a brother," Pereira said. "Why are you asking?"

"Just curious. How about Muniz Junior? You know him?"

Pereira looked down at his dirty tennis shoes, cheap ones that had never seen a tennis court and never would.

"That murdering fuck? Yeah, I knew him."

Knew?

Past tense. The word hung in the air.

"They found the body," Silva said. "buried on the top of that hill."

Pillar looked in the direction that Silva was pointing. Pereira didn't.

"Buried alive," Silva continued. "Old man Muniz, Junior's father, is at the gravesite. He'll be down here any time now and there's going to be trouble."

"Let the old man come," Pereira said. "I shit on people like him. He'll only be fighting for his personal interest. We fight for our principles. We'll win, because we have justice on our side."

"Save the rhetoric for the reporters, Pereira," Silva said. "If you've got a judge on your side, which isn't at all the same thing as justice, you might have a chance of winning this thing. Otherwise, by trespassing on his property, you're giving old man Muniz an excuse to react and, believe me, he'll be looking for one."

"Muniz is getting off cheap," Pereira said. "One life for four, five if you count the little seven-year-old that he—"

Pillar squeezed his companion's shoulder, silencing him. "Would you believe it, Chief Inspector? This was once the most peaceful of men. Preached a philosophy of absolute nonviolence. Now he's a firebrand."

"If I am, it's people like Muniz who made me that way," Pereira said. "Fuck him and all his kind."

"You see?" Pillar said. "If Roberto had been born forty years ago, he'd have been down in Bolivia, fighting with the *campesinos* and Che Guevara."

"Remember what happened to Guevara," Silva said. "He died for nothing."

The smile faded from Pillar's face. "We may die, Chief Inspector, but it won't be for nothing. The league is, by far, the largest *and* the most significant social movement in all of South America. We have the support of the entire world."

"Not when you invade private property, you don't."

"What else do you expect us to do? Back off? Well, we're not going to do that. We've waited long enough. We want land reform, and we want it now."

"Do you know how big this fazenda is?" Pereira chipped in. "More than half the size—"

"Of Denmark," Silva said. "Yeah, I've heard."

"Think about it. A piece of land half the size of the whole fucking country of Denmark and all of it owned by *one* selfish son of a bitch. Is that right? You tell me."

"I'm not a philosopher, Senhor Pereira. I'm just a cop. But, as a cop, I can tell you this: If you don't clear your people off his land, Muniz will evict you and I don't trust him to do it gently."

"We look forward to having him try," Pereira said. "We welcome it."

He'd raised his voice almost to a shout. Silva looked around. Sure enough, all of the journalists were looking at them, some of them were moving closer and a couple of video cameras were pointed his way. Had he said anything to Pereira or Pillar that the director wouldn't like to see on television? He didn't think so. In any case, it would be a good idea to cut the conversation short before he *did* say something compromising.

He looked around for a way to do it and caught sight of a familiar figure: a tall man in a league T-shirt and jeans, Father Brouwer. The priest was seated crosslegged on the ground in front of a tent. A little girl was in his lap, and he was feeding her with a wooden spoon.

"Excuse me," Silva said, and walked away from Pillar and Pereira, trailed by Hector.

The priest saw him coming, nodded, and went on feeding the child. She had big eyes, a swollen belly, and looked to be about four years old.

"Cornmeal mush, Chief Inspector?" Brouwer said, holding out the spoon.

"Thank you, no," Silva said.

"Maria likes it a lot. Don't you, Maria?"

The little girl nodded her head gravely and opened her mouth for another bite.

"You see the results of greed, Chief Inspector?" Brouwer said, gently tapping the fingers of his free hand on the child's distended belly. "Malnutrition." He pointed at her legs. "Rickets. This is what people like Muniz bring about."

"It turns out you were right about him," Silva said. "The younger one, I mean. He's dead."

The priest didn't seem in the least surprised. "Poor man," he said. "He should have changed his ways. Our Lord said it's easier for a camel to go through the eye of a needle than for a rich man to enter the kingdom of God. You'll find the same passage in Matthew, Mark, and Luke."

"Listen to me, Father. Old man Muniz is on the top of that hill where his son's body is. He's going to be down here any time now. He's got gunmen with him. He's got that bastard Ferraz and his men from the State Police with him. This is his property. Remember what happened last time?"

"Oh, yes, Chief Inspector, I remember. I remember very well. I was here."

"I didn't know."

"I've been fighting social injustice all my life. It's my vocation. I never learned to preach a good sermon. I'm not sure I was ever capable of writing one. But this, Chief Inspector, this I can do." He clucked at the child, gave her another spoonful of cornmeal mush and continued. "I sense you're a good man, that you want the best for everyone, but sometimes that's just not possible. Sometimes there has to be suffering to achieve progress. Jesus showed us that."

He smiled down at the child and the child smiled back, a smile so sweet that Silva found himself smiling too.

"There's really nothing you can do," the priest said. "So please, go away and let us get on with it. What's going to happen now is in God's hands, not yours."

Chapter Twenty-eight

THE UPPER-MIDDLE-CLASS CONDOMINIUM called Jardim Jericoara was less than ten kilometers from the favela of Consolação, but in socioeconomic terms it was in another galaxy. Access to the property was by way of two entry lanes, one of them labeled RESIDENTES and the other VISITANTES. A metal gate blocked each lane, and each gate was controlled from a guardhouse with what looked to Arnaldo like bullet-proof glass on the windows.

When the taxi stopped, the four rent-a-cops in the guard-house gave it a thorough once-over through the glass, and then three of them went back to watching a daytime soap opera on their little television set. The fourth, a husky fel-low with a revolver on his hip, carrying a clipboard, came out of the door and approached the taxi. He ignored the driver and spoke directly to Arnaldo.

"Senhor?"

The form of address was polite. The man's tone of voice wasn't. Arnaldo's taxi was a Volkswagen Beetle, not even a *taxi especial*. A resident (or a friend of a resident) of Jardim Jericoara wouldn't have been caught dead in one. The con-clusion was obvious: Despite his suit and tie, Arnaldo had to be either a household servant or some other kind of service provider. In either case, he didn't merit first-class treatment.

"I'm here to see . . ."—Arnaldo consulted the paper the old woman had given him—"Dona Marcia on the Rua das Bromelias."

The guard narrowed his eyes at the soap wrapper and made an annotation on his clipboard. "About?"

Arnaldo flashed his badge. "Police business."

The guard's attitude changed completely. He stood up a little straighter, the sneer on his face vanished, and a tone of respect crept into his voice.

"You want me to call?"

"That's what you're supposed to do, right?"

The guard nodded. "That's the procedure," he confirmed, "for any visitor."

"Then you'd better do it."

"Can I hold on to some ID? Sorry. But that's the procedure, too."

Arnaldo took out his national identity card and handed it over.

The guard walked into the shack, said a few words to his companions and picked up a telephone. Three pairs of eyes turned toward the taxi and stared at Arnaldo. Arnaldo stared back. They redirected their attention to the TV screen.

The guard returned in less than a minute. "Okay, she's expecting you." Then, for the first time, he addressed Arnaldo's driver. "Bromelias is the first right off the second left."

The driver nodded. Arnaldo sank back in his seat. The barrier lifted and the taxi started to roll.

The condominium was no housing project. Every house was unique, and every house was set well back on a tailored lawn. It was a little island of luxury in a sea of poverty. After the first turn, Arnaldo could no longer see the high walls that surrounded the place.

A group of teenagers was hanging around on one of the street corners. They were similar in age to the kids Arnaldo had seen in the favela of Consolação but there the similarity ended. These were wearing clean T-shirts with slogans in English and French. One of them, not older than twelve, was sitting on a motor-driven scooter, gunning the engine. There wasn't a dark skin among them.

The driver had no problem finding Dona Marcia's house. She was standing at the curb, and she started waving to them when they turned into her street. It wasn't a friendly wave. She was only doing it to get their attention.

Dona Marcia was a slender woman, closer to forty than thirty. Above her designer jeans she, too, was wearing a T-shirt with something written on it in English. This one said: FIVE REASONS WHY A BANANA IS BETTER THAN A HUSBAND, and went on to enumerate them. None of the first four were complimentary to males. Arnaldo, whose English wasn't that good anyway, couldn't read the fifth. It was tucked in under her belt.

The taxi driver offered his keys when Arnaldo got out of the cab.

"Keep them," Arnaldo said, and then to the woman, "Dona Marcia?"

"Sim."

She didn't ask him what he wanted, didn't ask him anything at all, just stood there frowning at him.

"You have a woman working for you? A woman by the name of Souza?"

"What's she done?"

"Nothing. She hasn't done anything. I just want to ask her some questions. Is she here?"

"Could I see your badge, or something?"

Arnaldo had his police ID ready.

She took a moment to study it, compared the photo with his face. "You're not from around here?"

"No, Senhora, Federal Police, based in the capital."

By which they both understood him to mean São Paulo, the capital of the state, and not Brasilia, the nation's capital, which everybody always refers to by name.

"Look, Agente, I've got a couple of young kids in this house, and my husband travels a lot. If Marly's been involved in anything illegal, I'll fire her so fast her head will spin. And I want you to tell me, right now, if she has."

She was a woman used to getting her way and not in the least fazed by being in the presence of a cop. She knew what cops were for. Cops were to protect people like her.

"She hasn't. I told you, I just have some questions to put to her."

Dona Marcia hooked a thumb under her jaw and tapped perfectly manicured fingers on her cheek. It wasn't a wholly unconscious gesture. She was wearing a gold ring with a large diamond—three carats, at least. After he'd had a good look at it she said, "I suppose you'd better come in."

He followed her through the front door. She led him through a sunken living room with white leather furniture and onto a wooden deck overlooking a swimming pool.

"Sit there," she said, indicating a plastic chair. "I'll get Marly. I think she's doing the bathrooms."

The woman she brought back looked to be a good deal older than her employer but probably wasn't. Marly Souza's best feature were her eyes, which were large and brown, and at the moment, fearful. She'd done nothing to conceal the streaks of gray in her black, kinky hair. Her lips were generous and still showed the signs of some carmine lipstick. Arnaldo thought she might have been quite pretty, once.

"I'll leave you to it," Dona Marcia said, and went away without so much as offering Arnaldo a cup of coffee.

"Bitch," he said softly to her retreating back.

One corner of Marly Souza's mouth twitched. A smile or a nervous tic? He wasn't sure. She brushed a strand of hair from her right eye with a hand that showed faint traces of crimson nail enamel.

"She'll fire me for sure," she said.

"Why? You haven't done anything, have you?"

Marly looked down at her ragged sneakers, once white.

She was wearing them without socks. Bits of the dark skin of
her feet showed through the holes.

"Have you?" Arnaldo insisted.

She looked up. "You don't get it, do you? I brought a cop
to her home. That'll be reason enough." She sounded angry,
and maybe she was, but the fear was still there. She still
hadn't asked Arnaldo what he wanted. And she didn't.
Instead, she looked around to make sure they were alone and
said, "Not yet."

"Not yet?"

"I swear."

Arnaldo caught on. "I don't work with Colonel Ferraz," he
said.

Her mouth opened in surprise.

"I'm from the Federal Police. Help me. We'll protect
him."

She started picking at one of her broken nails.

"I don't know what you're talking about," she said.

"Yeah, you do. We're talking about Edson. We're talking
about your son. If Ferraz gets to him first, he'll kill him."

With a brusque movement she ripped off part of the nail.
Her finger started to bleed. She stared at it, as if she'd had
no part in causing the injury. The expression on her face
didn't change.

"Help me," Arnaldo said. "Help him."

"I'll do what I promised," she said. "You go back and tell
the colonel that. Tell him I'll come and tell him where Edson
is. I'll tell him just as soon as I know."

"I doubt it," Arnaldo said. "I'll bet you're worried about all
of your children, not just the little ones."

He'd struck a nerve. Impulsively, she reached out a hand
and clutched him by the wrist. "No," she said. "A bargain's a
bargain. I'll keep up my side. Please. Tell him that. Tell him
to leave my babies alone."

"Marly?"

It was Dona Marcia.

Both of them looked up. The woman came forward and held out some banknotes.

"For today," she said, "and for last Friday. I won't be needing you anymore."

"Does this have anything to do with me?" Arnaldo said.

"No, Agente, it has to do with Marly, and frankly it's none of your business. Now, if the two of you are quite finished. . . ."

"We're not," he said bluntly.

"Then you can continue your conversation elsewhere. I want you both out of my home."

Arnaldo waited while Marly fetched her things, a purse and a shopping bag, and watched while Dona Marcia made a minute inspection of the contents of both to make sure that Marly hadn't helped herself to any of the family silver.

The taxi driver was where Arnaldo had left him, listening to a cassette tape of *musica sertaneja* and tapping his fingers on the dashboard. He didn't seem surprised to have acquired another passenger.

"Where to now?" he said cheerfully, shifting the meter from the waiting position to the basic rate for daytime travel.

His broad smile disappeared when Arnaldo told him to go back to the favela.

Chapter Twenty-nine

THEY ARRIVED IN A caravan, four vehicles in all.

Muniz led the way in his black Mercedes. His capangas were right behind it. Ferraz's black-and-white police sedan brought up the rear.

Muniz leapt to the ground and advanced on Pillar even before his car had come to a complete stop. A long-barreled .44 magnum revolver dangled from a holster on his right hip. He was carrying a 12-gauge pump-action shotgun.

The men he had with him grabbed their weapons, piled out of both vans, and formed a semi-circle behind him.

Hector reached under his jacket and wrapped his fingers around the grip of his Glock.

Muniz was so furious, and so intent on getting to Pillar, that he didn't even notice.

But one of his gunmen did, and tensed.

Silva addressed his nephew, speaking softly so that no one else could hear. "Don't draw that pistol. We're outgunned. Put your hands where that capanga can see them."

"He wouldn't dare—"

"He would. And then his friends will kill those reporters, Pillar, and me. Muniz will claim the league started it, and Ferraz will back him up. Do it."

Hector took his hand out from under his coat, but the capanga didn't take his eyes off him.

Muniz came to a stop, three meters from the group surrounding Pillar.

The journalists scurried back out of the way. A few of the league members did too, but only a few.

Pillar raised his hands to shoulder height.

Muniz pumped a round into the chamber of his shotgun.

"I'm sorry about your son," Pillar said, his voice even. "It's a heavy burden for any father."

"Don't give me that, you hypocritical, lying bastard. You made the biggest mistake of your life when you decided to tangle with me."

There was a screech of brakes. Vicenza and her crew piled out of their van, leaving the doors open and the engine running. The red light on the front of the camera was already blinking.

"No pictures," Ferraz said, extending his arms as if he was directing traffic.

Vicenza lifted her microphone, caught her breath and said, "You're looking at Colonel Ferraz of the São Paulo State Police, a man who evidently thinks he's still living in a dictatorship. Over his shoulder, and holding a shotgun, is Orlando Muniz."

The cameraman pushed a button, and the barrel of the zoom lens started to rotate, tightening the angle on Muniz.

"A few moments ago," Vicenza continued, "Senhor Muniz told us he's convinced that the Landless Workers' League is responsible for the death of his son. It appears he's decided to take the law into his own hands."

Pillar saw his chance. He raised his voice and started to talk, almost as if they'd rehearsed it. "The Landless Worker's League categorically denies any complicity in the death of Orlando Muniz Junior. None of us are armed. None of us want trouble."

"Well, you've got it anyway." It was Ferraz, his face crimson. "You're trespassing on private property. The owner of this fazenda, Senhor Muniz here, has the right to evict you. I authorize him to use force."

"Sorry, Colonel, you can't do that—"

"The hell I can't."

"—because we've got a restraining order," Pillar finished calmly. "We've petitioned the court. They've agreed to consider our case."

"Petitioned the—"

Muniz cut Ferraz off. "What court?" he said.

"A federal court and a federal judge," Father Angelo Monteiro said, stepping out of the crowd around Pillar. He held a smoking cigarette in his right hand and a document in the left.

Muniz lowered the shotgun, snatched the paper from the old priest, and stared at it. "Son of a bitch," he said, his eyes bulging as he absorbed the significance of what he was reading.

"No," Father Angelo said, "he isn't. That particular judge happens to be an honest man, unlike a certain local magistrate you have on your payroll."

Muniz ignored the priest and turned to Ferraz. "Can they do this?"

Ferraz opened his mouth, thought better of whatever he had planned to say and shut it again.

"May I see that?" Vicenza Pelosi took the paper from Muniz's unresisting hand and held it toward the camera. The cameraman adjusted his focus.

Muniz realized what was happening, snatched the paper back, and tore it to shreds.

"I got it," the cameraman said to Vicenza. "Sharp, but short. We'll have to freeze it."

Muniz started advancing toward him.

The cameraman stepped backward, zoomed out, refocused.

"Keep rolling, Beto," Vicenza said.

"Rolling," the cameraman confirmed, stopping when Muniz did.

Muniz, trembling with rage, spun around. He raised his shotgun and aimed it at the ground in front of Pillar. He shouted an epithet, but no one heard it. The blast of the weapon overpowered his voice. The hail of buckshot threw up a cloud of dust. Before it had settled, and while the report was still ringing in everyone's ears, he turned on his heel and walked back to his car.

Chapter Thirty

"SHE SAID SHE'S GOING to do *what?*" the director said, his voice loud and shrill.

Silva held the telephone away from his ear. "'Stick around for a few days while we catch the bad guys,' was the way she put it."

"*Ave Maria,*" the director said. "That's all we need. That woman is . . ." His voice trailed off. He apparently couldn't think of an adequate definition for Vicenza Pelosi. "She'll make us look like the Curbstone Cops," he finished lamely.

"Keystone Cops."

"Whatever."

"She didn't seem to like Muniz or Ferraz all that much," Silva said.

"Well, she wouldn't, would she? Her father was a union organizer or some such, and they killed him for it."

"She said her first report would be on the *Jornal de Noticias* at eight."

"Merda! I'm going to have to brief the minister. You got any *good* news?"

"Not yet."

Silva's boss grunted and did what he usually did when he was displeased. He hung up.

"You heard?" Silva asked his nephew.

Hector nodded. "He wasn't exactly whispering."

Arnaldo walked into the suite and caught Hector's last remark. "Who wasn't whispering?" he said.

"The director," Silva said glumly. "He just found out that Vicenza Pelosi is in town."

"No kidding? She's hot stuff." Arnaldo saw the expression on Silva's face and wiped the grin off his own.

Hector walked over to the little refrigerator and opened the door. "Who wants a beer?"

Silva shook his head. Arnaldo raised a hand.

"Glass?"

"Hell, no," he said to Hector. Then, turning to Silva: "I found Edson Souza's mother."

Silva had been studying the dust on his shoes. He looked up sharply. "And?" he said.

"And I could be wrong, but I think she knows where he is."

"Hector, give me one of those beers," Silva said.

"But she's not going to tell us. Thanks."

The last word was for Hector. Arnaldo popped the tab on the can.

"Why the hell not?" Silva said.

"Because she's got other kids, younger ones, and she's scared of Ferraz."

"She said that?"

Arnaldo took a swig of his beer and wiped his mouth with the back of his hand. "No," he said. "She didn't say it, but she is. The woman she worked for was a real bitch. She fired her for bringing a cop to the house."

"*Fired* her?"

Arnaldo nodded. "Right in front of me. I had a taxi waiting. I gave Marly—that's her name—a lift home. We talked. She told me Edson was earning money, but he wouldn't tell her how. Sometimes he'd sleep at her place. Mostly he didn't. She didn't say it, but I got the impression that he didn't like to see his mother being fucked by different people. She and the kids—there are three of them, two girls and a boy—all live in one room and sleep in the same bed, if you can call it a bed. Every now and then, she said, Edson would bring her a bag of groceries, sometimes presents for the little ones. One time, he even brought a television set."

"Stolen, probably."

"Marly says no. Says it was in a box with a guarantee and all. Says the kid swore he wasn't a thief."

"And she believes him?"

"Yeah. She does. Says he never lies to her."

Arnaldo gulped down the remainder of his beer, bent the can, and tossed it into a wastebasket. It landed with a clatter. "I've been giving it some thought," he said. "I've got a sister in Riberão. She works in one of those homes for battered women."

"So?"

"So, maybe she could take Marly and the kids. Ferraz'd never find them there. Once she's safe, maybe she'll open up."

"Worth a try," Silva said.

Arnaldo pulled out his address book and picked up the phone.

VICENZA PELOSI appeared, as promised, on the eight o'clock news and she spared no one.

She used the shot of Ferraz waving his arms and excoriated him for trying to deny to the public their "constitutionally guaranteed" right to the truth. She berated Orlando Muniz Senior for raising a private army of thugs and for threatening "physical violence to defend his property" instead of "availing himself of the recourse provided by law." She accused Luiz Pillar and Roberto Pereira of "demagoguery" and a "lack of respect for private property." She denounced Wilson Cunha, the local judge, for not implementing the appropriation of uncultivated land as "clearly prescribed in the Constitution of this country." She castigated the police— "both State and Federal"—for their lack of progress in solving the "brutal assassinations" of Dom Felipe Antunes, the journalist Diana Poli, and the landowner Orlando Muniz Junior. She took the President of the Republic and the Minister of Justice to task for not having taken preventive measures to defuse the "land wars that lie at the heart of all of the problems."

And she did it all in only three minutes and twenty seconds.

ABOUT A quarter of an hour after the broadcast ended there was a knock on the door of Silva's suite. Arnaldo opened it, and his jaw dropped.

It was Vicenza Pelosi.

She was fresh from the shower. Her long hair was tied up in a bun and held in place by oriental chopsticks. She came in smelling of freshly applied perfume, sat down without being asked, flashed her radiant smile, and ignored the fact that her host wasn't smiling back.

"I guess you didn't do that broadcast live," Silva said.

"No," she said. "Tape. Sit down, Chief Inspector. I have news."

Silva sat.

"Want a beer, Senhorita Pelosi?" Arnaldo said, recovering from his surprise.

"Or maybe a guaraná?" That was Hector.

Arnaldo was beaming. Hector was straightening his tie.

"A beer would be nice," Vicenza said.

Arnaldo and Hector bumped into each other on the way to the refrigerator.

"Muniz called me," she said to Silva.

"Did he?" Silva tried to sound uninterested. He didn't think it fooled her.

"Thanks," she said to Hector when he placed a beer on the coffee table in front of her. Arnaldo got a smile and a nod when he put a glass next to it. She opened the beer, poured it, and took a ladylike sip before she continued.

"Muniz," she said, "is offering a reward, a big one, for anyone who comes to him with information about who killed his son."

"How big is big?"

"A hundred thousand reais."

Silva sat back in his chair and frowned. "That's going to be a problem," he said.

"Yes, I know," she said.

A hundred thousand reais was more money than a landless man could earn in twenty years of working the soil. People would come forward for sure. Most of them would be telling lies that Orlando Muniz would be all too happy to believe.

"Muniz had it all worked out," she said. "He wanted to do it through me."

"Through you?"

"People trust me. He thought people would be more likely to come forward if I was the intermediary."

"What did you tell him?"

"I refused, but it didn't stop him. He had a backup. Says I can use the story on the midnight news if I choose to." She took another sip and seemed not to wet her lips. "He's asked me to come up to his suite and tape an interview."

"What are you going to do?"

"Go, of course. It's news, isn't it?"

"People are going to get killed, Vicenza. As soon as he gets information he finds credible, he'll turn loose his capangas."

"I suspect he will. That's why I thought you should know."

"Why didn't you just tell him you wouldn't do it?"

"Because it wouldn't change anything. He'd go to another network."

"Who's his backup? Who's going to be the intermediary?"

"A priest. Some guy called Gaspar Farias. He gets to tithe ten percent for the new church. The informer will clear ninety thousand."

"Jesus Christ," Silva said, "Doesn't that priest realize what he's doing?"

"Apparently not," she said. She put the glass down on the table and stood. So did Hector and Arnaldo. Silva didn't move.

"Sit down," he said.

"I have an interview to do."

"Please."

She sank back into her seat.

"I need your help," he said.

She picked up her glass and waited.

"There's a young man I have to get in touch with," Silva said. "He's gone into hiding. I want you to broadcast an appeal for him to turn himself in."

"Why?"

"I think he may know something about the death of the bishop."

"What?"

"I have no idea."

"Meaning that you really don't know, or that you won't tell me?

"I really don't know."

"Tell me more."

"Not now. It's a long story."

She put the glass back on the table.

"What do I get out of it?"

"A story, of course."

"What's this kid's name?"

"Edson Souza. He's a street kid."

"How did you—"

"I can't tell you anything else. Not yet."

"But you will?"

"Yes."

"And to me, exclusively."

"Yes."

She picked up her beer. This time, she drank off half the glass and left a mustache of foam on her upper lip. She took a paper handkerchief out of her purse and used it like a napkin.

"You've got a deal," she said.

"I TOLD you she was hot," Arnaldo said after he closed the door behind her.

Silva grunted.

Arnaldo pretended not to notice.

"Why didn't you tell her the rest of it, *chefe*? About Ferraz and all?"

"First of all," Silva said, "because I can't prove it. Second, because she'd start digging, and if Ferraz thinks she's digging, he'll kill her just like he killed Diana."

Arnaldo thought about that for a moment, then nodded. "You want another beer?" he asked.

Silva shook his head.

"You, Hector?"

Hector nodded. Arnaldo went to the refrigerator, fetched two cans, and handed one to Hector. "You made up your mind, then? You're sure Ferraz killed Diana?"

Silva nodded.

Hector took a long draught, wiped his mouth and said, "So how do we nab him?"

"We start by finding that kid," Silva said.

"You think Ferraz had anything to do with what happened to the bishop?" Hector asked.

"Do you?"

Hector thought about it. "No," he said at last. "How about

the murder of Muniz's kid? You believe Pillar when he says he didn't have anything to do with that?"

"Actually, I do," Silva said. "He's been doing his thing for years without killing anyone. Why should he start now?"

"Maybe because nobody ever nailed one of his people to a tree."

"Maybe. But they've done things just as bad. Don't forget, they've killed more than fifteen hundred of his compadres."

"But if it wasn't the league . . ."

"I didn't say it wasn't the league. I said I didn't think it was Pillar."

"Oh. So maybe that local guy, Pereira, and a few of his friends?"

"That would be my guess."

Hector tossed his empty beer can into the wastebasket. "So that gives us suspects for Diana and Muniz, but we're still no closer to the guy who killed the bishop."

"No, we're not."

"You think old man Muniz will try to kill Pillar?"

"He might, if he finds him, but Pillar's a wily old fox. My guess is that he'll make himself scarce."

"How about those people on Muniz's property?"

"That worries me more. There are women and kids there."

"So what's our next step?"

Silva looked at his watch.

"Too late for tonight, but first thing in the morning we're going to have a chat with that priest, Father Gaspar. I want to know what that telephone call from the bishop was all about."

Chapter Thirty-one

EUCLIDES, GASPAR'S MANSERVANT, WAS as welcoming as he'd been during Hector's previous visit.

"You again," he said, "Who's he?"

"I'm a chief inspector in the Federal Police," Silva answered for himself. "Who the hell are you?"

"We don't hold with profanity around here."

"And I don't hold with being kept waiting. Open the goddamned door."

For a moment, Euclides looked like he was going to slam it in Silva's face, but he didn't.

"I asked you who you are," Silva said, stepping over the threshold.

"Euclides Garcia. I work for Father Gaspar."

"Show me some ID."

"I haven't got any."

"You're required to have a national identity card."

"I mean I don't have it on me. I live here," Euclides said, defensively.

"Tell your boss we're waiting for him. Then go get it."

"Told you," Hector said, when Euclides had scurried off.

"Cheeky son of a bitch," Silva said. "What's that smell?"

"Lilac cologne," Hector said. "The good father drenches himself in the stuff."

FATHER GASPAR leaned over his desk to offer Hector a moist hand.

"Nice to see you again, Delegado."

He looked curiously at Silva.

Hector performed the introductions. The priest pronounced himself equally pleased to meet Silva and indicated the two cane chairs.

"Coffee?" he asked, resuming his seat.

"Thank you, no."

Hector had warned his uncle about Father Gaspar's coffee. Before they had a chance to initiate the questioning, Euclides returned with his identity card. He held it out to Silva, who passed it to Hector. Hector examined it, made a note of the number, and handed it back.

"Is there anything wrong?" Gaspar asked, puzzled.

"No," Silva said, deliberately addressing the master and ignoring the man. "He reminded me of someone, that's all. Apparently, I was mistaken."

"And to what do I owe the pleasure this time?" the priest asked when his servant had gone.

"That reward Muniz is offering," Silva said. "The hundred thousand reais?"

"Yes?"

"I'm told you've agreed to act as intermediary.

"Yes, Chief Inspector, that's right."

"Not a good idea."

The priest frowned. "Why not?"

"It's far too much money, Father. It's going to encourage people to lie. We want answers, too, but they have to be the right answers."

Gaspar started shaking his head.

Silva ignored it. "Muniz doesn't want justice, Padre, he wants revenge. He doesn't want the people who killed his son arrested. He wants them dead."

"Are you implying that he'd take the law into his own hands?"

"I am."

"Nonsense," Father Gaspar said.

"What makes you so certain?"

"Because we spoke about it. I enjoined him to put aside his bitterness. He assured me that he would. Orlando Muniz isn't after vengeance, only after justice. 'Vengeance is mine; I will repay, saith the Lord.' That's Romans, chapter twelve."

Silva was not in the mood for another scripture lesson. "Justice, hell. The man wants blood."

Father Gaspar held up his hand, signifying that he didn't buy into Silva's theory. "I pride myself on being a good judge of men," he said. "I'd be the first to admit that there've been rumors about him, but I'm convinced they're calumnies. Personally, I consider Orlando Muniz an exemplary Christian. He was a major contributor to the new church."

"That doesn't—"

Father Gaspar didn't let Silva finish. "And now, Senhor Muniz is offering the church ten thousand reais. All I have to do in return is perform a simple service. I'd be derelict in my duty if I didn't accede to his request."

"Listen to me, Father—"

"No, Chief Inspector, you listen to me. I have another reason to take issue with what you say. It obviously hasn't occurred to you that anyone bearing false witness would be violating the ninth commandment. That's a mortal sin. A perjurer puts his very soul in peril."

"Father—"

"I see we're unlikely to agree. Why don't we just drop the subject?"

"You're wrong."

"And you, of course, are entitled to your opinion."

Silence fell. Silva broke it first. "There's another matter: Have you heard of a young man, a street kid, named Edson Souza?"

"Edson Souza? No. Why?"

"I'm not at liberty to say. But I can tell you this: He placed a call to Dom Felipe. Immediately after they'd spoken, Dom Felipe placed a call to you."

"When was this?"

Silva looked at his nephew. Hector took out his notebook and read off the date and time.

Father Gaspar wrinkled his brow, checked his desk calendar and shook his head.

"If you could, perhaps, give me some inkling of the subject matter. . . ."

"I can't."

"Well, then . . ." Father Gaspar lifted his palms in a gesture of helplessness. "Do you have any reason to believe that . . . what was that young man's name again?"

"Edson Souza."

"That Edson Souza's telephone call to the bishop and the bishop's call to me are related?"

"I don't. But it's a possibility, and I'm exploring all the possibilities."

"Hmm. Sorry I can't help you.

Father Gaspar folded his hands over his ample belly and leaned back in his chair.

"During our first conversation," Hector said, changing tack, "you suggested that a priest might have been responsible for the bishop's murder."

"Yes."

"Father Francisco, the bishop's secretary, has another theory."

"Which is?"

"It might have been a landowner."

"A landowner?" Gaspar unclasped his hands and leaned forward. "A *landowner*? Why in the world would he say a thing like that?"

"Do you remember the last sermon Dom Felipe delivered in your old church?"

Gaspar nodded.

"'The Blood of the Wicked,' he called it. It concerned the murder of Azevedo, the league activist. He asked people to come forward. Not unlike what Orlando Muniz is doing, don't you agree?"

"No, Father, I don't agree. The bishop, to my knowledge, didn't mention money."

"Well, that's true. He didn't."

"I gather you disagree with Father Francisco."

"I most certainly do. The landowners of Cascatas are pillars of the community. None of them would stoop to violence."

"There's just one thing wrong with that argument, Father."

"What's that, Chief Inspector?"

"Judging by what happened to Azevedo, one of them already did."

WHEN FATHER Gaspar returned from escorting his guests to the door, Euclides was waiting for him.

"I don't like those guys," he said.

"But then, there aren't really many people that you *do* like, are there?" the priest said, sinking into his chair.

"I like you."

"Yes, my boy, I know you do. And I like you. You were, I suppose, up to your usual bad habits while those policemen were here?"

"If you mean was I listening at the door, then, yeah, I was."

"Good. So I don't have to explain. This Edson Souza? Who might he be?"

"He might be anybody. They've all got street names. I had one, too, remember?"

"Of course, I remember. But that's all behind you now. Let's see what the colonel can tell us."

He checked his watch.

"He should be in his office by now."

* * *

FERRAZ *was* in his office, and probably alone because he immediately took Gaspar's call. They exchanged pleasantries, then Father Gaspar asked, "Why do you suppose, Colonel, that the Federal Police are looking for a *menino de rua* named Edson Souza?"

"Who says they are?"

"Mario Silva does. He and that young delegado, Costa I think his name is, just paid me a visit."

"Yeah, Costa. He's Silva's nephew. Why do *you* care if they're looking for Pipoca?"

"Who?"

"Edson Souza. That's his street name. Pipoca. Why do you care?"

"Well . . . I thought I might be able to help."

"Take my advice, Father. Stay out of it. Let the Federal Police solve their own problems.

"Yes. Yes, I suppose you're right. No business of mine, after all."

"That's the attitude. Anything else I can do for you?"

"No. Nothing else. Thank you, Colonel."

"My pleasure."

Father Gaspar put the telephone back on its cradle and looked at Euclides. "It seems," he said, "as if the colonel knows the young man in question."

"He does, huh?"

"Yes, my boy, and so do we. It turns out that Edson Souza is the young man we know as Pipoca."

"Pipoca! Well, that explains a lot."

"It does, doesn't it? Something more: the colonel didn't actually say so, but he gave me the distinct impression that he's looking for him as well."

Euclides smiled. "Good," he said.

"Indeed. Let's hope he finds him before Silva does."

Chapter Thirty-two

SILVA COULD HEAR THE telephone ringing while he was still in the corridor. It stopped before he could get his key into the lock, then started again when he was closing the door to the suite.

"Finally," his caller said. "I must have called ten times."

Vicenza Pelosi.

"I should have asked you for the number of your cell phone," she said. "Hang on. Let me make a note of it right now."

And why shouldn't I give it to her? Silva thought, thinking of the director's admonition to keep the number confidential. *Everybody else seems to have it.*

"Okay, go ahead," she said.

He rattled off the digits, could hear her fumbling as she wrote them down. She was outside somewhere. There were traffic noises in the background.

"Good news," she said when the fumbling stopped. "The kid called."

Silva's hand tightened on the phone. "Edson Souza?"

"He wants to meet."

"Thanks, Vicenza. I'll take it from here. Where and when?"

"I'm not going to tell you."

"*What?*"

Vicenza started talking fast. "I know we've got a deal, and I know you gave me his name, but he doesn't want anyone else. Just me. Says he's scared but he's willing to talk."

"Vicenza, for God's sake, it's dangerous to be anywhere near that kid."

"Don't worry. I'll be careful."

"Vicenza—"

"No time to talk now, Chief Inspector. I'm almost there. I'll drop by your suite when I get back to the hotel."

"Vicenza, please listen—"

But she didn't. She hung up.

MAJOR OSMANI Palmas told the technician to rewind the tape and play it back. Then he told him to rewind it again, and picked up the telephone.

Ferraz answered on the first ring.

"The monitoring of the phone in Silva's suite paid off, Colonel," Palmas said without preamble. "Listen to this."

He put the handset next to the speaker and nodded to the technician.

When the playback ended, Palmas put the telephone back to his ear. "How about that?" he said.

"Where's she meeting the kid?"

"We don't know."

"Where is she now?"

"We don't know that either. Not at the hotel, that's for sure. You heard those traffic noises? She's on the street somewhere."

"She's staying at the same place Silva is, right?"

"Uh-huh. The Excelsior."

"Throw a cordon around it. Snatch her when she comes back. Don't let her get anywhere near those federal cops."

"And then?"

"And then bring her to the tobacco shed."

EDSON HAD told Vicenza to be on the northeast corner of Republic Square at four o'clock. Someone would come, pick her up, and take her to him.

In her blonde wig, dark glasses, and floppy hat she felt like a character out of a spy movie. Even disguised beyond recognition, she was still getting admiring glances from males.

Five minutes after the appointed hour, a battered Volkswagen taxi stopped directly in front of her. She waved him off, but the driver wouldn't take no for an answer. Ignoring the horns and catcalls from the traffic behind him, he climbed out and opened the door on the passenger side.

"I don't want a taxi," she said.

"You'll want this one, Senhorita Pelosi."

The driver was well above average height, with hair that had once been blond and intelligent brown eyes.

"I'm here to take you to Edson."

He didn't sound like any taxi driver she'd ever met. His elegant Portuguese bore a trace of a foreign accent.

"So who are you?" she asked, as they pulled away from the curb.

"I'll have to ask you to turn off your cell phone," he said. "It's been said they can be used to trace one's location."

No. Definitely not a taxi driver.

She took her phone out of her purse, switched it off, and leaned over to show him the blank screen. He reminded her of someone she'd seen somewhere before but she couldn't recall where or when.

And then she remembered. "Weren't you at the league encampment on the Muniz fazenda? Weren't you feeding a little girl with rickets?"

He glanced at her in the rearview mirror.

"I think you have me confused with someone else," he said. "We're going to follow a roundabout route. It will take some time to get where we're going. In the meantime, we're not supposed to talk."

"Who says so? Who says we're not supposed to talk?"

He didn't respond.

They drove into the countryside. He stopped at the top of

a hill where there was a view for kilometers in every direction. He must have been pleased with what he saw, or didn't see, because he gave a grunt of satisfaction, made a U-turn, and started back toward the city. Less than two kilometers later he came to a sudden stop and put the car into reverse. He'd missed the turnoff. It was a dirt road—not much more than a track, really—and almost obscured by vegetation. There was a sign, barely legible white paint on a wooden board: SEM SAIDA, it said. Dead end.

They drove through a little forest with tree trunks no thicker than her arm, and emerged into tobacco fields where leaves from the plants brushed both sides of the car as they passed. The track ended at a cylindrical structure, a standpipe or silo, with riveted metal walls and a domed roof. The driver stopped, got out, and opened her door.

"Edson will be along directly," he said, speaking for the first time in many minutes.

None of the tobacco plants in the neighboring fields were taller than knee-high. There was no trace of another human being.

"You'll be taking me back?" she asked, nervous now at the isolation.

He nodded. "But I can't stay here. This yellow car is too visible." He returned to the taxi and drove back the way he'd come, the wheels throwing up red dust. She watched the retreating vehicle until it vanished into the trees.

Behind her, someone cleared his throat.

Her heart skipped a beat. She put her hand to her breast and spun around.

"Don't be afraid," the young man said. He must have been hiding behind the tall metal cylinder.

Chapter Thirty-three

"THEY RAN THE ID from that guy who lives with the priest," Arnaldo said, handing Silva the printout of an e-mail he'd picked up at the hotel's reception desk.

"Euclides Garcia?" Silva asked, reaching for it.

"Yeah, him."

They were in Silva's suite, waiting for news from Vicenza.

"And?" Hector asked while Silva read.

"One minor charge for assault," Arnaldo said. "It happened during his army days."

"Compulsory military service?"

"Nope. Volunteer. Before that, he was a street kid. He used the military to get himself off the street, but once he was in he didn't like it. He took a swing at a superior officer. They gave him six months in the stockade and chucked him out. Other than that, nothing."

"Any news from your sister?"

"Yup. Marly and the kids are safe and sound in Riberão, and I was wrong. She really has no idea where Edson is. I talked to her by telephone."

"Too bad we haven't got a way to let the kid know his mother's safe," Silva said. "He knows that, he might come in."

"I've got the number of Vicenza's cell phone," Hector blurted out.

The two men turned to look at him.

"Really?" Silva said, raising an eyebrow. "Do you now?"

"I . . . I asked her for it. Just in case," Hector said, flushing.

"So call her."

Hector tried. But there was no response.

* * *

VICENZA PELOSI sensed that Edson was holding something back, but it didn't bother her overmuch. She had enough for a great story. All she had to do now was to figure out how to present it without getting the network sued for libel. She believed everything the kid had told her but he hadn't a shred of evidence to back him up. And then, to make it worse, he pricked her balloon.

"I'll say goodbye now," he said and pointed. "He'll take you back."

She heard the sound of an engine, turned, and saw the taxi appearing from among the trees.

"No, no, no," she said. "I need to get your story on tape. You have to come with me."

"With Ferraz out there?" The kid looked at her as if she had some kind of mental deficiency. "No way! I'll come in when he's locked up. Not before."

"A chief inspector from the Federal Police is in town. I'll get him to protect you."

The kid shook his head stubbornly. "It's not safe," he said.

"What if Ferraz finds you?"

"He won't. I've got friends."

"But . . . but without you there's no proof."

The kid met her eyes. "And *with* me, there's no proof. Just my word against his."

"No, it's not like that. It's—"

"It's *exactly* like that, Senhorita Pelosi. But now that I've clued you in on what's happening, all you need to do is to prove it."

He made it sound easy.

"Edson, listen to me. I'm a reporter, not a cop. It's the cops who have to get the proof, and you have to help."

"I already helped. I called *you* didn't I? You'd better leave now. Your car's here."

"But—"

"No, Senhorita Pelosi, I'm sorry, but if Ferraz gets his hands on me, he's gonna kill me."

The kid turned his back on her and started walking away.

"How will I get in touch with you?"

He stopped and turned around. "Like you did before. On television. From here on in, I'm going to watch all your broadcasts."

Behind her, she heard the sound of the taxi's door being opened.

ON THE drive back to town she applied all her skills to extract something from the driver. She got no response. Not a shake of the head. Not a smile. Nothing.

As they turned into Republic Square, she gave it one more try. "You must be one of those friends Edson was telling me about."

"There's a taxi stand over there on the Rua Garibaldi," he said, giving the first sign that he hadn't suddenly become a deaf mute.

"Why don't you just bring me to my hotel?" she said, trying to get more time to work on him.

He shook his head and pulled over to the curb.

The registration number, she thought as he pulled away. *I'll make a note of it. Silva can trace it.*

But he'd thought of that, too.

The rear end of the taxi had been liberally smeared with mud. The license plate was completely illegible.

Chapter Thirty-four

COLONEL FERRAZ'S PRIVATE LINE rang a little before six.

"That you, Palmas?"

"Yes, Colonel. Mission accomplished."

Ferraz grinned.

"I'm on my way."

The colonel hung up, took his holster from the hook on the wall and went out to his car. His driver opened the rear door, but Ferraz shook his head.

"I'll drive myself. Get a patrol car to take you home."

"*As ordens, Coronel.*"

Corporal Sanches showed no sign of surprise. It was a badly kept secret that the boss had frequent romantic engagements with a certain married lady of the town. On those nights, he drove himself.

FERRAZ'S TOBACCO shed was more than a kilometer from the main road, well removed from the other buildings on his fazenda.

The colonel no longer grew tobacco; he'd switched over to sugarcane. So the building was seldom visited. It was an oblong, wooden structure with a peaked roof and a fading coat of white paint.

Darkness had fallen by the time Ferraz arrived. His headlights illuminated the figure of his deputy, a dark silhouette against the white wall. Palmas stood with his hands on his hips and stared into the glare.

Ferraz didn't waste any time with pleasantries. "How did you nail her?"

"Stroke of luck, really," Palmas said, somehow managing

to convey that it wasn't luck at all. "One of the guys I posted saw her get out of a taxi on Republic Square. He called me, and then followed her over to the Rua Garibaldi. I got there in three minutes flat, just in time to see her get into another taxi. I flashed my badge, waved the driver down, and told him to come here."

"Where's the cab?"

Palmas shot a thumb over his shoulder. The double doors behind him were wide enough to admit a truck.

"Inside."

"The driver?"

"Taken care of. Watching me do it scared the shit out of her. You'll find her less bossy than usual."

"You question her?"

"Not yet. Waiting for you."

"Good. Let's see what the bitch has to say."

REDE MUNDO led the eight o'clock news with the story of Vicenza's disappearance. Silva's cell phone rang at seven minutes past 8:00, while the program was still underway.

"Hello. Who's this?"

"Who the hell do you think it is?" the director said. "Is this our private hotline, or not?"

"It's supposed to be, but—"

"Mario, if anything has happened to that woman, so help me God—"

"I assume, Director, that you're referring to Vicenza Pelosi."

"You're goddamned right I am! Did you hear what they said?" The director didn't wait for an answer. "They said she was involved in 'research that could have led to a solution of at least one of the murders.' She goes off to a so-called 'secret meeting' and poof, she's gone."

Poof? Silva thought, but he didn't interrupt.

"How come *you* didn't get the information she got? How come *you* weren't off to a 'secret meeting'? Do you have any idea, any idea at all, how this is going to look? First it was the bishop, then the son of one of this country's most prominent citizens, then the daughter of a press mogul, and now it's the country's leading telejournalist. For Christ's sake, Mario, when is it going to stop?"

"She was acting, Director, on information that I—"

"I don't want to hear it. You're always trying to bog me down in details. That's not my job. My job's the larger picture. What am I supposed to do now?"

Silva was tempted to suggest that Sampaio perform an anatomical impossibility.

But he didn't.

THE INSIDE of Ferraz's shed smelled of old tobacco leaves and fresh blood. The leaves themselves were long gone, but the blood was very much in evidence. It streaked Vicenza's naked body, stained the upright wooden chair they'd bound her to, and pooled on the dirt floor around her feet. There were drops of it on Palmas's uniform and traces of it on Ferraz's still naked torso.

The last few hours had started out with some fun for the two cops, but had, by now, degenerated into something else. The rape was fun. What they'd done with the pliers and the icepick had been fun, but she'd pretty much given up after that. It wasn't fun at all when she didn't resist, wasn't fun at all when the fear in her eyes turned to resolution and acceptance. And now it had become work. She was repeatedly passing out, and they had to keep throwing buckets of water in her face to make her come around.

I could use some of that water myself, Ferraz thought. It was hot in the shed. Perspiration had soaked his hair and was rolling down his face.

Palmas was feeling it, too. He had sweat stains on his chest and under his arms, darker gray against the gray of his uniform.

"I think that's it, Colonel. She's done."

His deputy lifted Vicenza's chin and looked at her face. Her eyes were closed. He pried one lid open, snorted, and went to fill the bucket.

Ferraz thought about it while he was gone. Palmas was right. She was done. There was nothing left to get out of her.

Palmas came back with the bucket and threw the contents into her face. The water wasn't cold. It was lukewarm, but it did the job. Ferraz waited until she blinked, then he said, "Finish her."

Palmas pulled his knife out of its scabbard and showed it to her. Her eyes were dull and listless.

"She doesn't even give a shit anymore," Palmas said, and casually cut her throat from ear to ear. He didn't seem to enjoy the act as much as he usually did. He was obviously tired from lugging all that water.

She started to bleed out. Even then she didn't react, just kicked out with one of her feet. It was more of a spasm than a conscious movement. Air bubbles appeared around the wound in her throat and frothed down her neck. For a while, the two of them watched her dispassionately. Then Palmas went over and picked up Vicenza's discarded panties. He'd laughed when he'd seen them for the first time. They were of white cotton, stamped with little brown teddy bears. He started using them to clean his knife.

"What do you think we should do about the kid?" Ferraz asked.

Palmas looked mildly surprised. The colonel seldom asked for advice.

"I don't think we have to do anything," he said. "One of his little friends will turn him in sooner or later."

Ferraz shook his head. "I don't like loose ends," he said.

"How about I have another chat with his mother? Maybe put a couple of guys to watch her house?"

"Good idea. Do it."

"How about her?" Palmas pointed at Vicenza's body. "You want me to bury her?"

"Not good enough. She's too well known."

"So?"

"So we've got to take the heat off and to do that we've got to blame somebody else. Finish cleaning the handle of that knife, stick the blade into her a couple of times to pick up some more of her blood, and we'll go harvest some finger-prints."

"Where?"

"Where do you think?"

"You want to use the team?"

"Yeah. And tell them to bring their hoods."

Chapter Thirty-five

CLEMENTINA FONSECA WAS THE most precocious and the most promiscuous of Eduardo and Nilda Fonseca's three daughters. If she hadn't been precocious she wouldn't have been interested in boys at all. If she hadn't been promiscuous she wouldn't have been lying out there on the bare ground with her panties off and with one hand wrapped around Rolando Pereira's cock.

Clementina was only two months past her twelfth birthday, narrow-hipped, small breasted and possessed of a flat posterior. If her charms had ended there, Rolando might not have given her a second look, but God had given Clementina other attributes to make up for what she lacked in voluptuousness. She had high cheekbones, café au lait skin, bee-stung lips, a small but exquisite nose, and the largest and most lustrous brown eyes that Rolando had ever seen.

Her charms saved his life.

They were lying in a field, some one hundred meters from the nearest tent, when Rolando heard the engine noises. Seconds later, there was a screech of tires followed by a spatter of gravel.

He disengaged himself from Clementina and looked anxiously toward his father's tent. Someone inside lit a lantern. Car doors slammed. Voices shouted obscenities. Armed and hooded men were spilling out of a van.

"My dress," Clementina said, in a whine Rolando hadn't heard before and didn't particularly like. "Where is it?"

He felt around in the dark, located the dress, and handed

it to her. Then he started pulling up his pants. If the men had arrived just a minute later he would have had an easier time fitting into them.

The men had powerful flashlights. They were walking from tent to tent, using machetes to cut the plastic sheeting, shining the beams inside, obviously looking for someone.

There was a shot and a woman's scream. Clementina got up to run, but he grabbed her by the ankle and pulled her down.

"Let me go," she said in a loud whisper. "I have to get home before my father finds out."

"Too late. Everyone's up, but they've all got their hands full. Let's just hope nobody notices we're gone."

Another shot. More screams.

"What is it?" she said. "Who are they?"

"The rancher's capangas," Rolando said, "come to run us off."

"Ai, meu Deus!" She wasn't whispering anymore.

Clementina's father had only recently joined the league, but Rolando, despite his tender years, was an old hand at this. His father, Roberto, was the head of the whole encampment, the leader of the league in all of Cascatas, the best friend of the now-legendary Aurelio Azevedo.

Clementina lifted her head to look. He pushed her nose back down into the dirt. "Don't move," he said, but he snuck a look himself. He was just in time to see his father come out of their tent. One of the attackers shone a light in his face and, recognizing him, called out to the others.

They gathered around him like a pack of mad dogs. He tried to throw a punch, but they overpowered him and forced him to his knees. Two men held him fast by the arms while others went into the tent and returned with Rolando's mother and his little sister, Lourdes.

"Where's the boy?" he heard one of them say.

Boy? That was him! They were looking for him!

"He's not in the tent, Senhor," one of the hooded figures said.

"Merda. All right, let's get it over with." The man who'd been called senhor had a voice hoarse from shouting. He was obviously the leader.

"Right," the figure holding Roland's sister said. He pulled out a knife and drew it across Lourdes's throat. She was so surprised she didn't even scream.

But his mother did: A long drawn-out wail of anguish, cut short by the blast of a shotgun.

They shot his father last, first in each kneecap, then in the abdomen and finally in the head, using a pistol for all four shots. His father didn't say a word, didn't beg them for mercy, didn't even cry out.

And yet all the time it was happening, Rolando heard his father's voice, coming to him from somewhere within his own head. *Keep quiet, Rolando. Too late for me, boy. Don't give them a chance at you. Don't die for nothing. Come back when you're older. Avenge me.*

The man who'd shot his father was wearing gloves. He bent over the body, pressed something shiny into his father's hand and took it away again.

The other people in the encampment were scattering in all directions, some of them toward the road, others dispersing into the neighboring fields. One group was coming directly toward Clementina and him.

She recognized her parents and both of her sisters. Before he could stop her, Clementina was on her feet and running to meet them.

A second later the hooded figures opened up with automatic weapons, spraying bullets into the dark. Rolando heard shots fly over his head like angry bees, heard one of them strike Clementina with a sound like the one his mother used to make when she beat a rug. Clementina staggered, turned, and looked back toward him. Her eyes were wide, the front of her pink dress dark with blood. He saw her lips move and thought she spoke his name. But he couldn't be sure. He couldn't be sure of anything except the chattering of the guns.

Chapter Thirty-six

THE CLOCK RADIO NEXT to Silva's hotel bed went off at three minutes past 8:00 in the morning. The voice that faded-in was a man's, and he was reading the news.

> . . . as yet unconfirmed number of dead and injured. The owner of the fazenda, Orlando Muniz, has been unavailable for comment, but a spokesman for the landowner denied any involvement in the massacre. Meanwhile, Emerson Ferraz, local Commandant of the State Police, had this to say . . .

Silva turned up the volume on the colonel's gravelly voice.

> Some people are saying that Orlando Muniz is responsible for this outrage. It might seem to many to be a logical conclusion to draw after what they saw on TV the other night. But anyone who does would be wrong. You have to evaluate Senhor Muniz's previous actions in the context of the situation at the time. He'd just been exposed to the body of his murdered son and he was, understandably, very upset. Now he's had time to consider and I can assure you—

Outrage. Logical conclusion. Evaluate. Context. The voice was Ferraz's, but the words weren't. The colonel made that doubly obvious by stumbling over some of them.

Silva shot out of his bedroom, crossed the suite's living area, and opened Hector's door.

"Hector?"

Hector opened his sleepy eyes and blinked.

"Get up. Ferraz was just on the radio. There's been some kind of a massacre on Muniz's fazenda."

Hector threw off the covers and got out of bed.

"And the son of a bitch didn't call us?"

Silva didn't bother to respond to that.

"Call Arnaldo," he said. "We're all going up to see Muniz."

LESS THAN TEN minutes later, Arnaldo was pounding his meaty fist against the door of suite 900.

There was no reply.

He pounded again.

A chambermaid came out of a linen closet at the end of the hall.

"Bom dia, senhores. Are you looking for Senhor Muniz?"

"We are," Silva said.

"He checked out."

"Checked out? Where's he gone?"

"I don't know, senhor. All I know is he didn't leave a tip."

THE CLERK at the front desk, the one who had Indian blood, was more helpful:

"He moved out to his fazenda, senhores. Said something about repairs being completed."

Hector and Silva went for coffee while Arnaldo fetched the car.

THEY ARRIVED to a beehive of activity. Dr. Ishikawa was squatting next to the body of a young girl. Two state cops were wandering around gathering up cartridge casings and putting them into plastic evidence bags. Father Brouwer, surrounded by a small group of adults of both sexes, was talking to an adolescent male. Ferraz was nowhere in sight.

Arnaldo and Hector each chose one of the cops. Silva walked over to Ishikawa.

"Doctor."

Ishikawa looked up and rose to his feet.

"How many?" Silva said.

"Ten. Six men. Two women. Two girls, one twelve, one nine. Three of them were from the same family, a father, a mother, and their daughter. She was the nine-year-old."

"Nine years old? *Nine?* That one had to be an accident."

"No. They cut her throat."

"Cut her—"

"Her father was the leader."

"Pereira? Roberto Pereira?"

"Yes. Him."

"Killed the whole family?"

"Not quite. The Pereiras also had a son. Fourteen. That boy over there, the one talking to the priest."

THE STATE policemen were no help. Ferraz had come and gone, and they didn't expect him back. The senior man was Menezes, the fat sergeant they'd met on the day Junior's body had been discovered, the one with the lisp.

"You woulda thought they'd have posted guards."

Posted came out like *pothded*, guards with a long sibilant "s."

"Could anybody identify the shooters?" Silva asked.

"Nah. They were all wearing hoods. Nobody has a clue."

Father Brouwer joined them just in time to hear the sergeant's response. "No clue? What do you mean 'no clue,' you fat fool? It was Muniz and those capangas of his. It had to be. Who else would have a motive?"

The sergeant didn't like the "fat fool" remark one bit. "Who the hell's talking to you?" he said. And then, to Silva, "Colonel thinks Muniz would never be that stupid. He's the first person everybody would suspect, right?"

"And so your colonel's conclusion is that Muniz wouldn't do it, just because everybody would suspect that he did?" Father Brouwer interjected.

"Colonel talked to him," the sergeant said, still addressing Silva. "He's got an alibi. Witnesses."

"What? Who?"

"I don't have to talk to you, Padre. Get lost."

"But you *do* have to talk to me," Silva said. "Answer the priest's questions."

The sergeant tried to stare him down, and lost. "Muniz was sleeping when it happened," he said, truculently. "He was in his bedroom. His bodyguards were at the door and all around the house. They're his witnesses."

"And the witnesses didn't hear any shooting down here? For the love of God—"

"Leave it to me, Father," Silva said. Then, to the sergeant, "It's less than a kilometer from here to the house."

"So?"

"And you're saying nobody heard a thing?"

"Uh-huh."

The sergeant looked from one to the other, not offering anything more. Silva turned on his heel and started walking toward their car. Arnaldo, Hector, and Father Brouwer tagged along behind. Silva didn't object when the priest climbed into the back seat.

"The house, right?" Arnaldo asked, starting the engine.

"Right," Silva said and turned around to address Brouwer. "I saw you talking to the boy."

Brouwer nodded. "He saw it all. He was in a nearby field, talking with his girlfriend. She's dead. Twelve years old. He blames himself for not holding her down. A stray bullet took her."

"What did he see?"

"As that fat idiot back there just told you, the men were hooded. They arrived in a van. No markings. No license plate. They had flashlights; cut into the tents with machetes;

were obviously looking for Pereira and his family. When they found them, they cut the little girl's throat."

"Did you see her body?"

"Yes."

"Did the wound look like the one that killed Diana Poli?"

The priest reflected for a moment. "As a matter of fact, it did. It looked exactly like that."

"All right. Go on."

"Then they killed his mother with a shotgun. The father was last. They did it with a pistol. His kneecaps, his stomach, his head." As Brouwer described Pereira's wounds, he illustrated by pointing to the appropriate parts of his own anatomy. "They wanted him to suffer."

"And the boy saw it all?"

"Everything. After they killed his family, the man who'd cut his sister's throat leaned over and did something with his father's hand."

"Did *what* with his father's hand?"

"The boy has no idea. He just saw one of them bend over with something shiny. Later he looked, but there was nothing there and no wound."

"I'll want to talk to him."

"I was sure you would. I doubt he has anything useful to add."

"The voices? Anyone have an accent? A speech defect?"

"No. I asked."

"Clothing?"

"It was too dark. The hoods looked like they were made of jute. You know, like coffee sacks."

Arnaldo rolled to a stop in front of the fazenda's main house. The new door was still unpainted. Two capangas, cradling shotguns, were seated in chairs on the veranda. Both stood when Silva got out of the car.

"Here to see the boss?" one asked. It was the one who'd stopped to speak to them on the hillside.

"Yes," Silva said. "Tell him."

The capanga turned and knocked. The door opened a crack. Words were exchanged. The door shut again. "They're letting him know you're here," the capanga said.

Thirty seconds later Silva heard the chain being slipped.

Inside, a man with a thick neck and biceps the size of Hector's thighs led them through the house and into the living room. Despite the heat outside, there was a roaring fire in the fireplace. Air conditioning kept the temperature so low that Muniz was actually wearing a sweater.

Their host didn't offer a hand or a smile. "You're not welcome here, priest," he said to Father Brouwer. "Go get your people off my property."

Silva opened his mouth to speak, but the priest beat him to it. "You've sown the wind, you fool, and now you're going to reap the whirlwind."

"You dare to threaten me? Get out!"

"It's not a threat, you bastard, it's a prom—"

"Shut up, Father," Silva said.

The priest turned furious eyes on Silva. Silva ignored him.

"Did you have anything to do with what happened down there?" Silva pointed in the direction of the encampment.

"No," Muniz said. "but I'm not sorry it happened."

"Two little girls died, Senhor Muniz. One of them was only nine."

"What's that got to do with me? Their damned fool parents shouldn't have brought them here in the first place. It was their fault, not mine."

"The other little girl was twelve."

"Why don't you get out of here, too, Silva? And take these other assholes with you."

Arnaldo grunted, but he didn't move. Hector took a step forward, but Silva closed a hand around his arm.

"All right, Senhor Muniz. You're within your rights. Let's go, senhores."

"That's it?" Brouwer sputtered. "You're just going to leave?"

"That's right, Padre. We're just going to leave. And so are you. Come on."

Silva released his nephew, took Brouwer's elbow, and turned him toward the door. The priest looked back over his shoulder and shot a vengeful glance in Muniz's direction.

But he went.

FERRAZ HAD left the matter of disposing of the two bodies until after his murderous visit to the league encampment.

Vicenza wound up in a culvert. They left the driver in his cab, his empty wallet beside him, as if another robbery had ended in murder.

It was almost 7:00 in the morning when the colonel got home. He'd still had to respond to the voice mail messages left while he'd been "asleep," change into a fresh uniform, and put in an appearance at the encampment. He'd called his media spokeswoman, explained how he wanted to spin it, told her to work up a statement, and picked it up on way.

It was past 10:00 when he was finally able to put his head on a pillow, so he was not at all pleased when his telephone rang at quarter to 11:00.

After the clear instructions he'd left with his secretary, no one at the office would have dared to disturb him. It had to be one of those pain-in-the-ass federal cops. But it wasn't. It was Orlando Muniz, and he, unlike the colonel, was in a very good mood.

"Hello, Colonel. How are you this morning?"

Ferraz swallowed his bile. "Just fine, Senhor Muniz. You?"

"I'm calling to commend you for a job of law enforcement well done."

"Uhh, what job is that?"

"The way you handled those trespassers."

"Sorry, Senhor Muniz. I don't know what you're talking about."

"No, Colonel, of course you don't."

There was a significant moment of silence. Then Muniz said, "I've just had some visitors. Those federal policemen that you're getting to know so well—"

"Fucking assholes."

"Yes. And someone else, too. That radical priest."

"The young one or the old bastard?"

"The younger one."

"Brouwer?"

"That's him. Brouwer. He threatened me, Colonel. I think it would behoove us both to keep a sharp eye on the son of a bitch."

Behoove? What kind of a word is that?

"I've known Brouwer for a long time, Senhor Muniz. A *very* long time. He's got guts, but he's harmless. He wouldn't hurt a fly."

"No? So much the better for him, then. If he tries anything with me, I'll kill him. You sound tired. A busy night?"

"I had a stomach bug that kept me up."

"Really?"

"Yeah. Really."

"You've got to be careful with stomach bugs, Colonel. They can be dangerous. I've heard they can even kill people."

Muniz was still laughing when he hung up.

Chapter Thirty-seven

A KID BY THE NAME of Bento Alves, the son of a tractor salesman, found Vicenza's body.

Ferraz called Silva to tell him about it. "He stuffed her in a culvert that runs under the road to Miracema," the colonel said in a matter-of-fact voice.

"What makes you so sure the murderer was a 'he'?"

"I'm getting to that. She could have been there forever, or at least until the rains came and they started looking for the blockage. As it is, we got lucky. The kid's dog was attracted by the smell, went in there to sniff around and, when the dog wouldn't come out, the kid went in after him. It's a real mess, the corpse is. Scared the shit out of the kid."

"When was this?"

"A little after four."

Silva looked at his watch. "That was more than three hours ago. And you're only telling me now?"

"That's right. I'm only telling you now. It's really none of your fucking business, and I'm only doing it out of professional courtesy. You want to hear the story, or not?"

"Cause of death?" Silva asked. He was damned if he was going to give Ferraz the satisfaction of provoking him into losing his temper.

There was a pause. Ferraz was taking his time in the telling, relishing every second of it. Silva heard the clink of ice cubes on the other end of the line, then the satisfied smack of the colonel's lips.

"Somebody cut her throat," he said at last. "Just like those two dykes."

"And just like Pereira's nine-year-old daughter."

"Yeah. Funny you should mention that. Ironic, huh?"

Silva was surprised to hear Ferraz use the word, surprised that he even knew what it meant. "What do you mean by 'ironic'?"

"We found a knife next to the body. Ishikawa says it's probably the murder weapon, and guess whose fingerprints are all over it?"

YOUNG BENTO Alves, the lad who'd discovered Vicenza's corpse, was good-looking and, for an eleven-year-old, eloquent, so he got to tell his story on the eight o'clock news. Even his dog, Snoopy, had a few seconds of fame and dutifully contributed a bark.

Then it was Ferraz's turn. Preliminary examination, he said, suggested that the victim had been raped. He related the discovery of the knife and revealed that Roberto Pereira's fingerprints had been found on the handle. He concluded that Pereira had committed a sexual assault on the reporter, then murdered her to conceal his crime. When he'd finished speaking, a solemn-faced news anchor headlined the next story, some kind of political flap in Brasilia, and promised to be right back after the commercial break.

Silva picked up his cell phone and waited for it to ring, which it did, seconds later. "Well, that's one down, no thanks to you or your people," the director said, getting stuck into it immediately.

"He didn't do it," Silva said.

"What?"

"Roberto Pereira didn't kill Vicenza Pelosi."

"What makes you so damned sure?"

"For one thing, Pereira's nine-year-old daughter was killed in precisely the same way. Her throat was slit from ear to ear, just like Vicenza's. It's like a signature. The same person killed them both."

There was a stunned silence from Brasilia. Silva waited it out. Finally, the director said, "Maybe he did his own daughter to protect her from being raped."

"No, Director. He didn't.

"All right. All right. So if Pereira didn't kill Vicenza, who did?"

"I'm working on that, Director."

"Not fast enough to suit me. Remember that goddamned Nazi? That whatshisname? The one they call the 'law-and-order deputado'?"

"Domingos Logullo?"

"Domingos Logullo," Silva heard the director snap his fingers. "That's him. He brought the whole business up not two hours ago in the Chamber of Deputies. Now it's a game of political *futebol* and the opposing team is scoring points off of us like crazy." The director was in rare form. He went on for another five minutes, made the usual blustering noises, and terminated the conversation as abruptly as ever by slamming down the receiver.

Silva stuck his forefinger into his ear, massaged the lobe, and swore that he wouldn't take another telephone call that night. But he reversed himself, some three hours later, when Hector told him it was Luis Pillar, calling from Brasilia.

"I just heard Ferraz is telling people Roberto Pereira killed Vicenza Pelosi. That's a bucket of shit."

"I'm inclined to agree with you."

That brought Pillar up short. After a moment of silence he said, "You are?"

"I am."

"Why?"

"I don't want to talk on this line. Call me back on my cell phone."

"Okay. Give me the number."

Silva did. Pillar called back immediately.

"I'm not used to having cops agree with me," he said.

"Well, this one does. Why are you so sure your friend Pereira didn't do it?"

Pillar paused, thinking about it, then said, "Look, Roberto wasn't an angel, okay? Maybe he did some bad things in his life—"

"Like killing Muniz's son?"

Another pause.

"Maybe. I'm not sure, but maybe. I talked to him before I left for Brasilia. He didn't actually admit to it, but . . ."

"But what?"

"Well, frankly, I didn't give him a chance to. When he touched on the subject, I told him I really didn't want to know."

"So you think he did?"

"No, I think he might have, but I know for a fact that he wouldn't have raped and killed Vicenza Pelosi. He was a good family man, loved his wife, had two kids he adored. Not in a million years would he do a thing like that. And besides . . ."

"Besides what?"

"Vicenza Pelosi was one of the few friends we've got. He liked her. We all did. What do you know that I don't?"

"One more question. Who, other than Orlando Muniz, would have an interest in raiding your encampment?"

"Nobody. There's no doubt in my mind that the murdering bastard is responsible for the massacre. Him and his goddamned capangas."

"I don't think so."

"What? Why?"

"I'm going to tell you why, but I want you to keep it confidential. Will you do that?"

"You have my word. Anyone who really knows me will tell you it's good."

"All right, then, listen: Rolando Pereira, Roberto's son, witnessed the murder of his father. I interviewed the boy. He saw one of the murderers grab Roberto's wrist and do something with his hand. It's my belief that what he saw was someone imprinting Roberto's fingerprints on the murder weapon."

"Jesus Christ. Can you prove it?"

"No, I can't prove it. Now, think about it. What advantage would Muniz derive from murdering Vicenza Pelosi and going to all that trouble to blame the murder on Roberto Pereira?"

"Maybe to discredit him?"

"Why discredit him at all? All Muniz wanted to do was to get rid of him."

"Hmm."

"So that leads me to believe that what was made to look like an attack by Muniz and his capangas was, in reality, something else."

"Which was?"

"An attempt to lay blame for the death of Vicenza."

"I see. Go on."

"So then I have to ask myself who would have had a reason to kill Vicenza and blame it on Muniz?"

"And you think you know?"

"Ah, yes, Senhor Pillar. I think I know. But I can't prove it."

"Who?"

Silva considered for a moment, and then decided to trust him.

"Colonel Emerson Ferraz."

"Why?"

"Because he's involved in some dirty business and Vicenza Pelosi found out about it."

"How?"

"By interviewing a street kid."

"That whatshisname? Edson? The one she mentioned a couple of times in her broadcasts? The one she asked to contact her?"

"Him. He *did* contact her. They spoke. Immediately after that, she was murdered."

There was a long silence on the other end of the line.

"Senhor Pillar? Are you there?"

"I'm here. So why trust me with all this?" Pillar asked suspiciously.

"Because I want your help. We've got no friends in this town, but you do, and I need to find that kid before Ferraz does."

Another silence, and then, "All right, Chief Inspector, I'll do what I can. What's that boy's full name?"

"Souza. Edson Souza. And I don't want it known *why* we're looking for him. All the rest of what I've just told you is confidential."

"Understood. You think Ferraz killed Diana Poli too? Her and that girlfriend of hers?"

"Yes, I do."

"The son of a bitch. If ever anybody deserved killing, it's him."

"There's no death penalty in this country, Senhor Pillar."

"For people like him, there should be."

This time it was Silva who remained silent.

Chapter Thirty-eight

SILVA REMAINED CONVINCED THAT Father Brouwer knew more than he was telling. After breakfast the next morning, he decided to pay him a surprise visit. They drove to the cottage, arriving a little after nine o'clock.

Methuselah was on the front porch with his head between his paws. When he saw them coming, he rose painfully to his feet and started to whine.

Arnaldo bent over to scratch his neck. The dog nuzzled his leg but the whining didn't stop.

Hector rapped on the doorjamb, got no response, and opened the screen door.

The dog brushed by him, went to the naked body on the living room floor and began to lick at the blood that had pooled from a massive wound in the corpse's neck.

Silva knelt down for a closer look. Arnaldo picked up the phone and started dialing. Hector took Methuselah by his collar and dragged him outside.

Father Brouwer's eyelids and genitals, and the soles of his feet, showed circular burns, some mere blisters, others much worse. In some cases, the flesh was actually charred.

"Too big for cigarettes," Hector said, coming back and squatting down next to his uncle.

"Yes," Silva agreed. "Cigars."

Arnaldo had the telephone against his ear. He put his hand over the mouthpiece and opened his mouth to say something, then dropped it again and spoke into the phone. "This is Agente Arnaldo Nunes, Federal Police. I'm calling to report a murder."

There was a squeak of hinges. All three cops turned to look. Father Angelo was standing in the doorway, his eyes fixed on his old friend's body.

Methuselah pushed past him and made a beeline for the blood, his tongue hanging out.

Hector headed the dog off and put him back on the porch.

Father Angelo walked forward until he reached the corpse and then dropped to his knees, as if he'd reached an altar.

For a while, no one spoke. Silva became aware of the distant chatter of a cicada, punctuated by the faint whining of the dog. He let a decent interval pass, and then cleared his throat.

"Father?"

The priest didn't answer.

"Father Angelo?"

The old man raised his head and spat out a single word. "Ferraz."

"Move away from him, Father," Silva said. "There might be some trace evidence. We don't want to contaminate it."

Father Angelo got slowly to his feet, turned, and took two steps toward them. There were tears in his eyes. "A lifetime of service," he said, "and this is the way he ends up. I should have . . ."

"Should have what?"

"Nothing, Chief Inspector, nothing. You must have questions for me. Go ahead and ask them."

"Thank you, Father. Did you spend the night at home?"

"No. I spent the night at the league encampment. Ever since the massacre, Anton—" His voice caught in his throat. He cleared it and repeated the name, "Anton and I have been alternating, each of us staying there for twelve hours at a time."

"When was the last time you saw him?"

"At around nine, last night. We always made it a point to

have breakfast and dinner together. He came home, we dined, and I left." He shook his head as if to clear it, looked again at the body, ran a hand over his bald spot.

"I always try to search for a meaning in things," he said, "but this . . ."

His shook his head.

"You mentioned Ferraz," Silva said.

The priest nodded. "Anton Brouwer, was my closest friend, Chief Inspector. We had no secrets from each other. I know about Ferraz's activities, and I know about the conversation Anton had with you. Look at those burns. Look how he was killed. Tell me frankly, do you really believe that someone else could have done this?"

"No, Father, I don't, but we have no proof, and without that . . ."

"Yes. I know. I know."

"Do you have any idea what Ferraz might have been trying to learn?"

The old priest reached for his cigarettes, put one into his mouth, and lit it. "Do you?" he said.

"My guess is that Ferraz was trying to find Edson Souza. He probably thought your friend knew where he was hiding."

"Perhaps. But if that was it, Anton didn't tell them."

"No?"

The old priest took another drag on his cigarette and reflexively looked around for a place to tip the ash. His gaze swept past, then returned to, the body of his dead companion. He sighed and flicked the ash directly onto the floor.

"No," he said. "Because, if Anton had cracked under Ferraz's torture, you would have found two bodies here instead of one."

Chapter Thirty-nine

THE "BOLTHOLE," AS FATHER Angelo called it, was directly in front of the fireplace.

"We built this," he said, rolling back the carpet that covered the entrance, "back in the days of the dictatorship. I told you we were tortured?"

"Yes, you did."

Father Angelo set the carpet aside and dusted his hands. "We were fearful they might come again. We set to thinking about how we could escape them if they did."

He inserted the tips of his fingers into a gap in the rough wooden flooring and started to pull, raising an oblong section about seventy-five centimeters long by fifty centimeters wide. "This was the solution. Anton's idea, inspired by the hiding places built for English priests in the time of the Tudors."

He set the section of floor aside, revealing a wooden ladder descending into a dark shaft. "We did all the work ourselves," he continued. "It took us seven months. We kept the earth we'd removed in baskets and spread it around the garden during the night. Those baskets were heavy, to say the least. Fortunately, I was younger and stronger then."

"Did you ever have occasion to use it?"

"Not until Edson came along."

"Edson? Edson Souza? He's down there?" Silva pointed at the shaft.

Father Angelo bent over and stuck his head into the hole.

"Yes," he said. "Thanks to Anton, he's still there. Come up, my boy. Come up and meet the people from the Federal Police.

Chapter Forty

EDSON SOUZA WAS A kid with shoulder-length hair and doelike eyes, more like a girl's than a boy's. He was dressed, as Father Brouwer had often been, in a pair of jeans and a red T-shirt bearing the logotype of the league.

When he saw Father Brouwer's body, a solitary tear escaped his right eye and rolled down his cheek. Silva had the impression he was looking at a kid who'd already done most of the crying he'd do in his entire lifetime.

Father Angelo put his arm around Edson's shoulders and gave him a comforting squeeze. Edson leaned into him like a dog seeking affection.

"We've been looking for you, son," Silva said. "We want to protect you."

Edson looked at him with contempt. "Yeah, I heard. And while you were looking, Father Brouwer got killed, and Senhorita Pelosi, and all those people from the league, and Diana and her friend Lori. Some cop you are. Protect me? What a joke! Go fuck yourself."

"Look, you little—"

Silva held up a hand, stopping Arnaldo in mid-sentence.

"Listen to me," Silva said. "The State Police are going to be here any minute and Ferraz might be with them." At the mention of Ferraz's name, Edson's eyes rounded in fear. "Arnaldo, get a cover from the bedroom. Put Edson on the floor in the back of the car, conceal him under it, and come back. Someone has to stay here until the State Police arrive."

"I'll stay," Father Angelo offered.

Silva waited until Arnaldo and Edson had gone outside, then said, "I'd prefer it, Father, if Arnaldo were to do that. Stay here, I mean. It would be better if you'd come with us. We might need your help with the boy."

"As you wish."

"And while Edson is out of earshot, let me say this: It was a stupid thing you did, hiding him like that. Look at the damage you've done. There are people who might be alive today if it hadn't been for that. One of them is your friend there."

Father Angelo's eyes flashed in anger. "It's easy enough for you to say that, Chief Inspect—"

"No, it's not, Father. It's damned hard to say, but it's the truth."

"Will you let me finish?"

"Make it quick. We have to get out of here."

"I understand that, but this will only take a minute, and it's important that you understand. Our concern, Anton's and mine, was for the life of the boy. We didn't know to what degree we could trust you, but there was one thing we knew for sure: As long as Ferraz was on the loose, Edson's life would be in danger. It still is."

"But—"

Father Angelo ignored Silva's interruption.

"Try to follow my reasoning. In order to put Ferraz and his colleagues away, you're going to need proof, isn't that true?"

"Of course it—"

"But you don't have any do you? Not even now."

"That's not true. Now it's different. Now we have a witness."

"I'm not a fool, Chief Inspector. I'll tell you what you have, and it's the *only* thing you have: The word of a street kid, nothing more."

"All right. I admit it's not much—"

"It's nothing at all. Edson's word against the word of a colonel in the State Police is nothing at all, and you know it."

In the silence that followed, there was the sound of a distant siren.

"State Police are coming," Hector said.

"Put that trapdoor back in place and cover it with the carpet," his uncle told him.

Hector had barely finished when a vehicle pulled up outside. The siren slid down the musical scale and died out. Car doors slammed. They heard Arnaldo's voice, and then heavy footsteps on the porch followed by the squeak of the screen door. Two state policemen entered the room.

"Father," one of the cops said, acknowledging Angelo's presence. Both of them seemed to know him. He nodded a greeting.

"Guy outside told us what happened," the other cop said, addressing Silva. "We saw his ID. How about showing us yours?"

Silva and Hector produced their wallets. The eyebrows of the cop who checked their warrant cards went up when he saw that he was in the presence of the Federal Police's Chief Inspector for Criminal Matters. Apparently, Arnaldo hadn't mentioned it.

"Father Angelo came in after we did," Silva said. "We found Father Brouwer's body just as it is. Nothing has been touched. There's no reason for us to stay here. If you want a statement, send an *escrivante* to my hotel and I'll give him one."

"Sim, senhor," one of the cops said with a sideways glance at Anton Brouwer's mutilated corpse. "You're at the Excelsior?"

"Yes, the Excelsior. Let's go, Padre."

THE TRIP to the hotel took them about fifteen minutes. Father Angelo kept one window open and smoked all the way.

They drove into the subterranean parking garage and succeeded in getting Edson up to Silva's suite without encountering anyone.

The kid tried not to show it, but he was impressed. A rather normal hotel suite was high luxury for him. He ran his hand over the fabric covering the couch and asked if he could use the bathroom. Hector showed him where it was. On his way back, Edson spotted the bottles behind the bar. "How about a whiskey?"

Silva poured him one. The kid had probably put much worse things in his body, and it might help him to relax. While he was drinking it, Silva nodded to Arnaldo, who took out his cell phone.

The agente dialed Riberão, got his sister on the line, and asked to speak to Marly Souza. The boy froze when he heard his mother's name.

When Arnaldo extended the telephone, Edson tossed off the rest of his whiskey and grabbed the instrument like he was afraid the agente was going to snatch it away again. The tough little street kid got a catch in his throat when he started to talk to his mother. He cleared it, then turned his back on them and talked for some time in a low voice. They didn't hurry him. When he finally hung up the telephone almost twenty minutes later he asked for another whiskey, and got it.

"Now talk to us," Silva said.

THERE'D BEEN a rumor on the street, Edson said, that Ferraz's men were looking for him. He couldn't think of another place to turn, so he'd sought refuge with the priests. He'd started out by sleeping on their couch, only bolting down into the hole if he heard a car stop or someone coming up the walk that led through the banana trees.

Then, after a couple of days, the bad dreams started. He

found himself waking up several times a night, always in a cold sweat. The priests wouldn't give him anything stronger than chamomile tea, so he'd tried spending a night in the security of the hole. He slept so much better down there that he'd taken to doing it all the time.

He didn't exactly know when he'd become aware of the footsteps overhead, but it had been sometime in the middle of the night. It was dark in the hole, pitch dark, and he didn't have a watch. After the footsteps there was the sound of a struggle, then the voice of Ferraz asking questions, and then the screams.

"That filho da puta Palmas was there too," Edson said. "I heard him. They hurt Father Brouwer bad, but he wouldn't tell them a fucking thing. Sorry about the language, Father, but it's the God's honest truth. Not a fucking thing. You would have been proud of him. I sure as hell was."

Father Angelo didn't comment. His hands were clenched in his lap. He was biting his lower lip.

Now that he was talking, Edson required little prompting. Ferraz, he said, supplied drugs to the street kids of Cascatas. To pay for them, the kids had to get money from somewhere. The ensuing crime wave caused a public revolt. Many townsfolk gave tacit support to what they thought was a death squad. In reality, it was Ferraz's gang of enforcers, killing the kids who didn't pay their drug debts.

No matter what anybody might have told them, Edson said, he didn't have a crack habit. And he'd *never* had a crack habit. He'd seen what the drug could do and it frightened him. But he was even more frightened of Ferraz, who demanded a regular purchase from every kid on the street. So he bought the stuff and pretended to use it. He didn't sell it to anyone. He just threw it away.

Then he lost one of his friends to an overdose and another to Ferraz's gang of killers. He wanted to do something, but he didn't know what. Finally he went to Father Brouwer and talked to him about it.

While Edson talked and talked, Father Angelo smoked and smoked, adding butt after butt to an already overflowing ashtray and filling the air with a thin haze. When Silva asked Edson why he'd called the bishop, the old priest raised his head and looked directly at the kid. This, it seemed, was something new.

Edson swallowed and looked down at the table. If his dark skin had been lighter they might have seen a blush.

"You called Dom Felipe?" Father Angelo said. "You never told me that."

"No, Father."

The kid squirmed in his chair.

"Was it something else about Ferraz?"

"No, Father."

"What then?"

Edson didn't answer.

"Immediately afterward," Silva said, "the bishop called Gaspar Farias. Gaspar says he can't remember what the bishop wanted to talk about.

"The fuck, he can't," Edson exploded. "He knows all right, the filho da puta."

Father Angelo leaned back and opened his mouth in surprise. Edson didn't notice. He was still looking down at the surface of the table.

"So you know why the bishop called Gaspar," Silva said.

"I don't want to talk about it."

Father Angelo put a hand on the boy's shoulder.

Edson swallowed. "Please," he said, and looked at the priest. "I don't want to talk about it. Not to you. Not to him."

Silva leaned back and locked eyes with the old man. Father Angelo blinked, gave the slightest of nods, and took over the interrogation.

"But you spoke to Dom Felipe, didn't you?"

"That was different. I didn't know him. And, besides, it was by telephone."

"What you told him, it's important, isn't it?"

The boy didn't look up. He swallowed again, nodded again.

"And you know that I love you and that Anton loved you and that nothing could ever change that, no matter what you've done?"

The boy searched the old priest's eyes.

"Yes," he said. "I know that."

"Remember how proud you were of Anton? About how brave he was?"

Another nod.

"Don't you think he'd be proud of you if you were to be brave now?"

The answer was some time in coming. When it did, it was only a single, strangled word: "Yes."

"Well, then," Father Angelo said, as if it was all settled, as if the boy had just agreed to speak.

And, after a good ten seconds of silence, he did.

Chapter Forty-one

IT HAD RAINED THAT night, a persistent, steady down-pour that cut visibility to no more than fifty meters and kept most of the kids off the street. But Edson was broke, and he had to work, so as soon as it slacked off a bit he grabbed an umbrella, went out to his usual corner, and started trolling for business.

The streetlights on Republic Square had been smashed since forever, so there was never much light even under the best of circumstances. That night, with the rain coming down, it was even darker than usual. But, light or no light, he wouldn't have been able to see much of the guy's face anyway because he was wearing a big rainhat, and he had it pulled down so that it almost covered his eyes.

Edson's customers normally didn't approach him on foot. On the rare occasions when they did, it generally meant that the John hadn't come out of the closet and didn't want to run the risk of having his wheels spotted.

"How much?" the man in the rain hat asked.

"A hundred and fifty," Edson replied, expecting a counter-offer.

"Okay," the guy said, surprising him, "but there are conditions."

"I don't take it in the ass," Edson said, "and I don't swallow. Find somebody else."

"*Your* conditions are okay," the man said, "you want to hear mine?"

"I'm listening."

"There are two of us, and my boyfriend's shy."

"Which means?"

"He doesn't want you to see his face. You have to wear a hood until we get there."

"And then?"

"And then you do us in the dark."

"Let's see the money," Edson said. The double act didn't bother him. He'd done that before.

"You see the money when we're in the car," the man said. "What do you call yourself?"

"Pipoca. How about you?"

"You don't have to know. Are you coming, or not?"

The car was a Passat, and not a new one. The inside stank of tobacco and of something else, too, something sweet and flowery. Once he was behind the wheel the guy lifted his ass to get at his wallet and counted out the hundred and fifty.

"You do a good job," he said, "and there's a tip at the end of it."

Edson folded the money and put it in the pocket of his jeans. "Remember the deal," he said.

"I remember. You suck, but you don't swallow. You fuck, but you don't want to be fucked, right?"

"Right."

Rainhat reached under his seat and came up with a plastic trash bag.

"What's that?" Edson said.

"You don't listen, do you? It's to put over your head."

"A hood, you said."

"What the fuck do you think we are? Seamstresses? Bite a hole with your mouth so you can breathe."

The plastic was resilient, and Edson had to put it on and take it off a few times before he got it right. The man waited until he did before starting the engine.

They drove for almost twenty minutes. The first eight turns were all to the left. Edson could feel his body being pushed to the right by the inertia. He figured the guy had taken him a couple of times around the square. After that, it got confusing. He soon gave up trying to figure out where they might be going. He really didn't give a damn anyway. He already had the money.

"Sit tight," the man said, coming to a sudden stop.

He heard a garage door open. The Passat rolled forward and then stopped. The door closed again. The man killed the engine, got out of the car, came around to Edson's side, and helped him out.

Edson asked if he could take off the hood.

"Not yet. Put your hands on my shoulders and follow me."

The guy had apparently done this sort of thing before. He warned him when they were coming to each of the two flights of steps and he told him exactly how many of them there were both times.

At the top of the second flight, he could feel carpeting under his feet.

"Now, stand still."

He heard a door open. And then he smelled it again: that same cloying, flowery smell from the car.

A new voice. "So this is our little whore for the night, hmm? I want to see your face, boy, but I don't want you to see mine. Shut your eyes. Are they shut?"

"Yes."

"Good. Keep them that way. There'll be more money if you do, trouble if you don't."

Edson kept his eyes tightly closed, felt the plastic bag slide off of his head, felt the new man's breath on his face: he was that close.

"Yes," the man said. "Well done."

The words weren't meant for him.

"I'm glad you approve," he heard the first man say. His voice sounded different, as if dampened by their surroundings.

Edson imagined a place with a lot of curtains on the walls. He heard a click. The light beyond his eyelids went out.

"Now you can open your eyes."

He did, not that it made any difference. Everything was pitch black.

"Move forward, until you feel the bed with your knees."

He did that, too.

"Now, slide to your right. No, no, you stupid boy, to your *right*. Good. Keep going until you feel the bedside table."

"Yeah."

"Do you feel it?"

"I said, yeah."

"Don't be insolent. Think of the money. Now disrobe."

"What?"

"Take off your clothes and drop them on the floor next to the table. That way, you'll be able to find them again when you leave."

The next ten minutes were strange and the five that followed them, a nightmare. To begin with, they didn't ask him to do any of the things he was used to doing. They just let him lie there while they did it to each other. When he started to join in, as he thought they wanted him to do, they pushed him away. And then, suddenly, it happened. They were all over him. Worst of all, one of them was *in* him. And not in his mouth, like he'd agreed, but where he'd specifically said he didn't want them to go. He tried to struggle, but he was just a boy and these were two strong men. One held him down, while the other did it to him. They didn't use any jelly or anything.

He tried to bite the one who was holding him down, but the man let go just long enough to give him a blow that made him see a white flash and then blue stars in the night.

"Keep still, you little bastard, keep still."

He stopped struggling. It was too late, anyway. The thing

he'd never wanted done to him *had* been done to him. He started to whimper, and that seemed to encourage his tormenters all the more. One of them climaxed with a long cry and, after a moment of satiated rest, made way for the other.

The second one reached under Edson's body, grasped his flaccid penis and squeezed it when he climaxed. And then it was over, and they were telling him to get dressed, and that he'd be taken back to where he came from.

Tears still creeping down his cheeks, he did what they'd told him to do: As a guide to finding his clothes, he felt for the table. And when he did, he touched a fat wallet. Without thinking twice, he palmed it, and as soon as he'd located his jeans, he stuffed it into a pocket.

His heart started to beat faster. If they turned on the light, they'd be sure to notice.

But they didn't.

"You dressed?" the first man said a minute or two later.

"Almost."

"You earned another hundred. Put this on."

He felt the plastic bag, took it, and slipped it on. He had to turn it to position the hole in front of his mouth.

"Okay. The same drill. Hands on my shoulders."

Fifteen minutes later he was back on Republic Square, 250 reais richer, feeling dirtier than he had in all of his young life and with the wallet still in his pocket.

Chapter Forty-two

EDSON CAME TO THE end of his story without meeting Father Angelo's eyes.

The old man put his hand on the boy's shoulder. "Look at me," he said.

Edson did, and something in the priest's expression must have encouraged him. His posture straightened and his sunken shoulders rose.

"Tell us the rest of it, why don't you?" Father Angelo said.

"The wallet belonged to that *canalha* Farias," Edson went on, faster than before, eager to get it over with. "There wasn't much money, but there was his identification card and his driver's license and even a credit card. I tried to use the credit card, but that was only the next day, in the afternoon. He'd canceled it by then."

"What did you do with it?"

"Threw it in the river."

"The wallet too?"

"All of it. Everything except the cash."

"Where?"

"I threw it off the Goulart Bridge."

Silva looked at Father Angelo.

"The river is deep there, and fast flowing," the priest said, shaking his head. "I think it's highly unlikely you'd find anything."

Silva addressed Edson directly: "What did you do then?"

"I sent a letter to Dom Felipe."

"Why didn't you tell Father Brouwer or Father Angelo?"

"I . . . I was embarrassed. I didn't want them to think . . ."

"Okay. Why the bishop?"

"Because I didn't know him, and he didn't know me, and he's the boss of all the priests."

"Did you tell the bishop everything you just told us? About what they did to you? About the wallet?"

"Yes."

"Do you think he believed you?"

"Maybe not at first, but after a while he did. He asked me to go with him to the police."

"That doesn't necessarily mean—"

"Yes, it does. Because I told him I was afraid of the police, and he said that he couldn't stop Father Gaspar without me coming forward, and I said I'd like to help, but I couldn't, and he said I had to, that it was my . . . Christian duty, yeah, that's it, Christian duty, and that it had to be stopped, because it had happened before and it would happen again if I didn't—"

"Happened before? It had happened before?"

"That's what he said."

"Why would he share anything like that with you?"

"How the hell would I know? But he did."

"All right, Edson. Stand right where you are for a moment. Gentlemen, a word."

Silva drew Arnaldo and his nephew into his bedroom and closed the door. "Well?" he said, lowering his voice. "Do we believe him?"

"I sure as hell do," Arnaldo said.

"The smell clinched it for me," Hector said. "Gaspar drenches himself in that lilac cologne. And when we check the army records of that surly bastard, Euclides, I'll bet we're going to find out he's an expert marksman."

"So here's how it probably went down." It was Arnaldo again. "The bishop talks to the kid, and he tries to get him to come in. The kid refuses. The bishop pressures Gaspar anyway. Gaspar gets nervous, and he gets Euclides to kill the bishop."

"Maybe," Hector said, "or maybe not. Maybe the priest didn't have anything to do with it. Maybe Euclides took the initiative himself."

"Not likely," Silva said. "The bishop talked to Gaspar. Why would Gaspar go whining to Euclides unless he expected him to do something about it?"

"Good point. Case solved?"

"Solved, maybe. But not proven and, therefore, not worth a damn. We've only got the kid's word for the motive, nothing else. Gaspar was on the steps of the church when the bishop was shot, and everybody saw him. The gun's untraceable, and there are no prints. Euclides doesn't have a motive unless we can prove that Gaspar had a motive, and we can't. All we've got is the word of—"

"A street kid who's just admitted to being a prostitute and a thief," Hector said.

"Precisely. And that, as Father Angelo was kind enough to point out to me earlier today, is the same as nothing at all."

"So where do we go from here?" Arnaldo said.

"You go rent a car."

"What for?"

"Never mind, just do it. Meanwhile, Hector and I will take the kid over to Gaspar's place and confront him. If we take him by surprise, maybe Gaspar will crack and say something stupid."

"What about Ferraz?"

"He won't crack. Not him. And I don't want him to know we've got the kid. We'll leave Ferraz for later. Let's go back and tell the kid."

"So AS soon as we leave Gaspar's place," Edson Souza said when Silva explained the plan, "you send me to my mother, right?"

"That's right," Silva said.

"Okay. But I want Father Angelo to go along, to Gaspar's I mean."

The old priest shook his head. "It wouldn't be appropriate, my boy. Just keep on being as brave as you are."

Edson's face assumed a sullen expression, but he nodded. He didn't like it, but he'd do it.

"As for you, Father," Silva said, "I wouldn't be at all surprised if you're the next one on Ferraz's hit list. How about accompanying Edson to Riberão?"

"Thank you, Chief Inspector. I appreciate the suggestion, but, no."

"You're sure?"

"Quite sure. I have unfinished business here. You *will* inform me, won't you, about what Gaspar has to say? I think I've earned the right to know."

"I don't think—"

"Please, Chief Inspector. It's . . . very important to me."

"Well, then . . ."

"Thank you." Father Angelo fished a small notebook out of one of the pockets of his cassock and made a note. "I'll be at this number," he said, tearing off the page and giving it to Silva, "waiting for your call."

Chapter Forty-three

WHEN EUCLIDES SAW EDSON standing between the two cops, his eyes started to narrow. When he noticed where Hector had placed his shoe, they became mere slits.

"There you go again," he said. "Take your fucking foot out of the door," he said.

"I thought you didn't hold with foul language," Hector said. "Where's your boss?"

"Not here."

"Really? Then we'll wait for him. Get out of the way."

"You can't come in here. You need a warrant."

Silva's patience, held in check since he arrived in Cascatas, took that moment to run out.

"We do like hell," he said. "All we need is this."

Euclides took one look at the gun and stepped back out of the way. They pushed past him and headed straight for Gaspar's study.

The priest was seated at his desk, a pair of reading glasses perched on his nose and a pen in his hand. When they burst in, he dropped the pen and whipped off the glasses.

"I tried to stop them, Father," Euclides said, "but the old guy pulled *that*."

Gaspar ignored where his manservant was pointing. He only had eyes for the boy.

"Recognize him, do you?" Silva asked.

He slipped the Glock back into its holster without taking his eyes off the priest.

"I've never seen him before in my life."

"It's him," Edson said, pointing a finger. "I recognize his voice. And he's using that same stinky stuff."

Gaspar tore his eyes off the kid and addressed Silva.

"What do you mean by bursting in here with this . . . this . . ."

"This what, Father? What do you think he is?"

"I have no idea. I told you. I've never seen him before."

"He says you have."

"Then he's a liar."

"You used me like a girl," Edson was shouting now. "I told you what I didn't like, told you what I wouldn't do, but you did it anyway, you and him." He pointed at Euclides. "He had a hat pulled down over his eyes, but I recognize his voice, too."

"Preposterous."

"*He* picked me up on Republic Square, and brought me up to your bedroom, and the two of you—"

"Outrageous."

"—fucked me in the ass."

"Disgusting."

"This boy's name," Silva said, grasping the kid firmly by the shoulder to quell his outburst, "is Edson Souza. You probably know him as Pipoca, and you also know that he's a male prostitute—"

"Aha!"

"Let me finish. He says—"

"I don't care what he says. He's a liar."

"He says," Silva repeated, "that he took your wallet."

"If he did, which he didn't, then he'd be a thief as well as a prostitute."

"He said the wallet was on the table next to your bed."

"I *lost* my wallet. On the street. Maybe to a pickpocket. Isn't that true, Euclides?"

"Yeah."

"You see? How *dare* you—"

"Did your man here kill Bishop Antunes?"

"What did you say?"

"I asked you if your man killed Bishop Antunes."

"I don't have to listen to any more of this."

"It's a simple question, Padre. Answer it."

"Of course he didn't. Why would he?"

"Maybe to help you conceal the fact that you're a pedophile?"

"A pedophile? *Me*, a pedophile?"

"Well? Aren't you?"

"Certainly not."

"No? *He* says you are."

"*Him*? That vagabond? You'd take the word of a whore and thief over that of a consecrated priest?" Gaspar's chin went up, and his back straightened. A little smile creased the corner of his mouth. "You haven't any proof, have you? Of course not! How could you? There isn't any to get. Euclides, show these people out."

Silva made a final attempt. "Look, Padre, you know what you did. So do we. Why don't you just make it easy on all of us and confess?"

Father Gaspar picked up his pen, put the glasses back on his nose, and went back to his papers.

Silva turned on his heel and walked out of the priest's study, followed by Edson and Hector. When they passed through the front door, Euclides slammed it behind them.

Silva took out his cell phone, searched his pockets for the number Father Angelo had given him, and made good on his promise to update the old priest on the results of his interview with Gaspar.

Chapter Forty-four

ARNALDO WAS NOT PLEASED when Silva told him why he'd wanted the rental car.

"Why can't we just send him by bus, like we did his mother?"

"Too risky," Silva said. "By now, Ferraz knows she's gone. He'll be checking the buses, looking for the kid. And we can't use one of our own cars because the colonel already knows what they look like."

Silva's cell phone chose that moment to ring.

"Wipe that smile off your face, you little punk," Arnaldo said to Edson. The kid had been looking back and forth between Silva and Arnaldo like he'd been watching a tennis match.

"Fuck you," the kid said.

Silva pulled the phone out of his pocket, wishing the damned thing had a caller ID. He pushed the call button.

"Mario?"

It was the director. Again.

"I've got to take this call," he said, putting a hand over the mouthpiece.

Arnaldo snorted, grasped Edson's shoulder, and propelled him out of the room.

"Hey," the kid said, "keep your paws to yourself, you big gorilla."

"Cut the crap," Silva called after them.

"What the hell do you mean, 'cut the crap'?"

"Sorry, Director, that wasn't meant for you."

"I should hope not. What's this business about somebody

offing a priest? What did this Brouwer guy have to do with what happened to the bishop?"

"As far as I know, nothing at all. I don't think the killings are connected. How, may I ask, did you find out about Brouwer?"

"Not from you, that's for damn sure. On the news. Ana heard it."

Ana. Silva liked the director's secretary, but sometimes . . .

"Has it occurred to you, Mario, that ever since you arrived things have been getting worse?"

"I take exception to that remark, Director."

"I don't give a damn what you take exception to. Are you one iota closer to solving the bishop's murder?"

"As a matter of fact, I am. He's a pedophile and—"

"Whoa. Slow down. The bishop was a pedophile?"

"No. The man who killed him is. Well, actually it wasn't the man himself, but this manservant of his who—"

The director, interrupting, cut right to the chase. He wasn't a man who cared about details, no matter how juicy they might be.

"Can you prove it?" he said.

"No. Not yet."

"What do you mean by *not yet*?"

"Well, we've got a witness—"

"To the killing?"

"Not to the killing, to the pedophilia. He's a street kid—"

"A street kid? And he's going to testify against a pedophile?"

"Yes, except that the pedophile is a priest and—"

"A priest? Did he confess?"

"No. He denies everything. But I'm sure he did it, as sure as I've ever been of anything in my life."

In a moment of silence, rare for him, the director reflected. Then he softened a bit. Not much, but a bit. "Well, I suppose we're better off today than we were yesterday. Wrap it up, Mario, wrap it up."

And, although he didn't wait for Silva's reply, he actually went to the trouble of saying goodbye.

Just before the handset hit the cradle, Silva heard him bellowing for the long-suffering Ana.

Chapter Forty-five

ORLANDO MUNIZ WAS POURING what he'd planned to be his last whiskey of the evening when the telephone rang. He kept on pouring and let one of his bodyguards pick it up.

"It's Colonel Ferraz, senhor."

Muniz picked up his glass with one hand and the wireless telephone with the other.

"What can I do for you, Colonel?"

"It's about that priest, Brouwer." Ferraz sounded worried. Strange. The colonel hadn't struck him as someone who worried easily.

"What about him, Colonel? You, yourself, said he was harmless."

"More than ever. Somebody killed him."

Muniz took a sip of his drink and swished the whiskey around in his mouth.

"You hear what I just said?"

Muniz swallowed. "Yes, Colonel, I heard what you said. Brouwer is dead. I'm delighted to hear it. Good riddance." Muniz took another sip. The whiskey in his glass was almost gone. Maybe he'd have just one more before he went to bed.

"Good riddance, yeah. But there's a problem. Angelo thinks we had something to do with it."

"Angelo?"

"Father Angelo. The old guy who lived with Brouwer."

"Thinks *we* had something to do with it? We? As in you and me?"

"Yeah," the colonel said again.

"And you think we should be concerned about that? Really, Colonel, I'm surprised at you. That priest, if he's the one I'm thinking of, is a weak old man. He must be pushing ninety."

"It doesn't take any strength to pull a trigger. He's got a gun."

"He said that? He said he had a gun?"

"He did. And he said he was going to use it on both of us."

"I'd like to see him try. I really would. The old bastard is just blowing off steam, that's all."

"You think so, huh? Well, I hope to hell you're right."

There was a newfound insolence in the colonel's voice. Muniz didn't like it.

He decided he'd definitely drink one more whiskey.

Chapter Forty-six

EMERSON FERRAZ TURNED A cold stare on his deputy.

A sheepish expression came over Palmas's face, and he looked down at the handcuffs shackling his wrists.

The fact that he let the old bastard get the drop on me, Ferraz thought, *is something I'm never going to let him forget. Never.*

The old bastard in question, Father Angelo Monteiro, had been standing out of sight, and just to the right of Colonel Ferraz's front door, when Palmas rang the bell. So the only person Ferraz had seen through the peephole was Palmas, and Palmas was one of the few people, maybe the only person, for whom Emerson Ferraz would have opened his door without having been given a damned good reason first. So he *had* opened the door and now here he sat, in his own house, wearing a pair of his own handcuffs, with his ankles firmly bound to the chair he was sitting in.

Palmas was in another chair, and he was even worse off. Father Angelo had forced Ferraz to run a long length of clothesline around and around Palmas's chest and to fasten him firmly to the backrest. When he was finished, the old man made Ferraz stuff one of his own handkerchiefs into Palmas's mouth. Finally, he was instructed to tie a second handkerchief around Palmas's head, and over his lips, to make sure the first one stayed in place.

Ferraz, in his fury, had made the second handkerchief a good deal tighter than it had to be. He could see that Palmas was feeling the pinch. *Well fuck him. He deserves it.*

The gun Father Angelo was holding looked like an

antique. It was a military revolver of some kind. There was a ring on the butt that you could hook a lanyard to, and the thing had a huge bore. The old piece of hardware seemed to be well-oiled, but a lot of the bluing had worn off. If the priest really knew what he was doing, he would have exchanged it for one of the more modern weapons Ferraz had in the house but the old goat hadn't thought of that. He obviously felt he was doing just fine with what he had.

And the thing that really pissed Emerson Ferraz off was that the priest was right. He *was* doing just fine. There wasn't a damn thing that Ferraz, or his deputy, could do to put him in his place which, as far as Ferraz was concerned, was two meters underground. The colonel was immobilized and angry but he wasn't afraid. Not much, anyway. He didn't think the old man would shoot him on purpose. The trouble was that the antique firearm was fully cocked. The damn thing could go off anytime, doing just as much damage as if the priest had meant to shoot him in the first place. With that in mind, the colonel had decided that his only recourse was to do the old bastard's bidding and be patient until he went away. *But once he does . . . once it's all over, I'm going to find him, and I'm going to hurt him really, really bad before I kill him.*

"You did well, Colonel," Father Angelo said.

"I don't get it. If you're going after Muniz, why did you tell me to warn him?"

"That needn't concern you, Colonel. Now there's just one more thing I want you to do for me."

"What's that?"

"I'm going to hold that telephone handset up to your ear again so that you can make another call. Just one, and then we're done. A little more than half an hour after you've made that call, I'll be gone.

"Who is it this time?"

"You'll be talking to one of your men, and you'll tell him exactly what I say. No tricks now, Colonel. Don't even think of trying to summon assistance. If you say one wrong word, I assure you that I *will* shoot."

Chapter Forty-seven

SILVA KNOCKED OVER A glass of water when he reached out for the phone. Fortunately, most of the liquid wound up on the hotel's carpet, not in his bed.

"That Chief Inspector Silva?" someone lisped.

Silva raised himself to a sitting position and glanced at the numbers on the face of the digital clock. It was 2:14 in the morning.

"Yeah. Who's this?"

"Sergeant Menezes."

Silva turned on the bedside lamp. "Who?"

"Sergeant Menezes. State Police. I took you up to the body of Muniz Junior, remember?"

It was that fat sergeant with the gap between his teeth, the one who'd gone up the hill puffing like a steam engine.

"I remember. What is it, Sergeant?"

"You know that priest, Gaspar?"

Some of the water was still dripping off the surface of the table. Silva looked around for something to mop it up and settled on the terrycloth bathrobe he'd draped over the back of a chair. The telephone cord was just long enough for him to reach it.

"What about him?"

"He's dead."

Silva sat down again, the robe still in his hand.

"What?"

"Dead. Shot his manservant and then killed himself. Colonel says you better get over here."

* * *

"OKAY, YOU old bastard," Colonel Ferraz said. "You talked about half an hour. Well, it's been half an hour. What are you waiting for? When the hell are you going to let us loose and get out of here?"

"I told you I'd leave, Colonel," Father Angelo said. "I don't recall having said anything about letting you loose."

"What's that supposed to mean?"

"Let's return to that subject in a moment, shall we?" The priest lifted the sleeve of his cassock and consulted his cheap plastic watch. "Moreover, it's only been twenty-seven minutes since you made the call."

He took another puff on the cigarette dangling from his lips, removed it from his mouth, and extinguished it in an overflowing ashtray.

"But twenty-seven minutes might well be long enough. Let's see."

He took out a pack of cigarettes, but instead of a smoke, he removed a small piece of paper he'd inserted between the pack and the outer wrapper. His reading glasses were inside some kind of a pocket accessible through the neck of his cassock. He fished them out, put them on his nose, and pulled the telephone toward him. Consulting the paper, he dialed a number. While it was ringing, he put a finger to his lips enjoining Ferraz to silence.

The colonel heard a faint click as someone picked up the receiver.

"I know it's terribly late," Father Angelo said, "but might I speak to Father Gaspar?" Then, after a short pause, "Father Angelo Monteiro. And you?" Another short pause. "Oh, hello, Sergeant. What in the world are *you* doing there?"

Ferraz couldn't hear a word of the other end of the conversation, but the man who Angelo had addressed as "Sergeant" went on talking for quite some time. When next the old priest spoke, his voice conveyed concern. "That's terrible.

Just terrible. But thank you, Sergeant, for telling me. I'll pray for them both. Yes. And a good night to you, too."

He put the telephone back on the cradle, fished out another cigarette, and lit it.

"Good work, Colonel. Your men are already there. I would imagine they've also called Silva by now."

"What the fuck have you done?"

Father Angelo secured the cigarette with his lips, dangling it as he spoke. A fine rain of ash fell onto the lap of his black cassock.

"Who killed Diana Poli and her roommate, Colonel? Was it you?"

The question took Ferraz by surprise.

"I didn't kill anybody," he said, sullenly.

"No?"

The priest picked up the revolver. It had been lying on the coffee table for the last twenty minutes and was still cocked.

Ferraz watched him like a hawk.

"So it was Palmas who killed both of them?" Father Angelo said, absently waving the muzzle of the antique weapon in the major's direction.

Palmas's eyes bulged and he leaned aside.

"Watch out for that thing," Ferraz said. "Stop pointing it at people. It could go off.

"Answer my question."

"Fuck you."

The explosion caught Ferraz by surprise. It was tremendously loud in the confined space of his dining room, seemed louder still because Ferraz hadn't been expecting it. Major Palmas slumped in his chair. There was a spreading stain on the front of his uniform. The stain looked black in the dim light.

"You see?" Angelo said, conversationally. "Just like me. Old, but it still works." He didn't seem to be in the least perturbed that he'd just shot a bullet into a man's heart. He put the revolver down while he fished out, and lit, another cigarette. "Answer my question, Colonel. I really want to know. Was it him, or was it you? Who killed Diana Poli and her roommate?"

For the first time since the priest invaded his home, Ferraz felt real fear. This was no longer the man he'd helped to string up all those years ago. This was a new Father Angelo Monteiro.

"He did," Ferraz said, inclining his head toward the body in the chair. "He killed Vicenza, too, and Pereira, and some of those people at the encampment. Not all. A couple of the other guys were shooting too. I wasn't. I didn't kill anybody."

"Who were these 'other guys'?"

Ferraz gave him the names: Tenente Lacerda, Sargento Maya, Cabo Cajauba, and Soldado Prestes.

Father Angelo took out a little notebook and asked Ferraz to repeat the names. Then he said, "You, Palmas, and another four men. Is that it? Are those all of the men who compose your death squad?"

Ferraz nodded.

Father Angelo leaned forward and closed his hand around the grip of the revolver.

"There are two more," Ferraz said hastily. "Soldados Porto and Najas. They weren't there that night. But they were there . . . other times."

Father Angelo made a note of those two names as well. Then he lit another cigarette with the still-burning butt of the one he'd been smoking. He crushed the butt into the ashtray.

"And lastly, Colonel, we come to the subject of my friend, Anton Brouwer. Who killed him?"

"Palmas."

"Come now, Colonel. There were cigar burns all over his body. Palmas didn't smoke cigars, did he?"

Ferraz didn't answer. His eyes swiveled back and forth.

"Did he?"

Father Angelo lifted the revolver and aimed it at Ferraz's heart.

"No. Okay, I admit I burned him, but I didn't kill him. Palmas did."

"Anton Brouwer was a good man, Colonel. You may find this hard to believe, but I think he would have forgiven you for what you did."

"Really?" There was a flicker of hope in Ferraz's eyes.

"Oh, yes—but unfortunately for you, *I* can't."

He stood, walked to within a meter of Ferraz, and pointed the revolver at his face.

"Wait," the colonel said. "What are doing?"

"In the name of the Father, and the Son, and the Holy Spirit—this."

And Father Angelo Monteiro put a bullet into Emerson Ferraz's forehead.

Chapter Forty-eight

EVERY HOMICIDE IS DIFFERENT, but the circus surrounding every homicide is pretty much the same. The circus begins with the arrival of the first police car and ends with the removal of the corpse. It's lit by flashing red and blue light, punctuated by the squawk of police radios, and isolated by yellow strips of crime-scene tape. The gatekeeper is almost always a grizzled veteran or an eager rookie.

This time it was an eager rookie.

"Hey, hey, hey, where do you think you're going?" he said, appearing from nowhere and blocking the doorway to Father Gaspar's home.

Silva waved his gold badge under the youngster's nose. "Where's the colonel?" he said.

The rookie leaned forward, read the lettering around the seal of the republic, and addressed Silva with newfound respect. "Sorry, Chief Inspector, he's not here. The senior man is Sergeant Menezes."

"And where is he?"

"In Father Gaspar's study, where the bodies are. If you gentlemen will follow me—"

"We know where it is. Thanks."

Silva led the way down the hallway.

"Where's the fucking medical examiner?"

The lisp was distinctive. It was the fat sergeant's voice, coming from inside the room.

"Just arrived," Hector said as they entered. "We saw him outside, talking to the paramedics."

Sergeant Menezes turned to face the two federal cops.

"You guys sure got here quick," he said. He didn't bother to introduce any of the other six men in the room, four of whom were in uniform and two of whom were not. One of the civilians was holding a digital camera. He gave Silva and Hector the once over, then went back to photographing the body of Euclides Garcia.

Garcia was face-up on the carpet with a small hole in his forehead. Father Gaspar was slumped at his desk. There was an equally small wound in his temple and a pistol in his right hand. There was little bleeding in either case. The room still smelled of lilacs, strong enough, even, to conceal the smell of death.

"Well, what a surprise," Hector quipped. "They must have been killed by someone from out-of-town."

"How do you figure?" Sergeant Menezes said.

"Neither one had his throat cut."

The sergeant frowned, maybe because he was puzzled, maybe because he was annoyed.

"Looks like a .22," Hector said.

Menezes nodded.

"Yeah, a .22. Just a little popgun. Hi, Doc. Glad you could finally make it."

This last, a weak attempt at humor, was directed to Ishikawa, who entered the room to a chorus of mumbled greetings. The medical examiner clucked his tongue a few times and squatted next to the body of Euclides.

"Colonel left already?" Silva asked.

"He didn't come," the sergeant said.

"Didn't come? But you said—"

"It's like this. I'm the senior man on duty tonight. A little after midnight, I got a call from the colonel. He said he got an anonymous tip that something had happened here. He said to check it out, and if there was really anything wrong to get in touch with you. As for him, he said, he's going back to bed and doesn't want to be disturbed before eight o'clock tomorrow morning."

"Doesn't sound like him at all."

"Oh, yes it does. You don't know the colonel. He keeps banker's hours. Likes a good night's sleep, the colonel does."

"I meant the part about calling me. He's normally not so cordial."

"Oh. Well, I wouldn't know about that. I just do what I'm told."

"How about Palmas? Where's he?"

"No idea, but you don't often see him without the colonel. They're like Siamese twins, those two. Anyway, I sent a patrol car over here. They found the house all lit up and the front door unlocked, but nobody was answering the bell. They tried calling on the phone. No answer. So I took a chance and authorized them to walk in. This"—he waved his arm, taking in both bodies—"is what they found. Murder and suicide. Pretty obvious."

"Not to me. Not yet," Silva said.

"Ah, but that's because you don't know," the sergeant said smugly.

"Don't know what?"

"About the note."

"What note?"

The sergeant wouldn't be hurried. He was enjoying the opportunity to show the big city boys a thing or two. "It was right here on the desk. I had my doubts at first. So what did I do? I went to that file cabinet over there and looked for samples of Father Gaspar's handwriting. Then, I put them side-by-side with the note, and compared them. No doubt about it. A perfect match."

"So Gaspar wrote something. A suicide note?"

"Not exactly," the sergeant said. "Something better. Much better. He confessed."

"Confessed to what?"

The sergeant dropped what he thought was his bombshell. "Killing the bishop," he said.

He was visibly disappointed when Silva showed no sign of surprise.

"So he confessed to that, did he?"

"Sure did. Turns out he was a pedophile. The bishop found out about it, and they killed him to make sure it didn't come out."

"They being?"

"Him and that guy on the floor over there. He was the one who actually pulled the trigger. It's all in the confession. Want to read it?"

"I sure as hell do. Where is it?"

"I'll get it."

Sergeant Menezes walked over to one of the crime-scene technicians, exchanged a few words, and came back with two plastic envelopes, a rose-colored page of stationery in each.

"So I guess the colonel was right," he said. "We didn't need you guys after all." He extended the envelopes to Silva. "Here. See for yourself."

Silva read both sides of the first sheet, passed it to Hector, and went on to read the other.

The confession contained details that only the murderer would know. There was information about how and where the rifle had been purchased, and even the price that had been paid for it. It revealed that Euclides, during his military service, had been trained as a sniper. What it did *not* say was that the writer had decided to end it all, or that he'd intended to take his manservant with him. It was, most definitely, a confession but it wasn't a suicide note.

Silva walked over to Ishikawa, who was examining the wound in Father Gaspar's temple. "Any preliminary conclusions, Doctor?"

"Two cases of death by gunshot to the head, inflicted with a small bore weapon, consistent with that one there." Ishikawa pointed to the semi-automatic pistol still clutched in Father Gaspar's right hand. Then he pointed to the area around the wound. "Powder burns. The muzzle was right next to his head when the shot was fired. Probably a .22 caliber short. No exit wound on either body. The bullets are still inside their skulls."

Silva reached into his pocket, pulled out a pair of latex gloves and put them on. "You already photographed this?" he asked the crime scene technician, pointing at the hand clutching the gun.

The man nodded.

"You painted the skin for powder residue?"

"Sim, senhor."

"And found it?"

"Also."

"Good. May I touch this?" He pointed to the weapon. The crime scene technician looked to Sergeant Menezes.

"Go ahead," the sergeant said with a verbal shrug.

Silva gently pried the weapon from Gaspar's grip, removed the clip, ejected the round in the chamber and counted all of the cartridges. He came up two short of a full magazine.

"You see," Menezes said. "Two wounds, two dead men, two shots. Case closed."

"Excuse us for a moment, Sergeant."

Silva put pistol and clip on the desk and drew his nephew aside, out of earshot. "What do you think?" he said.

"I don't buy it," Hector said. "A few hours ago Gaspar was denying everything. He knew damned well that we had no proof. Then he's suddenly overcome by his conscience, kills his accomplice, and shoots himself? Not likely."

"No," Silva said, "not likely at all. Conclusion?"

"Someone else did it."

"And the powder residue on Gaspar's hand, and the fact that there were only two shots fired?"

"Everybody who watches television knows that a pistol shot leaves residue on the skin of the person who fired it. Without it, it's not suicide. The killer would have wanted to make sure that Gaspar's hand had the necessary traces of gunpowder."

"Good boy. So?"

"The killer added another cartridge to the magazine after he shot them. Then he put the gun into Gaspar's hand, and pushed his trigger finger to fire off a third shot. That way, Gaspar would test positive for the telltale powder residue, but there'd still only be two cartridges missing from the magazine."

"Take it a step further."

"Somewhere in this room there's another bullet hole, and the bullet we dig out of it will have been fired from the same weapon."

"My thinking exactly," Silva said. "Let's find it."

Fifteen minutes later they did. It was in the wall, behind one of the curtains. Silva told the crime scene technician to remove the section of plaster and concrete, bullet and all.

"We'll want a ballistics comparison between the bullet in there and the ones that the M.E. is going to take out of the bodies."

"Of course. I understand."

The technicians had already discovered two empty shell casings. They now went on to search for a third, but they didn't find it.

"So three bullets and only two casings," Hector said. "The murderer must have taken it."

A careful search of the remainder of the room turned up nothing more of interest except for a box of ammunition and some stains in Gaspar's top right hand drawer.

".455 caliber," Hector said, rolling one of the cartridges from the box between his thumb and forefinger. "Very unusual."

Hector was the expert on firearms. Guns were nothing more than a tool to Silva, but for his nephew they were a hobby as well.

"What would they fit?"

"Nothing I can think of other than a Webley."

"A what?"

"A Webley. It's a British service revolver. They were made by the thousands and used in the trenches during the First World War. These cartridges, though, aren't antiques. Look, no corrosion. They're recent reloads."

Hector put his nose close to the drawer and sniffed.

"Nitro solvent," he said, "and gun oil. Offhand, I'd say the revolver was kept here too. But, if it was, what happened to it?"

"Maybe the killer took it," Silva said.

"Why would he?"

"Maybe because he had to leave his .22 to make it look like a murder/suicide, and he needed another gun?"

"For what?"

"I wonder. . . ."

Sergeant Menezes appeared at Silva's elbow and interrupted his ruminations. "You guys are something else," he lisped with admiration in his voice. "Without you, the son of a bitch would have gotten away with it. I wish I could be a fly on his wall when the colonel finds out we really needed you guys after all. He's gonna be pissed."

The last word came out "pithd." Menezes had come over to their side. His enthusiasm was beginning to carry him away.

"Now, let's go through it together, okay? The way I figure it, the same guy who killed Father Gaspar, and forced him to sign that bullshit confession, must have killed the bishop, too."

"That's what you think, is it?" Silva said.

The sergeant looked hurt. "Well . . . yeah, sure. Why else would he force Father Gaspar to slander himself?"

"Libel himself," Hector said.

"Huh?"

"Slander is spoken. Libel is written. It was a written confession, so if it wasn't true it would be libel, not slander."

"*If it wasn't true?* What do you mean by that?" Sergeant Menezes said indignantly. "It's as plain as the nose on your face. You just got through proving it. He didn't kill himself. Whoever forced him to write that confession did. Don't tell me you believe any of that crap?"

"As a matter of fact," Silva said, "I do."

"That he had his manservant kill the bishop? Come on, Chief Inspector. He wouldn't do anything like that. He was a priest, for Christ's sake."

Chapter Forty-nine

FOR THE SECOND TIME in seven hours, a ringing tele-phone jarred Silva awake. He rubbed his sticky eyes, put the receiver to his ear, and grunted.

"Chief Inspector Silva?" Father Angelo's distinctive rasp.

Silva cleared the phlegm from his throat. "What can I do for you, Padre?"

"We need to talk."

"About?"

"I don't want to discuss it over the phone. I'm leaving now to meet Orlando Muniz in the breakfast room of your hotel. How about nine o'clock, in the same place?"

Silva glanced at the bedside clock, blinking to bring the numbers into focus. He'd have half an hour to get ready. He threw the sheet aside and put his feet on the floor.

"All right. What do you want with Muniz?"

"It's a personal matter. Take a table. I'll come to you when I'm done."

IN CASCATAS, things follow the rhythm of the country-side. Nine o'clock is late for a country breakfast, so most of the hotel's guests had already gone about their business by the time Silva and his nephew arrived.

Near one of the windows, a middle-aged couple was lin-gering over their coffee. Arnaldo, back from his trip to Riberão, had taken a place in the middle of the room. Orlando Muniz, seated alone and devouring an omelet, was in the far corner opposite the door. The couple ignored them. Arnaldo waved. Muniz stopped chewing just long enough to give them a hostile nod. The fazendeiro had brought two of his capangas. They were leaning against the wall near his table.

"Good trip?" Hector said, slipping into a seat next to Arnaldo.

Arnaldo nodded.

"A little over seven hours, out and back," he said, and bit into a *pão francês* heaped with guava jam.

Silva gestured for the hovering waiter to pour him coffee. "Black," he said.

Arnaldo raised an eyebrow. Silva normally took his coffee with milk.

"You look like hell," Arnaldo said.

"So do you."

"Yeah, but I look like hell all the time. Besides, *I've* been driving all night. What's your excuse?"

"Up most of the night."

"So what? I hear you old guys need less sleep."

Silva snorted. Arnaldo was only two years younger than he was and both of them knew it.

"Gaspar and that guy Euclides are dead," Hector said. "Shot. Both of them."

Arnaldo gave a low whistle. "Any suspects?"

"Not yet," Silva said and flicked his eyes in the fazendeiro's direction. "How long has *he* been in here?"

"Not long. Maybe ten minutes." Arnaldo popped the last morsel of bread into his mouth and washed it down with some *café com leite*. "He came over here before he sat down. Asked me what the hell I was doing here."

"What did you tell him?"

"That I was having breakfast, which happens to be the truth. So then I asked him what the hell *he* was doing here."

"And?"

"He's waiting for Father Angelo. Said the old guy called

him. Told him he had information about his son's murder. Wanted to meet him here," Arnaldo glanced at his watch, "at nine. Yep, there he is. Only about five minutes late."

Silva looked over his shoulder.

Angelo Monteiro, a lighted cigarette in hand, was standing in the doorway. He nodded and smiled at the three federal cops, then focused on Muniz.

The capangas stopped leaning against the wall and moved a little closer to their boss. Muniz pointed at the chair in front of him. Father Angelo crossed the room and took it. For a long moment, the two men stared at each other. Then the priest deliberately reached across the table and ground out his cigarette in what remained of Muniz's omelet.

Muniz reddened and started to say something, but Father Angelo didn't wait for him to finish. He leaned forward and spoke. The hand he'd been using to hold his cigarette left the table and crept down to his lap.

Suddenly, Muniz's face contorted in fury. His hand, too, dropped out of sight. Less than a second later there was a sharp report.

Father Angelo's chair tipped over backward, spilling him onto the floor. He clapped his hands to his abdomen. Muniz's hand came out from under the table, gripping a revolver. The fazendeiro sprang to his feet, put the still smoking muzzle up against the black fabric of the priest's cassock and fired again.

The sudden violence took all three of the federal cops by surprise.

Arnaldo was the first to react.

"Drop it," he said, drawing his Glock.

Both of Muniz's capangas reached for their pistols.

"*Calma, garotos,*" their boss snapped, dropping his revolver and raising his hands.

The capangas froze, looking back and forth between Arnaldo and Muniz.

"Calma, I said," Muniz repeated. "Put the guns down."

The gunmen relaxed and lowered their weapons. It wasn't enough for Arnaldo. He went up to each man, relieved them of their pistols, and patted them down. Muniz watched it all with a confident smile, a smile that didn't change when Arnaldo went over and frisked him as well.

"Clean," Arnaldo said at last, and holstered his pistol.

Silva went to the prostrate man, knelt and placed two fingertips on the carotid artery. Father Angelo's skin was warm to the touch, but there was no pulse.

The room was filling with people.

Muniz took the opportunity to play to the crowd. "It was self-defense," he said, raising his voice. "Self-defense. He had a gun under the table."

"There's no gun, Senhor Muniz."

"What?"

"There's no gun," Silva repeated.

"No? Then what's he got in his hand?"

"A pack of cigarettes."

"*Cigarettes?*" Muniz said, mystified. "No. Look again. He said he was going to shoot me, said he had a gun."

"He said that, did he?"

"You're goddamned right he did." Muniz's surprise gave way to anger. "And that's not all he said. He said he killed my boy. Junior may not have amounted to much, but he was mine. Was I supposed to just . . . why are you looking at me like that?"

"You just murdered an unarmed man, Senhor Muniz."

"Murdered? Like hell! I shot him in self-defense. I *told* you what he said. Are you calling me a liar?"

"No, Senhor Muniz, I'm not calling you anything. Cuff him, Arnaldo. Take him up to my suite."

"Cuff me? *Cuff me?* Don't you dare touch me, you fucking Neanderthal. I'll have your goddamned job."

Arnaldo walked up to the fazendeiro and kicked his ankles out from under him. Before Muniz had recovered from the shock, the big cop's knee was pressing on his kidneys, and Muniz's arms were being forced behind his back. As Arnaldo led him away, Silva started going through Father Angelo's pockets. He found a cigarette lighter (a cheap affair in pink plastic), a rosary, a few folded bills of low denomination, some small change, two more packs of cigarettes (one of them almost empty), and a single cartridge casing. He brought the casing close to his eyes for a better look. It was a .22-caliber short. Other than that, there was nothing. No papers, no identification, no other personal effects. The priest's eyes were closed, his features composed, even content. There was no horror written there, no shock. He appeared to be sleeping.

Silva rose to his feet. As he did, someone touched his shoulder.

He turned and found himself looking into a pair of limpid gray eyes.

Merda! Silva thought.

His reaction had nothing to do with the eyes themselves or even the rest of what went with them: dark blonde hair, a flawless complexion, full, sensuous lips and a button nose.

No. His reaction had exclusively to do with the camera that some guy was poking over her left shoulder. There was a tiny red light on the front of that camera and the light was blinking.

"You were a witness to the shooting, weren't you Chief Inspector?" the blonde asked, holding a microphone up to his lips to capture his reply.

"No comment."

"Oh, *come on*," she said. "We were a couple of seconds too late, but *you* were right here in the room. You must have seen Senhor Muniz shoot the priest."

"No comment, Senhora . . ."

"Ferraz. And it's not senhora, it's senhorita, but you can call me Natalia."

"Ferraz. Any relation to—"

"The colonel? No. No relation. But, while we're at it, what's your comment about what happened to him?"

"Happened to him?"

"His murder."

Silva stared at her and blinked. She studied his expression.

"Hey, you didn't know about it, did you?"

"No," he said with a sigh, "I didn't."

She was going to make him look like an idiot. But then, to his surprise and relief, she let him off the hook.

"Cut it, João," she said to the cameraman.

The tiny red light gave a final blink and went out.

"To be fair," she said, "there's no reason why you should have known about the colonel. They only found him a little over an hour ago. Shot to death in his living room. Him and that adjutant of his, Major Palmas."

"How did *you* find out about it, Senhorita Ferraz?"

"Natalia," she said. And then, turning her gray eyes onto Hector, but still speaking to Silva, "Who's your friend?"

"Delegado Hector Costa," Hector said, before Silva could reply.

"Oh, yeah," she said, "you're the nephew, right?"

As Hector's smile faded, she turned back to Silva. "Heard it on the police scanner," she said. "His driver found the bodies."

"Whose driver?"

"The colonel's driver. He picks him up every morning. There's no sleep-in maid, so it's the driver who makes the colonel's coffee. He's got a key to the house. He called it in from the car radio. We picked it up. Got there just when everybody else did."

"And how did you get *here* so fast?"

"We got a tip somebody'd been shot."

"A tip? From whom?"

"Anonymous. He—it was a he—called it in to the network."

"When?"

She looked at her watch. "Maybe twenty minutes ago, which is at least fifteen minutes before it actually happened. Funny, huh? Maybe the caller was a psychic."

WITH THE colonel dead, there was no reason not to use the local jail, so that's where they took Muniz.

He was entitled to one telephone call and he promptly made it. His personal judge, Wilson Cunha, got there in five minutes flat, called for an immediate arraignment, and assured Muniz that he wouldn't have to spend the night in a cell.

Silva told Cunha that he intended to file federal charges and that, by law, he had twenty-four hours to do it. In the meantime, Muniz wouldn't be going anywhere.

"What federal charges?" Cunha sputtered.

"I haven't decided yet. I'm still thinking about it."

"I protest."

"Protest all you want. Your patron is going to spend the night in jail and I intend to make sure he doesn't get a cell to himself. Who knows? Maybe he'll find love."

Silva waited until Cunha had stormed out, then called a friend at the revenue service in Brasilia and initiated an audit of the judge's last five years of income tax statements.

Chapter Fifty

HALF AN HOUR LATER, a small crowd of the curious was still milling about in the lobby of the Hotel Excelsior. As Hector threaded his way through them, leading the way to the elevator, he spotted an unexpected figure: Father Francisco, the late bishop's secretary.

The priest's attire was rumpled, he was showing a day's growth of beard, and there were dark rings under his eyes. He tossed aside the newspaper lying in his lap, wearily pulled himself out of his armchair, and extended a hand.

Hector took it, introduced the priest to his two companions, and said, "I hope you'll pardon me for saying so, Father, but you look as if you could use a good night's sleep."

Self-consciously, the priest ran a hand over the stubble on his chin.

"I daresay I do, Delegado, but I'll have to put it off a little while longer. I've been waiting for you and the chief inspector. Have you time for a cup of coffee?"

"Of course. You heard about what happened to Father Angelo?"

"Yes. The desk clerk told me about it. He had it from some people who saw it all." The priest seemed neither scandalized nor surprised.

Hector glanced at the hotel's coffee shop. Yellow crime-scene tape still sealed off the entrance, and people were leaning over it, staring at the bloodstains on the floor.

"No coffee to be gotten here," he said. "Let's go upstairs and order it from room service."

* * *

WHEN HE was seated on the sofa in Silva's suite and the coffee had been ordered, the priest said, "Shortly after two o'clock this morning Father Angelo called me."

"He called you at two AM?" Silva asked. "You were awake?"

"Asleep, but I have a telephone next to my bed. Last rites, you see. I'm often asked to give them in the early hours of the morning."

"So you weren't particularly surprised to get a call?"

"Not until I picked up the telephone and heard Father Angelo's voice."

"What did he want?"

"To talk to me, he said, about a matter of the utmost urgency."

"What matter?"

"He refused to discuss it over the telephone."

"Sounds familiar. He did the same with me. Only it was hours later. Just after eight-thirty. He woke me out of a sound sleep and asked me to meet him in the breakfast room downstairs. He was shot to death before we could talk. I'm still wondering what it was all about."

"Perhaps I can shed some light."

At that moment someone rapped on the door. It turned out to be room service with the coffee. Father Francisco waited until everyone had been served, and the man had left, before he resumed his story:

"Angelo asked me to come here, to Cascatas. There was something in his voice, something in the way he made his request. It was . . . well, I hope you don't find I'm being too dramatic, but his voice was almost funereal. I told him I'd come immediately."

"To his home?"

"No. That was something else I found strange. He told me

to come to Santa Cecilia's. That's the old church, the one they're going to demolish to build a school. He said he had a key, and he'd leave a door open. He described how to find it."

"And you did as he asked?"

"Yes. We met this morning, a few minutes past seven." Father Francisco reached into his pocket and removed an envelope. "He gave me this," he said, "and asked me to deliver it to you, personally. He said you'd be in the break-fast room of your hotel. I was to hand it over at nine-thirty AM precisely."

Silva examined the business-sized envelope. It was sealed and unmarked. "What's in it?"

"I'm not sure."

"So why didn't you? Hand it over at nine-thirty, I mean."

"When he left, I sat down on one of the pews near the altar. I was exhausted from the journey and closed my eyes for a moment. When I opened them, it was almost ten. I hurried here, but you'd already gone off to the jail with Orlando Muniz."

"What did you and Father Angelo talk about?"

"I think it would be best if you were to read the letter, Chief Inspector. Afterward, I'll respond to your questions."

Silva tore open the envelope, perched his eyeglasses on his nose and began to read aloud:

Dear Chief Inspector Silva,
I am writing to confess to the murders of four men: Colonel Emerson Ferraz, Major Osmani Palmas, Father Gaspar Farias, and Euclides Garcia.

"Jesus Christ," Arnaldo said.

He looked at Father Francisco and reddened, but the priest ignored his interjection.

Silva continued reading:

Please note that I take no responsibility for the death of the fazendeiro Orlando Muniz Junior. The men who killed him are all dead, murdered by Colonel Ferraz in an unprovoked attack on the encampment of the Landless Workers' League.

"That's just too much of a coincidence," Arnaldo said. "And I'll believe it when I go back to believing in Santa Claus."

Silva cleared his throat and went on:

I staged the deaths of Father Gaspar and Euclides. My motive in misleading the police about the true nature of the crime was to sow confusion, and to thereby ensure that I would be given the time to carry out some other plans that I had on my agenda.

Gaspar's confession, although obtained under duress, is truthful. He planned the murder of Bishop Antunes and his manservant carried it out. There will be ample proof of this in the degree of detail set forth in his handwritten document.

In the case of Ferraz, his crimes are too numerous to list and many may never be known. They certainly include the murders of Diana Poli, Vicenza Pelosi, Anton Brouwer, various members of the Landless Workers' League, and at least five street children.

"That man Ferraz was a fucking murder machine," Arnaldo interjected. "Uh, sorry, Father."

"No apologies necessary, Agente. I happen to agree with you."

In all of Ferraz's crimes, his adjutant, Major Osmani Palmas, was a willing participant. In the case of the street children, Ferraz was also assisted by a death squad consisting of Tenente Lacerda, Sargento Maya, Cabo Cajauba, and Soldados Prestes, Porto, and Najas, the first four of whom also participated in the attack on the encampment.

"So that bucket of lard Menezes is out of it," Arnaldo said. "But there are still six of them. They'll be elbowing each other to be the first in line."

Silva nodded. As cops, Ferraz's men would be quick to recognize that the first of them to turn state's witness would get the best deal from the prosecutors. He adjusted his reading glasses and turned to the last page of Angelo's letter:

As for me taking the law into my own hands, I want to make one thing clear. I would have liked to have gone to my grave believing in Brazilian justice. If I regret nothing else, I do regret that I was unable to do that.

By the time you read this, I will have taken my own life. My last gesture before doing so will be to meet with Orlando Muniz in order to give him some degree of comfort by communicating to him what others have told me about his son's last hour.

God's blessings upon you, Chief Inspector Silva, and—to please my ghost—try to see that those as yet unpunished suffer the fate they deserve.

> Yours,
> Fr. Angelo Monteiro, S.J.

Silva folded the letter and looked at Father Francisco.

"A Jesuit, was he?"

Father Francisco nodded.

"Brouwer, too?"

"No. Franciscan."

"All right. Let's talk. Did Father Angelo ask you to come to Cascatas just to give me this?"

Silva brandished the priest's last letter.

"No, Chief Inspector, he asked me to come so that he could make another kind of confession. He did. I gave him absolution."

"So you *knew* he intended to take responsibility for the killing of four people?"

"I did. I would have expected no less of him. He was a murderer, but he was a good man. I know that sounds incongruous, but it's the truth."

"So you're sure he did it? Killed them, I mean?"

Father Francisco looked mildly surprised. "Of course he did. You just read his confession."

"I read it, yes, but don't you think it strange that the man lived a long life of peace and then, suddenly, went off on a murderous rampage? Was it because of what happened to his friend, Brouwer?"

"Father Angelo, Chief Inspector, was a very sick man. Lung cancer. He didn't have long to live. He authorized me to tell you that, and also to tell you that he wanted to make what he called 'a difference' in the short time left to him. He feared you weren't going to be able to bring certain people to justice, so he decided to help you."

"Help me?"

Silva remembered the times he, too, had taken justice into his own hands. Father Francisco studied the expression on his face and misinterpreted it.

"Yes, yes, I understand your feelings. At first glance, it really seems repulsive. I can't condone his actions—"

"I can," Arnaldo muttered. "Good for him."

Silva gave him a sharp look. Arnaldo, unrepentant, grinned at him. He almost grinned back. To hide it, he turned again to Father Francisco. "Is there any more you can tell me about the death of Orlando Muniz Junior?"

"No."

"Why not? Sanctity of the confessional?"

Father Francisco looked Silva in the eye and didn't answer but he might as well have.

"So Angelo had something to do with it after all," Silva insisted.

"I didn't say that."

"No, you didn't, did you?"

"Look, Chief Inspector, you're holding a letter in your hand in which Father Angelo confesses to four murders but quite specifically denies any responsibility for the death of Muniz's son. Wouldn't it be logical to assume, then, that he had nothing to do with it?"

"That's the way it appears, doesn't it?"

"It certainly does. So what reason might he have had to tell Muniz that he did?

"Are you also a Jesuit, Father?"

"As a matter of fact, I am."

"Then, just as an intellectual exercise, imagine this. Imagine that Father Angelo set Muniz up."

"Set him up?"

"Set him up. Provoked Muniz into committing murder with himself as the victim."

"All right. I'll try to imagine it. But first, tell me what motive Father Angelo could possibly have had for doing something like that. If he meant to hurt Muniz, why wouldn't he just shoot him like he did the others?"

"That's what's bothering me, too. Help me to think it through. As I said, purely as an intellectual exercise."

Father Francisco was silent for a moment. "Well . . . " he said.

"Yes?"

"Purely hypothetically, you understand?"

"Yes, Father. Purely hypothetically."

"Perhaps it could have had something to do with making the punishment fit the crime. After all, Muniz didn't actually kill anyone. He's not a good man, but he wasn't a murderer."

"Not as far as Angelo knew at the time. But now he is, Father."

"Yes, Chief Inspector, now he is. Or maybe. . . ."

"Maybe what?"

"Maybe Father Angelo believed that prison would be the worst punishment for a man like Muniz, worse than dying even. Remember what he wrote about wanting to believe in Brazilian justice?"

"Yes."

"Perhaps he thought he'd found a way to make it work."

"Make it clearer for me, Father. What do you mean by that?"

"How many rich men in this country actually wind up being convicted of a crime?"

"Unfortunately, very few. Our legal system leaves a great deal to be desired. There are those that say all of our judges have their price."

"Yes. But what would happen to a man, however rich, who shot down an unarmed priest in the presence of half a dozen witnesses, one of whom happened to be a chief inspector of the Federal Police? And what would happen to such a man if a reporter from Rede Mundo immediately arrived on the scene and had a chance to interview some of those witnesses? He'd be looking at a long prison term, wouldn't he? Whoever he was."

Silva took in a deep breath and slowly let it out through his nose. Arnaldo broke out in a broad grin. Hector turned away and looked out of the window. Silva was sure he was smiling, too.

He cleared his throat and glanced at his watch. It was almost noon, almost time for another one of those calls from the director.

For once in his life, Mario Silva was actually looking forward to speaking to him.

Brazil has a population of 180 million people occupying a land mass larger than the continental United States. It puts satellites into space, harnesses nuclear energy for peaceful purposes, boasts the world's second largest fleet of private jets, exports automobiles, weaponry, aircraft, and consumer electronics. It has millions of acres of arable land, exports agricultural products to every continent, ranks ninth among the world's economies—and has an unevenness of income distribution second only to Bangladesh.

The wealthiest 10 percent of the population enjoy more than 50 percent of the national income. Fifty-four million Brazilians live below the poverty line. A minuscule fraction of 1 percent of the population owns half the arable land. Twenty-five million agricultural workers survive on two dollars a day.

There is no organization called the Landowners' Association, but there is an organization called the União Democrátiva Ruralista (UDR).

There is no organization called the Landless Workers' League, but there is a Movimento dos Trabalhadores Rurais Sem Terra (MST) and a Movimento de Libertação dos Sem-Terra (MLST), now under the control of demagogues who have come to eschew peaceful means of protest and embrace violence.

No one really knows how many lives have been lost in Brazil's land wars, but documented cases exceed 1,500. One of them was Dorothy Stang, an American nun, shot twice in the face on the twelfth of February, 2005, four months short of her seventy-fourth birthday.

Turn the page for a sneak preview of

PERFECT HATRED

Chapter One

THE ACTION BEGAN AUSPICIOUSLY.

Salem Nabulsi had prayed for good weather—and God had rewarded him with a day of brilliant sunshine.

He'd hoped the woman's husband would leave at his accustomed hour—and the husband had departed fifteen minutes early.

He'd feared the woman would not admit him to her apartment—but she had.

And he'd feared she wouldn't die quietly—but she did.

By 8:15 A.M., he'd already washed her blood from his hands, injected her baby with the contents of the syringe and chosen, from among her clothing, the *hijab* and *abaya* that were to become his shroud.

God further smiled on their enterprise when He sent a taxi driver, punctual to the minute, but also so unobservant that he failed to notice how heavy the baby's carriage was when he folded it and stowed it in the cab.

The crowd, too, exceeded all expectations. It wasn't yet a quarter to nine when they reached the consulate, and yet the line already stretched to half the length of the security fence.

But then it all began to go wrong.

How could they have known, how could they *possibly* have known that babies attract Brazilians like flowers attract bees?

Salem hadn't been in place for more than two minutes before a grey-haired lady stuck her nose under the sunshade to have a look at the sleeping child.

She cooed at the infant and started telling him about her

grandchildren. Salem gave her no encouragement, but it still seemed an eternity before she abandoned her attempt to elicit a response and returned to her place in line.

Next to interfere was a fat sergeant from the Civil Police. Salem, fearing the cop's suspicions would be aroused by the difference in skin tones between himself and the baby, edged his hand closer to the detonation switch.

But the sergeant was wearing dark sunglasses and the baby was in deep shadow, so perhaps he didn't notice. After a few complimentary remarks, which Salem didn't respond to, the cop gave up and moved on.

He'd no sooner disappeared into an alcove fronting a leather goods shop when a third busybody appeared.

Salem was never to know it, but her name was Dorotea Candida. She was a sharp-eyed lawyer, the mother of three and the grandmother of two.

She was smiling when she bent over, but the smile quickly faded.

"Yours?" she asked, standing upright.

The Mullah hadn't prepared him for such a question.

"Yes," Salem blurted.

Her eyes narrowed.

"Uh-huh," she said.

Salem didn't like the way she said it.

Then, without another word, she turned and headed toward a cop, not the same one as before, another one. And this one looked a lot smarter. She spoke and pointed. The cop nodded and walked toward Salem.

Wait until nine, the Mullah had said. *The crowd will be biggest then.*

And it would have been. At least ten people had queued up behind him. More were arriving every minute. But Salem could wait no longer. Discovery was imminent. He put his hand on the button.

And pushed it, just as the cop reached him.

In Dudu Fonseca's law offices, a little more than three kilometers away, the shockwave from the explosion rattled the glass in the windows.

Fonseca held up a hand to silence his client.

"What was that?" he said.

"I don't give a damn what it was," Orlando Muniz said. "Answer my question."

The question had been *what's our next move?* And Muniz was sitting on the other side of Fonseca's desk, with his arms crossed, awaiting Fonseca's response.

Fonseca was the best defense lawyer in São Paulo. Not *one* of the best, *the* best, but on Muniz's murder charge, he'd been unable to deliver an acquittal, and Muniz was mightily displeased.

Fonseca picked up the mock-Georgian coffee pot and poured the last of its contents into his cup.

An honest answer would have been that further moves were a waste of effort. The hard truth was that Muniz would be spending the rest of his days in a prison cell.

But, at the moment, Muniz was still laying golden eggs, so an honest answer wasn't in the cards.

"I'll have to give the situation some deep thought," Fonseca said, taking a sip of the (cold) coffee. "Frankly, we're in a bit of a quandary."

"Quandary, my ass," Muniz said. "I can't believe this is happening."

Indeed, he couldn't. In his world, the rich didn't go to jail. Not in Brazil. Not even if they killed an unarmed, penniless priest, in the presence of a federal cop, as he had done.

The initial judgment, one that resulted in a conviction, carried with it an automatic appeal. Fonseca had arranged to plead the first instance before one of the best judges money could buy. He was about to do the same with the second.

But a public prosecutor named Zanon Parma, in a spectacular show of legal *tour de force*, had checked the man on the bench at every turn.

Parma was to prosecutors what Fonseca was to defense attorneys. The best. Muniz's remaining days of freedom were surely numbered. But this, Fonseca thought, was no time to be candid.

"How important is this guy Parma to the prosecution's case?" Muniz asked.

Fonseca didn't like where his client was going with this. He smelled trouble. But he was being paid for his advice, so he gave it.

"Very. Parma is brilliant, he's dedicated, and he can't be bought."

"And that federal cop? That Chief Inspector Silva? How important is he?"

"Perhaps even more important than Parma. In addition to being the principal witness against you, he's spearheading—"

"The witch hunt. It's a fucking witch hunt. But any witch hunt needs guys up in front with scythes and pitchforks, right? You take those guys out of the picture and—"

Fonseca, once again, held up a hand. "Stop right there, Orlando. I don't want to hear it."

Muniz stood up. "Then we're done. I won't thank you for your time. I'm sure you're gonna bill me for every fucking second of it."

Fonseca, as was his custom with departing clients, struggled to his feet. He was grossly overweight, and it was never easy for him to get out of a chair.

Muniz ignored the lawyer's outstretched hand. "One thing more," he said. "Keep your fucking mouth shut about this conversation."

He departed so quickly that Fonseca's hand was still hanging in the air when the office door slammed shut.

The blast had been the loudest thing Sergeant Flavio Correia had ever heard, louder than a crack of thunder, louder, even, than the stun grenades from his training days.

He rubbed his ears with his palms. One came away wet. He held the hand out in front of him and stared at it. It was red with blood.

His ears still ringing, Flavio stepped into the street.

A crater smoked where once a length of sidewalk had been. The windows in the buildings facing the American Consulate were blown out. The trees on both sides of the security fence were denuded. Small fires were everywhere.

A gas tank exploded, ruffling his hair with a pressure wave of hot air, as another vehicle joined the others already in flames. The woman slumped over the wheel didn't react. She was either dead or unconscious. Either way, she was a goner. There was no way he'd be able to get her out of there.

Flavio shuffled forward and stumbled over a severed foot still wearing a man's brown oxford.

A woman ran past him, her hair on fire, her mouth open in a silent scream.

A few meters away, a bloody arm rose from a legless trunk, waved once in wordless appeal, and fell back onto what looked like a pile of offal.

Flavio, his hands trembling, detached the transceiver from his belt, turned the volume to maximum, and put it to his ear.

But he couldn't hear a damned thing.

Chapter Two

CURITIBA, THE CAPITAL OF the Brazilian State of
Paraná, is a city without streetcars or a Metro system. Public
transportation depends entirely upon buses, but they don't
run between the hours of midnight and five in the morning.

Nora Tasca didn't want to spend a sleepless night in the
open air, so she did the next best thing: she got up at 4:30 A.M.
to make sure she'd be able to catch the first bus of the day.

It arrived in Tiradentes Square, as scheduled, at three
minutes to seven, but by then it was already too late. All
of the best places had been taken, but by dint of considerable pushing and shoving she was finally able to wedge
herself into a spot in the fifth row from the podium on the
right. It wasn't what she'd hoped for, but it was up against
a security tape that had been stretched on stanchions to
keep a path clear for the approach of the politicians. She'd
never seen her hero, Plínio Saldana, *really* close up. This,
she realized, with a flush of realization, was going to be her
chance.

The woman to her left was also a great fan of the Man of
the Hour, and she, too, had brought a collapsible chair. Nora
sensed kinship and, before long, they were seated side-by-
side, heads together, heaping praise on Plínio and pouring
vitriol on his opponent.

At a few minutes past nine, shortly after Salem Nabulsi
had detonated his bomb some 350 kilometers to the northeast, the sun appeared over the surrounding buildings and
banished the last of the shadows. The day was cloudless—
and likely to be a scorcher. The two women shared their

sandwiches, and Nora fought against her inclination to empty her entire bottle of water.

A small group of workmen appeared and draped the platform with bunting, emblazoned with the State flag, and interspersed with Plínio's campaign slogan, *SWEEP PARANÁ CLEAN*. A little later, a squad from the Civil Police arrived and inspected the platform for explosives; then a crew of technicians started tinkering with the microphones and speakers, creating a number of pops and a few ear-shattering squeals.

All the while, people continued to flock into the square. They were, as a TV reporter with a mane of blonde hair and an overbite gushed into her microphone, *turning out in record numbers for this, Plínio Saldana's last major speech of the campaign.*

The camera panned in Nora's direction. She and her companion picked up their brooms and gave them an enthusiastic wave. Nora's broom had a stick two meters long and bristles half the height of a man. She'd crafted it herself, and she'd had a devil of a time getting it onto the bus, but the effort had been worth it. The broom had proven to be an object of admiration. And it was a powerful statement of political allegiance. By 11:30 A.M., the entire square, all the way back to the twin spires of the Cathedral of Our Lady of Light, was a sea of brooms, but few were as attractive as hers. Her companion told her so.

The turnout that day was unprecedented. People had flocked into the city from all over the state. The Civil Police later estimated the size of the crowd to have been somewhere between 250 and 300 thousand—the largest ever to witness the assassination of a Brazilian politician.

BY THE time Hector Costa and Danusa Marcus arrived at the scene of Salem Nabulsi's martyrdom, the Civil Police had blocked off the street.

Janus Prado, his face intermittently illuminated by the

flashing red and blue lights of a nearby ambulance, was on the lookout. He waved when he spotted them.

Shattered glass crunching under their feet, they walked to meet him.

"Women," Janus said. "Kids. What kind of a sick fuck blows up women and kids?" He was badly shaken.

"Christ," Hector said. "What a God-awful mess. Any sign of Lefkowitz?"

Janus, who headed up the homicide division of São Paulo's Civil Police, pointed at the crater. "Poking around in there," he said. "You ever see anything like this?"

Hector shook his head.

"Once," Danusa said. "In Tel-Aviv."

"Well, I thank Christ I never have, and I hope I never do again. There should be a special place in hell reserved for people who do things like this."

"I agree," Hector said. "Who called it in?"

"One of our uniformed guys."

"He was on duty here?"

"Three of them were."

"Why three?"

"Crowd control. The Americans only admit a few at a time. The rest of them have to queue up here on the street."

"Queue up for what?"

"Visas, mostly. There's always a crowd."

"Have you spoken to your men about what they saw?"

"There are no *men*, Hector. Not anymore. Two of them were blown into little, tiny bits." Janus pointed in the direction of a leather goods shop. "The senior guy, a sergeant, was standing in that alcove over there. He survived."

"Badly hurt?" Danusa asked.

Janus shook his head.

"He's one lucky guy. Eardrums punctured, but that appears to be about it."

"Where is he?" Hector asked.

Janus pointed him out.

"But it's better if we go just the two of us," he said to Danusa. "No offense, but I already know his story, and he's going to be more forthcoming without a woman present."

"No problem," she said. "I'll go see how Lefkowitz is getting on."

"That woman," Janus said, admiring the view as she walked away, "is a knockout."

"She is," Hector agreed.

"You work with her much?"

"All the time."

"Doesn't Gilda get jealous?"

"She does," Hector said.

THE SURVIVING cop looked to be in his mid-thirties, and was fatter than any cop should be. A small trickle of blood, now dried, traced an irregular path from his right ear to his chin. He was pale, his hands still shaking. Janus introduced him as Flavio Correia.

"Flavio," he said, "this is *Delegado* Hector Costa. He heads up the Federal Police's São Paulo field office."

"You gotta talk louder," Correia said. "The explosion fucked up my ears. I can't hear for shit."

Janus raised his voice and repeated what he'd just said.

Correia stiffened his spine and snapped Hector a salute.

Hector acknowledged it with a nod. "Delegado Prado tells me you're a lucky guy."

"It's a miracle," Correia said. "And all because I fucked my wife's sister. Ironic, huh?"

Hector wasn't sure he'd heard him correctly.

"What? What are you talking about, Sergeant?"

Correia looked at Janus. "You didn't tell him?"

Janus shook his head. "I thought it would be better coming from you."

Thus prompted, Correia told Hector the story:

He would almost certainly have been killed, he said, if his wife, Marilla, hadn't taken the kids and flown to Rio to visit her mother. Flavio and his sister-in-law had been left alone in the house. They'd emptied a bottle of *cachaça*. One thing led to another, and they'd woken-up, nude, in the marital bed. Mutual recrimination and mutual repentance followed. And a pact of silence.

Marilla was unlikely ever to know what happened, but Flavio's guilt lay heavy upon him, and like many a wayward husband before him, he thought a present for his wife might help to alleviate it. Marilla, it seemed, was a handbag fiend. She could never have enough of them. Thus it was that, scant seconds before the blast, Flavio had stepped into the alcove leading to the front door of the boutique. He was, as he told it, admiring a cute little number in burgundy leather, with a brass clasp and zipper, when the bomb went off. The shock wave had toppled him, but the alcove had sheltered him from much of the blast and all of the shrapnel.

"I can't believe it," he concluded. "I thought God was supposed to hate adulterers."

"The Lord works in mysterious ways," Janus intoned.

Hector recognized the remark as sarcasm, but the sergeant took it at face value.

"He sure as hell does," he said. "Here I am alive, and that poor baby—"

"Baby?" Hector said.

Correia looked at Janus. "You didn't tell him about the baby either?"

"No," Janus said. "Tell him."

"It didn't fit," the sergeant said.

"What didn't fit?" Hector said.

"There was this woman, and she was pushing a carriage with a baby inside."

"Uh-huh. And?"

"And the mother, she was dark. Almost like a *mulata*. But the kid wasn't. The kid had really pale skin. Thinking back, I shoulda noticed there was something strange about it. But I didn't. It only hit me afterwards."

A baby carriage made sense. A bomb large enough to do the damage this one had done might have been too big to conceal on a person. Putting it within a carriage could have been the bomber's solution. And, if she was heartless enough, she might have used a child to complete her deception.

Hector was revolted by the thought, but he had to ask. "A doll, maybe," he said.

"No. I'm telling you, it was a baby."

"You're sure?"

The sergeant threw up his arms in exasperation. "Of course, I'm sure. I leaned over and had a good look. My kids are in Rio, and I miss them. And I like kids anyway. This particular kid not only looked like a baby, it smelled like a baby. It was sound asleep, but it was no doll."

Hector ran a hand through his hair. "So what did you do?" he said.

Correia frowned and blinked, as if he hadn't understood the question. "Do?"

"Yes. What did you do next?"

The sergeant scratched his head, vigorously, as if he was trying to kick-start his memory. "I looked at the baby, and I smiled at the mother. I tried to start a conversation, but she wasn't having it, so I walked away. That was all."

"Tell me more about her."

"What?" Correia pointed at one of his ears. "You gotta speak up. I can't—"

Hector raised his voice. "I said, tell me more about her."

"She was a Muslim."

"What made you think so?"

"She was dressed like one, that's what."

"Describe her. What did she have on?"

"One of those headscarf things. And a . . . dress, I guess you'd call it. It went all the way down to the ground. There was no shape to it at all."

"What do you mean by 'no shape'?"

"It was loose. You couldn't see what kind of a body she had. Why would a woman choose a dress like that? I mean, they usually want to show what they've got, right? Especially the young ones."

"And this was a young one?"

"Uh-huh."

"Where was she standing?"

"Behind the carriage."

"And where was the carriage?"

Correia pointed at the crater.

"Right there," he said, "where that big hole is."

AFTER SPEAKING with the sergeant, Hector went in search of Danusa and found her talking to Lefkowitz, the Federal Police's chief crime scene technician.

"Listen to this," she said and hooked a thumb toward her companion.

Lefkowitz turned to Hector. "I talked to one of the consulate's security guys," he said. "There were two video cameras on top of the building."

Hector looked up at the façade. "Well, they're not there now."

"Blown off," the diminutive crime scene tech said, "but it didn't affect the recordings."

His horn-rimmed glasses were slipping down his nose. He put a finger on the bridge and pushed them back into place.

"Two of them, huh?" Hector said. "Both pointed this way?"

"Uh-huh."

"Thank you, God, for small favors. Have you asked for copies of the tapes?"

"They're not tapes, they're video disks. And copies are being made as we speak."

"You find anything down in that crater?"

"I sure as hell did."

"What?"

"Let me have a look at the recordings first. Then we'll talk."

"I'm about to call the boss. He'll want to assemble a task force. And I guarantee you that you'll be on it. Keep your cell phone on."

"I never turn it off."

Hector withdrew to the alcove where sergeant Correia had been standing at the time of the explosion. There, somewhat sheltered from the noise, he took out his cell phone and called Chief Inspector Mario Silva at his office in Brasilia.

Silva was the Federal Police's Chief Investigator for Criminal Matters.

And Hector's uncle.

"You heard?" he said when he had him on the line.

"On the radio," Silva said. "On my way to work. Information is still sketchy. How many dead?"

"They're still counting."

"I've already reserved the jet. I'm leaving now. I'll swing by the house, pack a bag and go straight to the airport. I'll be in your office by noon at the latest."

"Good. Who do you want on this?"

"You, of course. Also Danusa, Lefkowitz, Mara and Babyface. I'll bring Arnaldo."

Mara Carta was Hector's Chief of Intelligence. Haraldo "Babyface" Gonçalves, so-called because he looked at least ten years younger than his chronological age, was one of the best investigators in the São Paulo field office. Arnaldo Nunes was Silva's longtime sidekick. The Chief Inspector seldom went anywhere without him.

OTHER TITLES IN THE SOHO CRIME SERIES